I0723681

The Singularity series:

Redshift
The Observer Effect
Uncertainty Principle
Quantum Entanglement
Event Horizon
Point Singularity

REDSHIFT

R.M. OLSON

To Grandpa Olson.
For all the nights you stayed up late to make sure we got in safe, for all the pancakes and buttered popcorn, and most of all, for showing me what the world looks like when you assume everyone is kind, and every stranger a friend.
And yes, your chocolate ice-cream sauce is still better than a peanut-buster parfait.

"This phenomenon, the faint redshift perceptible in virtually all observable galaxies, bears out what scientific observation has already told us—that our universe is constantly expanding. We may not be able to measure it with our eyes, but with each moment that passes the universe we see is more vast than the one we saw the moment before."

-From a first-year astronomy textbook, University of Sao Martim, Vila Nova do Sol, Colorida

1

Aran

Aran clung to the thin cable with both hands, swearing loudly and creatively.

Beneath him, molten rock from the northern Rim Mountains' most notorious volcano bubbled and gurgled like porridge mash left too long on the stovetop. As he watched, a particularly large bubble rose sluggishly, then burst, sending a spray of lava into the air with a thick glopping sound.

How the hell did he keep getting himself into these situations?

"Aran? Aran, are you alright down there?" Istvay's voice crackled through the wavelink. They sounded worried.

Then again, Istvay was usually worried.

And, Aran had to admit, in this case, his friend was probably right.

He tried to force his eyes away from the orange, dully glowing deathtrap fifty metres or so below him. It was harder than it should have been. Something about the simmering, hypnotic lethality of it drew his gaze inexorably.

There was a soft, delicate touch on his shoulder over the fabric of his high-temp protective suit, a curious, searching sort of gesture, and he managed a small smile.

"I'm alright," he called up through his link, dragging his eyes away from the certain death that waited below him. "I'm fine."

Istvay would be able to tell it was a lie. Still, Aran had told worse ones.

The tentative touch came again, inquisitive and questioning. He reached back, stroking the gently exploring tentacle with his heavy glove. "It's alright, Ani," he said in a whisper. "We've been through worse than this, you and me."

It was probably true, even.

His makeshift backpack shifted slightly as Ani flattened her bulbous body against the inside of it, as close to him as she could get. She stubbornly refused to stay behind, and the familiar weight of her was somehow comforting.

She, at least, didn't need protective gear. Her species was notoriously resilient.

Tendrils of heat twined insistently around him, searching for a gap in his gear, and the roiling, caustic steam fogged against the plex facepiece of his suit's hood.

He closed his eyes, bracing himself, then forced the fingers of one hand to let go of the cable hooked to his harness, currently the only thing standing between him and thorough, inevitable, uncompromising destruction. He fumbled in his pouch and retrieved his sensor, tapping it against his thigh. It grumbled unwillingly, seeming as unhappy with the conditions as he was, and then, grudgingly, hummed to life.

The dial spun lazily for a moment, and then snapped to attention, the low hum resolving into a quick, *beep, beep, beep*.

He stared at it. Then he stared at the volcano wall he'd braced his legs against, and then once more back at the sensor.

It couldn't be.

He'd hoped, of course, but he'd never actually dreamed—he shook the sensor to reset it.

Again, the dial spun, and he watched it intently, hardly able to breathe.

It beeped again, sharp and insistent, and a sudden giddiness bubbled in his stomach, excitement surging through his veins strong enough to banish any remnants of terror.

He squeezed his hand to activate his wavelink, and shouted, "Istvay! We were right! There's a life form down here!"

He could picture the look on their face, resignation mixed with cautious excitement, but he couldn't focus on it at the moment, because his whole attention was glued to the sensor.

"Aran, listen. You need to start back up." Istvay sounded distinctly uneasy. "I'm getting some readings—"

"Yeah, I'll be up in a sec," Aran murmured. He recalibrated the sensor to a more responsive setting, his hands trembling with excitement, every trace of his earlier terror now forgotten.

The dial's rotation was absurdly slow, but he hardly cared, lightheaded with exhilaration.

And then it beeped again, and he brought it close to his face, peering at the screen through the foggy miasma of the volcanic gases. He squinted, heart pounding quick and uneven.

Was he reading it wrong? Was it—could it possibly be—

"Aran!"

"Just a second." He rubbed the sensor's screen against his leg and looked closer.

No. He hadn't misread it.

He could hardly breathe.

"It's not something living in the volcano," he called, voice hoarse with excitement.

"For hell's sake, you can tell me about it when you're back on solid ground! There's something going on with the atmospheric pressure, and it's sending the readings I'm getting from the volcano off the charts—" Istvay's voice was sharp with worry.

Aran felt a momentary pang of guilt, but it was quickly subsumed by elation.

"That's the thing—it is the volcano. You know all those stories about this place? They make sense now! Whatever this thing is, it's alive!"

He was grinning so wide it hurt.

Beneath him, the molten rock—or whatever it was—gurgled restlessly, another sluggish bubble rising on the surface and popping with a loud, prolonged belch, caustic steam spraying from it like a cloud of smoke.

Well, if smoke would take the meat from your bones in three point two seconds.

He reached back and grabbed one of Ani's tentacles in delirious excitement. "We did it, girl! We did it! We were right!"

Ani's tentacle probed his glove gingerly, and she gave a small, questioning chirrup. Aran laughed, giddy with happiness, and loosened his hand on the cable, letting himself slide a few metres deeper into the volcano's mouth. His feet, braced against the inner wall of the volcano, slipped just a bit.

And under them, he felt, almost imperceptibly, something move.

Hardly daring to breathe, he bent his knees, letting himself closer to the blackened surface.

Ani made an uneasy sound.

"It's okay," he murmured. "Nothing to worry about. We're just here making a new friend."

The volcanic rock moved under his feet again, nervously, the faintest quiver.

He smiled. He couldn't stop smiling, honestly.

"Hello, beautiful," he whispered, brushing his hand across the rough stone. "Hello, you beautiful, beautiful creature, you."

There was a small shudder beneath his fingertips, and his pulse jumped, his grin almost too wide for his face.

"Aran!"

Something Istvay's tone made him look up, despite himself.

"If you don't get up here right now, I'm going to drag you up."

He frowned. It had been a while since he'd managed to make Istvay that irritated with him.

Something about the quality of the light above him had changed, the difference so subtle that he hadn't noticed until just then.

He squinted upwards, just in time for a flash of blinding light, like a star going supernovae, to sear across his eyeballs.

And then, the volcanic rock—or creature, or whatever it was they'd found—that had been vibrating under his hand in a slow, curious sort of way, stilled abruptly.

Beneath him, the molten rock bubbled, suddenly more menacing than it had been a moment ago.

Far, far beneath him.

A quick rush of dizziness washed over him, the terror he'd forgotten about moments earlier returning in a nauseating wave.

"I think Istvay might be right this time, Ani," he muttered, swallowing back the acid taste of vomit.

And then the lava below him exploded upward in a fiery shower of sparks.

"Aran!"

In the back of his head he could hear the panic in Istvay's voice.

He kicked off the rough stone in desperation, just as the section of the wall where his feet had been gaped inwards. Something caught the sole of his boot, sticking to it like particularly aggressive tar, and he kicked against it, struggling desperately.

The thing, whatever it was, was pulling him in. He swore and shoved the sensor back into his pouch, yanking out a short, sharp bush-knife. Ani whimpered softly as he slashed down, slicing the sole neatly from his boot upper. Then he was swinging free, the cable cutting into his hands with the tightness of his grip, and the wall of the volcano, or creature, or whatever it was, closed around the discarded boot sole with an unpleasant sucking sound.

"Pull me up!" he shouted, but above the noise, he wasn't sure Istvay would hear him even through the wavelink. "Pull me up, damn it!" Sweat beaded in his hair and dripped down his forehead under his goggles and mask.

"Great Mystery's sweet red eyes," he swore, squeezing his own eyes shut against the enveloping terror. Beneath him, the gurgling, bubbling sound of the lava was growing relentlessly closer. His right foot, now protected only by the thin lining-shield he'd slipped on before stepping into his boots, was starting to tingle from the effects of the caustic steam rising from beneath him.

Damn it to hell.

He should have thought to say goodbye to Istvay or something before he came down. He always meant to, and he always forgot, mostly because he was always fighting back sick, abject terror at the thought of what he was about to do.

But this time, he really should have done it.

He glanced down, then squeezed his eyes shut again.

At the rate the molten rock was rising, he gave himself maybe two minutes.

Ani whimpered again, and he took a deep breath, forcing himself to think calmly.

He wasn't the only one here. Ani had come along. She was depending on him, and she didn't deserve to be—well, he wasn't exactly sure what would happen to them, aside from the supposition that it probably wouldn't be pleasant.

He gritted his teeth, twisted the cable around his gloved hand, and, ignoring the way it cut into his skin, pulled himself up one painful arm's length.

His muscles shook. Pulling himself up hand over hand in this heat, with his gear and Ani's weight on his back, would be brutal—but it was better than certain death.

"Hold on, sweetheart," he whispered to her over his shoulder, trying to keep his voice steady.

He fixed his grip on the cable and pulled again, inching them upwards. Below them, the lava danced and spit like an angry tree-cat, steam hissing against his protective suit. He could feel it corroding away at the thin liner on his bootless foot, but there wasn't time to worry about that at the moment.

"Aran! I'm trying to pull you up, but whatever the hell you found has got a hold of the cable. I can't get it loose!" Istvay's voice was frantic.

Aran risked another glance beneath him. The lava was rising much more quickly than he was going to be able to pull himself up hand over hand.

He groaned inwardly, then, dangling from one hand, fumbled in the pouch on his waist. He pulled out a small, heavy cylinder. "I'm going to use the propulsion lift," he called. "Stand back."

He gritted his teeth and tried to keep his hand from trembling as he unclipped his harness. He really, really hated this. But … the lift had worked, mostly, the last two times he'd used it. Granted, he'd been using it to transport specimens up to their camp, not to transport himself and Ani, but …

Thinking about it wasn't going to help.

He closed his eyes and hit the base of the thing sharply against his thigh to activate it. It buzzed for a moment, then jerked upwards. He barely managed to let go of the cable with his other hand to grab onto the lift more tightly, and then it was rocketing him and Ani up the cliff face.

The air whipping past was the scorching heat of an oven, and Ani had pressed herself all the way down into the bottom of her pack. The boiling lava fell away below him, the small circle of sky above growing larger and brighter. Which was undeniably a good thing, but he had no way of steering the damn lift. There was at least an even chance that when the thing ran out of thrust, he and Ani would be heading back down towards the lava as fast as they'd come up.

He'd almost reached the lip of the volcano when the irritating buzzing from the device slowed and stuttered.

"Damn you to hell—" he gasped out.

Then hands grabbed the front of his jacket, and he was jerked over the lip of the volcano. His body scraped painfully against the sharp rock, then he was shoved bodily away from the edge and onto the knife-sharp blackened stone surrounding the volcano mouth.

Behind him, a thin spray of lava shot twenty metres into the air. He ducked, covering his head with his arms as the drips of molten rock landed hissing and steaming on the ground around him.

He scrambled to his feet, touched his back to make sure Ani's makeshift backpack was still firmly fastened, and looked wildly around. "Istvay?"

Then he caught sight of his friend, and despite the simmering heat of the air, his entire body went cold with dread.

Istvay was at the edge of the volcano, where they'd been leaning over to grab Aran. And the rock, or creature, whatever it was, had caught Istvay's legs, and sucked them into the solid rock up to their waist.

Istvay was coughing as the caustic volcanic gas swirled around them, and their eyes through the plex of their protective hood were terrified, but they gestured frantically at Aran. "Take Ani and get out of here!" they managed through a coughing fit.

"Like hell I will," Aran muttered, slipping Ani and her backpack from his shoulders and placing her gently on the safest bit of ground he could find.

He sprinted back towards where the struggling Istvay was being pulled ever deeper into the living rock, his mind racing.

What did he know about this thing?

He pictured, for a moment, his hand on the volcano's walls, the soft, curious humming under his fingers.

"Aran, for hell's sake, get back!" Istvay shouted, but Aran ignored them, yanking the sensor out of his pouch. He cranked it to its highest setting, the high-pitched hum of its vibrations setting his teeth on edge.

For a bare second, he hesitated—the creature would likely feel even worse about it, if its low-pitched natural vibrations were any indication.

Then again, it was currently swallowing his best friend alive, so humanitarian considerations would have to take a back seat for now.

"Hold out your hand," he called to Istvay, and shoved the sensor into it.

Istvay grabbed it desperately. The rock around them recoiled, but it didn't release its hold.

Below, the lava bubbled harder, an ominous grumbling rising from the depths of the volcanic pit.

"I don't think it likes this," Istvay said through gritted teeth.

"Hold it to your chest, tight as you can," snapped Aran.

That should send the rapid buzz of the vibrating sensor through Istvay's body. Hopefully.

Istvay didn't ask questions, just did as they were told.

Abruptly, the rock gave a quick shudder, like a shiver of distaste, and spat Istvay free.

Istvay staggered, falling into Aran and knocking both of them to the ground. There was a great, growling belch from below them, and another thin jet of lava sprayed into the air.

Aran rolled to his feet, grabbed Istvay by the hand, and yanked them up. "Run!" he shouted, and the two of them ran for their lives, Aran stooping to grab Ani's backpack as they sprinted past.

Molten rock fell around the three of them like glowing, flesh-eating rain, and they ducked, dodging around the livid orange drips that burned through the sparse vegetation at their feet.

They scrambled down the rock dome of the mountaintop, heedless of scrapes and bruises, and at last stumbled into the gentle grass of a small mountain saddle, outside the radius of the raining lava.

Then they collapsed in a heap, gasping for breath.

Istvay rolled over, pushing themself up on their elbow, and shoved back their protective hood, grabbing Aran's shoulder. "Are you alright? Are you hurt?"

They were breathing heavily, dark hair mussed and pulling free from the ponytail they always wore, cheeks flushed, brown eyes wide and frantic.

And for just a moment, as he stared into Istvay's eyes, the noise of the lava, the sting from Aran's bare foot where something must have almost eaten through the protective shield, the odd pressure on his back where a disgruntled Ani was trying to move into a more comfortable position, faded. All Aran could see were those brown eyes staring into his, with their impossibly long lashes, the concern on Istvay's face …

He shook his head and pulled his gaze away with an effort, clearing his throat. "I'm fine." His voice came out a little rougher than he'd intended. "Thanks for pulling me in. And—um, I'm sorry I almost got you—" he trailed off, gesturing vaguely at Istvay's battered protective suit, scraped and dirtied from where they'd been sucked into the rock.

Istvay shook their head and rolled over, sitting up and brushing ineffectually at their suit, then pushed themself to their feet. "Don't worry about it. I'm just glad you're alive. I—I thought you weren't going to make it this time." They paused, pulling off their heavy gloves and running an unconscious hand along the faint stain of a five o'clock shadow on their chin, then held out their hand. Gingerly, Aran pulled off his own gloves and shoved back his hood. He took the proffered hand, and Istvay pulled him to his feet.

He and Istvay were standing, he realized, very close, and Istvay's eyes on his were serious and unwavering.

And he could see, more clearly than ever, the dark circles under his friend's eyes, the way the skin of their cheeks pulled in around their cheekbones, more pronounced than it had even a few months back.

The slight tremble in their grip that hadn't been there a year ago.

"Why do you do this, Aran? I mean, I know this is your passion.

But these last few months—"

Aran tried for a smile. "Come on, Pishti, you know me."

Istvay didn't smile back, even at the childhood nickname. "I know what you're doing," they said quietly. "And it's not going to work. I'm sorry. People have been looking for a cure for centuries now. You getting yourself killed in—" they gestured behind them, "living volcanoes, or whatever the hell that thing was, isn't going to change that."

Aran shook his head, not meeting Istvay's eyes. "Maybe you're right," he said in a low voice. "But I'll be damned if I let you die without at least trying."

He turned away abruptly, bending over Ani's backpack.

She made small, discontented noises from inside as he unclipped the straps and pushed back the covering, but after a moment she peered up at him from the depths with her glowing, protuberant eyes.

He smiled despite himself. "Hello, sweetheart," he whispered. "I guess you're ready for some fresh air, aren't you?"

Ani hooked a delicate tentacle over the lip of the bag and pulled herself out, her colouring gone a deep, disgusted purple. Aran held out his hand, and she twined her tentacles around it sinuously, swarming up his arm and settling her bulbous body onto her preferred perch on his shoulder with a graceful, snakelike motion that he would never tire of watching.

Behind him, Istvay sighed. "Well, if we're going to—"

They stopped abruptly.

Aran glanced at his friend, then followed Istvay's gaze upward.

He stared.

Above them, the late afternoon sky was a clear, brilliant blue, like it had been that morning when he and Istvay were suiting up to explore the volcano.

But now … now, across a broad, open patch of sky, there was a ragged tear, a rip across the comfortable fabric of the afternoon. It was long, and jagged, and gaped open like a wound, a colour so thoroughly black that it seemed to suck the light into it like a vacuum.

Aran and Istvay stared at it for a long, long moment, then turned to stare at each other.

"What the actual hell," Aran said at last, carefully, "is that?"

2

Alba

"Madam Chief Justice! Madam Chief Justice, please."

Alba paused, drawing her expression into one of frigid attention. "Yes, Feliu?" she snapped.

The clerk had known her for far too long, though, and didn't have the grace even to look intimidated. He hurried towards her down the grand, echoing hallway of her front entrance, a bundle of holodiscs in his hand. "In case you need them. I put together all the numbers and statistics—"

She sighed, and took the discs from his hands.

He looked as if he hadn't slept for at least three nights. He was a good ten years younger than she was, but the dark circles under his eyes aged him far beyond his sixty-something years.

"There's nothing to worry about," she said briskly. "We've been preparing for this for almost a decade."

He nodded, but she could tell by the worry in his expression that he didn't really believe it. "He's dangerous," he said quietly. "And I'm afraid, Madam, you have a tendency to underestimate him."

Alba gave a derisive snort. "I'd like to see him outmaneuver me."

Feliu sighed heavily, and muttered something which might have been, "You may just get your wish."

Alba slipped the holodiscs into her reticule, straightened her stiffly starched collar, lifted her chin, and strode out the door, the heels of her boots clicking loudly off the marble floor.

She stepped out of the cool of her home and into the stifling heat of the courtyard. Even this early, she could feel the humidity trying to melt her firmly starched robes, and she crossed quickly to where a private transport waited to take her to the Council. As she stepped inside and took her seat, she found herself straightening her collar again.

She smiled, a small, wry smile.

Perhaps she was more nervous than she wanted to admit.

She stared out the plex windows as the transport hummed towards the Council Building, barely seeing the graceful old residences and elegant, tree-lined pedestrian walkways as the transport passed over them.

Despite Feliu's accusations, she didn't underestimate General Eniko Cavaco. He was dangerous—clever, ruthless, and obsessed with power. And he would be very unhappy indeed when he heard her proposal.

But she'd seen, firsthand, what someone like Cavaco could do with power. Ten years ago, when some of the Rim Mountain settlements had objected to a government proposal intended to ensure the education of their children—a proposal Alba had engineered herself—Cavaco had sent in the military.

The memory of the footage from the incident still made her shudder.

Morality aside, that type of brute violence undermined the

legitimacy of the entire government. And she was determined she'd not see it happen again.

The transport stopped in the courtyard outside the Council building, and Alba dismounted stiffly. The short ride from her residence seemed to be getting longer the more she aged, the seats of even the private transports growing harder on her aching joints.

The door stewards were already pulling the heavy doors open as she approached, tripping over themselves in their haste, and she stepped through into the massive, grandly domed entrance to the Council Chambers.

She paused for a moment before turning down the high-ceilinged corridor towards the Council room, where the door stewards once more would leap into action, terrified of making her wait one additional second.

She resisted the urge to straighten her collar again.

She'd been preparing for this moment for decades. She had gone over every possibility. There was nothing she'd overlooked.

At least, that's what she told herself.

She took a deep breath, and strode down the corridor to the Council room.

As she'd predicted, the door stewards leapt to attention so quickly they almost stumbled, pulling the doors back with an impressive alacrity, and nodding respectfully as she stepped through.

She allowed herself a small smile satisfaction.

What was the point, after all, of living seventy-three years if you didn't take some advantage of the reputation you'd spent those years honing?

She walked briskly across the massive rotunda of the Council room, the ancient stones of the walls polished to a lustrous reddish gleam and exuding an air of grander despite—or perhaps because of

—their age. The Council Chambers had been built in the first century after the generation-ships had brought their ancestors to this planet, one of the first buildings constructed in the new city. It had been renovated and repaired countless times in the five-hundred-some-odd years since then—it had even been burnt down to its bare stones once, a century and a half ago—but it still bore the ponderous weight of age and tradition.

At last, the rest of the Council had gathered, and the glowing, ancient screen set in the centre of the rotunda showed nine o'clock. The Speaker, a mousy-looking, middle-aged woman, stood and tapped the butt of her ceremonial staff on the floor, its holographic head glowing a deep purple.

"We wish to announce, in the presence of the citizens of the Joias system, and in the presence of all those in attendance here witnessing, and in the presence of the Great Mystery itself, the President-elect and Head of the People's Committee, Ander Seguer." She paused a moment for the small, ceremonial tapping of fingers on desks.

Alba leaned back in her seat, her hands firmly in her lap. The role of Chief Justice bore with it the role of Ceremonial Joint Head of the Council of Orthodoxy of the Church Unice Veritas of the Sacrament of the Great Mystery—a religious position which, in a modern society such as their own, was a position in name only, but still carried a satisfying ring to it—and, considering that any representative of the Great Mystery would not be expected to show respect for merely mortal authority, she was not expected to tap her fingers on her desk.

She took a perverse and undeniable amount of enjoyment in not doing so. Mostly because she knew it annoyed that twit Ander.

"And joining the President-Elect, the Head of the Judiciary

Committee, Chief Justice of the Joias system, and Joint Head of the Council of Orthodoxy, Alba Espina, and Head of the Military Committee, General Eniko Cavaco."

More polite tapping.

The General sent a cold glance in Alba's direction as he rose briefly to acknowledge the acclaim. He was in his mid-sixties, but his form was lean and muscular, his posture as straight as must have been drilled into him as a young man in military.

He may not know what she had planned for this morning, but their mutual hatred was long-standing and well-entrenched, and rather gratifying, truth be told.

The moment the noise ceased and the Speaker had taken her seat at last, Alba rose. "I approach the Council and request permission to address them," she snapped imperiously.

The Speaker bobbed back to her feet, looking faintly terrified, and murmured, "Permission granted, Madam Chief Justice."

Alba flipped on the holographic screen at her desk, broadcasting her face onto the screens of all the Council. "Esteemed friends and colleagues, I would like to begin today's business with a proposal."

She felt the weight of the Council's combined gaze, although, standing as she was at the front of the room and facing the Speaker as was ceremonially required, she couldn't see them. But she could hear the buzz of murmurs, some confused, others the low whisper of those waiting with bated breath for the explosion that was certain to follow.

She paused, allowing the whispers to die down before she continued. "Our people have a long and storied tradition, over our five-hundred-year history on this planet, of negotiation, adaptation, and a governance based on the unique circumstances in which we found ourselves. As we fought to survive and thrive upon this planet, and then spread to the surrounding planets and moons, we gradually created the system of government we now have—the elected Head of the People's Committee, the appointed Head of the Judiciary Committee, and the promoted Head of the Military Committee, together making up the General Council.

"In the wild chaos of our beginnings—the vicious animals and inhospitable terrain, and the inevitable conflicts that ensued amongst a group of people thus thrust into a stark struggle for survival—all three branches of the Council were indispensable. But, drawing on our tradition of peaceful resolution of disputes, and measuring intelligence as more important than brute force, we have evolved as a society. Our most recent conflict, between the Orthodox Church and the Corpus Dei sect, ended almost a century ago." She paused for effect, turning slightly to survey the room.

They were hanging on her words, as she'd hoped.

"I therefore propose that it is time now to take the obvious next step in our progression as a society. I propose that going forward, the government be comprised of the People's Council and the Judicial Council alone. While the military itself must be maintained, I propose that the Military Council as a branch of government be disbanded."

She turned to the Speaker, who was staring at her now with an expression of sheer horror. "I thank the Council for their attention, and resume my seat," she finished, and suited action to word.

The room was so still you could hear dust motes fall. Alba allowed herself the small, satisfied smile of a job well done.

This explosion was going to be legendary.

The reaction was swift and predictable.

After a moment of stunned silence, half the members of the Military Council, plus probably an equal number spread between the People's Council and the Judicial Council, leapt to their feet, talking and shouting over each other.

Alba sat back contentedly, and watched the Council's swift devolution into chaos.

The poor, harried Speaker was on her feet, pounding her staff against the floor, but no one was paying her any attention whatsoever.

"Silence!"

The woman's voice, broadcast over every amplifier in the Council room, boomed out with such force that it shocked the squabbling members, for just a moment, into some semblance of quiet.

"Silence," shouted the Speaker again, her amplified voice a little softer now. "A member has put forth a proposal for our discussion."

There was a heavy emphasis on the word *discussion*.

Alba raised an eyebrow, impressed despite herself. There was nothing mousy about the Speaker now.

"If anyone would like to add to the conversation," the woman continued, "they may do so in the proscribed manner."

She sat. The Council members looked at each other sheepishly, then slowly resumed their own seats.

With decorum once again restored, General Cavaco stood. No one tried to oppose him—everyone was almost certainly waiting to see the show.

"Madam Speaker, I would like to discuss the proposal put forward by my learned friend on the Judiciary Committee," he said icily.

The Speaker rose briefly and nodded, tapping the control on her ceremonial staff that turned the holoscreen broadcast over to him. "You may proceed," she said formally, regaining her seat.

Cavaco turned, and, although Alba didn't grant him the compliment of turning to face him, she could tell, even through the holoscreen, that he was glaring daggers at the back of her head. "Madam Chief Justice has made an … interesting proposal," he began. His tone was neutral, but undergirt with a sheer, icy hatred. "However, perhaps she has forgotten, or at least left out of her calculations, some rather pertinent information."

He held up a hand, ticking the points off on his fingers. "First, our world is not quite as peaceful as the Chief Justice wishes us to believe. There have been rumours of unrest in the Rim Mountain settlements, mainly among those who hold to the Mountain Dialect. There are, as we all know, pockets of Old Believer fanatics from the Corpus Dei sect, fixated on dredging up hundred-year-old grievances from the Cleansing. In the Rim Mountains, there are isolated Old Believer compounds that cannot be called anything but dangerous cults. We have information on the brainwashing they subject their members to—forcing them to watch century-old footage from the Cleansing, convincing them that there are plots by the Orthodox Church to re-ignite a holy war, preaching that their members must arm themselves for what their leaders call self-defence, and we know to be an attempt to re-create the Cleansing on their own terms. Between these groups, we're constantly one step away from a new war. If my intelligence is correct, the assassin who murdered Minister DaRosa is a member of one of the cults herself. The assassination could well be the first step of an attempt to destabilize the government, in preparation for further hostilities.

"Second, and perhaps more important, our solar system is light-years from the one in which our distant ancestors were born. While we have sporadic communication with our sister generation ships and the planetary settlements begun by them, we have no idea whatsoever whether or not there is other intelligent life in this galaxy. We need a strong military voice in the government against the possibility of hostile non-human life forms. But, of course, the honourable Chief Justice is, as we all know, aging. It's possible this could account for the lapses in the information she presented to you."

It was an entirely malicious dig, and Alba could see the Speaker shift restlessly, unsure if she should censure the General.

Alba simply smirked.

If he was resorting to personal insults, it meant he was worried. As he should be.

Besides, there wasn't a single member in this Council room, whether they loved Alba or hated her, who had any doubt as to her mental acuity.

Cavaco paused, probably for effect, but before he could draw a breath to begin his next talking point, Alba stood.

"Madam Speaker, I would be happy to respond to my colleague's queries, if you would be so kind as to grant me permission."

"Of course," said the Speaker, half-rising and tapping her staff on the floor, then flipping the holoscreen to Alba's desk. The woman was wearing a half smile—she clearly saw what Alba was doing, and was more than happy to play along. The General had not made himself friends of everyone in the Council.

"As to your first point," Alba began, smiling at the holoscreen on her desk, "there have been rumours of disturbances in the Rim Mountains for our entire history. And although there may be hyper-religious enclaves in the mountains, they're few and far between. While fanaticism in any form can be dangerous, it doesn't seem to me that sending the military after them would be an effective strategy to persuade such fanatics that they are in no danger from broader society. Education and time, I believe, are the best weapons against fanatics of any stripe. As far as the murder of the Councillor

—the woman who killed DaRosa may come from one of the heretical enclaves, but she appears to have been working alone. In fact, I have already instructed my personal clerk to assign the warrant for her arrest. I don't believe we need maintain an entire branch of government for something a warrant can solve."

She was much better at slipping in insults than Cavaco was.

He half-rose, trying to cut her off, but she continued smoothly. "To your second point, you are correct. It is a statistical improbability that we are alone in the universe. However, it is the conclusion of our leading scientists and philosophers that greeting an unknown entity or group of entities with the threat of force, without knowledge of their technology or capabilities, is a good way to get our entire planet destroyed. I am certain the Council will continue to fund the military, as required, in case protection should be needed. However, the decision as to when and in what circumstances military force will be used should be made by cooler heads."

She nodded to the Speaker, and resumed her seat.

Everything she'd said was good policy. She'd studied up on it for years now, weighing the benefits and risks. But she knew as well as anyone that what got passed within the wrangling Council was not policy, but politics.

And besides being certain it was good policy, she had made very, very sure of her politics before she presented this. They could argue all they wanted, but at the end of the day she knew exactly how many votes would go each way.

Still …

If she'd learned anything from her years in politics, it was that nothing was quite as certain as one might wish.

The squabble lasted until well after the time they would normally break for lunch. Alba leaned back in her seat, making herself comfortable as she watched the performance she'd orchestrated. At last, though, the Speaker rose, tapping her staff on the floor and shutting off the holoscreens at the members' desks.

"It's past midday break," she said. "And, while I am inclined to skip the afternoon break, as it seems you all have the stamina to continue for a full day of discussions, I am not willing to cede necessary breaks for food and water. I do not intend to be responsible for members passing out on the floor." She paused until the muttering had subsided.

"All are dismissed, and we will reconvene in an hour's time. At that time, the floor shall be re-commanded by Counselor Mateu, to give her an opportunity to finish presenting her views."

Alba glanced around at her colleagues as they rose, stretching and grumbling.

Cancelling the afternoon break, when most members dozed in their offices during the hottest hours of the day, would be a hard blow. The Speaker had likely done it calculatingly, either as a motivation to finish this fight as quickly as possible, or as petty revenge for the morning's chaos.

Either way, Alba looked at the woman with a touch more respect than she had previously.

As she stepped out onto the rotunda and made her way towards the door, she cast a glance over her shoulder.

Cavaco was still standing in the tiered seats, surrounded by ministers and counsellors from both the military and the other two branches.

No faces that she hadn't expected. But still … something about his face and posture worried her more than she wanted to admit.

It made logical sense to dismantle the military branch of the government. It hadn't been needed in a century, and it created far more issues than it solved. But Cavaco was the type to seize hold of power and not let go. And since he'd ascended to his position fifteen years previous, the stakes had only gotten higher. Cavaco's proposals, taken separately, were fairly innocuous, but there was a pattern behind them. He was trying, slowly, to strip the other two branches of any surplus power they might have, and consolidate it with himself—the one who was neither elected, nor appointed by an elected official.

She shivered as she stepped from the rotunda, warm from the midday heat and the crush of bodies and emotions, and into the cool hallway.

She told herself it was simply an effect of the change in temperature. But it wasn't.

Yes, she'd been preparing for this for a decade, and yes, she was confident in her ability to guide the outcome.

But not certain. Faced with an adversary like Cavaco, it would be foolish to be entirely certain.

When Alba returned to her private office, brushing past the nervous steward who pulled open the door for her, she sat at her desk and pulled up the discs Feliu had given her earlier. She scanned quickly through the reports he'd prepared, and paused at one—the warrant she'd mentioned to the Council earlier.

She pulled up a holographic copy, frowning as she read through it.

Reka Soler is hereby authorized by a judge duly appointed, to bring the underdesignated subject to face a court of justice, if practicable, and if not practicable, to execute the law on said accused, who has been, for matters of distinct urgency, tried in absentia and found guilty of the crimes of murder and political assassination. The holder of this warrant shall not be liable for any damage or death caused in pursuit of this aim, whether by her actions or the actions of another in her employ. Anyone thus injured may apply to the Judicial Council for recompense.

Underneath was a small, rotating hologram of a young woman with a wide, guileless smile, thick auburn hair, brown skin, and an open, friendly face. Her cheeks were round, her body pleasantly plump, and her overall appearance that of someone who had grown up far in the country, unspoiled by the intrigues of city life and politics.

She was also the most deadly assassin-for-hire in the system.

Alba leaned back in her chair, her eyebrows raised.

Reka Soler. Alba wouldn't have thought of assigning the warrant to her, but Feliu's judgement was, as always, impeccable.

Reka had worked under Cavaco, before rumours of a job gone wrong. The details had always been too hazy to parse, but Alba was well enough acquainted with Cavaco to know that the young agent had taken the fall for things she couldn't possibly have been responsible for.

Still, there were few in government who dared go up against Cavaco. Reka was undeniably the most talented government agent on the roster, but her name was poison in the government ranks these days.

Madam. Feliu's neat, careful handwriting popped up on the file attached to the warrant. *I took the liberty of assuring Ms. Soler that a successful completion of this warrant would clear her name, as you certainly have the influence to ensure it will. I felt it prudent, considering the likely difficulty of the task, to give her additional motivation. And, if you recall, Madam, I believe the job that went wrong involved the target of the warrant, Savina Moya, which should only enhance Ms. Soler's desire to complete the task in a satisfactory manner.*

Alba smiled faintly as she closed down the file.

Feliu was right—Reka was the perfect tool to stop Savina.

And then, from the corner of her eye, she caught a flash of blindingly bright light.

She blinked, and turned to the tall, narrow old window, its ancient plex faded by age and wear.

Outside, the day held the warm, hazy yellow glow of a late morning in early summer. But the entire courtyard seemed frozen, pedestrians, stewards, and clerks alike gaping upwards.

Frowning, she tapped the button on her desk to summon the door steward.

It was almost five full minutes before he appeared. His face was a sickly greyish, his expression a mixture of terror and shock.

"What just happened?" she snapped. "Was there an explosion? An attack?"

He shook his head mutely.

She could hear, faintly, over the amplifiers, the Speaker's voice. "I request that each member of the Council return to the Council room immediately."

"Well?" Alba demanded of the terrified young man. "What was it, then?"

The boy simply nodded towards the window, eyes wide with fear.

Alba glared at him as she stood, ignoring how her joints creaked at the movement, and crossed to the window, frowning upwards.

Then she stared.

There, in the middle of the brilliant blue of the sky, was a rent, as if someone had taken the sky in their two hands and torn it open.

"What is that?" she asked finally, her voice cracking just a little.

The steward shook his head. "The scientists are saying it's a portal of some sort. A gate, maybe, like a wormhole. Something that— something that—"

Alba stared at him, cold knotting in the pit of her stomach. "Something that someone—or something—could travel through," she finished grimly.

3

Savina stood at the plex window of the luxury ship and stared out at the gaping rift that cut across the glittering expanse of stars and nebula before her. Her expression was one of frank, wide-eyed astonishment.

She'd practiced it enough to be entirely sure.

And, truth be told, she was mildly unsettled. Whatever had happened outside, it seemed to be something completely outside anyone's experience. Still, whatever it was, it was unlikely to affect her in any material way in the near future.

The expression on her companion's face, she knew without looking, was one of greedy calculation. He'd come around the table to stand beside her, a glass of fine wine in his hand.

"My dear," he said at last, in the tone of a parent humouring a child. "Come, sit. My wavelink will be buzzing in about five planetary minutes with people either telling me what that is, or asking me to tell them what it is. If you have a business proposal for me, best tell me now." His words had an indulgent ring to them, and she turned her frank, wide-eyed gaze on him.

"I'm sorry," she said. "I got a little distracted. It's not every day I see something like that." She let her gaze drift around the luxurious room, and laughed, a little breathlessly. "Well, it's not every day I see something like this ship, to be honest. How long have you had it? It must have been quite a project."

He waved a dismissive hand and sank languidly back into his seat. "It's one of seven," he said, taking another sip of his wine. "Not the biggest, either. But she's a trim little thing, and comfortable for shorter trips. Now." He gestured her to a chair, pushing a glass of wine across the desk to her.

She took the seat and the wine, and leaned forward eagerly. "Alright, Mister Borges. I know you're busy, and I don't want to waste your time. So let me just …" She reached down, fumbling in her pouch, and pulled out a handful of holodiscs.

He'd crossed one leg over the other and was watching in mild amusement, but she caught the twitch of his face, the small hint of a frown that formed at one corner of his mouth.

"Mister Borges?" she said, looking up quickly and letting her own mouth turn down in concern. "Is something wrong?"

It was a good thing she had so much practice with her expressions. Because honestly, right now she could hardly keep from smiling.

This part of her job was always satisfying. But she wasn't always working with someone who was such an irrefutable bastard.

"No, nothing," he said, waving a hand again. But the gesture was not quite as smooth as it had been a moment before.

She stood, bumping the desk and barely catching one of the discs as it tumbled for the ground. "Mister Borges? You don't look well. Can I—"

"It's nothing, my dear." His voice was a little strained now, the frown on his face turned to something closer to a grimace. "I … I'm sorry. Perhaps I'll have to reschedule. I'm not … I'm not feeling entirely well …"

His hand groped for the button on his desk, and she watched, perplexed and worried.

Or at least, she looked perplexed and worried.

"Carolina," he called, finally hitting the button. "I need … I need a medic, I think." He released the button and waited, his pained grimace taking on a tinge of irritation. He hit the button again. "Carolina?" he asked sharply. "Dammit, why won't you—"

"She can't hear you," said Savina, smiling her wide-eyed smile.

He turned to her, a momentary confusion passing across his face. "What do you mean she can't—"

Savina smiled wider. "She can't hear you. Because I took the precaution of cutting off all the communication from this room before I came in."

The confusion on the man's cultured face was turning ever so slightly to fear. "You—" he croaked.

She strolled around the desk towards him, stopping to pick up one of the decorative figurines and glance at it in admiration before replacing it. She paused beside his chair, bending so she was eye-level with him. "Yes, me. I'm sorry. Oh, and before I forget, Clara Diniz sends her regards."

"Clara?" His expression was a mix of terror and fury and—well, whatever you called it when someone was choking to death on their own bodily fluids. She'd never found a satisfactory term for that one. "Why … does she want … to hurt me?"

Savina hopped up so she was sitting on the desk, still smiling. "She doesn't want to hurt you."

She glanced down at her hands. There was a bit of dirt on one fingernail, and she wiped it off daintily.

"She … she doesn't—" His words were barely intelligible.

"No, she doesn't." She looked back up at him and dimpled prettily. "She wants to kill you. And I believe she just has. Or rather, I have."

He struggled to push himself upright. His face was now an unattractive mottled colour, his muscles shaking, but he managed to bend down, reaching for something in his boot. When he straightened, there was a pulse pistol in his trembling hand. "You think … you think you can—" he gasped.

Savina slid down from the table in an easy motion, bringing the edge of one hand down on his wrist in a quick, disdainful gesture, and with the other, tapping the disc in her palm. A thin, sharp blade slipped out from its edge, and she grabbed him by the hair as the gun clattered from his nerveless fingers. She yanked his head back so his terrified, bloodshot eyes were staring into hers.

"I already have," she whispered.

She slid the blade along his throat in a sharp, practiced motion, stepping back fastidiously to avoid the quick spurt of blood.

She sighed as he went limp, surveying the mess.

They always had to try to fight back, these bullying boss-types. It would be easier for all concerned if they'd just go quietly, but no. And now some poor janitor would be stuck cleaning up a frankly unforgivable mess.

Still, it could hardly be helped. And if what she'd read up on him was correct, any janitor working on this ship would be more than happy to mop blood from the walls in exchange for not having to work for Borges.

In theory, there was no indentured servitude in the system, or so they said. In reality, people like Borges managed to find practical workarounds to such petty restrictions.

She tipped the chair forwards with an effort, allowing the limp body to slide off under the desk. It wouldn't do much for concealment, considering the walls and carpet were liberally doused in blood, but it was something. Then she wiped the tiny spatter of blood she hadn't been able to avoid off her hand, cleaned her concealed knife, and slipped it, along with her other rigged discs, back into her bag.

The rigged disks were her sibling's creation, and they'd come in handy countless times. They'd even pull up a holograph, although they didn't store as much memory as a regular disc—an unfortunate side effect of the space taken up by the hidden blade.

She paused a moment, then took the glass of wine Borges had offered her. She sipped it, closing her eyes to enjoy the flavour. It was delicious—a delicate bouquet of rare fruits that must have come from the off-planet settlements and grapes from the southern Rim Mountains, with a smoky undertone of something she couldn't identify. Since the poison she'd smeared on the inside of his glass was completely flavourless, he'd have had a pleasant few moments before death.

More than he deserved, really.

They didn't pay her to pass judgement on the people she killed, but really, she could hardly help it with Borges.

She glanced around one last time to be sure she hadn't forgotten anything, and once again, the empty, unsettling rift across the familiar vista of stars and nebula through the window snagged her gaze.

She shivered.

It was strange, that was all. Nothing she needed to worry about.

Still, best get off the ship and away before they closed down the ports or anything.

She stepped out of the room, shutting the door carefully behind her.

The grey-haired woman at the reception desk gave her a friendly smile. "Are you finished already, dear?"

Savina smiled. "I am. Thank you for setting this up! I really appreciate it." She paused, then added in a slightly embarrassed whisper, "He was, um, excited about whatever happened out there in space, and he, um … he might have had a little more wine than he should have. Probably best if no one disturbs him for a couple of hours."

The woman sighed, care-lines showing on her wrinkled face. "You're alright, though?"

"I'm fine," Savina said, making her voice bright. "I'm used to it. And he was very kind, all things considered."

"You got what you came for, at least?" asked the woman.

"I did," said Savina, letting her dimples show. "Thank you. You were a tremendous help. I couldn't have done it without you."

She started for the door with a slight skip to her step.

"Well, you seem the type to bring out the best in people. I hope we'll see you around here again sometime," the receptionist called after her, and Savina turned and gave her a little wave before heading down the corridor.

The corridors of the luxury ship were wide and elegant, and the people strolling back and forth had the air of those who were very aware of their own importance. And the servants, scurrying past them, had the air of people who were very aware of exactly how much their job was worth if they inconvenienced any of these very important people. Whatever had happened to cause the rift in space didn't seem important enough to bother the ship's guests in the slightest—assuming their underlings had even briefed them yet.

Savina smiled at all and sundry as she passed, receiving more than a few smiles in return as she made her way through the opulent ship's interior and down the sumptuous lifts.

Fifteen hundred, this job had earned her, and it had been easy as falling asleep.

She reached the port deck and found herself a seat in the finely decorated waiting room, glancing at the retinal screen on her wavelink.

A transport down to the grubby moonport below them would be arriving in about five planetary minutes.

A father with two young children sat in the waiting room as well. He looked harried, and the children, around five and seven, if Savina had to guess, were squabbling noisily.

Savina rummaged in her bag and pulled out two sweetmeats, glancing at the father for permission. He gave her a frazzled nod, and she smiled at the children, holding the candies out in the palm of her hand.

Within a minute, both children were at her side, sucking away at their sweets and each trying, through a sticky mouth, to be the first to tell Savina their entire life story.

They all jumped at the piercing, high-pitched wail of an alarm from behind them in the ship.

Savina tried to force her pulse to calm as the children scurried back to their father.

It was nothing. Surely it had nothing to do with her. She'd pulled off jobs like this a hundred times, and never once—

More alarms joined in, and a voice came over the ship amplifiers, stern and official. "I'm sorry to alarm you, but everyone must return to their cabins immediately. All staff to the muster stations to be counted."

The transport had just pulled up, its doors hissing open.

"No one is permitted to leave the ship."

Savina's heart pounded strangely.

They'd found Borges. Somehow, they'd found him.

She pictured again the smiling, grey-haired woman at the reception desk. The sharp intelligence in her eyes that Savina hadn't really taken note of, too busy charming, and being charmed.

Damn.

Two officers had stepped into the waiting room now, and were standing by the doors of the ship, taking the IDs of the shaken passengers.

Savina shot a pleading look at the children's father, and whispered, "My kids are down on the station. I need to get down there."

He hesitated a moment, then gave a slight nod and pulled something out of his bag. "Which one of you wants this?" he asked, and the kids began to shriek with delight, jumping for the toy.

"It's mine! It's my turn!"

"You had it last time!"

For just a moment, everyone's gaze turned to the children.

Savina slipped quickly behind the guards' backs, dropping into an empty seat before they'd turned back to their job.

She took a long breath and smiled at the woman beside her, who'd looked up as she sat down. "I was in the back, but I was getting a little airsick. I thought I'd move over to the window. I hope you don't mind."

"I don't mind," the woman murmured, turning back to watch the door guards. "Any idea of what's going on out there?"

Savina shook her head. "I don't know. But I'm not getting off if there's a problem. I'd rather go back down to port, come back another time."

The woman was hardly listening.

Savina allowed herself a small sigh of relief as the shuttle started up and purred off back towards the station.

She was feeling oddly shaky.

It hadn't even been a close call, to be honest. But she'd never underestimated someone like that before.

Maybe she was losing her touch.

"Savina!"

She jerked at the voice in her earpiece. "Beni?" she whispered back, activating her wavelink.

"Are you alright?"

Savina frowned.

Her sibling sounded worried.

There shouldn't have been any reason for them to worry. Surely word of the alarm on the ship wouldn't have reached the port yet.

"I'm fine, Beni. What's wrong?"

"We have a problem." Beni's normally calm voice was tight with agitation. "I've been tracking arrest warrants issued by the government. There was one signed just a few hours ago—for you. And it's under your real name."

Savina stared blankly out the black of the plex window in front of her.

This day had just gone from bad to a whole hell of a lot worse.

4

Alba

By the time Alba returned to the Council room, it was a scene of absolute chaos. People were talking over each other in tones that ranged from excitement to terror—shouting, arguing, waving their arms as if the world itself had ended.

And who knew, she thought grimly. Maybe it had.

She returned to her seat, ignoring the half-dozen counsellors trying to attract her attention, and sank into it.

She needed to think.

No, she needed information. What did this mean?

What it meant for the Joias system was certainly the most pressing question.

But she couldn't help but contemplate what it might mean for her proposal.

For half a moment, she'd been struck with the wild suspicion that Cavaco had engineered this himself. But looking over at him, the shocked disbelief on his face he'd been unable to hide, she knew he hadn't.

This was just incredibly bad luck, then, and incredibly bad timing. Worse timing than she really wanted to think about.

The immediate prospect of encountering an alien intelligence hadn't been a serious consideration when she'd calculated the timing of her proposal. But had it been something she'd foreseen, she'd have done everything in her power to ensure General Cavaco was off the Council before it happened.

He held an outsized amount of influence. And she knew exactly what his proposal to deal with the problem would be.

That proposal might well get everyone in the Joias system killed.

The Speaker called them to attention with the thump of her staff against the floor, and, when that failed to quell the noise, her voice, blasted through the amplifiers at a decibel level nothing less than painful.

"Thank you," she said, when order had once more been restored and the counsellors taken their seats. "I've taken the liberty of calling in a number of scientists who may be able to explain the unprecedented cosmic phenomenon you have all no doubt taken note of. After they have done so, the Council may then debate our next course of action." She glanced around, and when she received no objection, opened her mouth to speak again.

A heavy pounding sounded on the door, cutting off whatever she'd been about to say. The Speaker frowned, but gestured to one of the door stewards, who stepped to the heavy wooden doors. He pulled them back, and a woman burst through, her expression distraught, her clothing dishevelled. If Alba were to guess by her uniform, the newcomer was one of the scientists from the research facility of the Sao Martim University.

"What is the meaning of this?" the Speaker demanded, but the woman didn't wait. She strode to the podium in the centre of the room and half shouted, her voice ringing through the wall amplifiers. "Something's come through the portal!"

If the appearance of the portal had created chaos, this news was the equivalent of setting off plasma bomb. Even the Speaker, it seemed, had given up on trying to keep order as people leapt to their feet, shouting, screaming, demanding answers.

Alba sank back into her seat, something cold and numb in her chest.

This portal was no natural phenomenon, then. And there was something on the other side.

With Cavaco still in power, this was the worst possible development.

She noted the arrival of a security guard with only half her attention. The woman entered the rotunda, pausing to whisper something into the Speaker's ear.

The Speaker nodded, and the guard strode to the podium. She tapped the holoscreen controls, then her voice, sharp and worried, cut through the ringing panic and confusion. "The Security Head has determined that Council members shall remain in the Council room for their safety until we have determined the level of threat that the object sent through the portal presents."

This was enough to subdue even the loudest of the shouters.

The security guard turned briskly and strode out the door, the *click* of it locking behind her loud in the sudden silence.

Slowly, the counsellors resumed their seats.

The afternoon was hot. The sun pouring through the tall old windows did nothing to help the ancient cooling system, which creaked and groaned. A fly buzzed noisily somewhere in the rotunda, and in the sullen hush each clearing of a throat or shifting in a seat was clearly audible.

The holoscreens on the councillor desks showed the security officers standing at stoic attention outside the building. Although the guards' customary briefings were given punctually at fifteen-minute increments, they were curt and anything but reassuring.

Once or twice, a member hazarded a comment. No one seemed in the mood for a discussion, though, and the conversation quickly petered out.

Alba watched Cavaco.

Beneath the worry on his face, there was a glint of calculation.

Her proposal of that morning was trapped in orbit until the matter of the portal had been dealt with. And he knew it as well as she did.

She should be worrying about the fate of the system.

But it was entirely possible that in this instance, the fate of the system and the fate of Cavaco were the same thing.

It was almost two interminable hours later before there was the *click* of the door unlocking, and a male voice came over the amplifiers. "I will be opening the doors. Please don't panic. The threat, if any, has been neutralized."

A moment later the heavy doors swung open, and a security guard stepped through.

He was escorting a young man who appeared to be in his early thirties, with the manner and bearing of someone raised to privilege. In his hands, the man carried a small black box.

It wasn't anything to draw the eye—a long rectangle, battered and scored, perhaps the length of Alba's forearm. But from the way the man held it, Alba knew immediately it was important.

And considering everything that had just happened, she could make an educated guess where the object had come from.

The security guard crossed quickly to the Speaker and bent over, whispering something in her ear. She nodded and stood, tapping her staff on the ground.

"Members of the Council," she began, into the absolute silence. "This is Emeric Furtado, one of our lead biologists from the Sao Martim University. The scientists in his group have spent the past two hours analyzing the object that was transported through the portal. They have certified that it is safe, and he has requested permission to present us with a finding that he believes is highly important." She turned to the young man in the rotunda and gestured him to the podium. "Please, explain."

The young man strode into the centre of the room as the Speaker resumed her seat, his posture radiating nervous energy. Reverently, he placed the black box atop the podium, then turned the assembled Council.

"Esteemed counsellors," he began, a tremor of excitement in his voice. "This object was sent by an intelligent species. From our preliminary examination, they appear to be using, in some cases, technology that outpaces our own. For instance, the technology used to send this object such a distance so rapidly appears to be closer to theoretical quantum teleportation than regular space travel. However, they also demonstrate use of technology we surpassed centuries ago." He glanced down, and gently lifted the top of the object, like the lid of a box. As every head in the Council strained forward to see, he tipped the podium's holoscreen to broadcast a view of the box's contents.

Alba stared at her screen, frowning.

Inside the padded compartment were various samples, carefully packed, small items labelled neatly in a language which she'd never seen before. At least, she assumed it was a language, although there was no way to be certain.

"There are all sorts of specimens here," the scientist continued. "Sound patterns we assume to be music, and what appears to be a speech sample, although we are unable to discern what message, if any, it conveys. These we passed on to our linguists, and their team is working as fast as possible to decipher them. But—" he paused, the gleam in his eye almost fanatical. "Perhaps the most interesting thing of all is this." He indicated a small test tube in one corner, filled with a suspiciously red substance, his gesture reverent.

"It appears to be a blood sample," the man said. "Their method of stabilizing it isn't as advanced as our own, but it was sufficient to permit us to study it. Through DNA analysis, we were able to ascertain that whoever or whatever provided the sample was not human, but certainly related to humans. It was from a healthy individual of around sixty years old. And—" he paused, just for half a second. "And that individual carried the genetic defect."

Alba stared at the young man, almost unable to trust her ears.

For a moment the room went completely silent, as if every person in it were holding their breath. Then it exploded into noise, and the Speaker, for the third time that day, was forced to shout through the amplifiers to make herself heard.

"Order!" she snapped. When at last the furor had died down and everyone had returned to their seats, she continued, in a more modulated tone, "If there are questions or comments, I ask that they be presented with the decorum appropriate to this chamber."

An older member of the People's Council, a non-binary individual who, Alba recalled, had a granddaughter with the defect, stood and was granted the floor.

"Are you certain of this?" they asked, their voice shaking slightly. "Certain on both counts; the individual's age, and the presence of the defect?"

The scientist gave a wry smile. "It's difficult to be completely certain of anything. However, we are able to say with relative confidence that at the time of providing the sample, the individual had lived the equivalent of around sixty of Colorida's planetary years. As far as the presence of the defect—of that, we are certain."

A quiet, murmuring rustle travelled around the room.

Alba sat in silent shock, her thoughts tumbling over each other.

Five hundred years, and they still hadn't developed a cure for the defect. Early records indicated the defect had been present even on the generation ship that had brought them here. It was an odd combination of recessive genes, making it all but impossible to predict where it would pop up. But two things were quite certain—first, everyone was a potential carrier. And second, the current consensus was that the defect would manifest in about ten percent of the population.

One in ten children, who'd grow up perfectly healthy and normal until sometime in their late twenties.

There was no way to predict it. It might skip three generations in a family, and then three children born to the same parents would develop it. Two healthy parents might pass it to their child, or two sick parents might raise a healthy child to be left an orphan far too young.

Even with the best technology science could devise, the longest anyone with the defect had lived was forty. And that had been hailed as nothing less than a miracle. Most people affected died by their early thirties. It wasn't a pleasant death—a slow, agonizing wasting away, skin drooping from cadaverous frames, muscles weakening, heart pumping slower and slower until it inevitably failed.

"Does this mean whoever is on the other side of the portal has found a cure?" asked a woman from the Judicial Council, rising quickly to her feet.

"Unfortunately, it does not," said the scientist. "It could be a simple matter of physiological difference between species, like when a virus lethal in humans is only a minor nuisance to its animal host. But whatever it is that drives the aliens' resistance, it's possible that with additional samples and studies we could use it to create a cure of our own. As I said, from all indications, the specimen was in perfect health at the time of giving the sample."

President Ander stood as well. "If that is the case, obtaining these samples—possibly finding a cure—must be our top priority in any contact we have with these aliens. Above anything else." His face had gone slightly pale.

"Above *almost* anything else," came General Cavaco's sharp voice. "What must take overall precedence, I think, is ensuring that we are safe from whoever or whatever is on the other side of that portal. As of this moment, we have no indication whether they are friendly or hostile, nor of their capabilities, militarily, technologically, or otherwise."

The President frowned.

The young scientist cleared his throat, the noise loud over the amplifiers transmitting his voice. "I must agree with the General," he said.

Alba turned reflexively to glare at him.

A biologist turned politician? But now that she looked more closely, the boy's face was somewhat familiar …

Of course.

Emeric Furtado. The son of former councillor Alasne Furtado. The boy was a competent biologist, from what she understood, but he certainly owed his position more to his mother's name than to personal merit.

And looking between him and the General, she was very, very certain on whose payroll he was currently listed.

She rose briskly to her feet. "Madam Speaker. As the President has pointed out, this is a matter of absolutely vital import. I suggest that we gather the most capable individuals in order to pursue it. I suggest we summon—" she tapped her temple, bringing up the internal retinal screen of her wavelink, and scanned the information quickly. "Ines Madera and Matin Paredes, from the Sao Martim University, to lead the linguistics team. I suggest tasking Duarte Rios and Jakinda Veiga to study the implications of the portal itself and to verify whether it is posing any environmental hazard by its very presence. And I suggest that, in the search for a cure for the defect, we call Aran Romeu in from the field. I believe his reputation precedes him."

She caught scattered smiles on the faces of the other counsellors.

Perhaps Aran's swashbuckling reputation and harebrained expeditions were a touch flamboyant for her tastes, and perhaps the holographs of him in the news, with his brown skin sun-darkened to a burnt copper, his rakish black beard, his wavy, perpetually mussed hair and his soulful eyes—along with his reputation as someone who enjoyed an "evening of good company," as the saying went—did nothing to dampen the tales that had sprung up about him. But he was undoubtedly the best field researcher on the planet, and probably in the Joias system.

There was also the fact that she was unlikely to run up against argument as to his selection. He was popular and well-liked, and she'd already anticipated the need to forestall the eager young man in the rotunda from being peremptorily placed on the team by Cavaco.

The young scientist at the podium smiled as well, but the expression was less than genuine.

Alba snorted quietly. In her experience, professional jealousy did much less for one's chances than good old-fashioned hard work and talent. And, as much of a roguish thrill-seeker as this Aran was, hard work and talent he clearly had in spades.

"And why not Mr. Furtado?" asked the General, rising. His expression was hard, and anger sparked from his glare as he turned to her. "He has clearly shown his ability—"

"His ability to analyze samples in a lab," Alba interrupted tartly.

It spoke to the urgency of the matter that the Speaker didn't even send a dirty look her way at her disregard of formality.

"I am not, however, convinced that there will be ideal laboratory conditions on whatever alien settlement we find beyond the portal," Alba continued. "If you know of a more well-respected field biologist than Aran, I suggest you present their name to the Council for consideration."

A woman from the Military Committee, one of Cavaco's closest confidants, stood. "I understand Aran Romeu is currently involved in an important field study. I hardly think we can—" Her words faltered at Alba's quelling glare.

The older councillor who'd spoken earlier, whose granddaughter had the defect, rose to their feet. "Madam Speaker, if I may," they said in their trembling voice. At the woman's nod, they turned to the military councillor, their face taking on an expression of barely disguised disgust.

"If there's a scientific study more important than finding the cure for the defect, please explain it to me." Their voice cracked with age and emotion. "But if this is an excuse to express your pique at the Chief Justice at the cost of my granddaughter's life, I suggest you rethink your priorities."

The silence in the chamber was answer enough.

Alba allowed herself a small, tight smile.

In this, at least, she'd out-maneuvered the General, and it appeared he was intelligent enough to realize it.

After a desultory discussion, almost brief enough not to merit the term, a message was sent out to the various experts, and at long last the Council was dismissed.

There had been nothing else said about Alba's proposal to disband the Military Council.

She'd hardly expected there to be, not with developments as they were.

But as she stepped through the door from the rotunda and into the spacious, cool hallways of the council building, she couldn't help a quick glance over her shoulder at Cavaco.

He hadn't risen to his position by being timid, or stupid. He was a strategist by training and by nature. And if he wasn't already thinking up some play to use this new development to grab for power with both hands, and perhaps pull her fangs at the same time—then she wasn't the judge of character she knew herself to be.

5

Aran

The sleek government ship nosed its way into the passenger shipping lanes that wound through the old section of the city.

Aran stared out the plex windows at the colourful, noisy bustle of the streets below him, fighting back the wash of irrational panic.

There was absolutely nothing to be afraid of.

He'd been repeating that to himself under his breath for the last hour, ever since the transport had entered Vila Nova do Sol's airspace, and even running through the data he and Istvay had gathered on their most recent excursion hadn't been enough to hold back the choking dread.

It hadn't actually helped.

It also hadn't helped that he was bloody terrified of flying. And of heights. And of whatever the hell jiggly, gelatinous substance the unmanned government ship had spat out at them in fancy little dishes for their meals.

Istvay had eaten it with every sign of satisfaction. Aran had poked at it a few times, and then secretly slipped it to Ani when Istvay

50

wasn't looking. Which meant that now he was hangry, as well as terrified.

He sighed, leaning back in his seat and closing his eyes, trying to force his muscles to unclench.

Cortisol and adrinocorticotropin, obviously, as well as a flood of glucagon and catecholamines. An effective cocktail of hormones, if your future plans include running for your life, or fighting off a swarm of carnivorous common prairie snouts.

Less effective if your plans involved sitting in a damn unmanned government transport, to be brought into the city where you'd grown up and then spent the rest of your life trying to get away from. He could almost smell it—the confusing, heavy scent of cooking food, unwashed bodies, the ozone tang of the power generators and the dark, smoky fragrance of burning charcoal, all seasoned with the inescapable whiff of rotting garbage. The incessant noise and press and bustle, the feeling of wanting to crawl out of his own skin to get away from it all.

None of his long string of foster parents had ever understood it, but Istvay's mother had. And whenever he couldn't bear things any longer and escaped to the streets, the small makeshift shelter in one of the alleys, where she and Istvay lived and where he could take refuge from the chaos, had been the only constant, secure, safe memory of his entire childhood.

Until she'd died, of course.

He sighed heavily and squeezed his eyes closed, clenching and unclenching his fists to rein in the growing panic.

There was absolutely nothing to be afraid of.

Istvay had dozed off hours ago, head lolling back against the seat-cushions, but now they stirred and blinked their eyes open. "Aran?" Their voice was thick with sleep. "Are we there already?" They sat up, scrubbing at their eyes. "I thought you'd be sleeping."

Aran looked away, muttering something about not being tired.

Istvay sighed, still rubbing their eyes. "Aran. It'll be fine. We'll get in there, you'll talk to them, we'll leave. Easy as that."

"Yeah," Aran muttered, stroking Ani's tentacles, where she sat bunched in his lap. She gave a chirruping little purr and flattened her bulbous body with pleasure at the touch.

Istvay blew out a breath. "I'm not going to be able to talk you into leaving Ani behind, am I?"

Aran tightened his hand protectively on Ani's tentacle, then yelped, frowning down at her. "Ani, you know better. If you don't like something, we've talked about ways you can let me know." He looked ruefully at his hand, which was already swelling, and going an ugly greenish-purple where she'd nicked him with a tentacle-spike. "Look what you've done. Now I'll be wearing a bandage when I go in and talk to the Council."

Ani had the grace to look mildly ashamed, and tightened her tentacles protectively around his wrist.

Istvay was watching, shaking their head. "I suppose it's no use my reminding you that thing is considered an illegal method of biological warfare by the entire rest of the system?"

Aran rolled his eyes. "Ani's perfectly tame. And completely harmless, look at her."

She snuggled a little closer to him, her body now a delicate blue, her tentacles curling around his arm, the skin flaps she used for flying wrapped around him like a hug.

"She just poisoned you," Istvay pointed out, a trace of exasperation in their tone. "She literally just poisoned you, and the only reason that you're not convulsing on the floor right now is that she's done it so often you've built up an immunity."

Aran rubbed Ani's head affectionately, carefully avoiding the venomous line of serrated teeth that marked her second external mouth. "She only does that if she's upset, and it was my fault for upsetting her in first place. Besides, she's very intelligent. She'd never do it to someone else, and she knows it doesn't really hurt me."

Istvay looked meaningfully at Aran's hand, which had now swollen to almost twice its usual size, and was sending tingling pulses of pain up his arm.

Aran rolled his shoulder to shake it off, and sighed.

"And that group of bandits we ran across last summer?" Istvay prodded.

"They were trying to kill us," Aran said patiently. "The result wouldn't have been any different if we been travelling with a protection drone."

Istvay gave a disbelieving snort. "Last I checked, protection drones don't inject their prey with digestive fluids, then suck out the liquid afterwards so there's nothing left but crumpled husks."

Ani glanced up at the exasperated tone in Istvay's voice, and curled herself tighter around Aran's arm.

Aran stroked her soothingly. "Well, they were already dead. She was just following her instincts. I don't see that it makes any practical difference."

Istvay muttered something, shaking their head, and dropped back against the seat, glancing out the window as they did so. "Well, we're almost there. Then maybe we'll see what all this fuss is about." They closed their eyes, but Aran caught the tension in their posture, and the hint of pallor in their cheeks.

Perhaps Istvay wasn't as comfortable as they were trying to let on, either.

The craft navigated the streets of the elegant Old Quarter of the city, the buildings lining the wide streets crafted of elegant old stone, surfaces pitted from the centuries, but the soaring lines of their architecture showing the artistry of their construction.

Vila Nova do Sol was the oldest city settled when the generation ship had arrived here five hundred years ago, and this section of the city was still mostly original buildings. It was an elegant, expensive part of town, entirely different from the dirty, busy, squalid streets where he'd grown up. But somehow, it was no less terrifying.

They landed gently in a wide old courtyard, the ship touching down soundlessly on the elegant cobblestones. "We have arrived at our destination," said a pleasant male voice over the loudspeakers. "I have unlocked the cabin doors, and you may disembark at your leisure. Thank you for trusting me with this flight."

There was a pneumatic hiss as the doors slid open, and the thick, oppressive heat of a summer afternoon wafted into the ship with all the subtlety of a swamp blight's mating scream.

Aran swallowed hard, fighting back the nervous nausea, and stood. Ani slithered up his arm to perch on his shoulder, and Istvay eyed her askance before apparently deciding that any commentary would be ultimately a waste of breath. They glanced at Aran, shaking their head with an air of rueful fondness, then stepped forward onto the short loading ramp that led to the courtyard.

Aran took a deep breath, gathering his resolve, and followed.

It was exactly as bad as he'd been expecting—a line of politicians and small cluster of people who, he was very sure, were well-known names in the scientific community, and, ranged behind them like an unspoken threat, a swarm of reporters, mixed in with a crowd of gawking people pushing and scuffling for a closer look.

He slowed almost unconsciously, but Istvay, who'd probably been staying close in case of just such an occurrence, put a hand inconspicuously on his arm. Aran shot them a grateful glance and forced his legs to keep moving, and the two of them stepped out into the courtyard below.

"Aran! Is it true that the specimen you sent back a year ago—"

"Is it true you fought off seven wild harobeasts in the mountains of—"

"Is it true you're engaged to be married to—"

"Aran," said the politician in front, speaking loud enough to be heard above the clamour. He stepped forward and clasped Aran's hand, and Aran refrained, with an effort, from jerking it away. "So glad you could make it. As you can imagine, we were desperate for your expertise in this very exciting development."

Aran forced himself to breathe slowly, counting down from a hundred in his head. The politician didn't seem to notice.

He seemed the type of man not to notice anything he didn't want to.

"And Istvay!" He turned, shaking Istvay's hand warmly, then turned back to Aran and clapped him on the shoulder in a jovial manner.

Aran couldn't repress a flinch, and from his other shoulder, Ani gave a quiet hiss. "Easy, girl," he murmured, glancing back at her.

The man followed his gaze, then gave a yelp and leapt ungracefully backwards, almost knocking over an unlucky aide.

"I—that isn't—" he gave an uneasy laugh. "Aran, my friend, you didn't bring—"

Aran sighed and held out his arm. "Meet Ani," he said.

Ani hesitated a moment, then, body striated with a bright, angry orange, slithered warily down his arm to completely envelop his hand, her long tentacles twining up his arm and over his shoulder. She was making an angry, growling sort of purr, and he stroked her gently.

"Come on, Ani, be nice," he whispered, then turned back to the Councillor. "As you can see, she's perfectly tame."

Ani's growl turned into a hiss, and she shifted a little on his arm, puffing out the pouches under her bulbous eyes to make herself look bigger.

The man had a fixed, rictus grin on his face. He gave a forced chuckle. "Aran. That—that—surely you don't mean to—that thing could—"

"As Aran said," said Istvay mildly, stepping past Aran to insert themself between the insulted Ani, who was now hissing like a teakettle, and the terrified politician, "This is Ani. Her assistance on Aran's expeditions has been invaluable, and as she's a rare specimen, it's singularly impossible to leave her behind. When you extended the invitation, Aran and I both assumed she would be included, as she is, for all intents and purposes, a member of our party."

The Councillor's eyes flicked between Ani, Aran, and Istvay, but at last he gave a grudging, unwilling nod. "I suppose if it is, ah, a member of your party, and—" he shot a wary look at Aran. "And, as you say, tame enough not to pose a threat—"

"Perfectly harmless," Aran managed, tucking his swollen hand inconspicuously behind his back.

"Well." The man was sweating slightly, and he ran his finger under his collar in an unconscious, nervous gesture. "I suppose in that case, I'll let my aide show you to your rooms. I'm sure you'll wish to rest and refresh yourselves before tonight's gala in your honour."

Aran barely managed to bite back a desperate groan.

Damn it to hell, of course they'd have a gala in his honour. Of course he couldn't just come into the city quietly, talk to the Council, and leave. Because when in the hell had his life ever been that damn simple?

Istvay shot him a sympathetic glance. "There's no need for a gala, honestly," they said, turning to the man. "We have another research expedition planned, and it's quite time-sensitive, so——"

The politician brushed off Istvay's words with a wave of his hand. "No, no, I insist. It's no trouble at all, and the scientific community—not to mention anyone who's anyone in society—is dying to meet our friend Aran. He comes to the city so infrequently. Besides, the Council wanted to present a briefing to those who'll be in attendance, so it's all arranged."

The nerve-induced nausea was rising in Aran's throat in unpleasant waves.

"Now, Estel will show you to your rooms," the man continued, turning away.

Istvay slipped a comforting hand through Aran's elbow, eyebrow raised in rueful apology, and a thoroughly miserable Aran let Istvay lead him after the scurrying, terrified aide. They passed through the massive, elegant hotel lobby, up the lift, down a wide, airy corridor, and finally reached the doors of a double suite connected by a common area.

The aide gave a respectful nod and all but fled back down the corridor. Istvay closed the door firmly, and at last, they and Aran were alone.

"Sorry, Aran," said Istvay. "I did try."

Aran sank into a chair and put his head in his hands, then swore at the sharp jolt of pain. He tried again a little more carefully, this time letting his one good hand support the weight of his chin as he slumped in abject misery.

"It won't be that bad," said Istvay encouragingly. "We'll go early, and I'll think up some excuse to get us out as quickly as possible. You're famous enough that if you don't say anything the whole time, they'll just think you're stuck up." They dropped into the seat across from him. "Besides, you might meet someone interesting. You never know."

Aran gave a listless nod, not even bothering to look up.

It would be that bad. He could already tell.

A far-too-short time later, Aran jerked his head up from his palmscreen at a polite knock at the door.

The aide's nervous voice floated through, informing them that the gala would be starting in an hour, and she was more than happy to take them down whenever they were ready, just call her on the wavelink.

Damn it to hell.

He'd managed, somehow, to distract himself with his data, and he'd been pouring over the lines of the genetic readout from the beautiful, fascinating living rock/volcano that had almost eaten Istvay the previous day, the intricate details of it compelling enough that he'd almost been able to forget where he was, and what was waiting for him.

He groaned.

"I don't suppose we could tell them I died?" he called to Istvay.

Istvay's laugh floated out from the other bedroom. "Somehow, I doubt that'll work," they called back.

Aran closed his eyes for a moment, bracing himself, then stood, shutting down the palmscreen, and stumbled into his own bedroom to get ready.

He washed quickly, the luxurious warmth of the steam cleanser strange after months of bathing in river water unevenly warmed by a portable cleanser, or sometimes not warmed at all, depending on how hard their latest expedition had been on their supplies. Then he slipped into the most comfortable of the uncomfortable formalwear someone had stocked in his closet—a tailored cerulean-blue suit with a matching vest and a single-breasted coat—slipping the maroon cravat loosely around his neck and tying a haphazard bow.

Good enough, probably. It wasn't like anyone actually cared what he wore, any more than they cared whether or not he wanted to be there.

He stepped out, precisely forty-seven minutes later, just as Istvay emerged from their own room.

For a moment, Aran stood blinking.

Istvay's suit was a deep green, the cut accentuating their shoulders and slim waist, the creamy shirt underneath clinging loosely to their chest. The dark, elegant fabric of the suit brought out the light brown of their skin and the deeper brown of their eyes, and the smooth shadow of their beard emphasized the shape of their face, with its sharp cheekbones and prominent nose. Their black hair, still glistening from the steam cleanser, was pulled back in its usual ponytail and fell to their shoulders, and they were grinning their crooked grin.

Aran found himself unable to look away.

Hell, he was hardly able to breathe.

"Let me get that for you," said Istvay, their tone amused. They stepped forward, untying Aran's hasty bow and re-tying it in a practised motion. Their hands were quick, strong fingers deft and precise, and as they frowned down at the soft cloth, Aran was very aware of how close their face was to his own.

An uninvited memory flashed through his mind, of another time Istvay's face had been this close to his—the night of their university graduation, outside his tiny student dorm, both of them pleasantly drunk and Istvay's laughter sending an agreeable warmth through the pit of Aran's stomach. Istvay had been looking at him, their arm thrown around his shoulders, face centimetres from his, and Aran, caught in that gaze like he always was, had leaned forward impulsively.

And Istvay, instead of pulling back, had leaned in as well, laughing softly as their lips met, and they'd stumbled through the door to his room, Istvay shoving it closed behind them with their foot …

Istvay stepped back, examining their handiwork critically, and Aran let out a breath, his muscles suddenly far too shaky.

Istvay looked up, finally satisfied, and gave him a quick grin. "There. Now every person at the gala will be throwing themselves at you."

Their tone was joking, and Aran managed a grin in return.

Because what use would it be, telling them that the only person on the entire planet he had any interest in having thrown at him was standing right in front of him, examining his cravat with a critical eye?

He'd woken the morning after graduation to an empty bed. Istvay had avoided his gaze for the next few days, and they'd never spoken of it again.

And Aran had never figured out how to bring it up himself, or what had gone wrong.

Istvay gave him a sympathetic look. "You'll be fine," they said. They reached out a hand and paused, and when Aran nodded, placed it gently on his shoulder with a reassuring squeeze. "We survived a living volcano two days ago. It can't be worse than that, right?"

"Yeah," Aran muttered, still unsure of his voice.

Istvay laughed. "Well, just bring Ani with. I guarantee you we'll be invited to leave at the first opportunity."

This time Aran's grin in return was a little more genuine. "I've made her up a bed in the hotel room. But if she decided to come, I couldn't leave her behind if I wanted to."

"Yes, when your pet is something that's classified as a weapon of mass destruction, it tends to go where it wants," Istvay grumbled.

Despite their attempt at an early arrival, there were already hordes of reporters standing eager watch in the darkening courtyard of the grand old-stone building as the city transport pulled to a stop outside. Aran glanced quickly at Istvay, and Istvay shot a meaningful look at the tall stone walls surrounding the courtyard.

Aran nodded, grinning a little despite himself, and unbuttoned his suit jacket. Istvay had already strode around to the nearest wall, stripped their jacket off, and slung it over their shoulder, hands running along the rough stone calculatingly.

"After the things we've scaled, this is as simple as breathing," they whispered, eyes dancing. "I'd like to see the reporters' faces when they find they've missed us."

At the base of the wall inside, they both brushed off their suits, shrugged back into their coats, and, with Istvay trying with a notable lack of success to hide their mirth, blended in with the gathered dignitaries.

Even in the few short minutes before the two of them were noticed, Aran was miserable. The suit coat was unpleasantly warm, the cravat trapping the heat around his neck and causing sweat to trickle, itchy and uncomfortable, down his chest. The shifting mass of humanity, the drone and buzz of a hundred conversations, the overripe smell of wine mingling with the thick scent of cologne and perfume, started a dull ache behind his eyes and set every nerve in his body on edge, his muscles tightening unconsciously.

He stood slightly back from the crowd, trying to keep his breath from coming too quickly.

"Aran! There you are! People have been looking for you all night!"

He flinched, his hand tightening on his wineglass. A woman who he vaguely remembered from university—Mariana, maybe?—was pushing her way through the crowd towards him, and at her words, heads were turning in his direction from all around the room.

For a panicked moment he contemplated turning to run, but she'd already reached him. She tucked her hand firmly through his arm, drawing him towards an admiring crowd.

After an eternity of being introduced to people he didn't recognize and whose names he had no chance of remembering, he saw from the corner of his eye someone detach themselves from another group and start over.

Aran caught a glimpse of the man's face as he approached, and groaned to himself.

Just when he'd thought the night couldn't get any worse.

"Aran. What a pleasure to finally have you grace our company." Emeric's voice was rich and smooth, his smile as charming and effusive as it had been when they were classmates in university.

Maybe, Aran caught himself thinking, it wasn't as bad as it seemed. Maybe, after all these years, Emeric had finally realized this whole thing was a joke, that Aran hated his unwanted fame just as much as Emeric hated that Aran had it. That they were unconscious, unwilling allies, at least in this.

"I hear you've been busy," Emeric continued, his smile almost genuine. "Fourteen new specimens in six months. You must be very proud, especially for someone with a background like yours. Honestly, it must be nice being the token poverty student—I heard you got called in by the Council because they wanted some diversity on the task force. Oh, but you haven't been briefed on that yet, have you?"

"I—" Aran began, glancing around the room in the vague hope of a rescue. "I didn't mean to—"

Emeric brushed off his protestations with a wave of his hand. "Come now, you're among friends. No need to be bashful."

"I'd certainly like to believe that Aran is among friends, although the current company makes that claim a bit dubious," came another voice, and Aran's head jerked up at the obvious menace under the words.

"Istvay." Emeric's tone chilled noticeably.

Aran glanced between Istvay and Emeric, and noticed, with mild dread, Istvay's small, challenging grin, the way their eyes narrowed.

"Are you saying you regret trying to kill Aran the last time you two interacted?" Istvay's tone was light, but they were clearly furious, in a way that only Emeric seem to be able to provoke. "Is this an apology, then?"

"Istvay, it's fine," Aran whispered, trying to catch his friend's eye.

Istvay ignored him, smiling at Emeric with smooth menace. "Tell me, Emeric, how have things been in the research laboratory? Any recent successes? I haven't heard of any, but then, maybe it's just that Aran and I have been out of touch. I'm sure the news reports have been full of nothing but your discoveries."

Emeric stiffened as if Istvay had struck him, the look on his face pure malice. Aran knew, suddenly, that Istvay hadn't spent the entire time in the hotel room sleeping, either—they'd probably been combing through every single scientific report the news packets had run since the last time they and Aran had been in the city, in preparation for this precise interaction.

"Unlike some of my colleagues," said Emeric, his tone icy, "the research I am doing is delicate and precise. I simply haven't the leisure to announce myself in the news packets at every opportunity."

"Well, that's a relief," said Istvay, their voice amused and dangerous. "Of course, nor did Aran—reporters seem to seek him out, rather than the other way around—but then, I suppose when your work is as groundbreaking as his is, that's an unintended consequence of the job." They laughed softly, the sound carrying enough threat that Aran had to stop himself from stepping backwards. "But as you say, I'm certain your work is also—" Istvay paused, delicately. "Very important."

The glare Emeric turned on Istvay was the functional equivalent of a murder attempt.

"It was a pleasure to see you again, Aran," he said, pointedly turning his back on Istvay. "I hope we'll have a chance to reconnect when you're a little less occupied." With a final venomous glance in Istvay's direction, he turned and stalked off.

Istvay gave a low laugh. "Good riddance," they whispered.

In the brief lull, someone from the front of the room cleared their throat, the sound over the amplifiers loud enough to cut through the drone of the conversations. Aran and Istvay both looked up.

A councillor stood in the front of the room, looking somewhat nervous. He cleared his throat again, then said, "Friends and colleagues, I've been asked to inform you of the Council's deliberations. While no final decision as to a course of action has been made, please be confident that no effort is being spared to ensure that this unprecedented development is properly dealt with.

In fact, our valued guest, Aran Romeu, has come to the city precisely to assist the Council in their determinations ..."

He droned on, but it was clear he wasn't going to deliver any information of substance.

Istvay must have come to the same conclusion. They glanced around the room quickly, grinning their familiar, lopsided grin.

It would have made Aran's heart jump, just a little, even if he hadn't had two glasses of wine over the course of the last hour and a half. But he had, and now it made something catch in his throat, a little jolting gasp that he couldn't tell was pleasure or pain.

Istvay's eyes danced with mischief as they scanned the room, and there was a familiar knot in the pit of Aran's stomach, a warmth of desire that was far too pleasant, and far too hopeless.

As the Councillor finished and stepped down, Istvay turned back to Aran, their eyes still twinkling, their grin sending an electric jolt through Aran's entire body once more.

"Over there," they whispered, pointing across the room to where a tall, light-haired man with fair, freckled skin and an easy smile was watching them. "He hasn't been able to take his eyes off you all night." They winked at Aran, their dark lashes, especially after his two glasses of wine, almost choking Aran anew. "Go on. I can guarantee he'll be more than happy to talk about whatever you want to talk about. And if you don't like the look of him, there's a woman over there who's just about as enamoured, if I'm any judge—"

Aran managed a small smile and shook his head. "No, no, he looks ... fine—"

Istvay had been intent on Aran "finding someone" for as long as he could remember. Aran had given up on trying to make up reasons he wasn't interested that didn't involve him blurting out a confession of undying love to his best friend, and trampling all over their friendship, and … well, he'd never let himself think farther than that, because of the static white panic that flooded his brain at the thought of somehow hurting Istvay, or pushing them away.

Besides—well, at least spending the night with the inevitably pleasant people Istvay always seemed to find helped Aran push past the hopeless longing that seemed to have become as much a part of him as his own skin.

"Go on then!" said Istvay teasingly. "Can't be worse than listening to all your colleagues pretend not to be jealous all evening. And I'll bet he'll figure out a way to get both of you out of here soon as humanly possible, given the motivation."

Aran nodded grimly, took a deep breath, and started across the hall towards the man Istvay had indicated.

The man's expression brightened in delighted disbelief as he caught Aran's eyes, and he quickly excused himself from his conversation.

Aran sighed to himself.

He looked nice, at least. And Istvay was right—it was a thousand times better than any of his other current conversational options.

He glanced back at Istvay, who gave him a supportive wink that was enough to almost shut down the flow of blood to his brain.

Damn it, why hadn't he remembered what a bad idea getting tipsy around Istvay could be?

He gritted his teeth and turned resolutely back to his new companion, forcing a smile.

The man looked friendly, and more than eager to please. At the very least, he'd be better company than a group of envious colleagues. And perhaps, if the evening went the way Aran hoped it might, it would be enough to get the sight of Istvay's lopsided grin out of his brain for at least a few hours.

Istvay was, in fact, correct—the moment Aran telegraphed his intentions, his companion had, with impressive alacrity and creativity, managed to socially disentangle both of them, procure a bottle of wine and two glasses, and make their excuses to all and sundry. Now, an hour and another half-glass of wine later, they were sitting around a small table in Aran's hotel bedroom, and Tomas, who was, in fact, just as pleasant as his smile had promised, had a hand lightly on Aran's elbow, leaning in attentively as he spoke and smiling in genuine delight at Aran's replies.

Aran sipped his wine, enjoying the perceptible looseness spreading through his body. He calculated another half glass, and he'd find Tomas as attractive as the man seemed to find him. A glass after that and they both be laughing, and possibly one final glass before they'd end up in bed together. And the heady, intoxicating rush of testosterone, serotonin, and oxytocin would, with any luck, be enough to clear his traitorous brain of anything but his willing and pleasant companion, instead of a certain lopsided grin, rich brown eyes with a glint of mischief, and the absurd, electric spark that shot through Aran's body every time those eyes turned on him, especially if he had anything less than his full faculties at his disposal—

Tomas had finished whatever story he was telling, and Aran laughed. It had probably been funny, honestly, if he'd been paying attention. Now that he thought of it, Tomas was, in fact, more than a little attractive.

Aran finished his glass of wine, feeling a pleasant rush of desire, and smiled to himself.

Perhaps the evening wouldn't go so badly after all.

He reached out, letting his hand slide across Tomas's and linger there for a moment longer than necessary.

Tomas gave him a smile that sent a jolt of warmth through the pit of his stomach. "These formal shirts are always so hot," he said, loosening the top button of his shirt with a wink.

Aran grinned back recklessly. "I think it's late enough in the evening that we could find a way to get more comfortable," he drawled.

Tomas smiled, reaching down for his wine glass. Then he frowned in sudden concern. "Aran. You're hurt. What happened to your hand?"

Aran followed his gaze, and it took a moment for his wine-muddled brain to remember Ani's fit of temper that morning. Then, abruptly, he swore as, as if on cue, something tickled the back of his neck.

"Not now, Ani," he hissed over his shoulder.

"Aran?" Tomas's voice was now genuinely concerned. "Are you alright? Should I call someone?"

Ani, who'd wriggled up the back of his chair to settle herself in her customary place on his shoulder, poked her head up above his collar, and he could feel the gentle suction of her tentacles against his skin. He closed his eyes with a final, hopeless curse—when she was curious like this, she wouldn't be satisfied until she'd gawked her fill.

He could tell the exact moment Tomas caught sight of her, peeking out from behind his shoulder, and then, a second later, the moment when he realized what exactly he was looking at. The polite confusion on his face turned abruptly to terror, and he shoved his chair back, jolting to his feet.

Aran held up his hand helplessly. "Tomas, it's fine, it's only Ani, she's—"

Tomas was already backing towards the door, his expression frantic. He fumbled behind him for the switch, and when the door hissed open, he was through it and down the hallway as if the Void itself was at his heels.

Aran watched him go, and with him, any hope of an evening filled with anything other than himself and Ani.

Ani gave a curious little chirrup as the door hissed closed again.

Aran sighed, and stretched out his arm.

It hadn't been her fault—she couldn't have known how badly the sight of damn Istvay in a formal suit would leave him needing a night of pleasant oblivion.

She crawled down his arm, twining herself delicately around his hand, and he smiled despite himself. He stroked her bulbous body for a moment, then shook his head and pushed himself to his feet, glancing ruefully at the two wineglasses and the half-empty bottle of wine.

He'd clean up in the morning.

"And this is why we can't have nice things," he murmured, tickling Ani under the chin as she purred in contentment.

She, at least, seemed perfectly satisfied with the progression of the evening's events.

Aran, though, took far too long to drift off to sleep, and when he did, it was to a picture of brown eyes peering at him in familiar concern, full lips, the hint of a five o'clock shadow, and impossibly long lashes.

6

Savina

The moment the shuttle landed, Savina joined the pushing, shoving crowd, keeping herself tucked safely within the mass of panicking bodies as she stepped past two officers at the door, who were trying desperately to keep order, and out into the station.

She kept her walk brisk pace of someone with important things to do, rather than someone trying to avoid being picked up by law enforcement, until she was outside the shuttle block. Then, with a friendly smile at the door attendant, she stepped through onto the streets of the grungy, dirty moonport, glanced around once to make sure there were no officers following, and ran.

The moonport was small, and utilitarian at best. There was no terraforming outside the shuttle base itself, so the places tourists from the luxury ships could go were limited.

It wouldn't be a problem, usually. But if she was being pursued by the police, it would make things a lot more interesting.

She kept her head down, and forced herself to keep a slow, easy pace. But she couldn't help a slight smile.

Let them try to take her.

She strolled past the hangar bays, eyes running casually over the ships as she passed. On her retinal screen, each port showed the name of the ship, as well as its schedule and destination.

She paused in front of one—the *Dolphin*, apparently. It was a grungy, battered-looking ship, but it was headed to an outer planet. Which was exactly what she needed for now—a place to lie low until the furor with the government agent blew over. With funds coming into her account from the job she'd just pulled, she and Beni would have plenty to live off for a few months while they planned their next move, and enough to send back to the compound as well. A few months of forced inactivity should convince whoever had sent the agent after her that she was no longer a threat.

She'd spent her entire life persuading people she wasn't a threat, right up to the moment she killed them. A government official couldn't be that much more difficult.

A woman who must be the ship's captain stood at the base of the loading ramp, haggling over fuel prices with a man in shop overalls. She looked to be in her mid-forties, with light brown skin and thick black hair pulled into a shoulder-length ponytail, and was dressed simply in slacks and a white shirt. There was a no-nonsense air about her, and she wore an expression of weary resignation, the lines around her eyes and mouth evidence of a life that had aged her beyond her years.

Savina waited patiently until the woman came to some agreement with the seller, who nodded gruffly. The captain squeezed her hand closed, presumably activating her wavelink, and the fuel seller paused, eyes going unfocused for a moment as he scanned his retinal screen. He nodded, and turned to a handful of small drones behind him. They came to life, rolling backwards on the bay floor, and returning a short time later loaded down with heavy fuel cubes to deposit in the fuel port in the ship's belly.

Savina move closer, positioning herself so that when the captain turned from inspecting the fuel cells, she couldn't help but see her.

"Do you want something?" The woman's voice was rough, like someone accustomed to shouting orders, but her tone, although abrupt, wasn't unkind.

Savina smiled, widening her eyes in the innocent expression that had served her so well over the years. "Are you the captain of the *Dolphin?*" she asked, letting a Rim-Mountain drawl lengthen her words.

The captain gave a faint smile. "I am. But if you're looking for passage, you picked the wrong ship. I have a full cargo load to drop."

Savina dimpled. "I'm not looking for passage, exactly. I mean, I guess I am, in a way. But I was hoping to work for my passage. I'm a decent mechanic."

Considering the records her wavelink had pulled up on the ship, as well as its general appearance, the *Dolphin* needed a mechanic desperately.

"Well …" the captain hesitated, clearly torn.

Savina smiled again. "I won't be any trouble, I promise. I'm used to rough bunks." She let a trace of desperation show through her tone. "I was working up there on the yacht until last week. Sent my wages home to my family because they promised me a passage credit home. But when the time came …" She shook her head and trailed off.

The captain sighed. "And you wonder how people like that get so flush. It's by taking money off those who can't fight them for it." There was a hint of bitterness under her tone. She shook her head, looking Savina up and down. "Mechanic, you say?"

Savina nodded eagerly. "I can do other things too, if you need. I'm pretty handy around ships."

She managed not to let even a hint of a smile show. The fact that she couldn't tell a spanner from an inverter torch was irrelevant to this discussion. As long as the captain believed she could do the job, the rest would work itself out.

The captain chuckled ruefully. "Well, it just so happens I do need a mechanic. I have some issues with the thrusters, and I was going to pay someone to have it fixed at our next port. But if you're willing to work off your passage—"

Savina nodded again, eyes wide and earnest. "I'll work off my passage, I swear. I'm a hard worker, and I can get references if you want."

"Off the yacht, no doubt," said the captain dryly. "That won't be needed. I prefer to keep out of the way of those people if I can." She looked Savina over carefully and sighed again. "Well, I'd have starved to death half a dozen times if people hadn't given me the benefit of the doubt when I needed it." She shook her head. "You can come. But if you don't earn your keep, I'll drop you on the next planet with my cargo, and you have to find your own way home."

"Thank you," said Savina, her smile one of desperate gratitude. "I won't let you regret it."

These trustful, pay-it-forward types were always the easiest to dupe.

"Don't thank me until you see your bunk," the captain murmured wryly. "We don't have much space. I hope your kit isn't too large."

"I travel light," said Savina, smiling brightly. "It won't be a problem at all. I just left my things back at the port locker—"

The captain nodded. "Best bring them aboard then. We've got clearance to leave in fifteen planetary minutes, and I don't plan on being late. If you're not here by then, we'll leave without you."

She paused, and as Savina turned away, called after her, "I should warn you, I took on another stray who's working their passage home. You'll have to bunk with them, and they look like they're a little on the touchy side."

Savina turned her full smile on the captain. "I get along with most people. Don't worry about me."

She rolled her eyes as she walked quickly across the port to the small locker where she'd left her meagre bag of belongings. She paid a coin to the grumpy-looking attendant and grabbed her bag.

"There!" came a voice from behind her.

She turned in time to see a handful of police officers turning in her direction, the one in the lead pointing directly at her.

She swore, snatched up her bag, and took off down the moonports's maze of corridors.

"Map," she whispered, flicking her eyes to bring her wavelink online. A station map popped up, translucent in the left corner of her eye. She glanced through it quickly, then turned down a narrow street leading to the food court.

The officers were hard on her heels. If she was any judge, they'd be spreading out, trying to cut her off.

She smiled grimly to herself.

If they came all this way for a show, she may as well give them one.

She burst out into the food court, knocking over a table and several chairs and sending their occupants to their feet cursing. A rough-looking woman grabbed her by the shoulder, spinning her around angrily. "Where the hell do you think you're going?"

Savina gave the woman a terrified, pleading glance. "Some people are after me," she panted. "They're—they're dressed like police officers, but they're not, and I'm—I'm scared, I don't know what they're going to do to me—" she let her voice catch just a little.

"Or maybe it is the police," grumbled a man, but she could see by his face that she had him.

"Help me, please," she whispered. "I don't care, I'll wait somewhere for the real police to come. I just—" she blinked back a tear.

From the hallway where she'd emerged, she could hear police officers shouting.

The man sighed, shaking his head. "Look, if you go out that back way, we'll send them off in the wrong direction. It should give you maybe five minutes."

Five minutes. That should be enough. "Thank you," she murmured, her voice trembling.

The man gestured impatiently. "Go on. This won't last forever."

She gave him a grateful nod, and the woman released her grip on Savina's arm.

Savina ducked down the corridor the man had indicated as the police burst into the food court.

She was grinning to herself as she ran for it.

The man was as good as his word, it seemed—there were no sounds of pursuit from behind her, although like he'd said, it wouldn't last forever.

She slowed as she reached the *Dolphin's* docking bay, straightening her mussed hair and deliberately slowing her breathing until she was able to sound like she hadn't just been running for her life. She pasted on a charming smile and stepped around the corner, almost bumping into the captain.

"I got my things," Savina said with a friendly smile. "Do you mind if I bring them on board?"

The captain gestured up the loading ramp. "What took you? Get on and get your things stowed. Rafel is just finishing up the pre-flight checks." She shook her head. "After whatever the hell just happened, I'm guessing they'll shut down the ports soon enough, and I can't afford to miss this cargo run."

For just a moment, Savina felt a sick jolt of panic. And then she realized what the captain must be referring to—the rift, or whatever it was, that had so handily distracted her query on the yacht.

She'd have to look deeper into that, probably, figure out what the hell it was. But until then, getting out of this damn wreck of a backwater spaceport was as high on her priority list as it seemed to be on the captain's.

"I'm sorry," she murmured, stepping past the woman up the loading ramp. "It'll only take me a second to get stowed, don't wait on me."

"Don't worry, we won't," said the captain dryly, but she gestured Savina up the loading ramp. Savina skipped up quickly and glanced around.

"Your cabin's in the back," came a gruff voice, and she glanced towards it, blinking in the dim of the ship's emergency lighting.

A man stood at the head of one of the corridors, one leg obviously a cheap prosthetic, his belly bulging over his belt, and a sour look on his pale face. His face was creased with scowl-wrinkles, and his dark hair was going to grey. "Don't know why the captain let you on—she's too soft for her own damn good. But I'm not. You'll work off your passage, I'll to see to that."

Savina gave him a disarming smile. "You won't have to worry about that, I promise. I know she probably shouldn't have, but I'm so glad she was willing to give me a chance." She let her mountain drawl thicken just a little.

The man gave a sceptical snort, jerking his thumb in the direction he'd indicated. She nodded and started off down the corridor.

Time enough to get him on her side later, if it came to it. For now, the first item of business was staying out of the way.

"You're sharing a bunk with the other passenger." The man's voice echoed down the hallway after her, and she could hear an unpleasant glee in it. "I hope you're as good at making friends as you say you are."

Savina rolled her eyes and pulled open the door to what must be her cabin. It slid open, and she stepped inside, blinking at the sudden light.

Someone had already taken their place on one of the two cots. They were tall, and a little younger than Savina, their dark hair short and spiky, their features sharp and angular. Their clothes were all black, and they wore iron spite studs through piercings in every available part of their body—ears, nose, eyebrows, lips, tongue. They turned towards Savina as she stepped through the door, and their face wore an expression of disdain.

Savina grinned to herself. No wonder the captain had warned her.

She threw her small bag of belongings onto the unoccupied cot with a disarming smile. "Hello. I hear we'll be bunking together. Did you get off the yacht without a passage ticket as well?"

The black-clad figure gave her a quick smile. "Glad you made it out, sis."

Savina sighed and dropped onto her cot, feeling a weight lift from her shoulders. "I always do. What about on your end? Everything okay?"

Beni gave their usual small, genuine smile. "Smooth as always. That man tried to talk the captain out of taking me on. I even heard him whispering something about the fact I'm blind could be a problem—but honestly, the moment he said that, the captain told me it was fine if I came." They chuckled. "She sounded furious with him, honestly. Anyway, she seems very kindhearted." Beni paused a moment. "Vina? Do you think she and that crewman are in love?"

Savina snorted. "You say that about everyone. Have you been listening to those damn romance audios again?"

Beni pouted, and Savina grinned despite herself.

Under her feet, the ship hummed gently as the engine started up, and then there was a small jolt as the mag anchor released and the ship rose to hover outside the bay doors. Their cabin had no external plex windows, but Savina could tell from the sucking *hiss* from outside when the bay airlocks opened. There was another jolt that probably would have knocked her off her feet if she'd been standing, and then they were out, and into the sky.

There was a sudden feeling of weightlessness, and Savina swore and clutched for the edge of the cot as her belongings floated up beside her.

Beni laughed. "Forget to stow your things?"

Grumbling, Savina pushed her way awkwardly to the cupboard in the corner, the handle of her kit in one hand, and stowed her belongings as Beni chuckled.

But even as Savina rolled her eyes in a gesture her sibling wouldn't see, she couldn't help but smile—she and Beni had both made it. Maybe there was a government agent after her, but she'd pulled the job, and they were both off the station.

Everything else she could deal with when she had the leisure.

7

Alba

The Council reconvened early the next morning. Alba arrived at the Council room at seven o'clock, a full two hours earlier than usual, to find it already filled almost to capacity. Counsellors were gathered in small groups talking and gesticulating, standing slightly apart paging desperately through holographic tokens from the newsstands, or with the glassy, distant stare of people reading through the retinal screens on their wavelinks.

President Seguer stopped her with a hand on her arm as she pushed her way grimly towards her desk. He looked as if he hadn't slept at all the previous night, and Alba couldn't blame him.

Of the three branches of government, his was the only one whose mandate could be directly repealed by the system's citizens. Which meant the consequences of every decision, good or bad, would be his to bear.

She couldn't muster much sympathy—Ander had always been more concerned about maintaining his position than he had about what that might mean five or ten or fifteen years down the road. He was still in his late fifties, and didn't have the heavy weight of experience, good and otherwise, that had come to colour Alba's decisions.

"Alba. I know the General's been talking with the others, trying to convince them the Military Committee is best suited to deal with this —but do you think he may be right on this one?" Ander's face was pinched with worry, and drawn with lack of sleep.

Alba turned a scornful glance on him. There was a reason why she'd never been particularly fond of the man. "I stand by the statements I made when I presented my proposal," she said curtly. "Now, if you'll excuse me—" She brushed past him, but she couldn't ignore the hard knot of worry in her stomach.

If Cavaco had half-way convinced the President already, it wasn't a good sign.

The Speaker called them to order a few minutes later, and the sudden quiet, after the deafening buzz of voices, was an indescribable relief. Alba leaned back in her chair, aware, suddenly, of the weariness in her muscles, the stiffness in her joints.

"Madam Speaker, if I may." Cavaco rose to his feet, and the Speaker tapped through control of the holodisplay to his desk.

He didn't speak immediately, pausing to cast his gaze across his assembled audience. "My friends and colleagues," he began at last, his voice crisp and precise. "We are in the midst of a situation of unprecedented threat. The world as it existed when we stepped into this chamber yesterday morning is gone, irrevocably." He paused a moment, as if to judge the impact of his words, then, with a sudden, involuntary glance at Alba, he continued hurriedly.

She smirked.

"Only yesterday," he continued, "we were debating a proposal to disband the Military Committee entirely. Now it appears this very branch of the Council may be the only thing standing between our planet, indeed, our solar system, and destruction. I've been in consultation with our top scientists—notable among them Emeric Furtado, who presented the discovery yesterday—and it seems they are in agreement with myself and my associates. Based on what little we know of these aliens and their technology, our best, and perhaps only, hope is to attack first, while we can maintain the upper hand."

He paused again for effect, recalled himself, and tried to hurry on, but he was too late. Alba had been waiting for just such a miscalculation, and she rose and addressed herself to the Speaker before he could open his mouth.

When she'd been granted the floor, she turned a scathing glance on Cavaco. "The scientific community is in agreement with you," she repeated. Her tone dripped disdain, despite the quick pounding of her heart. "Then I assume you'll be more than happy for me to call them immediately to verify. It's always possible for messages to get distorted in the transmission." She made no effort to hide her contempt as she tapped the communication device on her desk to page the door steward. "Would you be so kind as to contact the Sao Martim University research laboratory and inform them that the Council wishes to speak with them via wavelink?"

If she was wrong, she'd just orchestrated her own grand failure.

But she was certain she wasn't wrong. Her past ten years of research couldn't have been upended overnight.

A moment later, a holoscreen popped up in the centre of the room over the podium.

The young scientist from the previous day, Emeric Furtado, appeared, looking dishevelled and uncomfortable. He was flanked by a handful of his associates.

"I understand you've been discussing this new development with my colleague, General Cavaco, and, in your infinite wisdom, have determined the most expedient course of action for our government," she snapped.

The other scientists looked even more uncomfortable, if that were possible, but Emeric rallied slightly. "Madam Chief Justice. We certainly had no intention of telling the Council its job," he said. "However, General Cavaco asked our opinion on certain matters, and we deemed it our duty to—"

"You're a biologist, am I correct?" Alba cut in.

He stopped, somewhat taken aback. "I—"

"And your field of expertise is molecular biology?"

"I—" he looked distinctly flustered now.

"The rest of you—" She turned her gaze on the hapless scientists gathered behind him, all clearly unhappy to be there. "Have all the molecular biologists in your department developed such strong views on how to interact with alien entities?"

There was a shuffling of feet.

She turned back to Emeric, who was clearly trying to gather his dignity. "Since you alone, out of all the molecular biologist of the research institution, seem to believe that your expertise compels you to recommend a course of action to government officials in matters of inter-species relations, perhaps you will enlighten us as to the information upon which your conclusion is based."

He cleared his throat, glancing around in vague desperation. "I, um—that is, I ... the biological markings on the blood sample we examined indicates what I believe to be a genetic predisposition to aggression," he finished finally.

Alba raised her eyebrows with a look she'd perfected over her years on the bench, eloquent enough to send a bloviating lawyer slinking back to their desk, head lowered in shame. "A genetic predisposition to aggression," she repeated, sarcasm veritably dripping from her words. "That is a groundbreaking discovery indeed. I assume you constructed this hypothesis based on thoroughly peer-reviewed research?"

He was silent.

"Come now, I'm certain you wouldn't advise this government to stake the survival of our entire system on a hypothesis not based firmly in data and fact. I'm simply inviting you to refer me to the materials upon which you relied on in coming to your groundbreaking discovery."

He shifted uncomfortably. "I—the, er, the research I relied on was something I've been—I—I intend to publish it shortly, and then, I'm certain, once it's gone through the peer review process, I'd be more than happy to—"

She cut off the line with a flick of her wrist, and turned back to the room. "General," she said, her voice losing none of its ice. "It appears the scientist who advised you may have been a touch precipitous in his recommendations, does it not?"

From the look on Cavaco's face, the young scientist would be hearing from his benefactor that evening.

"As I stated yesterday morning, from a world that, as the General has so poetically informed us, is gone forever, all the *reputable* research," she leaned into the word with just a touch of malice, "research, that is, done by scientists who are experts in the field, agree that the method most likely to be successful in initiating contact with an alien species, especially one of unknown technological and military capabilities and uncertain motives, is not to antagonize them, but to attempt to open a dialogue."

She turned to face her fellow counsellors in the rows of seat rising behind her.

Her hands shook slightly.

It wasn't that she wasn't confident in her factual position—she was entirely certain of it. But she was not accustomed to politicking without making sure of her political position first.

And the stakes of this particular political decision were unimaginably high.

"Friends and colleagues," she continued, in a voice loud enough to carry without the assistance of the amplifiers. "I submit to you that following the suggestion of my learned colleague, General Cavaco, and his molecular biologist consultant, would lead to what scientists in the field refer to as an 'extinction event.'" She paused a moment, letting the silence settle.

"The stakes here are doubly high," she continued at last. "In the one field in which our molecular biologist friend is, in fact, an expert, we have been told this alien species may hold the key to a cure for the genetic defect. This has been our plague, the silent tragedy that has stalked us since our ancestors first arrived on this planet—perhaps since the generation ship itself, if our records are to be relied upon. Millions upon millions of lives cut short, and millions more affected by their loss. In fact, I might venture to say there is not a person in the system whose life has not been touched by the defect in one way or the other. This contact holds the possibility of a cure. Surely threatening to destroy our potential benefactors is not the way to gain access to such sensitive information. I propose that we send out a diplomatic mission, in place of a military one—linguists, scientists, and above all, ambassadors. Negotiators. People trained in defusing conflict and opening communication. If that should fail, we always have my learned friend's suggestion to fall back on. But certainly you must agree that opening negotiations with a pistol to our counterpart's head is unlikely to lead to a mutually beneficial result."

She sat down to silence, marred only by the low murmur of voices as counsellors conferred in quiet tones. She could see Cavaco bending to consult with his advisors, but he didn't spring to his feet to offer a counterargument, as she'd expected him to.

One or two other members of the Council stood, almost timidly, to ask a question or make a statement, and from the tenor of their words, Alba judged that her speech had made some impact.

Her hands were trembling, and she placed them firmly in her lap, forcing them still.

At last, when the silence had stretched, she rose to her feet again. "I call for a preliminary vote," she said. Her heart was still beating too fast, but she managed to keep her voice steady. "The votes may be private, and need not be binding, but I should like a gauge of my esteemed friends' feelings on the General's and my respective proposals."

There was complete silence on the floor as the Speaker sent the tally-code through to their screens, and each Council member tapped their choice: diplomacy, or war.

Alba forced her hands to remain in her lap after she'd made her selection, forced herself not to adjust her collar or touch her face.

This would play out as it played out. She'd done everything she could to steer it, and she'd lived long enough to know that fretting wouldn't change the outcome.

But she'd also lived long enough to know there were some decisions the impacts of which would echo through generations.

She was uncomfortably certain this was one such decision.

At last the speaker hit the screen on her desk, and the tally flooded through to the councillors' personal screens.

Alba drew in a deep breath, almost dizzy with relief.

Her proposal had 347 votes to Cavaco's 64. Even accounting for those who would, perhaps, choose differently when their names were broadcast alongside their votes, and those who might be swayed to one side or the other by argument, it was a solid count.

She'd won this round.

Cavaco stood.

There was a look on his face that Alba couldn't read as he surveyed the room. If it had been anyone else, she'd have guessed that perhaps, faced with a decision of this magnitude, they were willing to put their own position second place to simple self-preservation—that the better angels of their nature, or even just base self-interest, had brought them to agree with her.

But this was Cavaco. And she knew him better than that.

"It appears," he said quietly, "that my respected peers have judged diplomacy our best chance at success. I bow to your collective wisdom." He glanced around again, and still she could read nothing from his expression.

The words should be comforting. But a trickle of unease was working its way up her spine.

The General was not someone to take defeat lying down. She'd expected more than this.

"Far be it from me to attempt again to persuade you. I've presented my position and you have all heard it." He paused a moment. "However, as a loyal member of the Council, I intend to do all I can to ensure the success of this venture. I wish, therefore, to present my recommendation for head diplomat—as I know of no one better at marshalling arguments and turning a clever phrase—" the wryness of his tone did nothing to hide the enmity in the glance he sent in Alba's direction, "I suggest this diplomatic mission be led by none other than the Chief Justice herself. As she has so eloquently argued, we can only afford to send the very best on a mission of such importance."

The unease crawling up Alba's spine crystallized into something akin to dread.

Perhaps it was only a matter of getting her out of the way, buying himself time to unpick the decades of delicate politicking it had taken her to marshal sufficient support for the restructuring of the government. Or perhaps he truly believed his assessment of the hostility of the alien civilization, and assumed they'd make her temporary removal from the council unpleasantly permanent.

Either way, there was a reason he wanted her off the planet, and this was a terrible time for her to be absent.

And yet—she glanced around the chamber at the terrified faces of her colleagues. If she, who'd advocated for this plan, refused to go— how would she find someone else willing? And forcing an unwilling diplomat onto a ship, and into contact with life forms the diplomat was convinced were hostile, was a recipe for disaster.

No. The General had very neatly backed her into a corner.

She took a deep breath and stood. "I am flattered by the recommendation of my learned friend," she said, though her hands were clenched tightly beneath the sleeves of her robe. "It would be remiss of me to send others on a mission that I am unconvinced will be successful, and, as the saying goes, if you want a job done well, best to do it yourself." She paused to allow the small, polite laughter to quiet. "I suggest we put this to a vote, as it is not my individual decision to make. But should the Council agree, I would be honoured to lead this mission, and will shortly present a list of the individuals who I would like to accompany me." She turned to the Speaker, who was staring at her, open-mouthed. "Madam Speaker, if you would be so kind as to call the vote?"

She sat gracefully. She was almost certain she'd managed to hide how her legs shook, so badly that the only reason she'd stayed on her feet was her hands clutched on the edges of her desk.

This didn't mean the situation couldn't be turned to her advantage, of course. But she had a feeling that there was much, much more riding on this mission than simple diplomatic contact with an alien species.

And that, in and of itself, was enough stakes for anyone.

8

Aran

When Aran stumbled out of his room the next morning, Istvay was still sleeping.

It was just as well. Aran wasn't sure he was ready to face them at the moment anyways, not with the nagging ache of a hangover pulsing behind his eyes and the uncomfortable memory of the way he'd stared at his friend, probably for far too long, while they were at the gala.

There was a steaming pot of coffee on the side table, and he poured himself a cup, wondering absently whether the hotel servers had guessed what time he'd get up by taking into account how long he'd stayed at the gala and the number of glasses of wine he'd drunk, or if they simply sent someone to replace the pot every half-hour or so.

It could have been either, honestly, for as hard as he'd slept.

"Time," he mumbled, tapping his wrist, and the AI voice from his battered palm screen said cheerfully, "It's 8:23 in the morning local time. Time difference between here and your previous location is two hours, so you'll feel like it's 10:23 in the morning."

He rubbed a hand over his face and swallowed a mouthful of coffee hot enough to scald his tongue, grimacing. Taking travel time into account, he had a little over half an hour to get ready if he wanted to make the Council meeting at 9:30 local time.

He didn't, it so happened. But the sooner he learned what this was all about, the sooner he and Istvay and Ani could get the hell out of this damn city.

He shook his head ruefully, swallowed another mouthful of scalding coffee, and stumbled back to his room to clean up.

An hour later he was being escorted through three layers of security drones and a sensor machine on his way into the Council building.

He'd been here exactly twice before. The first time was when his discovery of the breeding grounds of the lesser shriek had taken the scientific world by storm. The second time was when word got out that he'd managed to hatch out the egg of a great tree-dwelling venomous tentacled land-devil, and, instead of immediately destroying it, had tamed the hatchling and kept it as a pet.

It had been the first time he'd ever been grateful for his unasked-for fame, since that was probably the only reason Ani hadn't been immediately destroyed, likely by nuclear weapons of some sort. Land-devils were notoriously difficult to kill.

The decision, however, had not been unanimous, and he'd taken the precaution of leaving Ani in the hotel room this time.

At last he completed the security protocols and was waved through the heavy doors. He shivered a little as he stepped inside the Council Building. It was still early summer in Vila Nova do Sol, and the city hadn't yet achieved the scalding heat that would come later, but even so, the change in temperature from the warmth of the courtyard to the musty cool of the entranceway came as a shock.

It should have been pleasant. It probably would have been, in any other context. But in the current situation, the cool felt oppressive, rather than welcome. He took a deep breath and followed the two clerks, who'd been waiting patiently, down the echoing corridors.

When they reached the massive entrance to the council room, the clerks stepped aside and a door steward pulled open the doors.

Just like the last time, the grandeur of the place took Aran's breath away. It was large and spacious, with a domed ceiling of old stone and seats of luxurious dark wood descending in tiers to the circular floor, in the centre of which stood an ornate podium.

He stood there staring for probably far too long before the woman at the door gently nudged his elbow and gestured with her chin toward the podium.

He swallowed, and stepped through.

Rows upon rows of faces, framed in various-coloured robes and collars which probably all meant something important, stared down at him as he walked the impossibly long pathway to the podium. And while, considering his previous few months, the notable absence of weapons, fangs, claws, or venomous stingers probably should have been reassuring, it was distinctly not.

He bit back a hollow laugh.

It was always, "Aran Romeu single-handedly fights off red-frilled mountain cat" (it had been making off with his recently gathered data, and it hadn't really been a fight—he'd mostly just had to convince it that he wasn't a threat, and it would be best for both of them if it would just let go of his leg), and "Daredevil scientist scales ice-cliffs in the northern Rim Mountains" (he'd noticed the odd configuration of the ice caves at the top, which had turned out to be, as he'd hoped, the winter nesting grounds of the ruby-throated dicks, and hadn't really considered the height aspect of it until it was far too late), and "Well-known scientist/explorer and his assistant survive three days in a cave in the Coloured Desert in the midst of a once-in-a-generation swarm of spitting tarantula-snakes" (that one he actually couldn't remember how they'd gotten into. But the point was, he'd been so caught up in the unprecedented opportunity of observing the snakes' swarming behaviour, as well as occasionally treating himself or Istvay to avoid the worst of the venom-induced hallucinations, that he hadn't had time to notice the fact they'd been in actual danger until Istvay read the story out loud to him from the news packets several days later). It was never, "Aran Romeu barely manages to stave off an actual panic attack at the prospect of standing in front of the damn Council."

Venomous creatures, extreme conditions, large carnivorous mammals running off with your supplies—those were things he knew how to deal with. But this …

"Aran Romeu," said a woman, tapping a large holograph-topped staff, probably ceremonial, on the floor—although he could imagine it being used as an effective club, should the need arise. She turned to him. "The council has asked permission to speak with you."

For a moment, he wondered what would happen if he said no, turned on his heel and left through the doors he'd come in through.

In any event, the woman didn't pause for his answer, just nodded to the Council members and said, "I grant the members the floor," before resuming her seat.

Now that his eyes had adjusted to the light, Aran could make out some of the faces on the rows of Council seats. One specific face caught his eye—a petite woman in robes of deep scarlet topped with a stiff white collar.

He felt himself tense almost instinctively.

She had dark skin, white, close-cropped hair, and a severe expression he recognized immediately. He had the vague recollection that the people on the right were the People's Committee, the centre was the Judiciary Committee, and the Military Committee was on the left, but he didn't have to know that to know who the woman was.

Alba Espina.

She looked exactly as foreboding as he'd always pictured her. She'd been behind the legal reforms that had ended up sending him and Istvay, the foster-child and the homeless orphan, to university, and half of their friends to prison.

Apparently, intelligent homeless deserved to be educated, while the less academically gifted homeless deserved to be jailed.

"Aran." It was the President. He had thick brows, pale skin, sharp features, and an imperious scowl, and for a panicked second Aran wished desperately for Istvay to interpret—maybe he'd forgotten some sensitive ceremonial greeting, or maybe he was supposed to have come in a more formal suit—and then the man smiled, sharp features softening into an expression that was probably meant to be friendly. "I'm very glad you were able to come. As I'm sure you realize, the last few days have been … eventful."

"If you will permit me, President, I'd appreciate if we could cut straight to the point. Now that the Council has made its decision, time is of the essence." Alba had risen to her feet, an imposing figure despite her diminutive stature. She turned her sharp gaze from the President to Aran, and he had to hold himself from flinching. "Aran. I won't waste your time explaining events you are already aware of. What you don't know—or at least, what I hope you don't know, considering how hard we've tried to keep it quiet at present—is that something came through the portal. Something sent by sapient creatures, in what appears to be an attempt to communicate. And of what they sent, one thing is likely of the most vital import—a blood sample from a healthy individual, the equivalent of our planet's sixty years of age. An individual who possessed the defect."

Aran stared at her. The world around him had gone strangely fuzzy, and he had to clutch the edge of the podium with both hands.

"The genetic defect," he murmured finally, his voice coming out strange.

Alba nodded. "It's not a cure, unfortunately. But it holds the possibility of a cure."

Aran was still staring.

He could see Istvay's face from the evening before, the hollows in their cheeks that even the flush and colour of excitement hadn't been able to disguise.

The way Istvay's mother had looked when she died.

"The scientists who analyzed the sample—they're confident they read the results correctly?" he asked, when he could trust his voice.

"So I'm told," she said. "Although I shall ensure you have access to the sample, should you wish to verify."

Aran tightened his fingers on the edge of the podium, his stomach clenched with something between hope and nausea. "What—" his words came out slightly unsteady. He cleared his throat and tried again. "What do you want me to do?"

"The council has decided that I shall head a diplomatic mission to attempt to open contact with the aliens," said Alba briskly. "There were what appeared to be star maps in the container they sent, and our linguists are, as we speak, broadcasting messages through the portal in as many dialects as we know of to alert them that we would like to establish friendly relations. However, I am no scientist. Therefore, I requested that you accompany me on the mission, if you are willing. If there is the potential of a cure among the aliens, I would hope that a man of your reputation would be able to discover it, or at least inform the rest of the diplomatic party whether anything they presented us with was worthwhile."

Aran was still staring. He felt like he'd been pricked by half a dozen of Ani's tentacle spikes—his legs going weak, his head spinning, a wave of nausea rising in his stomach. A shock reaction, he found himself thinking absently. His thoughts were whirling, far too quickly for him to make sense of any of them.

A cure for the defect.

It was impossible.

People had been searching for a cure for five hundred years.

He'd been searching for a cure with every damn breath in his body, ever since he'd noticed those first telltale traces of gauntness in Istvay's face.

"There would be other scientists as well, correct?" he found himself asking. He wasn't sure if he'd decided to say it, or if his mouth had simply given up on his brain and was saying whatever it liked.

"Yes, we'd provide you with assistants, but you'd be the head scientist. They'd follow your lead, as you have by far the most experience with research in the field."

She spoke as if she thought he'd appreciate the sentiment.

He felt like he was choking.

They'd follow his lead. He'd be the head scientist. It would depend on him, everyone in the damn solar system who was suffering from the defect would depend on him to save their damn lives.

Istvay's life would depend on him.

He could see Istvay's mother, her sunken eyes staring out of her hollow face. She'd tried to smile at him as he'd knelt beside her makeshift cot, sobbing, a bottle of medicine shattered on the ground where she'd dropped it, her weak fingers unable to hold its weight.

He hadn't even been able to help. He couldn't even make her death easier.

Istvay was dying. They had a year, maybe two.

And now this. The first real possibility of a cure, and she wanted it to all depend on him.

"I'll … I'll have to think about it," he managed at last.

Alba nodded. "I know this is unexpected," she said crisply. "However, as I'm sure you will understand, this mission is of urgent, and vital, importance. We will be leaving first thing in the morning in two days' time. I will need your answer by eight o'clock tonight, in order to prepare an alternate choice should you decline." She paused a moment, and her gaze sharpened, so it felt like she was looking right through the centre of him. "There are other scientists I could ask. But believe me when I say not one of them has your qualifications. I requested your presence specifically because you are the person I believe will give us the highest chance of success. And I don't think I need explain to you how desperately we need this to succeed."

Aran gave a brief, stunned nod.

"I needn't remind you, I'm sure, that what's spoken of within these walls must remain confidential. You may tell those who you are obligated to inform, but that is all." She turned to the woman with the staff with a peremptory nod. "I yield my time."

There were a few scattered questions from a few other counsellors. Aran answered, but he couldn't have explained what he'd said.

He knew he was breathing, but he couldn't seem to get enough oxygen to allow his brain to function properly.

At last, the woman with the staff turned to him. "Thank you, Aran. We won't take up any more of your time."

He nodded again, and stumbled from the council room.

9

Aran

When Aran reached his hotel suite again, somehow, he locked the door firmly behind him, glanced around, and grabbed the coffee set off the table. He was swearing, muttering a litany of curses under his breath like a damn Orthodox prayer. He stepped into his bedroom, locked that door too, then, hands shaking, poured the still-scalding coffee down the drain in the small bathroom sink. Then he picked up one of the coffee cups—made of a smooth, fine porcelain, as delicate as an eggshell—and threw it as hard as he could against the far wall.

It shattered with a satisfying tinkle, and he picked up a second cup.

By the time the third cup had met a similar demise, Istvay's voice drifted through the closed door.

"The meeting went that well, did it?" Their tone was wry.

"Yes," said Aran shortly, picking up another cup and throwing it with all his might.

A couple of delicate shards stuck in the wall, which now glittered with fine porcelain dust, and the rest slid to join the growing pile of fragments on the floor.

"Is everything alright?"

Aran threw another cup. "It's fine," he said through his teeth.

"Alright," said Istvay. They paused. "Tell me when you want to talk about it."

Aran picked up the last cup, weighed it in his hand, then hurled it after the others.

Damn it to hell.

He'd been so discombobulated in the council meeting he hadn't even considered the additional fact that this would, of necessity, mean going into space.

Of course it had to involve getting on a damn spaceship and going out into space.

He hated crowds, and he hated heights, and he hated closed-in places. And he hated space, with a visceral, stomach-clenching dread —something cold and lifeless and foreign, something waiting patiently for a chance to kill any organic lifeform with the temerity to venture into its domain, a place where everything that he knew and everything he was remotely good at would be completely irrelevant.

And this mission? It wrapped all his personal nightmares into one neat package.

He picked up the empty coffeepot, hefted it in his hand for a moment, and sent it after the cups. Then he closed his eyes and sank into a chair, dropping his head into his hands.

Dammit, dammit, dammit.

There was a small, soft chirrup, and he glanced over in time to see the tips of Ani's tentacles and part of her bulbous head, flattened comically, poking through the crack under the door.

"Sorry, Aran," came Istvay's voice from outside. "I tried to tell her you wanted to be alone, but you know how well she listens to me."

Aran found himself smiling, despite his irritation.

Having wriggled her way through the narrow space, Ani's body resumed its normal shape, protruding eyes blinking at him in a look of such innocence that he shook his head, smiling ruefully, and held out his arm. She raised delicately up on her tentacles and skittered along the ground until she reached him, then swarmed up his arm and settled herself on his shoulder. Her nervous colouring told him she'd picked up on his distress, although she had no idea of the reason for it, and she was ready to kill whatever was causing him problems.

"It's alright, sweetheart," he whispered, and she gave a little grumble and settled farther down on his shoulder. He could feel her tentacles suctioning down on his skin, and he clicked his tongue reprovingly. "Ani, gentle," he said in a stern voice, and she loosened her grip reluctantly.

Just as well—he didn't actually have the time to spend the probably twenty-four hours in a coma that being jabbed by multiple tentacle spikes on his torso and neck would entail, even with the immunity he'd built up.

"Why, Ani?" he whispered, stroking her. "Why space, why this, why me? What the actual hell did I do to deserve this?"

Istvay tapped on the door again. "Look, Aran, take as much time as you want, but I'm going out to get some food. You want me to bring you back something?"

Aran mumbled something, and Istvay chuckled. "Well, I'll bring you something anyways. You'll feel better after you've eaten."

Their footsteps faded, and the door clicked shut behind them. Aran stared at his own closed door in abject despair.

If only eating something would solve a fraction of the damn

problems that Istvay seemed to think it would, his life would be a hell of a lot easier.

It wasn't fifteen minutes later that there was a tentative tap on the outside door.

Aran sighed and pushed himself to his feet. Istvay had probably bought out the entire street vendors' market in an effort to find something that would tempt him, which, honestly, was very sweet, but also mildly exasperating. "Ani, stay here," he said in his sternest voice, placing her gently on the seat he'd just vacated. "I don't need you stealing Istvay's food again."

She grumbled to herself, but obeyed, bundling herself into a sulky heap in the corner of the chair.

He shot her a warning look, then unlocked the door to his private suite and crossed to the door of the suite's common room, pulling it open. "Istvay," he began, "you didn't have to—"

He stopped abruptly.

The man outside the door was not Istvay.

"Aran," said Emeric. He was dressed more casually than he had been at the gala the night before, but still far more finely than Aran could ever have hoped to emulate, even if he'd wanted to. "I'm sorry to intrude. May I come in?"

Aran watched him, contemplating simply closing the door in his face and then pretending he couldn't hear the insistent knocking that was sure to follow.

"It's about this morning, with the Council," said Emeric delicately. "The mission they told you about."

Aran sighed, and pulled the door open wide enough to let him through. Emeric stepped inside and took a seat on one of the two overstuffed armchairs, gesturing graciously to the other as if Aran had come to visit him rather than the other way around.

"I see they put you up in decent lodgings, for once," he said, glancing around. "Must've been a bit of a shock, I imagine. Not really the side of the city you're used you, is it?"

Aran remained standing, and glared at Emeric. "Why are you here?" He didn't bother to hide his annoyance.

"Straight to the point, as always," said Emeric, with an indulgent smile. "That's something I always liked about you, Aran."

"If I remember right, you liked it so much you tried to kill me a few years ago," said Aran.

Emeric laughed, leaning back in his chair and crossing one leg over the other. "Don't be absurd. I wasn't trying to kill you, I was just trying to give you a leg up. You've been listening to Istvay too much, I think."

"In fairness, Istvay's never tried to kill me," Aran pointed out.

Emeric laughed again. "Well, I'm not going to convince you I didn't either, so I guess this is one of those things where we'll have to agree that reasonable minds can differ." He glanced around. "Aren't you going to offer me coffee? This place is famous for its coffee." He frowned. "Don't tell me they forgot to bring you any."

"I finished it off," Aran muttered.

Emeric gave a philosophic shrug. "I suppose down to business it is, then." He leaned forwards, face serious, and rested his forearms on his knees. "Listen. I know what the Council talked to you about this morning." He waved a hand dismissively as Aran opened his mouth. "I know, I know, they probably swore you to secrecy. But the reason I know that is I headed up the group of scientists analyzing the alien artifacts."

He sighed. "They told you they wanted you along, I know that. But I've known you since college. You're … skillful at what you do, in your own way. But I also know your reputation is a lot larger than

your work deserves. And, I know how much you hate space travel."
He leaned a little farther forward. "I'm not trying to disparage you.
You've done some good things. But do you really think you're
qualified to head up something like this? You've been out in the field
for—how many years now? Since we graduated college, essentially.
This isn't like that. This is working with people, collaboration,
negotiation. And I don't think you need me to tell you that isn't a
strong suit of yours. I know Istvay thinks you drink rainbows and piss
gold, but you and I know better. You're an adventurer, I suppose, but
not really a qualified scientist. And how much time have you spent
keeping up with all the latest advancements in the scientific
community?"

"I … read as much as I can," Aran mumbled, but Emeric cut him
off.

"You know as well as I do that's not the same thing as the hours of
studying that those of us who are more centrally connected put in."
He shook his head. "If you go on this trip, the life of every person in
this solar system with the defect depends on you. And if you mess it
up, or you don't know what you're doing—how often do you
collaborate with other scientists, Aran? How much of this sort of
work have you done?"

Aran stared at him, teeth clenched.

Istvay would have been offended on his behalf. Hell, Istvay would
probably have picked up one of the egg knives and tried to stab
Emeric in the throat by this time.

But Emeric hadn't said anything Aran's own brain hadn't been
telling him, painfully and in-depth, since he'd listened in stunned
shock to Alba's offer.

"Listen. I'm not supposed to tell you this, but I think I can trust
you to keep a secret," continued Emeric. "If you turn this down, I'm

the next one slated for them to ask. I tried to tell them why it might be a better idea for me to go in the first place, rather than drag you back from whatever research you were in the middle of when they sent for you, but—" he shrugged. "They're not scientists. They don't understand how these things work. So I thought I'd talk to you."

He looked Aran straight in the eyes, his expression as serious as Aran had ever seen it. "You decline, Aran. I'll go. And then you don't have to worry about any of this. I'll take care of it. I have a team all picked out, and they know me, I've worked with them. We'll find this cure and get it back here and develop it, and you can go back to whatever it is you were doing. I know you want to. I know how much you hate this—the people, the noise, the close quarters. It'll be a million times worse on the ship. But that's exactly the kind of environment I thrive in. I'll be good at it. And you'll be free."

Aran watched him for a long moment, then finally sank down into the chair opposite.

The offer was like a cold drink of water after a day in the Coloured Desert.

But he knew Emeric. Had known him since they'd been in college together.

"I assume you have some … financial backing for this?" he asked at last, cautiously.

He always felt slightly awkward asking those questions. But, awkward or not, it seemed to be expected practice in his field.

Emeric grinned, leaning back in his chair again. "Is that what you're worried about? You don't need to be. I have a very well-connected backer, and I'm certain they'd pass on any excess funding to put towards your pet projects, if I spoke a word in their ear."

Aran frowned. There was something about the way Emeric had avoided saying his backer's name …

"That's … generous," he said cautiously, feeling out the words as he spoke them. "But I'd need a little more security before I'd be comfortable with something like that. Who's backing you?"

Emeric glanced around. "I don't like to say. I'm sure you appreciate the delicacy of the situation, when I haven't officially been signed onto the expedition." He hesitated a moment, watching Aran's face, then shook his head. "Listen, I always trusted you. I'll tell you, but you can't breathe a word of it." He leaned forward. "It's Eniko Cavaco."

Aran looked at him, puzzled, before the pieces clicked together, and he half-jumped from his chair. "General Cavaco?"

Emeric frowned, clearly not expecting the reaction. "I wouldn't think his name would mean much to you," he said. "I didn't realize you followed politics. Is there a problem?"

Aran shook his head. "No, no problem," he said quickly. He stood. "Look, Emeric, I appreciate you coming. Give me some time to think on it and I'll let you know."

Emeric was still frowning, and still ensconced in the chair. "Is something the matter?"

"Nothing's the matter, I … I just need some time to think."

At last Emeric stood, still watching Aran carefully. "If there's anything that's bothering you, anything I can do to reassure you—"

"No, no, it's fine." Aran practically shoved him towards the door.

Emeric went, finally, with many a backwards glance, and when he was gone, Aran shut the door firmly behind him and sank down in one of the chairs.

General Cavaco.

He should have guessed. With Emeric's family connections, it wasn't exactly unexpected. And Emeric was right—Aran didn't keep up with politics, generally.

But he knew General Cavaco. He kept his ears open for news of the man in the same way as, in the desert, he kept his ears open for the soft rattle of a tigersnake. It didn't do to ignore something that could kill you.

Even before he'd become head of the military branch, Cavaco's name had been an unspoken threat, hanging smoky and insubstantial over Aran's life. Cavaco had been the one who'd backed the proposal to re-introduce the ban on the Mountain Dialect.

There'd always been an uneasy relationship between the people who spoke Mountain Dialect and the rest of the planet, a ceasefire, maybe, after centuries of outright hostility, but not really a peace. The rest of the planet saw people like his mother—like him, if he hadn't learned to hide his accent and never speak his childhood language—as slightly sub-human. But it had been General Cavaco who'd re-ignited the tensions.

He hadn't realized, as a child, it had been that which provoked such violence from his foster families. He'd been small, and alone, and bewildered, and it was only when he'd met Istvay out on the streets, where he'd run to escape yet another beating and was crying from hunger, that someone had finally explained it to him. Istvay's mother, who'd known a few words of Mountain Dialect, had made him feel safe, shared her and Istvay's meagre meals, told him he'd always have somewhere to run to when he needed to get away. Warned him that people could be cruel, and that until he learned to hide who he was, he'd be hurt.

She hadn't liked teaching that lesson, he'd seen it in her face. But he'd needed it, nonetheless.

And he'd learned to pay attention whenever General Cavaco's name was mentioned.

If General Cavaco was funding Emeric's bid—whatever cure the mission came back with wouldn't be used for people without names and connections. People like Istvay.

The General would never waste resources like that. And cure or no, Istvay would still die.

He felt shaky, and slightly sick.

It had been a long time since he'd thought about Cavaco, or about his own childhood. The memories weren't ones that quieted easily.

He took a long, deep breath, and squeezed his palm to activate his wavelink. "Hello," he said, when the hotel receptionist answered. "I … need a message delivered to the Council."

He received a message back short minutes later, containing a copy of the data they'd retrieved from whatever had come through the portal. He took a deep breath and opened the file.

If he was going to do this, he may as well get started on the data.

He wasn't sure how long it had been when there was another tap on the door, this time followed by Istvay's voice.

"Hey, Aran, open up! My hands are full."

Aran blinked, then shut down his palmscreen and pulled open the door, feeling like he was walking in a daze.

Istvay stood there, grinning their lopsided grin, their arms full of bundles from which seeped a plethora of mouth-watering smells. "I didn't know what you were in the mood for, so I thought I'd—" they broke off, frowning. "What's the matter?"

Aran shook his head and took some of the parcels from Istvay, depositing them in a heap on the table.

Istvay followed him in, dropping the rest onto the table beside them. "Did something happen while I was out?"

Aran hesitated. "Emeric stopped by," he said at last.

Istvay's face clouded, their expression growing sharp with anger.

"You didn't let him in, did you? Aran, for hell's sake, he's not a good person. He tried to kill you! That should be a bigger deal to you than it is, I feel like."

Aran shook his head wearily. "He just wanted to talk."

"About what?" Istvay snapped, pulling a chair around angrily and dropping into it.

"About … what happened in the Council meeting this morning," Aran said at last, in a low voice. "I—Istvay. They … something came through the portal. Some alien artifacts. And a blood sample."

Istvay was still frowning, but they just watched him, waiting for him to continue.

"I … anyways, the point is, they analyzed the DNA, and they think … they think the aliens might hold the key to a cure for … for the defect."

Istvay's face went bloodless. "They think—" they began at last, their voice a whisper.

Aran nodded. "The DNA sample was from an individual who had the defect. A healthy individual, about sixty years old."

Istvay's hands were clutching the arms of the chair tightly enough that their knuckles were white, but they didn't say anything.

"They're sending out a diplomatic mission to try to find the cure and bring it back," said Aran. "They asked me to come with as head scientist."

Istvay shook their head slowly. They looked stunned, almost sick. "You … said no, of course. We both know how much you hate space travel." Their voice was strange, and quiet.

Aran gave a quick, sharp shake of his head. "I'm going. I already sent back word. I'm leaving in two days."

Istvay was still shaking their head. "No, Aran. I can't let you do that. You'd be miserable. I know you'd only be doing for me, and I

—"

Aran stepped over to the chair and grabbed Istvay by the shoulders. "Istvay," he said through his teeth. "Just shut up, for once, and stop being such a damn idiot."

He closed his eyes for a minute, letting his hands drop to his side.

They were shaking, just a little, and it wasn't going to help matters for Istvay to know.

But Istvay just sat in silence for a few moments, their face looking suddenly much older than their years, and inexpressibly weary.

At last they stood. "When are we leaving?" they asked quietly.

It was Aran's turn to stare. "I'm leaving in two days. I thought you and Ani could—"

Istvay shook their head, the trace of a wan smile appearing on their face. "I'm not going to be able to talk you out of this—I know how damn stubborn you can be. But you're not going by yourself, either." They paused a moment. "I know I complain about Ani sometimes, but the fact is, she's the best protection you have. And as for me—" their grin widened, just a bit. "Well, if you try leaving me behind, I'll hide myself in your suitcase and smuggle myself aboard. If you go, Ani and I are coming with you."

Aran stared at Istvay, their face still drawn with shock, their eyes deadly serious despite their joking tone. A lump was forming in his throat, and he tried to clear it away, but Istvay shook their head and stood, placing a hand on Aran's shoulder.

"Whatever you're going to say, don't bother." They straightened, suddenly all business. "If we're leaving in two days, I guess we'd better get packing. Have you started on your list of what equipment you'll need? I'll put one together as well, since I usually do the shopping for our expeditions anyways. And will Ani be alright with the food they'll have along? I assume so, but let me know if there are any nutritional supplements I should ask for."

They half turned away, then turned back to the table with a forced grin, pulling open one of the bags of street food. "Before I forget. We'd both better eat, since it looks like we'll have a busy day ahead of us."

Their tone was light, but Aran could see the expression on their face they were trying to hide—a painful hope, mingled with a sort of dread.

Aran took a deep breath.

He couldn't say he blamed them.

He felt almost the same way.

10

Savina

When she was sure they were well away from the moonport, Savina made her way out of the cabin and through the ship's corridors to the main deck. The vessel was apparently too small and too old to have artificial gravity, but she found she could move easily enough using the handholds that had been placed for the purpose.

The captain was on the flight deck, along with the irritable man from earlier. She looked up at Savina's entrance and gestured with her chin to the pair of clunky boots on the deck. "Use the mag boots, it'll make your life easier. Guess you're not used to flying on a ship too small for its own gravity generator."

Using the handholds, Savina somehow manoeuvred herself into boots. When she was finally able to stand, she straightened, smiling winningly at the captain.

"So," she asked. "Any word on what was causing all that commotion this morning?"

The captain gave Savina a wry look, jerking her chin towards the plex window.

Savina crossed over to it with some difficulty in the unfamiliar mag boots, and glanced outside.

That long, ragged gash in what looked like the fabric of the universe itself, the thing Savina had seen on the yacht, still stretched across the vastness of space, a gaping hole of inky black that should have been filled with the bright pinpricks of stars.

The sight, now that she had the leisure to study it, was disconcerting, in a visceral way she hadn't expected.

"Quite the sight, isn't it?" said the captain softly, coming up beside her. "It's all they're talking about through the news packets. It appeared out of nowhere, and no one knows who made it or why."

Savina turned quickly. "'Who made it?' Not 'what made it?'"

The captain gave her trademark reluctant smile. "They're saying it's a 'who.' The unofficial chatter is something's come through it."

Savina turned back to the plex window, unable to draw her eyes away from that empty gash of nothing.

The captain sighed. "We keep the standard ship's time. Which means I'll expect you to be up at 0600 in the morning with the rest of us. You may as well get some sleep while you can."

Savina nodded silently, unable to pull her eyes from the rent in the sky.

It didn't matter. Whatever this was, it was irrelevant to her current situation.

But she couldn't help the uneasy spark of something between curiosity and dread as she watched it.

"Did they say what came through?" she asked at last.

The captain raised an eyebrow. "The government's keeping it quiet, I hear. There's supposed to be an announcement sometime tomorrow. But rumour has it, the announcement has something to do with the genetic defect. I'd guess whatever came through the portal might suggest a cure—it's not like it hasn't been the holy grail of science for the last five centuries. I suspect that's enough to keep everyone interested, if the portal itself wasn't."

Savina turned abruptly to stare at her, trying not to let the sudden fear show on her face. "That's what they're saying?"

The captain shrugged, turning away. "Right now it's only rumours. But we can always hope."

Savina nodded again, not trusting her voice enough to speak.

She pulled her feet from the mag boots, unlatching them with trembling hands, then made her way down the corridor back to her bunk, a cold, sick knot in her stomach.

Beni was waiting for her back in the cabin. "Did you find anything interesting about our captain?" they asked. "I pulled her records, but there's not much—just cargo shipping, nothing special." They paused. "And she's not married. So it's possible that she and the crewman—"

Savina sighed and shook her head, strapping herself to the seat. "Nothing. She's close-mouthed."

"She seems nice, at least," said Beni.

"Tell her who you are and see how far 'nice' gets you," muttered Savina.

Beni raised an eyebrow. "What, that we're an assassin-for-hire and her accomplice?"

Savina scowled, even though she knew her sibling couldn't see. "Corpus Dei. Old Believers. Heretics." She couldn't hide the bitterness in her tone.

Beni shook their head, but didn't say anything.

The two of them had had this argument a thousand times.

But then, Beni had always been sheltered. Even when the two of them were home in the compound, Savina's reputation ensured that people left Beni alone. Beni hadn't experienced the things Savina had. Beni hadn't done the things Savina had.

Which was the point, after all.

Savina could still see the flames licking up the roof of the small farmer's cottage, hear the screams from inside. Feel her fingernails digging into the flesh of her palms as she watched the fire take hold.

She'd only been twelve. But it wasn't something you could ever forget.

"Did you find out what everyone was so upset about?" asked Beni at last, when the silence had begun to stretch.

Savina sighed, unease sitting heavy on her chest. "The news packets are saying it's some sort of portal. And … that something came through it."

"What's wrong, Vina?"

Savina shook her head. She'd never been able to hide anything from Beni. Maybe her sibling couldn't see her expressions, but they could hear it in her voice and in the way she moved. "There's … rumours. Whatever came through the portal made people think there might be a cure for the Curse."

"Is it true?" Beni asked at last, quietly.

"I don't know," snapped Savina. "It's only rumours. It might be nothing."

"That's—that would be a good thing, though. Right?"

Savina took a deep breath, pressing the heels of her hands into her eyes. "Beni. If the Officials of the High Mystery in the Orthodox Church think they can prove that the Curse is just some natural phenomenon, with a natural cure, do you think they'll let it go? They've been looking for an excuse to wipe out people like us for centuries."

"You don't believe the Curse is actually a curse."

"That's not what matters," said Savina through her teeth. "If they have proof the Old Believers are wrong, they can take that to their High Council, the one the Chief Justice sits on. They want us dead, and all they need is an excuse. And when they find one, do you think you and me can just say, 'oh, we never believed that, honest'—you think that would save us? Nicolau's alive because we got him out and no one knows where he came from. We're safe because no one knows who we are. That's all. Don't mistake their ignorance for kindness."

The two of them were silent again, for a long moment.

Beni's grin had faded, and Savina's conscience twinged.

"Maybe it's nothing," she said finally. "It's just rumours right now anyway. We'll find out what's happened in the morning, and we can figure things out from there." She sighed, maneuvering herself into position on the cot and strapping herself in. "I'm going to bed. We'll worry about it when we know more. It's probably nothing."

But the thick knot of worry in her stomach, and the unease buzzing in her brain, told her she didn't really believe it.

She didn't sleep well that night. Judging by the rustling from the cot across from her, she doubted Beni had slept any better.

The tingle of an alarm buzzing through her nervous system from her wavelink jerked her awake. She groaned, blinking owlishly, and unstrapped herself from her cot, kicking off to grab the handhold on the ceiling.

Beni was already up and dressed.

"I'll meet you in the mess hall," they said over their shoulder as they made their unerring way out the door.

Apparently, the echolocation function in their wavelink worked as well for finding handholds in a zero-grav spacecraft as it did for navigating the mountains around the compound back home.

The captain was leaving the mess hall as Savina arrived.

"Good morning, Savina," the woman said. She, at least, didn't seem to have lost sleep. She had no reason to. "I've asked Rafel to show you what needs repairs later this morning, but I thought you might want to orient yourself to the engine room first."

Savina nodded, trying to smile. "I'll head down after breakfast." She paused. "Have you heard anything? About the portal?"

The woman raised an eyebrow, her weathered face softening slightly. "You have someone you care about with the defect? I guess most of us do." She paused a moment. "They did say something on the packets. Good news, I think—they're sending out a diplomatic mission to go through the portal. And they confirmed that what was sent through the portal does hold out the possibility of a cure." Her face twisted in the hint of a wry smile. "And you'll never guess who they sent as head diplomat. The Chief Justice herself."

She frowned. "Savina? Are you alright?"

Savina gave a faint nod, trying to paste a smile back onto her face. "I'm sorry. It's just—"

"It's a lot, I know," said the captain softly. "Two days ago, we were alone in the universe, and the defect was a death sentence. Now we have company, and they might be bringing the cure."

"I'm—I think you're right, I'd better go down to the engine room. To get familiar with it," Savina managed, turning away. From the corner of her eye she noticed the captain watching her in mild concern, but she didn't have the attention to care.

Beni met her in the engine room a few minutes later. "Vina," they said in a tight voice. "I have bad news."

"So do I," said Savina, not looking up. "I heard it from the captain. They're sending a mission through the portal, and they sent the Chief Justice to head it. The Joint Head of the council of the Great Mystery. The one that the Book of the Heretics says should preside over the heretic trials."

There was a long pause. Beni was facing away from her, but she could see the tension in their posture.

"What did you want to tell me?" Savina asked at last, when the silence began to stretch.

For a moment, Beni was silent. "I found out who issued that warrant, and who accepted it," they said at last. "There's a government agent after you."

Savina's hands stilled on the spanner she'd been turning over and over. "A government agent?" Her voice shook, just a little, despite her best efforts.

Beni nodded. "Yes. And not just a low-level agent. They sent Reka Soler."

Savina stared at them, then swore. "Reka Soler? Are you sure?"

Beni nodded again. "You know her reputation, right? She's never lost a warrant. Seven years with the agency, and she's their top agent. She has a reputation for bringing home bodies."

"I know," said Savina, in a low voice. "Who signed the warrant?"

Beni frowned, and for a moment, Savina wasn't sure if they'd answer. But at last they took a deep breath and released it slowly. "The Chief Justice. Alba Espina."

Savina thought for a moment she might throw up.

"She's a government official, too, not just a religious leader," Beni said finally, breaking the silence. "It's not that strange for her to sign a warrant. Besides, we've spent plenty of time outside the compound, ever since …" they trailed off. "And no one seemed to care what religion we were. Maybe back in the compound—maybe they're wrong."

Savina leaned forward and rested a hand on her sibling's knee. "Beni," she said quietly. "You can't honestly believe that. You know the stories. You've heard about great-great grandmother Miram and her family—three of her children burned alive, one of them thrown into boiling water while she watched, to force her to deny her faith."

"That was a hundred years ago," said Beni.

Savina shook her head. "Do you honestly think anything's changed? Do you think they sent the Judge of Heresy into the portal by chance? Do you honestly think that her signing the warrant for me, the only warrant they've issued in my real name, is chance? They're biding their time. Waiting for their opportunity. I've—" she paused a moment, not wanting to speak the words that seemed to lock up in her chest. "I've seen what they do to Old Believers, Beni. I've seen it on the recordings.

"They want you to believe no one cares how you worship. They want you to believe the holy war is over. But those memorials, those statues, those fine words about tolerance? They're a trap. They want you to let down your guard. And then, when they're ready, when they've finally made their preparations and found their excuse— they'll kill us all." She broke off abruptly. Something ached and burned in the corners of her eyes, and she had to blink it back.

Beni was silent.

"They've found their excuse," Savina said finally. "And now they're coming. They're coming for all of us. Reka Soler is only the beginning."

"What do we do?" Beni's voice was soft, and for just a moment, Savina's heart gave a small, painful stutter.

Beni was her baby sibling. Beni hadn't asked for any of this. They came along because Savina was their sister, and they'd never leave her alone. And in return, Savina had protected them, as best she knew how.

But if this agent caught her, she'd find Beni, too. And with the DNA tech the agents carried, it wouldn't take her long to figure out that Beni and she were siblings.

And more than that. It was possible that if Reka found Savina and Beni, she'd find Nicolau as well.

Savina had stayed in the compound her entire life, made Beni stay as well, to keep him safe.

She'd killed to keep him safe.

Savina took a deep breath. "We go back to Colorida. It'll be easier to hide there, and we'll have options—we can split up to confuse the agent if we have to. We'll warn the others back at the compound. But we can't afford to waste a single moment."

Her parents had always told her this day would come. They'd beat it into her from when she was too young to remember. She hadn't believed at first—it had seemed too absurd that whether or not the Great Mystery had a corporeal body was an idea worth fighting over.

But then they'd showed her the footage from the Cleansing—the heresy trials, the gatherings to watch the sentences being carried out. They'd forced her to watch it over and over, an infant's screams from a cauldron of boiling water, her great-great grandmother sobbing and screaming like it was she, along with her child, being murdered.

Savina wasn't sure she believed in the Great Mystery anymore, embodied or not. But she'd learned soon enough that you didn't need to believe for people to want to kill you for who you were.

She ran her hand over her thick hair, glancing at the dark stain it left on her skin. She couldn't use permanent dye without risk that a security sensor would pick it up, but shoe-black worked just as well.

Even if she didn't believe, she was marked—the combination of dark skin and red hair, some genetic fluke that, a hundred and fifty years ago or so, had sprung up in the colonies of Old Believers.

This was who she was. She could choose to believe, or disbelieve, and it wouldn't matter.

"Will they even listen to us?" asked Beni.

Savina glanced up. "They're going to have to," she said brusquely. But Beni's words made fear tighten in her stomach.

What she'd done to save Nicolau—what they'd both done, although Beni had mostly just followed her lead—Savina had always told herself it was worth it.

But if everyone in the compound was killed because of it, because they wouldn't believe her after what she'd done?

She took a deep breath, pushing the thought away.

She wouldn't regret it. The memory of her baby brother's tiny, chubby face, tear-streaked and covered in mud and dirt, his small body cradled in her arms, the soft fuzz of black hair on his tiny head, wouldn't let her regret it.

She'd get away from the agent. Government agents weren't omnipotent, and surely if she made it hard enough for the woman, even Reka Soler would give up. And then Nicolau, at least, would be safe, no matter what happened to the rest of them.

"They'll have a record of you on the yacht. A government agent will be able to check the records of every ship that left the moon port since then. Even if we catch another ship off the next port, they'll be able to track us." Beni was suddenly businesslike, and Savina breathed a small sigh of relief.

She could handle this if they both treated it like another job. She wasn't sure if she could if she stopped for even a moment to consider what it really was.

Maybe things had gone sideways badly in the last twenty-four hours—maybe more sideways than she'd experienced in a while. But she didn't trust to luck. She trusted to her wits, and her weapons, and Beni. And despite everything that had gone wrong, she still had all three.

Slowly, she smiled. "Beni. I know what we'll do."

Beni frowned suspiciously. "Savina," they said. "You can't solve all your problems by killing people."

Savina raised a sceptical eyebrow. "It's worked pretty well so far." She grinned at Beni's expression. "Besides, I don't necessarily need to kill anyone yet. We still need someone to fly the ship."

Beni gave a long sigh. "Fine. But no killing. I like the captain."

Savina's grin widened. "No killing unless absolutely necessary."

The captain looked up as Savina stepped onto the flight deck with mag boots firmly fastened on her feet.

"There you are," the woman said, rising with a small, friendly smile. "I was just about to send Rafel down to—"

"I do appreciate it, Captain," Savina broke in, "but I'm afraid there's been a change of plans. We need to head back to Colorida, immediately."

The captain frowned. "I'm sorry. I told you when you signed on, I've got a cargo drop to make on Rochosa. When we get there, if you need a ship that can take you back, I'm sure you'll find something, but—"

Savina pulled the gun from the pocket of her sundress, still smiling. "I don't think you understand. That wasn't a request."

The captain froze, her face going suddenly completely still.

When Savina had started this job as a teenager, she might have felt a pang at the woman's expression. But she'd learned better, by now.

The captain was drumming her fingers together, and suddenly

Savina remembered, and cursed under her breath.

The captain's wavelink was a wrist implant, the kind people without the money for a decent temple-implant wavelink used.

"Beni," she called, raising her gun and levelling it at the captain's head. "Watch the crewman."

She turned back to the captain. "One move from you or that other idiot, and there won't be enough left of either of you to send back to your families."

A moment later, Beni stepped into the cabin, pushing the paunchy man in front of them. He had his hands over his head, and a deep scowl on his face.

"Smart of you," said Savina, still with that friendly smile. "Now I think it's time the ship has a change of ownership. And then it looks like we'll be plotting a new course."

11

Alba

It was late the evening by the time the Council disbanded.

Alba made her slow way out of the Council room and into the courtyard, fixing an expression on her face that would hopefully keep away any well-wishers or questioners. But it appeared it wouldn't be necessary—her colleagues, the young clerks, the door stewards, all avoided her in the vaguely respectful manner they might avoid someone with the defect, whose sunken face and wasted muscles told all and sundry they wouldn't live to see another season. Someone around whom it would be not just impolite, but impossible to speak to without some reference to death.

There was a reason, she thought grimly, that their ancestors had viewed a death's head symbol with cautious superstition. No one wanted the reminder that they could be next. And now, in the course of a single day, she'd become a death's head. A grinning reminder of their own mortality.

It was just as well. She was exhausted, and in no mood to speak with anyone, least of all some curious gossip who wished only to pass her reaction on to their friends.

She felt numb.

Seventy-three years. She'd lived on this planet for seventy-three years—a long time for anyone. Surely she couldn't begrudge death at this age.

She allowed herself a wry smile. Apparently, she, too, was convinced that this was more a death sentence than a diplomatic mission.

She sighed.

It was late enough in the evening that the oppressive warmth of the day had faded, and the cool of the evening air was comforting. She hailed a transport, and on the ride home, watched the city pass below her. This city was where she'd grown up, made a name for herself, become who she was—Madam Chief Justice, head of the Judicial Council, perhaps the most influential woman on the planet. She'd made her mark on these streets, subtly shifted the shape of the entire system over her forty-odd year tenure. Vila Nova do Sol, for all its changing, was as familiar to her as her own name. But now she watched the streets slip past—the old stone buildings fading into each other, the confusing, noisy, beautiful, colourful, fascinating cross-section of life, from the beggars at the street corners, their guttering holotokens broadcasting their pleas and accepting pledges, to the well-dressed and wealthy, taking the air on the pedestrian walkways and old city parks, jostling to see and be seen—as a stranger might. As an alien, unfamiliar with their civilization.

She found herself smiling slightly. Humans, for all their unpredictability, their intelligence, their scheming, were just another animal, really, preoccupied with status, with mating, with food and shelter and protecting their young.

She sobered.

It would be her task to convince whatever lay on the other side of that portal that these noisy, squabbling, colourful animals were worth saving.

This diplomatic mission was their best chance. The best theoretical minds on the planet all agreed. But now, with the outcome of their theories become not theoretical at all, Alba found herself more nervous than she'd imagined she'd be.

By the time the morning dawned on the day they were to finally depart, neither she nor Feliu were in a state to be spoken to.

The Council had sent a transport, and the poor woman piloting it looked thoroughly beleaguered as a company of movers and transport drones loaded her craft with enough bundles and boxes to suffocate the entire crew of them.

Alba had a reputation, she knew—a reputation of someone who did not lightly suffer fools. But even she was not brave enough to reprimand Feliu this morning, or to question the quantity of items he'd arranged to be packed for them.

Feliu was accompanying her—she'd offered him the chance to decline, and despite the fact she wasn't quite certain how she'd function without him, she'd almost hoped he would. He'd been looking more and more weary these last few years. But he'd given her that icily formal glance of his and said stiffly that he was sure his ability as a clerk wouldn't be entirely useless on a diplomatic mission.

She hadn't had the heart to say anything more.

When they were all on board at last, the driver informed them, meekly, that she had been instructed to bring them to the Council Building prior to their departure so that Alba could address the citizens of the system. She handed Alba a holographic disc, commenting deferentially that it contained the speech Alba was to give.

Alba snorted, giving the woman a look so sharp it almost brought her to tears, and dropped into her seat.

Her bones ached. She was feeling every one of her seventy-three years this morning.

She opened the disc and gave its contents a desultory glance. The speech had been written by Ander's speechwriters, almost certainly, and was full of maudlin platitudes and vacuous, vaguely hopeful assertions.

She tapped the disc off and dropped it onto the seat next to her.

If she was going to speak, she was going to use her own damn words.

They came to a halt in the courtyard of the council building, and Alba stepped down onto it with a strange sense of unreality.

She'd stepped into this courtyard almost every day for the last fifty years of her life.

Now she found herself wondering if she'd ever set foot in it again.

There was a crowd of gathered reporters and government officials, standing as if they'd been hastily gathered for show. As Alba disembarked from the transport, someone started a nervous cheer.

She turned the full force of her glare on the cheerer—a middle-aged man who she knew vaguely by sight, and nothing else—and he stopped abruptly, shrinking under her withering gaze.

A podium had been set up, and two nervous assistants herded her gingerly towards it. Waiting behind it were a handful of others who she assumed would be her diplomatic retinue. None of them looked particularly promising. She recognized a few as government officials and aides, and some bland-looking young people who were probably scientists.

Aran, the head scientist she'd specifically chosen, was not present.

Instead, the individual who apparently acted as his assistant was standing in Aran's place, scowling, their expression forbidding enough that Alba almost allowed herself a smile.

It appeared, then, she wasn't the only one who didn't relish the prospect of being paraded in front of the news cameras. Although unfortunately she, unlike the young scientist, had not been able to browbeat someone into coming in her place.

Perhaps, rather than Chief Justice of the entire Joias system, she should have been angling for the position of wandering itinerant biologist, since apparently that gave one a clout that she did not yet possess.

She took her place in front of the podium. From the row of seats, Ander cast an imploring glance in her direction, his eyes darting towards her bag, then back to the podium, as if wondering where she'd put the holographic token.

She gave a grim smile.

This may be the last time she stood in this courtyard, in front of this podium, facing this audience. If she was going to use it to raise a figurative middle finger to the President, she doubted anyone would try to stop her.

A hush fell over the gathered crowd as she activated the holoscreen on the podium and glanced around with her most quelling stare. Every eye in the crowd was fixed on her, their attention focused like a laser beam.

She cleared her throat. "Friends, colleagues, and citizens," she began. "Today, I leave on a ship headed towards the unknown."

She caught the faint flash of panic on Ander's face as he realized she had no intention of following the script he'd laid out, and she had to bite back a satisfied smirk.

"I volunteered for this mission because I believe in our chances of success," she continued. "As all of you are aware, over the past few days we've gone from being, insofar as we knew, alone in the universe, to being one among a potentially countless number of intelligent beings. We've received communication from something not human. What they are and what their intentions may be, we do not know. But I, for one, am optimistic." She paused, looking out over the crowd, trying to judge the impact of her words.

This could be the last chance for influence she had before her voice was muffled, or silenced entirely.

"I am optimistic, despite the unknowns, because it is my belief that our best hope for humanity is, as it always has been, our ability to cooperate. Our intelligence, our curiosity, our willingness to step forward into the unknown without giving in to fear. We have a unique and unparalleled opportunity to open a dialogue with a new intelligent species, an opportunity which has not come in the history of our presence in this solar system." She paused again.

"And we will take this opportunity," she continued at last, each word deliberate. "Because our progress, our innovation—perhaps our very survival as a species—depends on it." She glanced around again, and this time her eyes found Cavaco. He was scowling, and she was suddenly very certain he'd influenced the direction of the speech that Ander had prepared for her. She raised her eyebrows at him in slight challenge and continued, loudly and slowly enough for the news recorders to pick up every word. "There are those among us who believe that the answer that will best serve us is violence. There are those who believe that, when faced with a new challenge, an opportunity that could lead us to new heights, new understanding, new knowledge, we should meet it with fear and hatred. There are those who wish humanity to live in constant dread, constant suspicion, constant wariness, a grinding daily terror that wears us down until we are no more than crawling worms. But I believe we are better than that."

Cavaco looked as if he'd like to step across the podium and strangle her. Which was gratifying, considering it was his manoeuvring that had led to her standing behind this podium in the first place.

"I believe we are better than that," she repeated. "But that is not the only reason I believe this mission to be our best chance. Because if our first instinct is to attack rather than talk, to fight rather than cooperate—to give up the one thing that raises us above mindless beasts—what happens if the unknown has sharper teeth than we do? Those who advocate for force will tell you they are advocating caution. I say they are advocating wonton destruction. They are advocating a self-immolation that will echo through the annals of our history—if, at the end of it, there are any left to keep that history. Remember this: we may not always be the strongest. And those who advocate for that course advocate for a path that will lead, inevitably, to destruction."

They were watching her, hanging on her words.

She shook her head brusquely. "What I have said behind this podium is something I believe in, enough to place my life behind my words. I don't ask for your gratitude for what I'm about to do. I don't ask for sympathy or for accolades. I merely ask that you remember what I've said here today. And I ask that you beware of those who would wager your lives to back their words, instead of their own."

She stepped down from the podium, and the crowd parted silently for her.

Ander rose and addressed a few words to the reporters, followed by some clearly irritated words from Aran Romeu's assistant. Aran himself must be meeting them at the docking bay, and again she wondered, with a hint of jealousy, how he'd arrange that.

She managed, only just, to keep her legs from giving out under her until she was back inside the transport and could collapse into the relative comfort of the seats. The others joined her soon afterwards, and Feliu shepherded two of the least likely looking individuals from the courtyard in her direction.

"Madam Chief Justice," he said stiffly, as the shuttle lifted from the courtyard. "I would like to introduce you to your newest members of staff."

Alba cast an unimpressed glance over the two of them.

"This is Ines Madera," said Feliu, gesturing to a young girl with dark skin and a halo of black hair, wide, timid eyes, and a nervous expression. "She will be acting as linguist, and your personal translator."

Alba frowned at the girl. She'd heard the name, of course—she vaguely remembered recommending an Ines Madera to head up the attempts to translate the alien markings. But this girl looked like she'd needed a permission slip to be absent from her prep school.

Feliu must have noticed her expression, because he cleared his throat. "She is among the most talented linguist in the department, and her study had been entirely focused on theoretical languages. She has an immense amount of practice in deciphering unknown communication methods and has been the lead on the team attempting to decipher the alien artifacts."

"And have you been successful?" asked Alba sharply, turning the full weight of her glare on the girl.

The girl swallowed visibly. "N—no, Madam Chief Justice. Not—not yet. But—"

Alba gave her a repressing glance, and she fell silent.

"And this," said Feliu, gesturing, "is Yosip Coelho. He will be acting as your diplomatic advisor."

He was an older man, with light brown skin darkened by the sun and a grey bristle of hair shaved close to his head. Alba couldn't tell his age at a glance, but it was likely near her own, possibly even older. His face was friendly, creased with smile-wrinkles, his eyes mild and good-humoured. He was looking at her with unabashed curiosity, and when he caught her gaze, he gave her a friendly smile. "Madam Chief Justice," he said, with every indication of pleasure. "I'm happy to meet you in person at last."

Alba narrowed her eyes. "Yes, well, I'm certain they warned you about me," she snapped.

For some inexplicable reason she wanted to see that cheerful quirk of a smile wiped off his face, replaced with the mixture of respect and apprehension she was accustomed to provoking.

His smile broadened. "I don't generally believe warnings." The twinkle in his eye felt almost as insolent as a wink might have, and she found herself momentarily taken aback.

But of course he hadn't actually done or said anything that she could object to, so she was forced to retreat into a silent glare that seem to have no effect whatsoever.

"I assume, then, that you have diplomatic experience," she said, her tone cutting.

He smiled. "In alien diplomacy, no more than the rest of us. But human diplomacy—I've accompanied a number of ambassadors to the Rim Mountain settlements, as well as the outer planets and moons."

"He is, in fact, in high demand as a diplomatic advisor," Feliu put in. "I had to work very hard to get him for you."

"And I was delighted to be asked," said Yosip, still smiling. He was disturbingly, disarmingly friendly, and the kind twinkle in his eye seemed the most genuine part of him. He seemed the type of person one would expect to find leaning on a plow on a farm in one of the Rim Mountain settlements—aged and wrinkled, but satisfied with the hand life had dealt him.

It must be a front. No one could be that open and friendly, and also be a diplomat.

She nodded brusquely. "Thank you. I shall look forward to working with you." She allowed her tone to communicate her heavy doubt.

As they left, though, she saw Yosip give the girl—what was her name? Ines?—a small, encouraging wink. And she saw how the girl's shoulders relaxed perceptibly at the kindliness of the gesture.

Feliu stood beside her, watching after them. "They're not much to look at, I know," he said in sotto voce, "but I can assure you, I went through every record of every candidate, and these two are by far the most qualified."

"Thank you, Feliu," she said, voice less curt than usual.

He sighed, his shoulders slumping, his posture slack with weariness now that he wasn't trying to hold his usual formal posture. "Do you think it will be enough?" he asked quietly.

She looked over sharply.

He must be very tired indeed; it had been a long time since he'd addressed her so informally.

But then, perhaps he was thinking the same thing she was—if they were all to die in a matter of days, or weeks, or months, it hardly mattered anymore.

She glanced out the plex window of the shuttle, watching the streets she'd grown up on spool past beneath her, and was hit, suddenly, with an unexpectedly sharp pang of regret—for all the things she hadn't done, all the things she'd neglected, all the things she'd put off for a more convenient time.

She sighed and turned away, straightening her shoulders. At seventy-three years old, she should be used to the possibility of things changing, irrevocably and without warning.

"We shall simply have to hope that it is," she said.

They reached the loading dock, and a predictable bustle and confusion ensued. They had to unload passengers and cargo from the shuttle into the transport ship that would take them out of atmosphere, and get said passengers and cargo arranged properly. In the harried confusion and noise and shouting, she almost didn't have time to take note of the moment the ship left the docking bay. The sudden acceleration was offset by the interior ship systems, but still enough to make her stagger slightly, and there was the rush of air past the ship that she hardly noticed until it fell abruptly into silence as they broke through the atmosphere.

But when at last they'd transferred to the massive ship that would be their home for Mystery-only-knew how long, and she was finally alone in her cabin, seated on her cot—the small, neat room nothing like the comfortable ancient townhome she'd left—she let herself slump, her head dropping into her hands.

"We shall simply have to hope that it is," she whispered again, to no one in particular.

12

Aran

There was a sharp, insistent tapping on the door to the tiny ship's cabin that would be Aran's home for the foreseeable future.

Aran contemplated ignoring it, but he'd run out of both despairing swear words and things to throw. So instead he turned from where he'd slumped hopelessly on his cot and called, "Come in," in a hollow tone.

"You have to unlock it," said Istvay, a hint of amusement in their voice.

Aran groaned, rolled over, and fumbled for the controller to unlock the door.

Istvay stepped inside. They stood, hands on hips, and surveyed Aran with a mixture of sympathy and exasperation.

"So," they said. "You plan on spending the entire flight curled up on your cot?"

Aran glowered at them weakly. "That was the idea, yes."

The realization that all around him, outside the fragile shell of the ship, was nothing but a cold, blank, lifeless vacuum, had set the walls of his small cabin closing in on him until he thought he'd scream.

Istvay cracked a smile. "How about this: I'll bring you lunch. You eat it. I'll leave you alone for another planetary hour. Then I expect you to at least come look around the ship with me. You owe me, after I showed up at the damn reporters' meeting this morning for you. The President was furious."

Aran groaned again, and Istvay laughed.

"Come on. It'll be good for you. Get your mind off things."

"You do realize," Aran grumbled, "that we're currently both hurtling through a frozen vacuum designed specifically to be lethal to organic life forms, and also completely surrounded by people."

Istvay laughed again. "This from the man who just got back from abseiling down the inside of a living volcano."

"That was different," Aran muttered. "It was research."

Istvay gave him a skeptical look, and Aran sighed heavily. He'd agree sooner or later, because he couldn't damn well out-stubborn Istvay, so he may as well save himself the hour of badgering.

"Alright," he said. "I'll eat the damn food, and I'll go out afterwards. But you promised me an hour."

Istvay nodded, grinning. "An entire hour to mope around and contemplate your upcoming demise." They stepped out the door. "I'll be back in a shake with lunch."

Istvay was true to their word. After he finished eating, Aran had an entire hour to stare at the wall in hopeless despair. But exactly an hour later, Istvay's cheerful tap sounded once more on the door.

"Aran," they called. "You promised."

Aran sighed, pushing himself heavily to his feet, and unlocked the door.

When it hissed open, Istvay stood behind it, an expression of repressed delight on their face. "I have a surprise for you, grumpy-pants," they said. They stepped back to reveal a woman, maybe a little older than the two of them, with long, wavy black hair and striking, light-brown eyes.

Aran stared at her for a moment, then at his friend.

Istvay was always trying to set him up with people. But surely they hadn't thought that the midst of an existential crisis was a good time to introduce a new date—

Istvay was laughing, softly at first, then hard enough that they had to bend over and brace their hands on their knees. "Aran," they said at last, wiping their eyes on the back of their hand. "Your face—" They brought their expression into seriousness with an obvious effort. "Aran, this is Gilda. She's one of the assistant scientists for the mission."

The woman smiled at him, a friendly sort of smile. He nodded back, still faintly confused. Istvay knew him well enough to know the idea of working with some stranger would hardly fill Aran's heart with joy.

The woman cleared her throat. "Aran. As this expedition was put together in a rather hurried fashion, I'm not sure you were briefed on all the parameters of the mission." She smiled at the confusion on his face. "I see I was correct. Our first and most important task is, of course, to bring back anything that could help us develop a cure for the defect. But it would be rather waste to spend an entire mission of an unknown duration without at least attempting to gather additional data."

Aran looked up with a faint stirring of interest. "You're planning on running experiments onboard the ship, then?"

She nodded, her smile widening. "We are. To begin with, we brought several different species aboard to see how they react to various conditions inherent in space travel. Although we've run such experiments within our own solar system, it's entirely possible that the results will be dramatically different when travelling through the portal, and in the space of the other side. We simply don't know what's out there, so we want to take every opportunity to observe."

Some of Aran's earlier panic was dissolving as she spoke, curiosity taking its place.

"Could you talk me through the variables you're studying?" he asked cautiously. "I'm fairly familiar with field work, so I may be able to add something."

Her smile broadened. "We've all been hoping you'd stop by laboratory once you were settled. We wanted to get your insights on some of the experiments we had planned, although I know you're probably extraordinarily busy with work of your own."

"I—" he began lamely, shooting Istvay a poisonous glare. Istvay shrugged innocently, grinning.

He cleared his throat. "I'd very much enjoy going down to the lab."

As always, now that his brain was focused on an item of scientific curiosity, rather than his impending doom, the noise and bustle of the ship was much less overwhelming than it would have been otherwise. And when he stepped inside the lab, which sprawled across half the third-floor port deck, he forgot everything else.

He'd always been a field scientist. Not only did he prefer studying nature in its proper setting, it also meant he could avoid the internecine politics he'd never really understood no matter how hard he tried.

But this lab, with its smooth, clean surfaces, its pristine, state-of-the-art equipment, its scales and timekeepers that were accurate to the microgram and the millionths of a second instead of the rough counting and guesswork he usually had to resort to when his equipment inevitably failed under whatever conditions he'd happened to subject it to, was like something from a children's wonder-tale.

Istvay stood back with a satisfied smirk, but Aran was too interested to spare them a scowl.

The woman—Gilda, he should probably remember her name if he was going to be working with her—led him to a remarkably genuine terrarium in the corner, where various small creatures and insects had been placed in simulated habitats. They were arranged so everything from the oxygen the creatures consumed to the most minute fluctuations in weight and caloric consumption could be measured constantly, with remarkably minimal disruption to their living patterns.

At his questioning, she began walking him through the parameters of the experiments. It wasn't long before he was surrounded by eager scientists, all engaged in a hearty conversation about variables, and the best way of measuring them, and potential additions to the experiment.

"And here," said Gilda at last, leading him towards desk upon which sat a mass spectrometer that looked to be even more powerful than the ones at the university, "is the other experiment I was hoping to get your insight on." She smiled. "Whatever opened the portal was fuelled by an extraordinary amount of energy. They did tests back on Colorida, and it appears that space debris from behind the portal was pushed through into our solar system when the portal opened. Some of us have posited that there's a potential for remnants of organic matter within the debris. It's not certain, of course, but there were traces of something that may have been carbon-based on the scoring on the outside of the container that was sent through the portal, and from the score-patterns it's likely the fragments were accumulated on the trip through space rather than from the box's point of origin."

Aran stared at her, then down at the mass spectrometer, a delighted grin forming on his face. "And if there are," he said slowly. "Then they may well belong to life-forms none of us have ever encountered before."

She nodded.

"Have you found anything yet?" he asked, glancing down at the collection boxes on the table.

She shook her head. "We're having issues with the equipment. We can send our harvesters a short ways from the ship, but they're not strong enough to withstand an impact from any larger debris, and we can't risk ruining them in the collection process, since we have no idea when we'll be in a place to get more."

Aran bit his lip, frowning down at the small containers. "I think," he said slowly, "I might have an idea."

From the corner of his eye, he caught a flicker of movement, and at the same time Istvay shouted, "Aran!"

He looked up just as a scientist, who had been lifting a stack of crates to pack into a storage cupboard, stepped back, tripping over the hem of his trousers.

The crates tumbled out of his arms, and Aran recognized the label on them and leapt to his feet. He caught Istvay's eye, and Istvay gave a quick nod, stripping off their jacket and starting at a sprint towards the fallen boxes, which had begun to hiss dangerously, smoke seeping through the edges.

Aran yanked his shirt up over his mouth and nose and his goggles down over his eyes, and grabbed the scientist, who'd landed on the floor, lifting him bodily to his feet and shoving him out the door. "Out! Everyone out!" he shouted, turning back to herd the rest of the panicked people to safety.

"What are you going to—" Gilda began, coughing, but he grabbed her arm and shoved her through the door, slamming it after her.

"Aran—"

He spun.

Istvay had thrown their jacket over the boxes and turned, grabbing a handful of lab coats to add to the pile. "The med cupboard is by the door. I'll get the terrariums, don't worry."

Aran turned to the cupboard, yanking the door open. He scanned quickly through the labels on the bottles inside, then grabbed an armful of laxatives and antacids, yanking off the lids.

Istvay was leaning against the terrariums, coughing, but they'd managed to cover the cages with a couple lab coats, which hopefully would protect the delicate creatures inside for just a few more moments.

Aran started forward, then staggered at a wave of light-headedness.

"Aran?"

"I'm fine," he managed. He took a deep breath and held it, then sprinted the last three steps to the boxes. Istvay pulled back the pile of coats and shoved the tip of their bush knife under the lid, their other arm covering their mouth and nose, and pried it open to reveal the cracked hydrogen fluoride canister inside. Aran poured the contents of the bottles over the mess, then he grabbed Istvay's arm, dragging them backwards. The canisters steamed and smoked, and, leaning on each other, Aran and Istvay staggered to the door. Istvay yanked it open, and the two of them fell out into the corridor beyond.

"Hit the ventilator," Aran gasped, kicking the door shut behind them. One of the scientists, who'd been staring dumbly, jumped to attention and stepped over to the controls.

"We can't ventilate that, it'll—" Gilda began sharply, but Aran shook his head.

"We neutralized it with magnesium hydroxide. It'll be fine."

She was staring at them. "You—how did you—"

"The laxatives and antacids from the med cabinet. This isn't the first time we've dealt with a hydrogen fluoride leak," said Istvay, raising their head finally. "Like Aran said. It'll be fine." They turned to Aran, looking him over. "You didn't get splashed, did you?"

Aran shook his head and straightened, still trying to catch his breath. "You?"

"I'm good."

There was something in their tone, though, that made Aran glance at them a little more closely.

Gilda's voice was heavy with concern. "I'll talk to the people who packed this. All the dangerous chemicals were supposed to have been padded and protected, although with the rush to get everything on board ..." she trailed off, shaking her head. "Why don't you two head into the med bay, get checked out? We won't be able to do anything in the lab for a couple hours anyways."

Istvay and Aran exchanged glances.

"We should probably head back to our cabins and wash up," said Istvay. "I still haven't finished unpacking, and Ani's probably missing Aran by now." Their words were light, but there was something forced in their tone.

Gilda nodded reluctantly, and the two of them started down the corridor, Aran trying to ignore the admiring, slightly awed glances the other scientists were shooting in their direction.

* * *

When they were out of earshot, Istvay stopped, catching Aran by the arm. Aran turned, startled.

"Listen," Istvay said in a low, strained voice. "There's something wrong. Right before the hydrogen fluoride spilled, I saw a note tucked in between two of the boxes. The handwriting on it—I'm sure it was Emeric's."

Aran stared, not quite sure he'd heard right. "I … what?"

Istvay's scowl deepened. "Emeric? You know, our former classmate, who hates you? You remember him? Look, Aran, do you know these scientists? Any of them?" They shook their head. "This is too much of a coincidence. He could have … I don't know, he could have had something to do with choosing who was assigned to the mission. Or with choosing the supplies that got sent along. Right?"

"I … guess it's possible. But I don't see why he'd want to—"

"Aran." Istvay was speaking through their teeth. "He wanted to come on this trip instead of you. He tried to talk you into trading places with him, but couldn't. He clearly has some personal stake in this. And, I cannot emphasize this enough, he. Has tried. To kill you. Before."

They looked like they were on the verge of a stress-induced cardiomyopathy.

Aran hesitated. "Istvay," he said at last, cautiously. "You just saw a note, right? It's been how long since either of us has seen Emeric's handwriting? Are you sure—"

Istvay sucked in a long breath. "You're not even trying to take this seriously. I heard you talking to Gilda before the accident. You said you had a suggestion. What was it, exactly?"

Aran frowned in confusion. "I—thought of a way to collect samples."

Istvay's eyes narrowed. "They don't have equipment durable enough to survive the conditions out there. We don't know if Emeric has tampered with anything. And you bloody well intend to put on a bloody space suit and go out there yourself. That was your plan, wasn't it?"

"To collect samples," said Aran patiently.

Istvay rolled their eyes in utter exasperation. "Why the hell do I think this is ever going to turn out differently than it does?" they muttered.

"Look, I'm … sorry. But Pishti, if we find something? Some life-form, some fragment of a creature that no one has ever seen before?" He couldn't keep the excitement from his voice, although he felt slightly guilty about it.

"No, Aran, I don't know! I haven't spent the last seven damn years since we both graduated university tagging along on your bloody expeditions trying to keep us both alive!" snapped Istvay, turning away.

Aran frowned.

Even for Istvay, this was a bit of an overreaction.

He hesitated, then put a hand on Istvay's shoulder. "Pishti. I—"

This time Istvay did look up, and for just a moment, their eyes met Aran's. There was an odd, pained expression on their face, and Aran dropped his eyes abruptly, suddenly very certain that whatever had been about to come out of his mouth was something that was probably better left unsaid.

"I'm sorry," he finished lamely. "You're right, we should both probably get unpacked,"

For a few moments, neither of them spoke. Then Istvay gave him a small, forced grin. "Come on. We should go, before Ani gets impatient and decides to come looking for you."

They turned away, and Aran let out a long breath.

He wasn't sure what was wrong with him these days.

Istvay was quieter than usual as the two of them walked down the corridor, and Aran glanced at them out of the corner of his eye. They looked thinner than they had, even though he knew they were eating.

Maybe Istvay was right. Maybe there was something wrong, and he should be more careful.

But he was going out to collect samples regardless. Because if there was organic matter, and it had come from behind the portal, it was just possible that it would give him a head start on looking for a cure. He'd spend the rest of this damn trip outside the ship in a space suit if that's what it took.

How much time did they have left?

It had to be enough. It had to be. The universe couldn't be that unfair.

13

Savina

Savina saw the small slump of the captain's shoulders, the way her eyes flicked quickly to Rafel, as if to be certain he was unhurt. When she turned back to Savina, there was something weary and beaten in her eyes.

"I'm not going to fight you," she said quietly. She gave a small, wry chuckle. "As if I had anything to fight you with in the first place."

Savina nodded, but didn't holster her pistol. "Then I'm sure you won't mind signing the ship over to make it legal," she said. "I'd hate to be stopped by someone and have some incongruence in the paperwork cause a misinterpretation as to who is the ship's rightful owner."

"That would be unfortunate," said the captain dryly. She hesitated, then sighed and reached into her jacket, pulling out a disc Savina recognized at once as the ship's official papers.

"Toss it," Savina instructed, her smile never wavering. The captain's answering smile was grim, but she tossed the disc in a light underhand, and Savina caught it neatly.

"I'm so glad we could come to an understanding," she said pleasantly, tapping the disc open.

It appeared she'd judged the women correctly. She wouldn't risk her crew's life, no matter the cost.

Savina scrolled quickly through the documents, pulling the retinal filter over her gaze with a quick flick of her eyes. The documents scanned as genuine, and she tapped her fingerprints to the owner's panel and let it scan her face. When she finished, she smiled at the captain. "I just need your signature," she glanced back at the papers, "Joska, and then we'll be done."

The captain—Joska—nodded again, and Savina tossed the disc back to her. The woman added her fingerprint and facial scan, and after a moment the disc whirred, beeped, and flashed the green of a successful transmission.

"There," said Joska quietly, tapping the disc off. "The ship's yours. No need for your friend to point their gun at Rafel anymore. Every database in the system will have you as registered owner as soon as the ship's system syncs in."

Savina took the disc, tapping it on and examining the documents to be sure the captain was telling the truth.

She was.

Savina tucked the disc into the front of her jacket with an insincere smile. "I appreciate your cooperation, Joska."

The captain's smile was unreadable, and Savina frowned.

Joska might be kindhearted, as Beni put it, but she wasn't stupid. She'd taken defeat with a suspicious amount of calm. And there was something about her expression that made a hint of unease twist in Savina's gut.

Still, the woman didn't try to fight when Savina clipped a restraint around her and Rafel's wrists. And when Savina tapped the disc into the ship's control board and the retinal scanner scanned her, everything in the ship came online at her command, exactly as it should.

Savina clipped herself into the captain's seat and smiled up at Joska. "I have you on restraint, but I'm no sadist. I have no interest in hurting you as long as our mutual goals align. So, what I suggest is, you agree to pilot my ship under my direction. Once Beni and I reach our destination, I'll be more than happy to sign the ship back to you. For a small price, perhaps, but what's that between friends?"

The captain was still watching her with that small, unreadable smile. "And as you've gathered, I'm no masochist," she said dryly. "So I agree to your proposal." She paused a moment. "I assume I won't be talking you into making my cargo drop before we head off to wherever you plan to go?"

Savina gave a delighted laugh. "I admire your sense of humour, Captain."

The captain nodded in resignation. "Very well. Send through the coordinates of where you like me to take you."

Savina leaned forward. "Of course. But to avoid any embarrassing misunderstandings ... You may be tempted to try to send word ahead. I've asked Beni to encrypt the communications lines—anything you send out will be unintelligible. So don't bother."

Joska nodded again. "I understand," she said quietly.

Savina dimpled prettily. "I do appreciate that." She blinked to activate her wavelink, and said, "Coordinates for Colorida ports, please."

A line of text scrolled across the retinal screen at the corner of her eye, and she flicked her eye to adjust down to the coordinates she was looking for—a port about three hours' transport journey from the compound. She could bring them down closer, of course, but this port was more central, and would make it less easy to guess why she and Beni had chosen to put down there.

"Sent the coordinates through," she murmured, and the captain tapped her wrist to accept the transmission, glancing down at the screen on the pilot's dashboard.

"I assume you'll have no problem getting us there," said Savina.

The captain studied the display. When she looked up, there was the slightest quirk of amusement in the corner of her mouth. "I can pilot us there easily enough," she said. "But since you're the owner of the ship, I think it's my duty to brief you on a few items."

Savina narrowed her eyes, her hand reaching inconspicuously for her gun.

The captain reached into the ship's controls and tapped something twice, bringing up a list on the ship's main screen. "Getting into the port itself shouldn't pose a problem," she said. "But as you'll see here, the ship's two port thrusters are almost gone. We can make it to Rochosa, where I was planning to drop the cargo, but we won't make it much farther than that without new thrusters. I don't have the funds to fix them, and I was hoping that this cargo drop would give me enough left over to at least give them a temporary patch-up. But for the length of trip you're suggesting, I'm guessing you'll need to replace them completely. And, since you're the captain—" she shrugged. "Shouldn't take more than a couple thousand, I would think, if you get some good-quality used ones."

Savina glared at her. "Why the hell would I put a couple thousand credits into this floating junkpile?" she snapped.

The captain shrugged again. "Your choice. But if you don't, I'd lay a wager we don't make a week's travel before we're stranded, right in the middle of deep space. And if we do get stranded, it'll take at least a day or two before someone can get out there to tow us, and the towing fees—" she shook her head. "Cost you more than a couple thousand, that's for sure."

Savina shot the woman another glare, then tapped her wavelink. "Interface with the ship's database, give me a reading on the thrusters."

"The thrusters are currently working at five percent of capacity," said the friendly male voice into earpiece.

"How far will they take us?" she snapped.

"The only planet within an acceptable-risk flight range for the thrusters is Rochosa," the wavelink answered cheerfully. "At distances farther than that, you will run an exponentially increasing risk that the thrusters will fail. I can send you a graph of the likelihood of failure over distance, if that would be helpful."

Savina's scowled deepened, and she avoided the captain's eyes.

"Inventory the supplies, check for the ability to repair the thrusters," she growled.

"There are materials for basic repairs, but not enough to change the analysis," her wavelink responded.

Savina held herself back, with an effort, from swearing, and forced her mouth into a thin smile. "Well, Captain," she said finally, "it looks like you get your wish after all. We'll stop at Rochosa and put down, I'll unload my cargo from my ship, and I'll use my profits to offset the cost of the thrusters."

The captain nodded, but there was still that hint of a smile playing about the corners of her mouth. "As you say," she said, her voice carefully neutral. "But I should mention, too, that, as funds have been a bit scarce, I'm about eighteen months behind on my permits." She gave a small chuckle. "Some ports will let you unload anyway, on credit. At least, they would on my credit, because they know it's good. But they don't know you, so I doubt they'll be inclined to be accommodating. They'll read the ship's registration, see the fees are behind, and impound the whole thing, cargo and all." She gave a small shake of her head. "The fines are a bit exorbitant, I think, but what can you do? That's the government."

This time, Savina couldn't hold back a curse. "And how much are these eighteen months' worth of fees?" she asked through her teeth.

The captain tapped her palmscreen. "Looks like about fifteen hundred, plus interest."

"Fifteen hundred. Plus interest," repeated Savina icily. "Another any other surprises you'd like to spring on me?"

This time, the captain couldn't hold back the smile that lifted the corner of her mouth. "None I can think of at the moment. Although with you being eighteen months behind on permits, they'll probably ask you for the next year of permits paid in advance when you go in."

"Let me guess. Another thousand," said Savina in an acid tone.

The captain shook her head. "Prices went up as of last month. It'll be twelve hundred for the year. But no interest, at least."

For a long moment, Savina glowered at the captain. The woman's smile in return was polite and friendly, but it had an unmistakable overlay of amusement.

She could try to sign the ship back over the captain, although looking at the woman's face, Savina doubted she'd agree to it even if Savina were to offer. And Savina knew better than to offer. If Joska had command of the ship again, it would take no effort at all for her to unencrypt the ship's wavelink, send off a warning, and then idle them outside the docking bay on Rochosa, far enough back to make it next to impossible for Savina and Beni to get away until someone came to pick them up.

She could use the restraint, see if watching Rafel scream in agony was enough to make the captain volunteer to pay. But she'd checked the ship's register. From the records, the captain was exactly as broke as she proclaimed herself to be. The ship had shown some profit five years back, but then it had taken massive damage in a space storm. When it was towed back to the nearest port, every credit of profit had been sunk into fixing it up.

Savina ground her teeth, swearing quietly.

There was nothing she could do. She'd walked into a trap as neat as any she'd set herself. Even docking the ship and sneaking off, trying to wheedle a passage on another ship, would be ultimately unsuccessful—she was registered as the *Dolphin's* owner now, and while she could change aliases, changing fingerprints and facial features was more difficult. She wouldn't get past the spaceport.

She drew in a long breath.

Joska would live to regret this.

Or perhaps she wouldn't. That would be infinitely enjoyable as well. For a moment, she enjoyed her small fantasy of the captain begging for her life as Savina stood over her, pistol in hand …

Either way, the bastard certainly wasn't getting her ship back now, even if Savina had to blow the damn thing up to make sure of it.

But in the meantime …

With an effort, she forced her face into a pleasant expression. "Well," she said. "I appreciate you briefing me." She stood. "Set a course for Rochosa, please. If you deviate from it, or try to send off a communication, or do anything else other than what I've specifically ordered you to do, I've programmed the restraint to send you a level ten shock."

"Of course, Captain," said Joska, still with that hint of a smile.

Savina turned on her heel and left the bridge, swearing savagely under her breath.

14

Alba

Alba was exhausted, bored, and thoroughly cranky. "If the captain tells you again that he cannot receive the news packets from the planet, tell him I shall come speak with him myself," she snapped.

"Yes, Madam Chief Justice," said Feliu, his posture stiff, but still reluctantly respectful.

He was as cranky as she was.

He moved towards the door, irritation in every line of his posture, but as he reached it, it opened of its own accord. Feliu paused a moment, then gave whoever it was a brief nod and stepped out into the hallway.

Yosip stood in the doorway, with his eternally twinkling smile and bright eyes. "Madam Chief Justice," he said. "I have the latest diplomatic briefing that the staff has put together." He paused a moment, glancing around, and she felt the sinking dread that he'd suggest they go over it.

She wasn't certain she could keep a civil tongue in her head at the moment.

But instead he smiled, his expression much too perceptive. "I'll leave it here for you to study at your leisure."

"And why not go over it now?" she snapped, suddenly irritated.

She might be exhausted, yes, but she certainly didn't need some old fool insinuating it.

He raised his eyebrows, his mouth quirking good-naturedly at the corners. "We could. But I'm a little tired, and I'd take it as a kindness if you'd give me some time to wander the decks and recover."

There was nothing she could say to this, since his words were perfectly polite and sensible, and it seemed almost too petty to scold someone for a smile. Besides, she wasn't sure how exactly she'd go about that in the first place without making herself look the fool.

So instead, she gave a stiff nod. "Very well. But I'll expect you first thing tomorrow morning. We'll finish up then."

He nodded in agreement, his eyes bright with good humour, and turned to the door.

She watched him leave with a strange mix of irritation and gratitude.

He was the only person in her acquaintance who was not intimidated when she snapped at him, and she wasn't entirely sure how to take it. Was he truly that oblivious? Certainly not, or he'd hardly be a highly sought-after diplomatic aide.

Perhaps he was he trying to outwit her? Play her in some way?

That was most likely option, but …

But in his quirk of a smile, his dancing eyes, she'd never caught a hint of either the cunning, or the malice, that she'd expected. Instead, every word and every action seemed glossed with an unfeigned and entirely unexpected kindness.

She sighed.

The thought of the diplomatic briefing had only driven home her lack of information on the parties with whom she'd be negotiating—not for a political advantage, but possibly for the lives of everyone in the system.

The thought weighed more heavily on her every day. If she'd admit it, that was the most likely source of her recent irritation, not Feliu, despite his aggravating mannerisms.

She shook her head, glancing around. The small cabin felt suddenly far too confining.

Feliu would likely be furious with her for wandering about the ship —he'd probably make some stiff comment about the dignity of her position, or some such thing—but honestly, at this point, she was about to lose the dignity of her position anyway by dint of going out of her mind with sheer boredom and pent-up anxiety.

The sterile hallway was empty as she stepped out—two cleaning drones, humming busily to themselves, were the hallway's only occupants, although she knew that there were security guards posted at regular intervals. The corridor itself was clean and swept, completely void of any personality. Perhaps the entire ship was, honestly.

But, she realized, she wanted very much to find out.

When she was very young, long before she'd decided to go into law, she been fascinated by ships. And yes, that had been sixty-something years ago, but she couldn't, somehow, remove the hint of romance the image still brought to mind.

She raised her chin.

If she couldn't, as Chief Justice of the system and head of the diplomatic mission, explore the ship if she so chose, she wasn't sure who could.

She activated her wavelink as she walked. "Ship schematics, please," she said crisply, and a moment later, a map of the ship's decks appeared on her retinal screen. She flicked her eye upward to reorient the map, and said, "Direct me to the main deck."

A small dotted line appeared on the map, indicating the most direct route, and a translucent indicator superimposed itself on her vision, pointing the direction she should go.

After three lifts and several minutes of walking, the corridors she was travelling down began to take on an entirely different character than the ones outside her cabin. They were undeniably older, with an air of use about them, the paint peeling slightly, the dents in the walls not fully covered, crew hurrying past on some errand or another, far too busy to take note of her. But there was an undefinable flavour to the place that the cleaner, quieter diplomatic section of the ship lacked. It was the sort of thing she was accustomed to when walking the Old Quarter of do Sol—the marks not only of age, but of joy and sadness, triumph and sorrow, conflict and worry, the small building blocks of day-to-day life that seeped into the walls and floors and left a mark as indelible as the coal-fire smoke from outdoor cooking fires—each individual instance completely unremarkable, but cumulatively, enough to change the colour of the buildings around them with its residue.

She was arguably the most powerful woman in the Joias system, and her influence couldn't be overstated. But she wondered, sometimes, about the lives of the people on whose behalf she made the laws—the women and men huddled by the charcoal cookfires, almost identical to the ones their great-grandparents may have sat beside, sweating in the full-bodied heat of summer or shivering in the damp winters. Or crews on ships like this, whose entire lives, sometimes from childhood, were spent in the deep reaches of space, and who, after decades of travel and back-breaking labour, could hardly return planet-side at all, their bones become so brittle that they scarcely could hold them up in full gravity. She'd been told they often died longing for space, for the very weightlessness and radiation that had slowly killed them.

She'd done her best to do well by them, but sometimes she felt their lives were as foreign to her as these aliens with whom they were going to speak.

When at last she stepped out onto the main deck, her breath caught for half a moment with a sudden, unexpected rush of wonder.

The scene was everything she'd imagined as a child—the crew bustling back and forth across the open space, redistributing fuel cells, organizing the carrier drones and the cleaning drones into workforces, shouting orders or obeying them, or else clustered in small groups, laughing and talking loudly.

"Excuse me," said a voice from behind her, and as she half-turned, someone stumbled against her, knocking her out onto the main deck.

She barely managed to keep her feet, her heart pounding at the unaccustomed, casual violence that had almost sent her sprawling. The man who'd pushed her stepped around her without a glance back, and for a moment she was almost speechless with anger.

"Out of the way," someone else growled, and despite her outrage, she stepped back quickly against the wall to catch her breath.

She became aware, gradually, of the quiet conversation from the group of crew nearest her.

"… sending us on a bloody suicide mission, is what it is," someone muttered.

"Maybe if I was raised somewhere like that damn judge, with everyone bowing to kiss my kneecaps, I'd feel the same way she does," another of the crew responded. "Never mind she's not the one who'll be thrown to the aliens if things go sideways. Always have an escape plan for the important people."

Alba frowned, and listened closer.

"I don't think it's all bad," said another, a young man with bright auburn hair and brown skin. He had the cheerful exuberance of the young, who still believed firmly in their own invincibility. "Like she said, better to talk than to fight until we know what we're going up against. You remember when Benat tried to take me on when I first joined up?"

There were scattered chuckles at that.

"Be that as it may, have you heard what they're saying on the news packets?" another of the crew put in. "They're saying we're being sent in as some sort of sacrifice. There's no way we're coming out of this alive. We should have shot a phaser missile through the portal, not sent a crewed ship."

Alba leaned against the wall, trying to process what she'd just heard.

No one should have had access to the news packets yet—at least not for a few more hours, if her information was correct. But the crew members were talking as if they were up to date on the latest packets.

"And who might you be?"

Alba turned, startled, and to find a woman glowering down at her. She had a fuel-cell propped on one broad shoulder, her muscles showing clearly through the thin undershirt. But there was something about her bearing, a straightness to her posture, that set her apart from the crew members Alba had been listening in on.

Alba gave the woman a haughty stare. "I'm sorry, but I don't see that it's business of yours. Surely you have other duties besides asking unnecessary questions."

The woman's eyes narrowed, the hint of an unpleasant smile playing about her mouth. "Don't worry. I know who you are, Madam Chief Justice," she said softly. "I know that you're responsible for tying General Cavaco's hands, when he was the only person who could possibly protect us against whatever the hell is out there." She glanced around the deck at the group of crew members, who'd broken off their conversation and turned to watch the show. "Shall I tell these others that the person who sent them all this way on a suicide mission is standing right here behind them?"

Alba narrowed her own eyes, although her heart was beating faster.

She'd never really stopped to consider, until this moment, the possibility of physical danger here, on the ship.

"I would thank you to get back to your work," she snapped.

Another of the crew came up behind the woman, a middle-aged man with the skin creased from radiation. "What's happening here?" he asked gruffly.

The woman turned and shot him a quick grin. "Unauthorized person on the main deck," she said, her voice lazy with confidence.

The man looked closer at Alba. "Who are you?" he asked.

"That's just what I was asking," said the woman, and there was a purr of menace in her tone, and triumph in the glance she shot at Alba.

Others of the crew were gathering as well, forming a small semi-circle around them.

Alba forced her breathing to steady, but her palms were damp with sweat.

This was ridiculous. If the crew knew who she was, the most likely thing to happen was that they'd stammer out apologies and escort her safely wherever she wished to go.

But—

She'd heard the way they talked, when they didn't realize who was listening.

The way this woman had spoken of Cavaco.

"Go on," said the woman, "why don't you tell us."

Alba took a deep breath.

There was nothing to be afraid of, surely.

And yet, the rapid pounding of her heart told her she didn't really believe that.

She braced herself, opening her mouth to speak, when a sudden commotion came from the back of the crowd.

The man facing her turned, frowning, and then she saw his eyes light up.

Alba followed his gaze and saw a pleasant-looking young man who appeared to have just stepped out on the deck. He had dark, wavy hair, a close-cropped beard, and a dreamy expression, and it took her only a moment to recognize the young daredevil scientist she'd earmarked for the mission.

He looked surprised, and not particularly pleased, at the attention.

"Aran?" the man said with a broad smile. "I was hoping to run into you. I wanted to tell you how much I admire what you do."

"I. Um. Thank you," Aran muttered, the smile on his face obviously forced. "I'm sorry to disturb you. I'm just looking for some calcium carbonate. My, um, my pet is—she needs something to settle her stomach, and I thought—"

"I can get some for you," said an eager-looking young woman. "Come with me, I have a friend on mess duty. He'll get you sorted."

"I'll come along," said the young man with auburn hair. "There's half a dozen of us who'd like to buy you a drink anyway."

Aran had a desperate look on his face, like he'd rather be

anywhere else in the system at the moment, but he gave a hopeless sort of nod. "I have to get back to my work, but—"

"Just one drink, then," the young woman proclaimed, slapping him on the arm. He flinched, but tried to smile.

"One drink, then," he said. "I … I appreciate your help—"

"It's nothing," said the man who'd been speaking to Alba, grinning. "Our pleasure."

Aran's eyes suddenly stopped on Alba, and he frowned slightly. She caught his gaze and shook her head firmly, hoping she didn't look as shaky as she felt.

He raised an eyebrow, but gave a faint nod and turned away, allowing himself to be led away by the exuberant crew.

At last it was only Alba and the woman who'd confronted her.

"You're lucky, Madam Chief Justice," the woman said in a low voice. "But I suggest in the future, you stay where you belong."

She turned on her heel and strode off, her straight, formal posture contrasting sharply with the comfortable slouch of the rest of the crew.

Alba frowned after her, too shaken to feel properly outraged.

By the time she reached her cabin again, Alba was exhausted. Her heart still pounded strangely, and a sudden light-headedness made her sit down abruptly on the edge of her cot. Her joints ached, and her feet ached, and the muscles in her legs ached.

She should call for that woman to be disciplined, probably. But she didn't know her name.

And the obvious disrespect in the woman's eyes had shaken her more than she cared to admit.

A short time later Feliu arrived, tapping lightly on the door before stepping inside. "Madam" he said. "You were right—I was able to retrieve the news communications."

"Good," she said shortly. "Thank you. If you'd see fit to give them to me—"

He nodded, handing over a small stack of holodiscs, then frowned. "Madam? Are you quite well?"

"I'm fine, thank you. That will be all," she said.

He was watching her with faint concern, but at last he nodded and stepped out of the cabin.

She glanced down at the holodiscs in her hand and closed her eyes for a moment, trying to slow her racing heart. Then she tapped first disc open, pulling up the news packets for the last week.

As she paged through them, though, the unease that had started at the crew's overheard conversation sharpened into a sort of dread.

"—alien threat of unknown proportions—"

"—military potential unknown—"

"—technology sent through the portal indicating the alien culture is almost certainly developed for war—"

No wonder, listening to this, the crew had been terrified.

She would have been, too, in their place.

This couldn't be accidental. This, then, must be Cavaco's strategy —stir up the populace. Frighten them. Terrify them. Turn the whole system into a simmering reactor. And then the first small thing that went wrong on the diplomatic mission would be the catalyst, the excuse for war, and the citizens would swallow down the burning result like strong liquor.

When she'd finished going through the reports, she sat on the edge of her cot for a long, long time. The numbness gripping her had spread through her body until she could feel it in her fingertips.

She couldn't afford to let anything on this mission go wrong then. Not one single thing.

Perhaps once she would have stated with confidence that nothing would go wrong. That she was perfectly capable of carrying this off flawlessly.

But that was before the portal had opened. Before her grand, legacy-making proposal had been derailed, before Cavaco had made his move and forced her into leading this mission.

She could still feel the sudden, sharp realization from earlier that day on the main deck. That moment where she'd been facing the tall, muscular woman, and realized, with a sudden, hard certainty, that if the woman wanted to, she could hurt Alba.

And there was nothing at all Alba could do to prevent it.

15

Aran pulled the fasteners closed on his spacesuit, trying to keep his hands from trembling.

He was cursing quietly to himself.

Istvay was right. They'd always been right. He was stupid. Why the hell was he doing this?

Except—the last time he'd gone out, the samples he'd collected had showed traces of something, a fragment of organic material with a DNA sequence he hadn't been able to identify.

And so of course he had to go out and collect more. And of course he had to insist on going himself, because he was a damn idiot and had no sense of self-preservation, just like Istvay said in their more exasperated moments.

He closed his eyes, trying not to think about what would come next: stepping into the airlock. Watching it close behind him, hearing the *click* of the lock sealing him in to the small, air-tight space. The *hiss* of the outer door as it opened, the sudden weightlessness, a sense, all around him, of a grinding, icy vacuum, an implacable nothingness that wouldn't rest until every piece of organic matter it could touch was obliterated.

"Are you ready?" asked one of the scientists, a normally quiet young woman with pale skin and straw-coloured hair.

Normally quiet, except when she looked at Aran, when her expression took on a tinge of giddy infatuation.

He groaned quietly to himself. If only she could hear what he was thinking—

"Aran?"

He managed a smile. "I'm ready." His voice was muffled in the stifling confines of his helmet.

"The airlock's ready for you," she said. "And Gilda is waiting there with your equipment."

He gave a sickly nod and made his way forward, his movements awkward and constricted by the suit. Sweat beaded on his forehead, and he forced himself to breathe.

This would be fine. He'd done it before, it would be fine.

Gilda handed him his collections equipment at the entrance to the airlock. He fumbled with it for a moment, then gave up and tapped the controls, loosening the seal on his gloves. He pulled them off and dropped them beside him while he stowed the equipment on his belt.

Gilda smiled, retrieving them. "I suppose when you're as experienced as you are, you need everything just so," she said, holding the gloves in place while he resealed them.

He shook his head in despair. Why in the hell …

"Good luck," she said.

He forced himself to nod, grateful that the helmet at least partially obscured his expression. Then he stepped into the airlock, and waited for the sick finality of the door sealing shut behind him.

The external door hissed open, and, biting his cheek so hard it hurt, Aran forced his hands to let go of the handholds and stepped out into nothing.

The abrupt sense of weightlessness that came when he left the ship's gravity field was an odd shock, and for a moment, he found himself struggling to remain upright—as if 'upright' was a concept that had any meaning in space.

With shaking hands, he tapped the small propulsion unit on his suit, pushing himself farther out from the ship. The farther out he could get, the more likely he'd find particles undisrupted by the ship's path through space. But the sight of the ship shrinking behind him, his only connection to it a long line that looked terrifyingly delicate against the vastness surrounding him, was enough to make him swallow hard to avoid being sick.

Then the line went taut, and, tapping off the propulsion, he carefully unclipped one of the collection canisters from his supply belt, and clipped it, just as carefully, onto the edge of his glove. Then, holding his arm out in a way that would have been exhausting if he'd been somewhere there was actual gravity, he settled back to wait.

Around him, the stars burned tiny and brilliant, glowing specks in the vast void surrounding him. From the opposite side of the massive ship, Colorida glowed as bright as a moonrise. He sucked in a long breath, trying to force his tense shoulders to relax.

He was out here for research. There were particles out here, particles that had come through the portal. Possibly fragments of life forms. Once he got back in, he'd get the samples into the centrifuge, then feed the screens into the mass spectrometer, and maybe this time he'd get some solid readings …

He felt his panic slowly draining away as his mind slotted into the familiar, comfortable rhythm of research.

If he found something—

The genetic sample, at least, had proved there was a species behind the portal similar enough to humanity that with any luck, whatever resistance the aliens had developed to the genetic defect could be recreated in humans.

There was a familiar tightness in his stomach at the thought, a mix of desperate hope and abject terror—hope that perhaps, just maybe, there might be something, somewhere, that could save Istvay.

And terror that after everything, he'd fail. That he'd watch Istvay die, the same way he'd watched Istvay's mother die when he was ten years old, and she and Istvay were the only safe and happy things in his frightened, confused, miserable young life.

He frowned, pulled out of his thoughts.

There was something tickling at the back of his spine. Something that wasn't simply nerves.

He stayed very still, focusing on the odd sensation. His mind ran rapidly over potential causes. Nerve damage, obviously, but he hadn't suffered the sort of physical trauma that would induce something like that. Pressure, applied at the wrong place for a long enough time, could do the same thing, but—

The crawling sensation had moved up his spine now, to his shoulder.

He risked a quick glance.

He couldn't see anything through the suit, obviously, but whatever it was seemed to be crawling up his neck. He tilted his head to one side and craned his eyes.

And then he felt suddenly very, very cold.

He couldn't see the insect's entire body. But the two brightly coloured antennae, with their distinctive orange and purple patterning, told him everything he needed to know.

He let out his breath very, very slowly, holding his body completely still to avoid alarming the creature.

He'd seen, in the experimental tanks, the male speckled death moura. And in the next room, under protective watch, the creature herself.

If he were observing her in the wild, he would have been stilled with sheer admiration for her beauty and deadliness—one bite could inject enough poison to kill a full-grown adult within minutes. But death mouras were shy, quiet creatures, and generally, seeing one in the wild, he'd have no fear.

But they were highly, highly sensitive to changes in pressure, or to changes in temperature.

And he was acutely aware of how the discovery had sent his heart pounding, adrenaline pumping through his veins, the temperature in his suit rising as his body prepared to fight or flee.

He took a deep breath and let it out carefully.

She was probably just as frightened as he was, bewildered and confused by her new surroundings.

"Hello there, sweetheart," he whispered, hoping his voice didn't shake.

The waving antenna paused for an instant, then resumed their slow movement.

Speaking would, he hoped, let her know there was another creature in here with her, show her that he didn't intend to be a threat.

Of course, he'd worked with venomous creatures long enough to know that their perception of a threat could be very different than his own. He couldn't blame them, honestly. But that wouldn't make him any less dead if she happened to put him in the threat category.

The creature hesitated, then started delicately up the side of his neck. He could feel the hooked spurs of her legs on his bare skin, every sensation amplified by the adrenaline pumping through his body.

Her steps were slow and cautious, and he closed his eyes for a moment, trying desperately to slow his heart rate, steady his breathing.

The colouring of her antennae suggested that she was almost ready to lay her eggs. Which would make her exceptionally sensitive to potential danger.

He couldn't see her now, could only feel the slight scrape of her legs on his skin as she explored, the occasional brush of her antenna. From the feel of it, she was at least ten centimetres long.

There were some insects whose venom was more potent the smaller they were. Speckled death mouras, though—the larger the specimen, the more venom available to pump into their hapless prey.

The insect climbed slowly along his neck and paused at his hairline, then he felt the brush of its legs against the corner of his jaw.

He closed his eyes, hardly daring to breathe for fear of pushing her against the plex of his helmet faceguard.

He had to get back to the ship. She'd be far too agitated in these unfamiliar surroundings, and far too easily frightened by any movement on his part.

But turning on the propulsion unit would mean a sudden hum and a rapid acceleration, which would almost certainly frighten her as well.

At least she was in his helmet. At least here he could keep an eye on her, and perhaps get some warning if she became alarmed.

Moving with almost glacial slowness, he reached out, grasping the anchor line carefully in one hand. Very, very gently, he pulled, dragging himself a fraction of a metre back towards the ship.

She didn't react, and he almost breathed a sigh of relief before catching himself.

Another grip, agonizingly cautious, another pull. His movement towards the ship was so slow he could only judge the distance he'd travelled by the loose tangle of anchorline behind him.

She seemed to have settled now, her legs gripping his cheek, her waiving antennae brushing almost at his eyelashes. But at least he knew where she was, and there was no danger of—

There was another small, unmistakable tickle along his left hip.

He stopped himself, barely, from jerking in surprise, and swore quietly through his teeth.

"So," he said, in the calmest voice he could muster, "you brought your boyfriend along."

There was a chance it wasn't the male speckled death moura—it could be any number of venomous creatures. It could, even, be a nonvenomous creature, but that possibility seemed almost laughable, considering how things had gone so far.

The male wasn't as venomous as the female. But he was still venomous enough to put Aran in a coma, or paralyze him permanently.

And if there were two of them in here, there could be another, hiding in his gloves, or his boots, or—

He fought down his rising panic. He was pretty sure they'd only brought along two specimens.

"I'm just going to keep moving slowly," he murmured, in the same voice he used on Ani when she was in a particularly bad mood. "I'm just going to pull us in. You two probably don't like it out here any more than I do, and if you kill me, they'll drag me in when my vitals flatline, and you'll get smashed in all sorts of different ways."

The ship was definitely closer now than it had been, but still much too far away.

Sweat beaded on his forehead, and he took a long, shallow breath, trying once again to slow his racing heart.

Anything, even something as innocuous as a trickle of sweat, could be enough to set off his nervous guests.

He could see the female's slender, speckled body from the corner of his eye, distorted by nearness, and he had the half-hysterical thought that he was lucky to have her to look at—the males were a drab greyish-brown.

Reach, grip, pull. Reach, grip, pull.

"Aran?"

Gilda's voice through his earpiece almost made him jump, and he cursed quietly. He could feel the creature on his cheek stir uneasily at his inadvertent movement.

Very, very gently, he pressed his wrist against the inside of his gloves, activating his wavelink. "There's been a bit of a problem," he said quietly. "I'm on my way back in. Nothing to worry about, but please don't—"

"I'll get you in right away—" Her tone was suddenly concerned.

"No," he said quickly. "Just—get Istvay."

Istvay was the only one he could think of who'd trust him to come up with a solution, instead of trying to come up with one for him and getting him killed for it.

"I can—"

"I have the situation under control," he said, praying it was the truth. "I just need you all to make sure that no one accidentally interferes."

Reach, grip, pull.

He was getting closer, almost imperceptibly.

And then, to his horror, he felt a faint vibration as the automatic line winch activated, snugging the line back into his suit and pulling it tight.

He could feel on his hip the quick, darting half-charge of the male death moura, now clearly perturbed, and the female was dancing her front legs from side to side, body reared up in alarm.

And maybe he was close enough that if he got bitten and they dragged him in, they'd still be in time to use the antivenin, stored in the laboratory. But—he could see from the corner of his eye the female's bright body, her markings a glorious celebration of colour, the nervous twitch of her movement.

These two were only trying to do the same thing he was, stay alive. They were the only two death mouras the scientists had brought along to observe, and the unique way they metabolized sulfur was a trait none of the other creatures in the menagerie possessed. He might survive, possibly, but the death mouras would die—if they weren't crushed against the inside of the suit by his senseless body, they certainly would be once anyone on the ship pulled the helmet open and saw them.

The female's head was weaving in the rhythmic, snakelike pattern that meant she was about to strike.

He took a deep breath, and pulled the bush-knife from his equipment belt, flipping it open against his leg.

He was a damn bloody idiot.

Before he could think about it any farther, he sliced the blade cleanly across the vibrating anchor line, cutting himself loose.

The anchor lines, of course, were heavily reinforced, threaded with fortified steel. But the honed blade of his bush-knife was tougher still.

For a moment he sat frozen, watching the cut anchor-line drift away. But at least the vibrations had stopped.

Slowly, the female's nervous dance slowed, and at last she came to rest again tucked against his cheekbone. The male's movements, too, grew slower, and finally stopped altogether.

He forced himself to look ahead at the ship—the ship from which he was now completely detached.

He was drifting, however slowly, towards it. The anchor-line pulley had started him forward, and with no atmosphere or gravity to check his momentum, he was still drifting in the right direction. Slowly, yes, but that wasn't important, as long as he was getting closer.

Then he bit back another curse.

What did matter was the fact that he'd been nudged off course somehow. He wasn't going to hit the airlock door straight on. And somehow, without an anchor-rope or mag boots, he'd have to make his way into the airlock, all without disturbing his two passengers.

Damn it to hell.

Carefully, he scrabbled in his supply belt for something—anything —and at last pulled out a magnetic wrench.

Not much, but it just had to be enough.

His body bumped up against the ship, and he slapped the wrench against the hull.

If the magnet wasn't strong enough to hold—

The slow drag of his body's momentum pulled his weight against the magnet of the wrench.

He sucked in a quick, panicked breath …

It held.

He let out the breath in a sigh of relief that came from the very depths of his damn soul.

"Aran?" Istvay's voice through his earpiece was sick with dread.

"I'm sure you're busy dealing with whatever the hell is happening out there, but for the love of all that's holy can you please let me know that you're alive and conscious?" They sounded like they were on the verge of donning their own spacesuit to come out after him.

Aran wasn't sure if the realization was touching, or horrifying.

"I'm—fine," he said quietly through his teeth.

He pulled out a second wrench and very carefully placed it along the hull a little closer to the airlock, then pulled himself forward.

He pulled a little too enthusiastically, and managed to break both wrenches free. He slapped both back on again, his heart pounding.

They stuck, and he let out a shallow breath of relief.

"Get—the outer airlock door—open, please. And make sure no one comes into the airlock until I tell them it's safe."

"Got it," said Istvay, voice tense.

There was a *hiss* as the airlock door gaped wide before him.

They didn't usually leave the doors open like this, but he could picture Istvay's face, the stubborn set to it as they argued with whoever was in charge, informing them the damn door was going to stay open until Aran got in, and if anyone didn't like it, that person could step out the airlock themself.

Aran had been on the other side of that stubborn expression more than once in his life, and he knew how hopeless arguing was.

And then he was there, clinging on to the external handholds of the airlock.

Now that he'd made it, his muscles had gone shaky and weak.

And then something twitched against his face, and he remembered that he hadn't made it, not yet.

In his thoughtless relief, he'd let himself slump inside the suit, and the female death moura was now pressed between his cheek and the plex visor of his helmet.

He waited, hardly breathing, for the sharp sting that would kill him—but it didn't come. He squinted one eye half-open, and realized, with the mixture of relief and panic, that she hadn't struck, because her stinger was pressed up against the plex.

Which meant for the moment, he was safe—or at least, relatively safe, considering the male was still perched on his knee.

But the moment he shifted, even accidentally, he was a dead man.

Very, very gently, he pulled himself along the handholds and into the airlock. And very, very gently, he raised a hand and tapped on the airlock door in the code that he and Istvay had developed as children, while with his other hand he held his helmet in place.

Istvay must have been listening, because the airlock door slid shut behind Aran, the room re-pressurizing as the gravity from the ship's grav control kicked in.

He'd been bracing himself for this, but even so, the abrupt change in the pressure around them made the male move uneasily.

With trembling fingers, Aran unsealed his helmet with his free hand. He felt the hiss of the normalizing pressure, felt the creature squirm against his cheek, but he was holding her steady with one hand, pressed up against his face like they were lovers.

The male danced uneasily on his knee for a moment, then settled.

Very, very gently, Aran bent his right knee, enough to allow him to unzip the front of his suit. It wasn't actually designed to be taken off before the helmet, but now seemed like a damn good time for improvising.

From the corner of his eye, he could see the entire group of scientists, their faces pressed against the plex of the airlock as they watched him, and behind them, Istvay, their ferocious glare probably the only thing keeping everyone else out.

For a wild second, Aran almost laughed. What this must look like people who didn't know what was going on—

He got the fastenings undone, and carefully, with one hand, peeled the suit off his shoulders and down his arms, trading hands for just a moment to get the sleeves off. Then, with infinite care, he slid his left leg, with its passenger, out of the suit.

From the corner of his eye, he could see the sudden furor among his assembled audience.

He leaned down, and very, very gently, pulled one of the collection bins from the supply pouch on his crumpled suit. Moving with glacial slowness, he brought the container's opening up to the feet of the insect on his leg.

It waved its antenna at it in uncertain fashion, but made no move to go inside.

Gritting his teeth, Aran gave his leg a sharp twitch.

The creature, startled, made a mock charge, directly into the collections bin. Aran flipped it up neatly with his free hand, slamming the port shut against his hip, legs so weak with relief he wasn't sure how he remained standing.

But he didn't have time for relief just yet—he still had to survive the next phase.

He stooped, placing the collections bin on the floor beside him carefully, so as not to jar it—the poor creature had been through enough trauma already—then moved his free hand to the lip of his helmet.

This had to work. It absolutely had to work. Because even if they got to him with the antivenin in time, a sting this close to his eye would leave him permanently blind, and possibly paralyze his vocal cords as well.

And that was assuming the antivenin would work quickly enough to save his life, which wasn't a given, considering the way his airways would immediately swell up.

He took a deep breath. Then in one swift movement, he yanked off the helmet and gave a quick shake of his head, and the insect, whose grip on his face had been loosened by her unwanted confinement, went flying across the room to land in a corner.

He grabbed for a collection bin, holding up his hand as he saw Istvay moving for the lever that would open the door, and sprinted across the room towards her. She was still dazed, but she was hissing, her tail raised in threat.

Before she had time to regain her equilibrium, he slapped the open collections bin over the top of her, scooped it up in one practiced motion, and slammed the lid shut.

He placed it gently on the floor, then leaned back against the wall, his legs too shaky to hold him. He could still feel the ghostly touch of her rough legs on the skin of his cheek, the anticipatory twitch of his skin against the painful venom.

When he'd recovered enough to manage it, he squeezed his hand to activate the wavelink, the familiar tingle spreading up the nerves of his arm and shoulder, and said in a shaky voice, "You can open the door now."

Then he dropped back against the wall again and tried to remind himself to keep breathing.

The door hissed open, and then there was a confusing, noisy chaos as at least a dozen people tried to shove into the room at once. One of them, he saw, was heading towards one of the collection bins, and he lurched to his feet, grabbing at it.

"No," he snapped. "It wasn't her fault. They must have got free somehow and gone looking for a dark, quiet place. Just put them back in the habitat, please, carefully, and check to make sure they can't get out again."

There was a fair amount of looking at feet and awkward shuffling before one of the scientists finally stepped forward, gingerly, and took the two collection boxes as if they contained live explosives.

"Those were in your suit?" one of the older men asked, his voice awed. "How are you still alive?"

And then everyone was surrounding him, asking questions, wanting to touch him or clap his shoulder or shake his hand, and he had to focus very, very hard to keep from losing his actual crap. He wished desperately for Istvay—and then, from across the press of bodies, he saw the look on Istvay's face.

It was unadulterated fury. Angrier than Aran had seen them in a very, very long time. And suddenly, he wasn't entirely sure that seeing Istvay would be a net positive at the moment after all.

Istvay waited until the other scientists had finally left—or at least, until Aran had made his excuses loudly enough and frequently enough that they stood back to let him pass.

Aran hesitated for a moment. Then, with almost the same feeling of dread as when he'd realized there was a speckled death moura in his spacesuit, he stepped forward.

Istvay's face was grim. They caught Aran by the shoulder and marched him down the hallway towards his cabin. They didn't say anything, and after a look at their face, Aran didn't either.

When the two of them reached the cabin, Istvay shoved Aran inside, slammed the door, and grabbed him by the shoulders, looking him up and down. "Are you alright?" they demanded in a harsh voice. "You got out without getting bitten, or stung, or anything else?"

Aran nodded wordlessly.

Istvay closed their eyes, face going slack with relief, and pulled him into a rough embrace.

Aran was too startled to react.

Then Istvay let go of him and stepped back, arms crossed, glowering. "What. The hell. Happened out there?" Their voice was low, and so furious that Aran almost found himself flinching at the words.

"There, um, was something in my suit," he said stupidly. "That's all. I just—I had to—" his words trailed off.

Istvay sank into a chair and dropped their face into their hands. When they spoke again, their voice was trembling. "Aran. You almost died. You were almost killed. When I saw you'd cut the anchor line —" they broke off.

Without really thinking, Aran put his hand on Istvay's shoulder. They looked up, and without meaning to, he met their gaze.

Their eyes were dark with concern, and more frightened than he remembered seeing them in a very long time. And he knew how to work with Istvay and push his feelings aside, he'd done it his whole damn life, but there was something about the unaccustomed vulnerability in Istvay's expression, the worry, and damn it to hell—

He forced himself to look away, suddenly as shaky as he'd been back in the airlock. "It's fine," he managed. "Not that big a deal. Just an accident."

Istvay stared at him with a mixture of astonishment and disbelief. "I saw the cages those things were kept in," they said at last. "There's no way they just accidentally got out. And even if they had, there's no way in hell they ended up in your space suit by accident."

Aran frowned.

Istvay threw up their hands in exasperation. "Aran! Someone is trying to kill you. Someone on the ship wants you dead. And whoever it is, I have a pretty decent suspicion who might have put them up to it."

Aran stared at his friend. "Emeric?" He asked last, incredulously. "You honestly think Emeric would—"

Istvay let out a heavy sigh. "He wanted to come on this expedition himself. You took his place. And, as I keep reminding you, he has tried to kill you before. This isn't unprecedented."

The idea was so absurd that for a moment Aran almost argued.

But—the memory of the feeling of those legs on his cheek was far too clear in his mind.

And now that he had time to think about it, Istvay was right—it should have been next to impossible for the creatures to escape.

"And you wonder why I didn't want to become a lab scientist," he muttered, dropping down onto his bed.

For the first time since Aran had made it back to the airlock, Istvay cracked a small smile. "Of course. It's because you're so damn risk-averse, right?"

Aran rolled his eyes, and Istvay managed a chuckle. But there was something forced in their laughter, and the stark panic of earlier still lingered under their expression.

And a small trickle of unease crept up Aran's spine, as prickly as the legs of a speckled death moura against his skin.

16

Savina

Savina's temper had not improved by the time they reached the Rochosa port and docked, but she managed a thin smile at the captain as she stepped past her and onto the loading ramp. "I programmed your restraint to allow you access to the ship's main deck, and your cabin," she said. "You could try to get off and warn someone, but——" She gave a small shrug.

"Of course," said Joska in a dry voice. "You have the restraint pulses set to level ten. Don't worry, I remember."

Savina gave her frigid nod, then stalked down the loading dock and into the port.

She made her way to the dockport duty-master's office. She'd radioed in ahead of time and sent a deposit of credits, and with that assurance she'd been allowed the land—although her docking bay had not been authorized for access yet, which meant no repairs, no unloading, and no additional fuel cells until she'd paid the full price.

She had it, but barely. This would wipe out everything she'd earned from her last job, plus most of her savings.

But …

She gave a small shiver.

But if she didn't get back in time, that may not actually matter.

There may not be any family to send money back to.

The port duty-master seemed charmed to make her acquaintance, and after a friendly chat, where Savina explained with wide, innocent eyes that the captain she'd acquired the ship from hadn't bothered to explain that the port fees hadn't been paid until the transfer was complete, the older woman even waved some of the interest. She did frown a little, though, when she looked at the records. "I wouldn't have expected that of Joska," she murmured. Then she shrugged. "I suppose that's what happens when you go through enough hard times for long enough. Poor woman's certainly had her share of bad luck, and if she was willing to sell her ship …" the duty-master shook her head, and Savina tried to appear sympathetic.

It was more difficult than it should have been.

Then she made her way out of the dock, after calling Beni on the wavelink and instructing them to have Rafel get the cargo unloaded and the fuel cells loaded up.

The bustling streets of the enclosed hive of a city were a haven of poverty, misery, and degradation of every type.

Exactly the kind of place Savina felt at home.

She put on her most innocent smile, and let her walk take on the odd skip of a provincial who'd never been in a docking port city in her life and was unaccustomed to the unfamiliar artificial gravity.

It worked—within a couple streets, three rough-looking individuals were following her, making almost no attempt at concealment. She allowed them to herd her into a small back alley, and when she emerged a few minutes later, sheathing her knife, her purse was a good deal heavier and her temper a good deal restored.

Finding the thrusters was more of a problem—she'd never had any interest whatsoever in knowing the inner workings of a ship. She'd still have no interest in knowing the inner workings of a ship, except that this appeared to be the only way she'd make it back home. At last, she had to resort to calling Joska on her wavelink and getting brand names of used models that might do what she needed.

When she reached the used-parts dock, she tapped her wavelink to connect with Joska's, so the captain's palmscreen would show everything Savina was seeing. "Tell me which ones we want," she whispered as she wandered up and down the aisles.

Judging by what the dock master had said, Joska wasn't the type to knowingly sabotage her ship, no matter how irritated she may be. Besides which, if the thrusters failed, all four of them would be stranded together. Joska certainly must have guessed that, should that happen, when a ship came to tow them back there'd likely be only two passengers awaiting rescue.

"Those ones," said Joska's voice in her earpiece, as Savina's eyes fell onto a heap of unpromising scrap metal. "Ask for the B73 model thrusters."

Savina wandered in the direction of the stall, keeping her eyes on everything except what was in front of her. She stumbled into the pile of parts, gave a soft little exclamation of surprise, and looked up innocently into the face of a large man with a scowl on his face.

"Damn," came Joska's voice. "Best keep walking. He'll try to skin you for everything you have, if he doesn't do worse."

"What you want, girl?" the man growled.

Savina gave him a wide-eyed smile and a slightly embarrassed laugh. "I'm looking for ships parts," she said. "I just—I don't really know what I need. Do you think you might be able to help me?"

The man's dour expression was rapidly changing to one of calculation, then greed. "I … may be able to," he said cautiously. "What are you looking for?"

"I just bought a ship, and the thrusters aren't working," she said, letting a little disgruntlement show in her tone.

He nodded brusquely, but she could see the gleam in his eye. "And what sort of price can you afford?"

"I'll need used ones, I know that," she said, with a hopeless shrug. "I just—I don't know enough about ship's parts to even know where to start."

"What model's your ship?" he asked.

She repeated what Joska whispered into her earpiece, making her voice a little uncertain, and he nodded, stepping over the two thrusters she'd been watching from the corner of her eye, and straight towards a heap of thrusters that even Savina's untrained eye could tell were garbage.

"Those'd last you may be one day's flying," whispered the captain's voice in her ear. "I think the ones I have now are in better shape."

"Since you're looking for top quality," the man said, turning around and patting one of the ancient thrusters, "this is the best you'll find around here. I don't generally offer guidance to my customers—let them figure it out themselves—but you look like a decent person, and I'd hate to see you cheated somewhere else."

Savina widened her eyes. "Oh, thank you! I was so worried I wouldn't be able to find something. How much?"

He studied her for moment, calculating. "Normally I'd ask five thousand," he said. "But seeing as you got fleeced when you got the ship, I'll cut the price down to four and a half."

Savina moved over to stand beside him, running her hands down the scored sides of the thruster as if in indecision. "You say these are the best?"

He nodded. "I wouldn't advise going with anything less. You don't want to get yourself stranded."

She sighed, still running her hands along the thrusters. "Well, I agree with you. But I just don't have that kind of money." She made her voice as regretful as possible. "I guess I'll have to take my chances."

He frowned slightly as she glanced around her, then pointed to the two thrusters the captain had indicated.

"I'll take these instead. For fifteen hundred, since, as you say, they're in such terrible condition." She gave him a sweet smile.

His face darkened in anger as he stepped over to her, his fists clenching. "What you're going to do is—" he began, in a voice heavy with menace.

Savina, whose hand had strayed to her pocket, pulled out the small shock-tranq and slapped it against the back of his neck.

His eyes widened for just a second, and then he went down, convulsing.

Savina bent over him and delicately detached the device, calling loudly, "Somebody help! This man's collapsed! Get a medic!"

People glanced up in alarm, some calling for a medic while others crowded over to help or gawk.

In the confusion, Savina shouldered the two thrusters, smiling in satisfaction. "These are the ones you wanted, right?" she whispered as she started back for the ship.

There was a moment of silence on the other end of the wavelink, and then Joska said, her voice tinged with humour, "And if you'd been wrong? You'd have gone back and knocked him out again?"

Savina smirked. "Don't tell me he didn't deserve it."

This time, the captain actually chuckled. "Oh, he absolutely deserved it. I haven't enjoyed seeing someone get taken for a ride that much for a very long time. But yes, those are the thrusters I wanted—or rather, you wanted, assuming you intend to get the ship back to Colorida without breaking down on the way."

Savina slipped out of the used-parts dock, still smirking. A woman brushed past her, and Savina turned in irritation.

Then she almost dropped the thrusters.

The woman was a little taller than Savina, her dark hair cut in a sleek half-shave, her figure lithe, the muscles of her back and shoulders defined even through her clothing. And there was something about the way her hips moved as she walked, the way her grey suit clung to her curves, that made Savina's mouth go completely dry.

She'd seen plenty of attractive women before. Mostly on her way to kill them, of course—an unfortunate hazard of her chosen career—but still … she'd never allowed herself more than an appreciative glance.

This woman, though—even from the back, there was an undefinable air of danger to her every movement, a magnetic allure that pulled at Savina like a fishhook through her gut.

Savina shook her head sharply, and stopped herself with an effort from starting after the woman like a dog following a steak.

This was ridiculous. She had a ship to repair, and a trip back to Colorida to make posthaste. And here she was, staring like a hormone-addled teenager.

She forced herself to turn away.

But she couldn't resist a glance back over her shoulder.

And she couldn't avoid the visceral jolt of disappointment when the woman had already disappeared into the crowd.

She'd almost reached the loading docks, still distracted by the memory of the woman, when she caught the faintest movement from the corner of her eye.

Her mind snapped back into focus, and instinct sent her diving to the ground. A shot slammed into the edge of the stall where she'd been standing, the shockwave that would have cut through skin and muscle like a projectile ringing harmlessly through the metal instead.

She scrambled beneath the shelter of the stall as the surprised owner gaped at her, and after a cautious moment, she peered out into the crowded market, which had gone suddenly silent at the sound.

Not an ordinary occurrence, then.

"Beni," she hissed into her wavelink. "I need you to get the thrusters back to the ship. Get Rafel to help you—use his restraint if you need to. I'll send you the coordinates. I ran into some trouble."

She glanced around, then tucked the heavy thrusters into a small gap between two of the venders' stalls. "My sibling will be coming for these," she whispered to the stunned stall owner. Then she started forward at a crouch, keeping her body low.

When she'd gone twenty metres or so, she took a deep breath and straightened cautiously.

Another shot hissed out into the silence, but she'd been waiting for it, dropping back down even as it dispersed against the wall behind her.

Well, that solved any uncertainty about who the target was.

Damn her inattention to hell. She hadn't even noticed she was being followed.

"Joska," she hissed into the wavelink. "Once you have the thrusters, how long will it take to get the ship running?"

There was a moment's pause, then Joska said, "Rafel says if he's working fast, he could maybe get us ready to go in an hour."

Savina shook her head grimly. "Tell him I'll give him half that, and if he can't do it, he won't have to worry about me killing him, because someone else will. If they're after me, they'll damn well gun down anyone who's with me, and that includes you and Rafel at the moment."

She shut off her wavelink, yanked a tiny cylinder from her pocket, and tossed it into the air. Even with her face turned away and her eyes squeezed shut and pressed into the crook of her elbow, the flash of brilliant white light was enough to make her see stars. Anyone looking directly at it—for instance, someone watching for Savina to poke her head up again—would be seeing nothing but that flash for the next ten minutes.

She jumped to her feet and ran, ducking past stalls, leaping over stacked ship parts, and dodging down narrow corridors, grimy from disuse. She gritted her teeth against the stitch in her side as she ran.

She hated running. She'd always hated running. And she'd been doing a damn lot of it these last few days.

At last, when her chest ached and her heart felt like it would pound out of her chest, she slowed, panting heavily.

"Time," she gasped into her wavelink, and glanced quickly at the readout on her retinal screen.

Fifteen minutes since the first gunshot. Maybe she'd lost whoever it was.

And then something hissed through the air behind her, and again, it was only instinct that made her leap to one side. A thin wire bolas clattered against the corridor walls in front of her, and she swore and took off again at a run.

She glanced at the readout of the station on her retinal screen, swearing through her teeth.

She couldn't run for much longer. Besides, better to wait for her pursuer somewhere she'd have the advantage.

She turned down a narrow corridor, then another, people jumping out of her way as she ran, until she was in a part of the station that was almost deserted. She dropped down behind the corner of one of the hallways, forcing her breathing to slow, and peered carefully out the direction she'd come.

She had every intention of killing whoever this was, but she'd rather ID them first, get some idea what was going on.

She waited for what seemed like an extraordinarily long time, but still no footsteps.

She closed her eyes for a moment, her breathing finally steadying out.

Had she actually lost them? It didn't seem possible, but—

A small sound made her jerk her head up, just in time to see a tiny gas cylinder bounce off the wall in front of her and roll around the corner, hissing malevolently.

She swore through her teeth. The gas was already thick in the corridor behind, and the best way out was clearly in the direction she'd already been running. But she hadn't lived as long as she had by doing the expected.

She yanked out a knife, launching herself around the corner in the direction the cylinder had come from, and rammed into someone, hard. The woman turned with a startled curse, and for a heartbeat, their eyes met.

Savina swore again, her voice choking in her throat.

It was the woman she'd passed earlier.

She looked to be around Savina's age, her skin a few shades darker than Savina's own, her hair still sleek and unmussed despite the pursuit. Her lips were pulled into a cold half-smile, her features sharp and elegant and as coldly beautiful as Savina would have expected.

But what caught Savina's gaze and held it were the woman's eyes —an icy slate-hazel, as cool and ruthless as a mountain cat's. They were the eyes of a predator, calculating and merciless and utterly mesmerizing, and for a moment, as those eyes met hers, Savina found she couldn't breathe.

And then the moment passed. The woman grabbed for a weapon. Savina slapped her hand away, raising her knife, but the woman grabbed Savina's wrist and twisted. The knife clattered to the ground, and Savina kicked out hard at the woman's knees, swearing through her teeth. The woman stumbled back, but her free hand was coming out from behind her back, and Savina caught the glint of a pulse gun. Desperately, Savina yanked out another flare, shoved it in the woman's face, and set it off.

The resulting flash knocked both of them completely sightless. Savina groped for the wall of the passage, swearing silently, then, keeping a hand on the dirty wall and trusting to luck, started off at a run.

The woman's footsteps were close behind her, but she wouldn't be in any better shape than Savina was—worse, probably, since Savina had at least squeezed her eyes shut before setting off the flare.

"Get me back to the loading dock," she muttered into her wavelink. "Auditory directions. And don't let me bump into anyone."

She could hear, as she turned a corner, hand still firmly pressed to the wall, the noise and voices of people around her.

She yanked out a knife in her free hand and twisted her face into what she hoped was a threatening expression, and kept running, praying that whoever was in her damn way had quick enough reflexes to jump aside.

"Tell Rafel he'd better be ready," she muttered into her wavelink as she ran. "I'll be there in ten minutes, and I'll be bringing company."

"What happened? Are you hurt?" Beni's voice was worried.

"I'm fine right now. But none of us are going to be fine if those damn thrusters aren't ready to go when I get there," she snapped. "And you can tell Rafel I'll shoot him myself before the bastard behind me has a chance to."

Her sight was returning slowly around the edges, and although the centre of her vision was still obscured by a white starburst, she could tell she was approaching the port docks. She took her hand from the wall and started into the crowd, shoving her knife back into her belt as she pushed through the throngs of embarking and disembarking space passengers.

The woman was probably still after her. But her sight wouldn't be any better than Savina's, and she wouldn't dare shoot into a crowd like this.

Probably.

But as Savina played the attack back in her mind, something cold settled into the pit of her stomach.

"Beni. There's no way that government agent could be here by now, could they?" she asked abruptly into her wavelink.

There was another pause. When Beni spoke again, their voice was sick. "They issued her a ship with a new drive tech. If the yacht sent your information back immediately, and she guessed where you'd come, it's … possible."

Savina swore.

This wasn't good.

She'd been raised on stories of government agents, the horrors and the atrocities they'd carried out on the Old Believers through the centuries.

And they were notoriously good at it.

By the time she reached the *Dolphin*, breath tight and legs aching from weariness, the ship was already running. The loading ramp was down, and Beni stood at the top, face creased in concern.

"Savina?" they began.

There was the *hiss* of a pulse rifle, and a searing pain blossomed in Savina's shoulder. She stumbled, with a whimpering, shocked little scream.

"Savina!" Beni's face was frantic.

"Get down," Savina panted. She was still on her feet, somehow, her shoulder burning like fire. "Get down, dammit!"

Beni dived to the ground as another shot hissed through the air, ringing loudly against the wall of the loading ramp where Beni's head had been. Savina yanked out her own gun and fired blindly over her shoulder, then scrambled into the ship. She grabbed Beni and shoved them ahead of her as the ramp closed behind the two of them, running up the narrow corridors towards the flight deck.

"Joska, go!" she shouted, hooking into the ship's wavelink. "Go now!"

The ship was already rising gently from the bay floor, making the captain's curt acknowledgement scarcely necessary.

They reached the flight deck, and Savina shoved Beni into one of the launch seats and pushed the strap into their hand, then dropped into the one next to her, strapping herself in with her good arm. The ship shot forward, the acceleration pushing Savina against her seat, the pain in her shoulder sharp enough that she had to fight against the black crowding the edges of her vision.

The bay's outer airlock doors hissed open, and then they were out, the station shrinking rapidly behind them.

Savina let out a breath of relief, and blinked back a light-headedness that she wasn't sure was from the zero grav, or shock from her injury.

"I hate to bring this up, but if you want me to keep us alive, I need to know," said the captain grimly, looking up from the controls. "What the hell was that about?"

Savina took another deep breath and let it out slowly. The pain from the pulse shot was radiating hot through her shoulder, and now that she was safe, her muscles had gone weak and shaky. Her legs ached, and her chest burned from running.

"Government agent," she said finally.

There was a moment of silence.

"That's not good," said Joska. "A government agent isn't going to give up that easily." She glanced down at her screen, then swore quietly, shaking her head. "You might want to take a look at this, Savina."

Groaning, Savina slipped her feet into the mag boots and unstrapped herself, then made her shaky way over to the ship's screen.

She could see the shape of the station behind them, clear on the screen.

And in front of the airlock doors of the station, just hissing closed, there was a small, compact ship. One that looked incredibly fast, and incredibly dangerous.

"Damn it to hell," Savina muttered.

17

Alba

"Don't tell me it's impossible," Alba snapped impatiently. "I know exactly what that word means—it means you don't want to put in the requisite effort."

Feliu looked uncomfortable. Ines looked horrified. Yosip looked unperturbed, but she could sense concern in the creases around his eyes and mouth.

"I didn't say it was impossible, Madam," Feliu said stiffly. "I said, the captain of the ship informed me that until we're several days' travel further on, it will be impossible to create and maintain the secure communication line required by protocol. And he has also informed me that he doesn't have the authorization to break protocol, not without significant—"

"If I may," broke in Yosip, his voice as mild and friendly as always. "I know we don't have authorization to break protocol, but I know someone in the communications bay. She's offered to let me call back to speak with my son if I ever want to. I can't imagine she wouldn't do us a favour if we asked nicely."

They all turned to stare at him.

He shrugged, a broad smile wrinkling his face. "She has a daughter who's around the age my grandson would have been, and we got to talking."

They all were still staring.

Alba recovered first. "Alright, I suppose if she's willing to break every regulation in the books to allow you to talk to your son, she may be willing to do the same to allow the Chief Justice of the entire Joias system to speak with the President," she said bitingly.

Yosip's friendly smile broadened. "I can't see why she wouldn't. I'll take you to her, and we can ask."

The trip down to the communications bay took an absurd amount of time. Yosip seemed to know every person they passed, whether officer, crew, or maintenance, and he greeted them as if he and they were old friends.

Alba gritted her teeth in annoyance. But still, if this ridiculous habit of Yosip's of striking up a conversation with every person he met was the thing that would allow her to get word back to Ander, she supposed she couldn't complain.

"It's six o'clock in the morning back on do Sol," said the woman at the communication booth. She'd introduced herself as Adela, after she'd greeted Yosip and they'd talked for an absurd amount of time about Adela's daughter, who was apparently staying behind with Adela's wife and her parents just outside the city—details Alba had had no desire to know, and would endeavour to forget at the earliest possible opportunity. "Will your friend be awake, do you think?"

They'd all judged it prudent not to be entirely forthcoming about Alba's identity, or the identity of the person she wished to contact back on Colorida, and she wore a shawl over her hair, the shadows of which did a decent job of obscuring her features.

Alba shot the woman her iciest glare. "If he's not, he certainly will be when I'm finished."

The woman stared at her for a moment, taken aback, then chuckled softly, apparently believing it was a joke. She tapped through the codes to open the line and stepped back, gesturing Alba to the seat. "You'll need to put in the security code for the line."

Alba stepped up, tapped in the code, and then let the scanner read her thumbprint and face.

The woman checked her controls, then smiled. "Perfect. That should get you through, as long as your friend answers."

Alba narrowed her eyes and murmured, "He'd better answer."

The woman chuckled again, a soft, comfortable sound, and turned to Yosip. "I suppose we should leave your friend to talk in peace. Oh, and you'll love this—the other day, my wife sent Nina out on her own to the market for the first time, and on her way over—"

The door closed behind them, and Alba turned back to the screen.

After far, far too long, it brightened, and she saw the President's face, his eyes puffy with sleep, hair flattened on one side.

"Madam Chief Justice?" His voice came out gravelly. Alba glanced behind her reflexively, but she was alone.

"I saw the news packets," she snapped. "What's happening down there?"

Ander shook his head, looking slightly more awake now. "It's … not good." Worry winkles creased his face, deeper than they had been when she'd left. "I've tried to keep the government speaking with a united front, but Cavaco insisted that all viewpoints must be able to have their say, and he convinced enough of the ministers to back him that I wasn't able to stop it. And it's not just that—he must have plenty of non-government people on his payroll. Every other news packet is a report from a scientist, or a security expert, or someone similar, giving an opinion that a pre-emptive strike against the aliens is our only option for survival."

"You can't counter it with genuine scientists?" she asked, worry sharpening her tone.

Ander shook his head wryly. "Somebody's threatening any of the scientists who might be willing to speak out. I've contacted a dozen of them to ask if they'd give an interview, no restrictions on what they could say, but at the last minute every one of them either backed out or disappeared." He sighed. "We can't even pay them off, like Cavaco does. The counsellors in my jurisdiction and yours might be self-interested, but most of them aren't completely corrupt. If we tried something like that, someone would grow a conscience and report it. But Cavaco is military, and so are his people. They do what he orders, and that's that."

Alba nodded silently.

"This was damnably bad timing," said Ander grimly. "You know my voice doesn't hold the same sway in the Council that yours does. I don't know how to fix this. Things are moving too quickly. If you'd held back on that proposal of yours until after we'd dealt with the portal, he may not have felt the need to—"

Alba cut him off sharply. "If my proposal had come after we'd dealt the portal, the situation would be exactly the same. You know as well as I do he's been looking for any excuse to expand his authority."

Ander hesitated for a moment, then nodded wearily. She couldn't tell if he didn't dare argue with her, or simply knew it would be no use.

Then he frowned. "I'm glad you called, actually," he said, voice uncharacteristically grave. "I was trying to think of a way to get a hold of you." He turned and rummaged through the drawers of what was probably his bedside table, emerging at last with a holodisc. He tapped it on and expanded the screen.

She leaned closer, squinting at the wavery lines of text.

"This is the list of the people we sent with you," he continued, running his fingers down a string of names. "And here, on the side, are their qualifications."

Alba nodded impatiently. "Yes, you gave that to me before I left."

"Except one of my aides came in two days ago," he said quietly. "She'd been looking through some of the information, preparing a report on the mission. And—" he paused, and she could see the unease in his face. "Their backgrounds were forged," he finished at last. "Most of these people belong to Cavaco. And … that's not all."

"Oh for the Mystery's sake, spit it out," she snapped, trying to hide her sudden, sick dread.

He looked even more worried, and even more miserable. "The ship's lists. They may not be accurate."

"What does that mean?"

"It means," he said, even more quietly, "that there are likely people the General smuggled aboard. People who aren't on the ship's lists. Who he'd send along, and why, I have no idea. All we know is, the ship's passenger lists were tampered with."

There was a long moment of silence. Alba closed her eyes for a moment, the flutter of her heartbeat quick and dizzying in her chest.

She took a deep breath, pulling on her iron control. "And what does this mean for the mission, then?" she asked briskly, proud of the fact there was not even a tremor in her voice.

President Ander shook his head. "I … don't know. I don't know what he's planning." He paused. "Alba, you need to come back. This mission is a disaster in the making."

Alba watched him for a moment, forcing her face into a chilly impassivity.

Cavaco had set her up.

What his end game was, she still didn't know. Perhaps to sabotage the mission, then spin it as a failure, and use that as a final impetus to take control. Or perhaps to get her to abort the mission herself.

If she didn't guess correctly, she'd be playing into his hands.

"I shall consider the matter and get back to you," she said at last.

The President nodded, worry still cut deep into the lines of his face.

"Do you know exactly who is compromised and who is not?" she asked.

He shook his head miserably. "We know some names. I'll send them through to you. But whoever forged their credentials was talented, and there's no way of knowing if we found them all. I can't definitively tell you that you can trust anyone on the ship."

Alba gave a short nod.

She'd have to figure it out on her own, then. Ander had always been a bit useless.

She pictured the woman from the main deck, her military bearing, her contempt for Alba. That entire situation made much more sense now than it had a few minutes before.

There was a cold fear in her chest that she wasn't entirely sure what to do with.

What the hell was Cavaco playing at?

"I'll contact you shortly, then," she said at last.

"Don't take too long," he said quietly. "Whatever he's planning—if we don't act quickly, I'm not sure we'll be able to stop it."

He tapped the screen off, and his picture faded.

For a few moments, Alba sat staring at the blank screen. At last she rose, her muscles and joints stiff and aching, her body tight with unease.

When she opened the door, Yosip was still deep in conversation with the woman, both of them smiling broadly. But when he caught her expression, Yosip cut the conversation short with a friendly excuse.

"What happened?" he asked quietly as they walked back down the now silent hallways.

She gave a brusque shake of her head.

She had no idea, now, if she could trust even him.

She should be used to it, after a career in politics. But something about the creeping menace of the situation—trapped on a ship in deep space, the unimaginably high stakes riding on the outcome—made a cold, unfamiliar fear coil itself deep into the pit of her stomach.

"He what?" Feliu's voice was equal parts shock, worry, and outrage.

"He, or someone near him, falsified the credentials and backgrounds of at least some of the people on our expedition," Alba repeated grimly. "And the President couldn't tell me whether they'd found them all. The upshot being, we have no idea who we can or cannot trust. Furthermore, it appears there are passengers on this ship who do not appear on the ship's lists."

Feliu shook his head and leaned back against the wall, looking suddenly very weary. "He certainly couldn't have gotten to everyone on the ship—that would be impossible, especially considering the short the timeline. But he could have gotten more than I'd like to think about."

"In the end, it hardly matters. One is enough to poison the entire batch," said Alba. "As long as we're not certain, we don't dare trust anyone."

Feliu shook his head slowly. "That's not entirely true. Your personal staff—I looked into them myself. There's no way the General would have known I'd do that, and no way he could have falsified the amount of data I went through." He paused a moment. "As I think of it, there were some suspiciously attractive candidates that I hadn't expected, but I make it a habit not to go into things with merely a surface understanding of the subject." A bit of prickly pride had returned to his tone.

Alba nodded, fighting back the hint of a smile.

She had been on the receiving end of his reports for years now, and she could verify, with no doubt whatsoever, the veracity of Feliu's words. He'd probably looked into Yosip's and Ines's hospital birth records, and possibly those of their parents as well. Even Cavaco would have no way of pulling one over on someone as thorough as Feliu—if mundane details were an art form, he was a master artist.

"Alright," she said. "That's two. Well, four, if you include the two of us."

Feliu was shaking his head again. "That scientist that you asked to be placed on staff, Aran. He's been a planetwide celebrity for years. I think we can be certain he is who he says he is. Even if we're not certain about his relative sanity," he added wryly.

Alba thought of the quiet young man who'd inadvertently rescued her the previous day, and nodded slowly.

He certainly wasn't one of the General's creatures, unless his ability to hide his connections was unparalleled. She knew the thoroughness with which every news reporter on the planet had looked into his background.

"And I suspect his friend must be trustworthy as well," she said. "They came in with him, and I hear they've been travelling with him for years as an assistant. In fact, I understand the two of them were friends in university."

"They've been friends since childhood, actually," said Feliu absently. "I looked it up." He turned to her. "That brings the number of people we can trust to six. So, Madam. What do you intend to do next?"

"I intend," she said grimly, "to do my utmost to find out exactly what our friend the General is planning."

The young man stood awkwardly in her cabin, looking as if he'd rather be anywhere else in the system, including off the ship with no space suit. Now that she had the leisure to study him, she could see his sweet, slightly dreamy half-smile and a wistful air that belied the daredevil man-of-the-world reputation synonymous with his name. His friend, with their challenging glare and stubborn expression, was the one of the two she would have guessed closer to the reputation the news packets had given Aran.

Although if she were being honest, neither of them looked particularly likely.

Ines, however, was staring at the two with a look of something like hero worship on her face.

Aran frowned as Alba finished a succinct summary of her conversation with the President. "General Cavaco," he said, glancing over at Istvay as if confirming a suspicion. "That means—"

From the look on Istvay's face, they found the news both worse, and less unexpected, then Alba had anticipated. "Emeric," they said shortly, something murderous in their expression.

The two shared a long, meaningful glance.

"As you are standing in my presence, I would appreciate being let into the conversation," Alba snapped.

Aran looked up, startled, then mumbled something she couldn't make out.

"Speak up!" she snapped. "You know how to behave in company, I assume? Or are you some homeless beggar?"

The young scientist flinched, looking like she'd slapped him, and from behind her Alba could hear the hiss of Ines's indrawn breath.

Istvay turned their murderous glare on her. "Don't talk to Aran like that," they said, their voice quiet with menace. "And don't use that as a damn insult."

Alba was so taken aback that for a moment she couldn't summon words.

No one had dared to talk back to her since she'd been a young law clerk, and they'd hardly dared even then.

"I will say exactly what I—" she began, drawing herself up.

Aran's eyes darted between Istvay and her in a sort of hopeless dread, his shoulders hunching slightly, and Istvay's glare became molten.

"Come on, Aran," they said, turning abruptly. "We don't have time for this."

Alba's gaze sharpened. "Do you know who I am?" she asked, her voice carrying a low, dangerous undertone to it that every lawyer in the system knew and feared.

"Istvay—" Aran began, putting a hand on their arm, but they ignored him completely.

"Yes," they said, turning back, the heat in their glare equivalent to the ice in hers. "You're the one who threw half the kids Aran and I grew up with in jail for the crime of not having a home to go back to. Funny, back where I come from, we use the term 'Chief Justice' as an insult."

Alba blinked at them in shock, then sucked in a breath. Aran flinched. And then a mild voice said, "Istvay! Aran!" in tones of genuine delight.

They all turned, and the fury in Istvay's face was replaced, suddenly, with a hint of a smile, the tension in Aran's shoulders releasing slightly.

Yosip stood in the doorway smiling, Feliu behind him.

"Yosip," said Istvay, and although the irritation was still clear in their voice, it was muted under what could only be called friendliness. "I didn't expect to see you here."

"I heard you'd come up to our section of the ship, and I couldn't pass up the opportunity to say hello," Yosip said, shooting Istvay and Aran a friendly wink. "Aran. Collect any interesting samples lately?"

Aran's posture loosened farther, the hint of a smile starting on his lips. "One or two look promising, but I haven't had time to go through them yet. I'm hopeful, though."

A delighted smile creased Yosip's face, and Alba realized, with absolute certainty, that he was exactly as interested in the lives of these two idiots standing in front of her as he been in the life of the woman at the communications bay.

It wasn't an act at all—he genuinely liked these people.

Yosip turned to Alba, his old eyes twinkling, his grin infectious. "I apologize, Madam Chief Justice. I think I interrupted something."

At his words Istvay stiffened again, but somehow the antagonism, which had been sparking through the small cabin like static electricity, had diminished, and Alba found her own voice slightly softer when she spoke this time.

"Aran," she said stiffly. "I ... apologize for getting off on the wrong foot."

Aran glanced at the floor and mumbled something, but, with a sideways glance at Yosip, who'd taken a seat and was now smiling beatifically at the room in general, Alba bit back her sharp retort.

"If you know anything about the General, or his plans," she said instead, "I would appreciate you sharing that information with me."

Aran sighed. "There's a scientist Istvay and me went to university with, Emeric Furtado. When I got back from meeting with the Council, he came to find me. He wanted to convince me to give up my spot on the mission so that he could go instead, and his backer was General Cavaco. He … knows I'm scared of space travel, so he thought—"

Alba blinked at the young man, whose hands were clenching and unclenching nervously as he spoke.

Aran Romeu. The swashbuckling, daredevil hero of legend.

Frightened of space travel.

She shook her head. This pair was not what she'd been led to expect.

"And was that all?" she prompted, when it became apparent Aran wasn't going to keep talking.

Aran hesitated, glancing at Istvay.

Istvay heaved a sigh, turning to her with clear reluctance. "Possibly," they said. "Aran and I disagree on this, but I suspect Emeric was the one behind the recent assassination attempt on Aran."

Everyone in the room turned to stare at the two of them.

"Assassination attempt?" said Alba at last, her voice a little sharper than she'd intended.

Aran, too, gave a weary sigh, and from the look that passed between him and Istvay, Alba surmised this was a conversation they'd had more than once. "We don't know for sure it was an assassination attempt," he said at last, turning back to her. "But two days ago when I was out collecting samples, two of the insects that we brought along for research ended up in my spacesuit. The, um, the speckled death mouras."

Everyone was still staring, and Alba found herself once again at a loss for words.

"How are you still alive?" whispered Ines breathlessly. "Aren't those things—"

"Poisonous, yes," said Aran wearily. "But they're actually very shy creatures, and I was able to calm them down and get back into the airlock. No harm done."

"And then you killed them, of course," began the girl, but Aran frowned as if she'd suggested cannibalism, or something equally unsavoury.

"No, they went back in their cages. I've been trying to keep everyone else away for a few days to let them settle down. I'm sure it was just as unsettling for them as it was for me." His demeanour, now that he was talking about his field of expertise, was competent and matter-of-fact, every trace of nervousness gone.

Alba was struck with a sudden, dawning realization of how Aran might have gotten the reputation he had, and so clearly did not appreciate.

Most people would not only have told the tale with much more relish, but would have saved it to pass on to their grandchildren.

Aran didn't seem to realize that he'd said anything extraordinary at all.

Istvay was watching their friend as well, shaking their head with a sort of fond resignation.

And then Alba realized the implications of Aran's story, and her mood darkened. "You say you can't agree as to whether it was an assassination attempt," she said. "But it could have been?"

Aran hesitated a moment. "I … suppose. I just can't imagine why anyone would do something like that."

Alba studied him for a moment, then turned her attention to Istvay.

From the way they were watching Aran, sharp worry in their face, they, at least, clearly believed that this had been no accident.

"Thank you very much, both of you," she said, managing to make her tone gracious despite her lingering irritation. "I must say that in this, I agree with Istvay. We know General Cavaco falsified the information of a number of people on this trip. We don't know who, and we don't know why. Why they'd attempt to kill the mission's lead scientist I don't know. But please, be careful."

Aran had dropped his eyes again, but Istvay nodded, their gaze meeting hers. And for the first time, she noticed the hollows under their cheekbones, the way their large, dark eyes were accentuated by the dark circles underneath, the traces of exhaustion in their face that they couldn't completely conceal.

She knew that look—she'd seen it far too often. They had a year, maybe two, to live.

And for the first time, she thought perhaps she knew why Aran had agreed to come, despite his fear of space travel.

"Thank you," she said at last.

Istvay nodded, then turned to Aran, and she saw the way their face softened, the faintest hint of a smile turning up the corners of their mouth. "Well, I suppose we'd best get back to work. Come on, Aran."

They slid the door open and followed Aran out into the corridor. Alba watched the two leave, something cold in her chest.

"If Istvay is right, and someone did try to kill Aran, then we may be in a much more serious situation than we previously realized," said Feliu, voicing Alba's own fears as she turned back.

He was correct.

But what did Cavaco want? Did he want them to continue, or turn back? She would be playing into his hands if she made the wrong move—but what was the right one?

Someone had tried to kill Aran. She couldn't rule out the possibility that they'd wanted to force the expedition to turn around. But neither could she rule out the possibility that they were meant to continue on, and that every person in this room was in grave danger.

18

Aran

Istvay didn't speak until they were back in Aran's cabin, and after one look at their clenched jaw and forbidding expression, Aran didn't say anything either.

Once they and Aran were inside and the door closed behind them, Istvay paced back and forth for a few moments, their hands in fists, every muscle in their body tight.

Aran tried to ignore the way the muscles in Istvay's arms and shoulders stood out, how their shirt clung to their chest. This was really, really not the time to be thinking about that. There were other things he needed to worry about at the moment—namely, who Istvay was going to kill first, him, or the Chief Justice.

Ani seemed to sense the mood as well—she slunk out of the nest he'd made for her under the bed, and took shelter behind Aran's right leg.

"I knew this trip was a bad idea," said Istvay at last, voice tense. "I knew it. Did you hear what that idiot said?"

Aran glanced up. "By 'idiot,' you mean the Chief Justice of the entire Joias System?"

Istvay glared at him. "Yes. Anyways, the point is, if she's right, then this entire mission may well have been a setup."

Aran sighed and reached down to pick up Ani. "Istvay. Look. It's going to be alright. The entire mission can't be a setup—I saw the genetic material that came through the portal myself, and they let me run my own tests. Besides, Emeric was practically drooling over the chance to be the one to find the cure for the defect. We know he's on General Cavaco's payroll. If the whole thing was a setup, why would he be so eager?"

The mention of Emeric did nothing to improve Istvay's mood, which, in retrospect, Aran should have predicted. Their eyebrows lowered farther, their expression growing even more grim. "I have no idea what Emeric may or may not want. But if that woman thinks there's something wrong with this mission, there probably is. She has access to better information than we do."

Aran nodded absently, still stroking Ani.

His hands were shaking, just a little.

The thing was, he was already scared to death of this mission. Every damn part of it terrified the hell out of him, and so honestly, the thought that General Cavaco had some nefarious scheme to interfere with it was hardly enough to register on the radar of things he was terrified of.

But there was one thing, he'd discovered, that still had the power to tip him over the edge—and it was the thought that maybe, somehow, Istvay was right. That this had been a setup after all, that there was no cure for the defect.

He'd gone over every bit of information they had on the alien blood sample, run every test, studied every result of the research lab's tests. He still had no idea what was behind the specimen's survival. But he couldn't bring himself to believe it was nothing.

He'd spent his whole life hoping for a miracle. There had been so many times in his life he'd damn well needed one, and it had never come. But this time … this time, he had to believe it would work.

If he lost Istvay—

He cut off thought quickly.

He couldn't. That was all, he couldn't.

"Aran! Are you even listening?"

Aran glanced up guiltily. Istvay sounded even more perturbed than they had a few minutes ago.

"I—sorry, I was just—"

Istvay glared at him for a moment in exasperation. "Then tell me what I said just now."

Aran racked his brain frantically, and came up with nothing.

Istvay sighed through their teeth. "I was saying, Aran," they said, with exaggerated patience, "that this means what happened to you is probably not an isolated incident. You can't afford to let down your guard."

"Istvay. Listen. I—"

"No, Aran! You listen to me, for once! I just want—" their words trailed off, and they closed their eyes for a moment, jaw clenched. "I just want you to be alright," they said at last, their voice barely audible.

Aran stared at them, his heart pounding.

He didn't know how to deal with this type of situation. He'd never really known how. Istvay was the one who dealt with things like this.

But now it was Istvay, not him, standing in the middle of the room, fists clenched, eyes closed, clearly on the verge of falling apart.

"Istvay," he tried tentatively.

Istvay opened their eyes at last and tried to smile. "I'm—sorry,

Aran. I—"

"No." Aran's heart was still pounding. "Sit."

Istvay gave him a puzzled look. Aran shook his head and dropped to the ground, his arms around his knees, and gestured to Istvay.

Istvay sighed, but at last, slowly, they lowered themself until they were sitting on the floor back-to-back with Aran, like they did when the two were out in the field after a long day of walking, and there was nothing to lean back against but each other. From the corner of his eye Aran saw them stretch one leg out in front of them like they always did, their other knee pulled up against their chest.

Aran closed his eyes for a moment, the familiar warmth of Istvay's back against his comforting. He could feel the rise and fall of their breathing, quick and strained at first, but gradually slowing.

"Pishti," he said at last. "What's wrong? And before you say it's that we might be killed, we've almost been killed about a million times before."

"That doesn't mean I have to like it," Istvay muttered through their teeth.

"Pishti …"

Istvay took a deep breath, and was silent for so long that Aran wasn't completely sure they'd answer him.

At last, though, they tipped their head back against Aran's wearily. "Aran?" they asked in a low voice. "Do you ever wonder … I mean —imagine there was something you'd been scared of your whole life, so scared of that you—that you damn well gave up the one thing you wanted most because of it. You spent your whole life being so damn careful, making sure you didn't make any sort of impact on the world because you wouldn't be there long enough for it to count. And then you found out one day that maybe that thing you were so afraid of might not be real. It probably was real, the most likely outcome was that it was real, but there was just a chance it wasn't. Would that make it better, do you think, or worse?"

"I—" Aran stopped. He wasn't completely sure how to answer.

"Worse," said Istvay, their voice almost too low to hear. "It would make it a million times worse."

Aran closed his eyes and tipped his head back as well, pulling in a long breath.

Even when he and Istvay had both realized—when it had become far too apparent for either of them to ignore—that Istvay carried the defect, Aran had been the one to panic, while Istvay remained calm, patient, stoic.

But now Istvay was looking more exhausted, more strained by the day.

Watching them fall apart was more frightening than anything else on this damn mission.

And Aran found he couldn't keep his mind on anything, not even a potential assassination attempt, except for the stabbing, beating, painful hope that maybe, through the portal, there was something that would fix this.

Istvay was technically right—it was technically more likely than not that what had happened with the speckled death mouras hadn't been an accident. But—

He ran his mind over the small contingent of scientists.

It was hard to imagine any of them actually trying to kill him. Besides, Istvay had always been suspicious of basically everything. It could have just been a fluke, unlikely as that seemed at present.

There was a tight knot in the pit of his stomach, and it took him a moment to realize that it wasn't fear, but an aching impatience.

It didn't honestly matter what was happening on the ship, or if someone was trying to murder him—at the end of the day, the only thing that mattered was getting through the portal, and finding something that might let Istvay live longer than another year.

That was the only damn thing he cared about right now.

"It's been my whole life too," he said at last. "I've spent my whole life worrying about you dying. But don't you see? That's the point— we have a chance now."

Istvay stood quickly, facing away from him, their body tense.

Aran's muscles were oddly shaky.

Damn it to hell, he had no idea how to handle this sort of thing.

"Listen," he said at last. "You … should get some sleep, okay? You'll feel better once you get some sleep."

Istvay turned to glower at him. "I don't need you to be worrying about me right now. I wasn't the one who was almost killed, for hell's sake!"

"Istvay—"

Istvay rolled their eyes heavenward. "You know what? The whole point of all this is, I've been trying to tell you to be careful, and I don't think you're even listening. We'll talk in the morning. Because right now, I can't deal with this." They turned abruptly and stalked out of the room.

Aran stood restlessly, shoving his hand through his hair.

He should go after Istvay, probably, apologize for whatever the hell he'd said wrong. But they looked like they needed some time to cool down anyways. At this point, he'd probably only make it worse.

So instead, after a moment's hesitation, he lifted Ani onto his shoulder and slipped out the door into the hallway.

The ship never really slept. Out here, where day and night were abstract concepts, there was no reason for one watch to be busier than another. But it was that quiet time between watches that had long since become his favourite time, and since most of the scientists kept their schedules synced, the lab would probably be empty.

There was no way Aran was going to fall sleep anyways, not now. And the quiet of the lab would be welcome.

He flipped the lab's lights on and bent over the small table where he'd left the samples he was preparing to analyze. He dropped one of them into the centrifuge unit and flicked it on, the steady purr of the machine soothing and almost hypnotic.

There had to be a solution behind the portal. There had to be. That was the only option.

If he were being honest with himself, he'd been working so hard on these damn samples mostly as a distraction, something to keep him from losing his mind from impatience.

The centrifuge came to a stop, the red light flashing green, and he carefully unhooked the sample bag and pulled out the inset screen. Gently, he cut the screen in two, and carefully slipped half into the feed of the mass spectrometer on the table beside him, and the other into the feed of the accelerator mass spectrometer beside it.

He tapped his palmscreen against the mass spectrometer as the machine stripped the particulate matter from the collection screen. He pulled up the readout, then the analysis calculator, his shoulders relaxing at the pleasant familiarity of the routine. The lines on his palm screen flickered as the machine worked, and he turned, pulling up the lab holoscreen and tapping the data through.

Slowly, the dancing lines on the screen came into focus.

Aran sucked in a quick breath, fighting to reign in his excitement.

Carbon. There were carbon-based compounds present. That meant the possibility of remnants of life forms.

His heart skipped, just a little, as he dialled up the magnification, studying the readout more closely.

Then he frowned.

There was inorganic matter mixed in with the organic matter. That wasn't unexpected, necessarily, but … according to the composition of the readout, at least some of the inorganic matter came from metal alloys that looked unsettlingly familiar.

It was a metal commonly used in spacecrafts.

And unless he was entirely mistaken—

No. He wasn't. That was a cluster of particulate signatures unique to burned fuel cells.

His heart was racing, although this time it was more from dread than excitement.

Organic matter, defused through the refuse of burned fuel cells and particles of ship metal.

What had happened behind the portal? Had it opened by a horrible accident, rather than on purpose, as they'd supposed?

There was a chill rising up his spine.

An accident, maybe—or maybe an intentional sacrifice. Really, what did they know about whatever was behind the portal? Nothing, except the most important thing of all—that it might hold the key to saving Istvay.

He stood abruptly, tapping his palm screen against the accelerator mass spectrometer. If he could get a date on the particulates, it might give him a better idea.

He tapped the readout, sending the data through to the large screen on the lab table, then scrolled quickly down the lines of data.

The dating on the debris was entirely inconsistent—some particles were dated a few months back, some almost a century.

The longer he read, the farther up his spine the ice crawled.

Whatever had caused this—whatever the tragic story behind these bits of mingled organic and inorganic debris—it hadn't been a single occurrence.

Aran sank slowly into his seat. At last, numbly, he tapped his wavelink.

Istvay's answering voice was short and irritated. "I was almost asleep. This had better be important."

Aran didn't have the energy to respond to Istvay's tone. "Pishti," he said quietly. "I think you'd better come down here."

"Where are you?" Istvay's voice was now sharp more with worry than irritation. "Is something wrong?"

"I … think it might be," said Aran. "I'm in the lab."

Istvay swore. "You're in the lab. By yourself. After I just spent twenty minutes lecturing you about—" they cut off their words, and Aran could almost picture the pinch of their lips. "I'll be there in a minute," they said, and the communication was cut.

Aran leaned back in his chair, his mind spinning dizzily.

He had to be wrong. He had to have guessed wrong. When Istvay got here, they'd look at the data and come up with a completely innocuous reason for all of this. They'd laugh at his panic, and he'd apologize, and they'd both head back up to their rooms.

There was a light tap on the door. "Aran, it's me. I'm coming in." The door slid open, and Istvay stepped inside, their expression a struggle between irritation and concern. When they caught sight of Aran, concern quickly won out.

"What's wrong?" they asked, striding quickly over to him. "Did something happen? Are you hurt?"

Aran shook his head numbly, and gestured Istvay over to the mass spectrometer readout. Istvay frowned, but glanced down at it, then back up at Aran. "You found some organic matter mixed in with the particles. That's—what you were hoping for, right?"

"Did you notice the composition of the inorganic matter?" Aran asked.

Istvay gave him an odd look, but bent over the readout again.

When they looked up again, Aran could tell from the look on their face that they'd seen what he'd seen.

"What—" they began slowly, an undercurrent of unease in their voice.

"Now look at this," said Aran. He tilted the screen on the table and ran his finger down the line of carbon dating.

Istvay looked at the line of numbers, then back up at Aran. "What does this—"

They broke off, a look of burgeoning horror in their expression, and it was that, more than anything, that told Aran his gut feeling had been correct.

"Ships," he said distantly, turning back to the screen so he didn't have to look at his friend's face. "Something vaporized crewed ships, that's why there's organic matter mixed in."

"And it didn't just happen once," Istvay finished, glancing back at the list of dates. "It happened over, and over, and over." They shut their mouth in a grim line, glaring at the screen in the centre of the table. "What's the latest date on these?"

Aran glanced quickly through the readout. "Maybe ... six planetary months before the portal opened."

They looked at each other for a long moment. Istvay looked almost sick.

"Then there's something behind that portal that's been killing ships. Has been for a long time," they said in a low voice. "I'd say a war, maybe—but if so, it's been going on for a long damn time."

Aran nodded. "Whatever's behind that portal, I don't think we can assume anymore that it's peaceful."

Istvay straightened, their expression grim. "We'll have to let the diplomatic team know." They glanced at the time display on the screen. "That idiot Chief Justice will probably be in bed, but I think this is worth waking her for. Although I expect she won't like it much." There was a hint of undeniable satisfaction in their tone.

Aran sighed ruefully.

Istvay was right, though. The Chief Justice needed to know, and she needed to know as soon as possible.

The portal was only days away.

"Explain that to me again, please." The Chief Justice's voice was as cold as deep space, and just about as welcoming. She was sitting primly on the chair next to her desk in her small cabin, her hair wrapped in a colourful wrapper, a sleeping-robe draped over her shoulders. Feliu, looking slightly rumpled, stood stiffly at the door. "As you might imagine, having been just woken up from a very sound sleep, it will take me a moment to process this information." There was no mistaking the irritation in her tone, and it was clear that she did not mean for there to be.

Aran glanced at Istvay's narrowed eyes and self-satisfied smirk, and sighed. "This evening, when I was looking through the samples I'd gathered from outside the ship, I found particles of both organic and inorganic matter. Since that's not usual in our system, we assume the particulate matter was blown through the portal when it opened, and has been travelling outward since then. And the inorganic particles—"

"The inorganic material was likely from some sort of spacecraft, I did understand that part," said Alba bitingly. "Please explain why you thought this discovery was interesting enough to wake me up in the middle of the night to discuss."

Istvay opened their mouth, and Aran continued hurriedly before they had a chance to speak. "I dated the samples. At first, I thought perhaps whatever energy source opened the portal—possibly an explosion—may have been the source of the particle. But that's not it. The dating didn't bear me out. The dates on these range from about six planetary months ago to about two hundred planetary years."

She was still watching him, as if waiting for a better explanation.

He sighed. "We can't be sure what this means. But one thing that I think we can be relatively certain of is that the particles came from ships that had been destroyed. Crewed ships."

He saw the realization dawn on the old clerk's face first. "So there's something behind the portal destroying ships," he said slowly. "And has been, for a very long time."

Aran nodded.

For a long, long moment, the cabin was utterly silent.

"If that's the case, then I believe it would be prudent to pause and reassess our options," said Alba at last. Her voice shook slightly, and under the stoic expression on her face, he could see the sort of sick shock that might accompany a dangerous injury.

He'd never imagined the Chief Justice looking like this.

Worried.

Frightened.

She turned to Feliu. "Put me through to the captain, immediately."

He nodded, and the four of them stood in utter silence as the wavelink buzzed, then at last broadcast the captain's face onto the main screen in the cabin.

"Madam Chief Justice." The captain's tone was surprised, but not unpleasant. "To what do I owe the pleasure of this conversation?"

"Captain," said Alba. "I will provide you with a more fulsome explanation shortly, but the crux of the matter is this: our lead scientist has discovered signs of a potential threat beyond the portal. I suggest we find a planet where we can stop and gather more information before we proceed."

There was a long pause from the other end of the line. "I'm sorry, Chief Justice," said the captain, an odd note in his voice. "I'm afraid that's not an option. Getting to any planet that could host us would take us a significant distance out of our way."

"Then take us a significant distance out of our way," Alba snapped.

"I'm sorry, Madam Chief Justice. With the strictures of fuel and supplies, it's simply not feasible."

Alba and Feliu exchanged glances, and Aran could see the worry in Feliu's eyes.

Alba closed her eyes for just a moment, and for just a moment, she looked old, and slightly frail.

Aran had always seen her before, on the news packets or in the Council chamber, as someone as ageless and invincible as the planet itself. Now for the first time he saw the weariness in her face, the exhaustion in the lines of her posture.

Then she straightened, her expression hardening once again into its haughty mask. "Very well, Captain. If, as you say, it is impractical to find a place to wait while we take the measure of our destination with the new information we've procured—" she hesitated for just a moment, and for just a moment, Aran saw the indecision flicker across her face. Then it was gone. "Then I order you, as head of this mission and the most senior government official on board the ship, to take us back to Colorida."

Aran stared at her in cold panic.

They couldn't turn around. This was his only chance to save

Istvay. She couldn't do this.

The look on Istvay's face was a sick mixture of despair and relief.

"I'm sorry, Madam Chief Justice." The captain's voice was still soft and friendly, but there was a note in it Aran couldn't read. "I'm afraid I can't follow that order."

Alba frowned. "Captain, shall I remind you of my position? You may be the senior ship's officer, but I remain in charge of this mission. My orders are to be obeyed."

"I'm sorry," said the captain again, in that same soft tone. "I have other orders. We're going through the portal as originally planned."

"Captain, wait," Feliu began. "The information we've discovered indicates—"

There was a click as communication was shut off.

Aran glanced around the cabin, his heart pounding strangely.

They were going on, then. It didn't seem that what he'd found would make any difference at all. But the stunned looks on the faces around him told him exactly how serious the situation had suddenly become.

19

Savina

"Savina. I need access to the defence systems." Joska's voice was grim.

For half a moment Savina hesitated. But there wasn't time for mistrust right now. She spoke a command into her wavelink, turning the ship's systems over to the captain.

Immediately, a low hum started deep in the ship's interior, and on the screen she could see the shields flicker on.

"These won't hold for long, not if that ship has the weapons I think it does," said the captain. "These were built for pirate attacks, which tend to be light-range and a quick in-and-out attack. I doubt your agent friend is going to be quite so accommodating." She let out a short sigh, and Savina could hear the strain in her tone. "I'm no A-rank pilot. But this ship's got me through some rough scrapes before. I'll do what I can."

Savina gave a brusque nod. "Um. Thank you."

The words felt awkward—after all, it hadn't been too long ago she'd held the woman at gunpoint and stolen her ship. But Joska just nodded, her face set, and turned back to the controls.

The pain from the pulse-shot wound was radiating outwards from Savina's shoulder in hot, dizzying waves, and if gravity had been an issue she'd have had to grab onto something to keep from swaying on her feet. Still, lack of gravity couldn't help the nausea rising in her stomach, or the way her head spun.

"Savina?"

She turned quickly to see Beni standing beside her.

"Are you alright? What happened out there?" they asked in a low voice.

Savina tried to make her voice light, thanking whatever luck she still possessed that Beni couldn't see extent of the injury. "Nothing much. A shot grazed me."

Beni frowned. "It did more than that. I know your voice when you're hurt, Vina."

"Either way, we don't have time to deal with it right now," Savina snapped. She brought her wavelink online. "Pull up specs on the ship following us," she said, tapping into the ship's command system.

A few moments later, a readout scrolled across the bottom half of the ship's screen.

Joska looked up from her work for long enough to scan through it, and gave a low whistle. "Whoever wants you dead, my friend, they are very serious about it. I could have hauled cargo for decades and saved every penny of it and I couldn't have afforded a ship like that."

Savina, who'd seen the ship's financials, bit her tongue against a retort involving Joska's inability to buy her own damn thrusters, and instead, frowned at the readouts.

She wasn't an expert on ships, but she knew weapons. The ship that was coming after them was loaded with them, and coming up fast.

"If we can hold out until we have time to switch over to auxiliary power, we might surprise her," said the captain quietly. Her knuckles were white on the controls, her posture tense. "I'm sure she'd beat us at a burst of speed, but the *Dolphin* moves along at a fair clip on auxiliary power, a hell of a lot faster than we're going now. If we can hold out until I can switch us over, it may buy us time to switch course and lose her before she can switch over to her own auxiliary power and follow."

Savina gave a tight nod, gritting her teeth against the pain pulsing from her shoulder through her entire body. "How long until we can switch over?"

Joska frowned. "Twenty planetary minutes, maybe? Half an hour? I've never had to use it in a hurry."

Savina glanced down at the screen again, and stiffened. Two blue dots had detached themselves from the pursuing ship and started after them. "We might not have twenty minutes," she said in a low voice.

The captain followed her gaze, and swore. "Of course. You're the only one on the ship's port records, aren't you? You wouldn't have wanted to list passengers, get people suspicious. So they have no idea they'd be shooting down anyone but you." She gave a small, humourless laugh.

Her words, and the bitterness under them, sent an unexpected jolt of guilt through Savina. She quickly shoved it down.

"Get me statistics on how long it will take the missiles to reach us," she snapped into the ship's command, and a moment later the answer appeared on the readout.

Savina swore, and the captain embellished on her curses.

"Any possibility we can pull the auxiliary power systems on in ten minutes?" Savina asked without much hope.

Joska shook her head. "No way in hell. Our only chance is for our shields to hold. And they won't, not with the kind of weapons they've sent after us."

Savina gritted her teeth and turned to Beni, who'd been listening silently. "Two missiles," she said shortly. "I'll sent the specs through to your wavelink. We need to keep from being blown to space dust. You're the planner. Make it work."

Beni shot Savina a glare, then turned to the captain. "You have missiles on this ship?"

Joska nodded. "Nothing to match that, though. And even if we could hit the agent's ship, it's too late—they've already launched the missiles."

"Are the missiles on this ship self-directed?" asked Beni, their voice brisk and businesslike.

The captain shook her head. "Manual aim. Sorry."

"But you can fire them with shields on."

"Yes."

Beni turned to back to Savina. "How badly are you hurt? I need you to tell me the truth."

The captain frowned, her eyes traveling to Savina's injured shoulder as if she hadn't noticed.

Savina shot her a warning look. "I'm fine. I told you."

"Then I need you to do what you do best."

Savina raised an eyebrow. "Kill someone?"

Joska cracked a smile, and Beni rolled their eyes.

"No, shoot things. You won't have much of a target, and there won't be time for a do-over. You'll have to fire them straight into the oncoming missiles, and it'll have to be a direct hit both times. But if you get it right, our shields should be enough to take the resulting explosion." They paused a moment. "I think, anyway," they added.

"I damn well hope you're right," said Savina through her teeth.

Joska raised an eyebrow. "You can do that?" she asked.

"I guess we're all going to find out," Savina grumbled.

The captain sighed, turning back to the controls. "Take Rafel with you. You'll need someone to load the missiles while you sight in, and they can be a bit touchy."

Savina give a short nod and slipped out the door, her teeth gritted against the pain, without bothering to check if Rafel was following.

He caught up her with outside the weapons bay door. He didn't look happy, but he didn't say anything, just hit the code on the door panel. When it hissed open, he stepped past her and set to work yanking at one of the two lockdown handles holding the missiles in place.

"Captain says you need to be able to aim," he grunted, not bothering to look at her. "Shooting seat and scope are up there. May as well get yourself used to them while I set the missiles."

Savina glanced towards where he'd gestured, then pulled herself up to the narrow seat and strapped in. It looked like the controls could be worked one-handed as well, which was a damn good thing. The thought of trying to move her injured arm made her almost want to pass out.

She pulled the scope to her eyes and adjusted it. "Are the sights set dead on, or high?" she snapped.

Rafel gave a surly shrug. "Haven't fired it in years. But I seem to recall them being pretty close to dead on. Missiles are online, so you can fire when you're ready. Hope you're as good as Beni thinks you are."

She turned to glare at him, but he ignored her. She turned back to the scope, tapping her temple to pull up specs on the incoming missiles into her retinal screen.

She'd have to hit precisely in the centre of the explosive head for this to work—the armouring on the rest of the incoming weapons' bodies was far too strong for the *Dolphin's* tiny missiles to do any good.

She drew in a shallow breath, trying to ignore the throbbing pain in her shoulder and the knot tightening in her stomach.

The missiles were five minutes from contact and closing.

She tapped through to Beni's line. "When do you want me to fire?"

"I'll give the word," said Beni tersely. "At the rate they're travelling —" they paused a moment. "I'd say wait for three minutes to contact, or under. We get one chance at this."

Savina glanced down at the small screen on the weapons control panel.

At this distance the following missiles looked almost peaceful, curving a serene path through the black expanse of space. But she knew full well how quickly that illusion would shatter the moment they made contact with their target. Or, by the Mystery's goodwill, her missiles made contact with them.

"Be ready to fire in twenty seconds," came Beni's voice in her earpiece.

Savina readjusted the sights, dialling them down to adjust for the ever-decreasing distance, and rested her fingers lightly on the controls.

"Five seconds."

Savina drew in a deep breath, forcing her tense muscles loose.

"Two. One. Now."

She let out her breath gently as she squeezed the control, pulling the trigger with a motion as gentle as the air escaping from her lungs.

"First missile off," she said, keeping her voice steady.

Rafel yanked the other missile into place, locking the lever, and she readjusted the sights, drawing in another long breath.

She fired again on the exhale, holding herself perfectly steady.

And then it was off.

She let herself slump in her seat. Nothing to do now but wait and watch.

From the quiet through her earpiece, she knew the two in the control room were watching as intently as she was.

There was a moment of utter silence, then a brilliant, shocking flash, then another.

She'd hit.

Savina had time for a quick, relieved breath before the shockwave slammed into them.

The ship spun and tumbled, and Savina was thrown against her straps. She choked back a scream as the pressure hit her injured shoulder, and then everything went dark.

When she blinked her eyes open, she was on the flight deck, strapped down into a reclining seat, and the captain and Beni were both bending over her.

"What—" she began groggily, then she gasped as the pain in her shoulder re-asserted itself on her consciousness.

"Why didn't you say you'd been shot?" Beni snapped, their voice harsh with worry.

Savina groaned. "We … made it?"

The captain managed a small smile. "We're on auxiliary power as of five minutes ago, and I've been pushing every bit of power I can spare through to the auxiliary system. It won't hold our friend off forever, but it'll give us a few minutes' breather. And if we pick a course they're not expecting, they may overshoot us and lose our trail."

Savina let out a shallow breath, closing her eyes for a moment. When she opened them, the captain was still watching her.

"You did well back there," the woman said at last. And for some reason, the praise, unexpected and brusque as it was, made something warm stir in Savina's chest.

"Now," Joska said, turning to reach into a med kit that was opened and anchored to the wall. "Why don't you lie quiet, and between Beni and me, we'll try to get you patched up." She was smiling, just a little, and when she turned, their eyes met. And just for a moment, Savina felt something that was almost camaraderie in her glance.

"Where are we going?" asked Rafel gruffly, as the captain sprayed a generous portion of med foam into the wound and fixed a bandage to seal it in.

The captain glanced at Savina, raising an eyebrow in question.

"I don't know this part of the system very well," Savina said finally, somehow unable to meet the captain's gaze. "I ... don't suppose you have any ideas?"

Joska gave her a long look. "You stole my ship," she said quietly, at last. "You threatened to shoot my crew. Now you want me to find you a safe place to hide?" Her tone wasn't angry—more curious.

"You need to get away as much as we do," said Savina, trying to make her voice carefree.

"No," said the captain slowly. "No, that's not necessarily true. Because the moment you fired those missiles, whoever's after us knew you weren't the only one on the ship. One person can't lock and fire those missiles alone. Maybe you have hostages, maybe you've smuggled yourself onto a crew. So I think she'll try to disable us and get aboard. And then you and Beni will go with her, and I'll get recompensed by the government for any damage to my ship. And hell, hard to tell exactly which damage was caused by the agent, and how much was there in the first place. I might end up coming out ahead."

Something cold had started in Savina's chest, mingling with the burning pain from her shoulder. "You can't be sure of that," she said sharply. "You can't be sure she won't just take the ship down, kill everyone on board. Even if you're right, the ship's in my name. The government will probably confiscate it."

"Perhaps you're right," said Joska, considering her. "But it seems like it might be a risk worth taking. After all, I can't be sure you won't shoot me the moment we reach your destination."

Savina turned her head away abruptly. "I can use the restraint. Order you to do what I say."

"You could," said Joska. "You can force me to follow the orders you set into it or get whatever level of shock you've set it at. But you can't force me to come up with ideas about where you can hide. How would you know I was telling the truth? I could take you into the middle of a shipping lane and you'd have no idea, not if you're not familiar with this part of the system."

Savina closed her eyes for a moment, sickness roiling in her stomach.

"What do you want?" she asked finally, in a low voice. There was a sharp sting in the corners of her eyes as she said the words, and she squeezed her eyes tighter shut to push the tears back.

She didn't cry. She never cried.

But somehow, the strain and exhaustion and pain of the past three days had cut through her defences.

The portal. The government agent. The judge and her "diplomatic mission." The sick knowledge that if she didn't get back in time, there may not be anywhere to get back to.

At last Joska sighed. "Listen. As much as you deserve it, I don't relish the thought of watching two kids like you get killed. And I'm sure you'll make me pay for that sooner or later. But as you said, I can't be sure that if the agent shoots at you again, Rafel and I won't be caught in the crossfire, or that I'd get my ship back at the end. So." She shook her head. "If I were to agree to take you somewhere out of the way—for starters, I'd need some guarantee that I will, in fact, be getting my ship back when I get you back to the planet, and that Rafel and I will be getting out of this alive."

Savina blinked, staring up at the captain in confusion.

The captain raised an eyebrow.

At last, Savina gave a long sigh and pulled the ship's disc out of the inside pocket of her jacket.

"Fine," she said through her teeth. "I can do that." She flicked it open with an impatient gesture, pulling up the ship's articles. "I do hereby transfer all my interest in the *Dolphin* to the undersigned, but such transfer shall not come into force until one planetary hour after the ship reaches a port on Colorida and hooks into the main system."

Reluctantly, she handed the disc over to the captain, who took it without a change of expression, added her signature at the bottom, and handed it back to Savina.

"Satisfied?" said Savina bitterly, turning away.

She could feel the captain's eyes on her back. "That's a start," said the woman at last. "But I'm going to need more than that. I'm going to need you to answer some questions."

Savina turned, startled.

The captain's gaze was steady and piercing. "Why is it so important that you get back to Colorida? Why the hurry?"

"Does it matter?" snapped Savina.

The captain shrugged. "Maybe. I don't know."

For a long moment, Savina glared at the woman, seething quietly.

She could just kill her here. It would be so easy—

But Joska was right. Savina needed her, at least for now.

"I got some news," she said at last, the words choking in her throat. "A warning. If I don't get back, my—my family is going to be killed. I can't reach them through my wavelink, and the compound where I grew up isn't hooked into any general lines. They don't just let you call in or out whenever you want. And if the agent finds me, she'll find Beni too." For some reason, the tears she thought she'd pushed back took that opportunity to well up, and she turned her head away quickly.

For a long moment, the captain didn't speak. At last she said quietly, "Beni. You two are siblings, I'm guessing, yes?"

Savina gave a brusque nod, not trusting herself to speak.

Joska watched her for a few moments longer. Finally she straightened, turning back to the controls. "Well," she said. "A villain like you, just trying to keep your family safe. Can't exactly say I wouldn't have tried to hijack a ship myself if those were my options."

She hesitated, and Savina could see the tension in her shoulders. "I … know a detour we could take," she said last. "I've used it more than once to avoid pirates. It might keep us out of the way of your friend." She shook her head and chuckled softly. "I must be an absolute idiot. You stole my ship and threatened to kill me. But, since it looks like this is my only chance of getting my ship back—I'll take you there. If you give me your word as a lying, murdering criminal that you won't spread the coordinates around."

Savina turned to stare at her. And then she found herself breaking into a smile of relief, something tightening in her throat just a little.

"On my word as a lying, murdering criminal."

Joska shook her head with a rueful smile, then turned back the controls.

Savina cleared her throat. "Um. Thank you," she said, for the second time that day.

The captain turned back with a sharp look, but there was a kindness under it that Savina hadn't expected.

"How did you grow up, Savina?" she asked at last. Her voice was quiet, as if she were talking to herself more than Savina. "What did they teach you about life in that compound of yours, where you can't call in or out?"

Savina narrowed her eyes and looked away.

She knew better than to trust kindness.

She must have drifted off at some point, despite the throbbing pain in her shoulder, because when she opened her eyes again, that captain was standing, stretching out the kinks in her muscles.

She glanced over as Savina's eyes opened, and gave her a small smile. "We're in behind the remnants of an old dead star. The debris field and residual magnetics make it almost impossible to track anyone back here." Her gaze, as she watched Savina, was a little too perceptive. "It wouldn't be a bad thing for you to get some more sleep. I've set us a course, and the autopilot should take us from there. Nothing more for us to do at the moment, and if you're in a hurry to warn your family it'll be easier if you're not passing out from pain." She paused, then added, "I guess murdering people and stealing ships takes more out of you than you'd think."

Savina stared at her, too shocked to respond, and Joska chuckled, turning away.

"Do what you want. I'm smart enough to take my sleep when I can get it. Rafel, wake me up at midnight watch."

Rafel give a terse nod from the copilot seat, but Joska was already gone.

"I'll take first shift, Vina," Beni whispered. "Their restraints are set, so the two of them shouldn't cause problems." They paused. "Vina, are you—"

"I'm alright," said Savina. "I'll be fine."

It still hurt like hell, but between the medifoam and the bandage, she no longer felt like she'd pass out the moment she tried to move.

Beni nodded, although they were clearly still unhappy. "Joska said there's a cabin just off the flight deck. Come on." They leaned over, fingers fumbling for the straps, and helped Savina sit up, guiding her feet into the mag boots.

"Wake me up if you need anything," said Savina.

"I will. Just go."

Savina's shoulder ached, and her muscles were heavy with exhaustion. She shuffled into the small cabin, and was asleep almost before she managed to strap into the cot.

It wasn't a noise that woke her, although the noise came soon after.

It was the way the ship shuddered, a small, incongruous movement in deep space, and one she might not have noticed at all if her nerves hadn't been so on edge. As it was, she jerked awake, blinking, and it took her a moment to reorient herself to the interior of the *Dolphin*, rather than the soft bunks and artificial gravity of the luxury ship she'd spent the last week on.

There was a shout of pain from outside, and Savina was suddenly wide awake.

She unstrapped with her one good hand, snatched up her gun, clipped her feet into the mag boots, and grabbed for the door control. From outside there was a grunt, and the hiss of pulse-fire, then she was through the door and out onto the flight deck.

For a split second, she took in the scene in front of her—Beni against the wall, face terrified. Rafel, eyes closed, body listing oddly against the straps on the copilot seat.

And in front of Beni, a small smile on her face, the woman whose face and figure had been carved into Savina's memory the day before, in the grungy hallway of the small port city.

The woman's posture was casual, but she must have heard the door open, because she was already turning, the barrel of her gun swinging towards Savina's face. Even in zero gravity her movements bore the smooth, easy grace of a predator, her body twisting in a fluid motion. And for a moment, as those deadly hazel-grey eyes turned on her, Savina was completely frozen, her throat dry in a sick combination of magnetic attraction and dread.

The woman's face still bore the cool ruthlessness that Savina remembered from the station, but there was something else underneath it.

A vicious, icy hatred.

"Vina!"

Beni's shout brought her back to herself, and Savina ducked, using the leverage from the mag boots to pull her down as a pulse blast rippled over her head. Then she was up and lunging forward, grabbing the stranger around the waist and shoving her against the controls.

Without gravity to offer resistance, they didn't fall so much as bounce against the console, the woman's hands scrabbling for Savina's throat. Pain rolled in nauseating waves through Savina's body at the impact, but she yanked a foot out of the mag boots, kneeing her opponent's hand and sending the woman's gun flying off towards the ceiling.

The woman's other hand was already coming up, and Savina could see the glint of a knife in it. She jerked her body to one side as a knife slid past her, missing her neck by centimetres. It was so sharp that it took a moment for the pain blossoming across her shoulder blade to register, blood welling in odd sticky globules along the line the knife had cut in her shoulder. She grabbed the woman's wrist and twisted it, gritting her teeth against the pain, and yanked a thin, sharp knife from her belt with her injured arm, driving it upwards towards the woman's rib cage.

It skittered across the woman's suit, the strange fabric turning the blow, but a thin line of blood followed the blade upwards. Savina let the tip of it catch in the fabric, then shoved it home with all her might. The woman gave a quick, startled gasp, her eyes widening in shock. Then, with surprising strength, she pulled her wrist free and slapped her hand against Savina's arm.

An agonizing pulse of electricity jolted through Savina's body, freezing her in place. Her jaw was clenched, muscles shaking, and she could feel the cords standing out in her neck, but her body wouldn't obey her commands.

The woman stepped back, breathing heavily, and reached for a holster on her thigh, pulling out a small, deadly looking pistol in a smooth, easy motion.

Savina was going to die. She was going to die here, in a beat-up ship in the middle of nowhere, and her family was going to die too—

Then there was a soft *hiss*, and the woman jerked back, blood forming in a perfect, rapidly swelling globe against her shoulder.

"Drop your weapon," said Joska from the doorway, in her dry, sardonic drawl.

The grey-clad woman hesitated. But there was a quality to her movements that told Savina that, between the knife wound and the shot, she was hurt worse than she was letting on.

She moved as if to obey, but Savina caught the way her muscles tensed. She tried to shout a warning, but her jaw was clenched too tightly, so she could only watch helplessly as the woman leapt forward, catlike, slipping past Joska and disappearing through the door, tossing something behind her as she went.

The small, round device hit the ceiling with a faint, metallic *ting*, a gaseous cloud roiling lazily from perforations in its sides. Beni and the captain both dived towards it, the intruder forgotten, and a moment later the cloud of gas was contained, the emergency filtration system kicking in with a low growl.

"Savina?" Joska stepped over, tapping the butt of her pistol against the tranq device on Savina's arm. It dropped loose, and the force holding her disappeared.

Savina leaned her head back weakly, an odd mixture of relief and disappointment flooding through her. Her muscles were rubber, her body hanging limply from her remaining mag boot. She felt oddly numb, the throbbing pain from the gunshot wound blending with the clean, sharp pain of the knife like two colours of paint mixing and spreading. She turned her head to see that the wobbling, ruby-coloured line of blood on her shoulder had grown, and she watched, fascinated, as a globule broke free.

"Savina! Savina, answer me. Are you alright?"

Savina blinked and turned back to the voice. Beni's face was frantic, and they were moving their hands gently down Savina's shoulders. Savina wanted to stop them before they reached the blood and got it smeared everywhere, but her tongue was oddly heavy—

And then Joska was there, speaking in Beni's ear in calm, soothing tones, and reluctantly, Beni stepped aside. The captain peered into Savina's face, sighed, and stepped over to the med kit. She returned a moment later and tapped a disk against the back of Savina's neck.

Savina gasped, the icy shock bringing her back to herself.

"Better?" asked Joska.

Savina nodded, although she felt a little like she was going to vomit—which would not be pleasant in zero gravity. "Where—where did she go?"

The captain stepped over to the ship's display, and Savina followed, a little unsteadily.

From the base of their ship, a tiny dot detached itself, falling quickly behind.

"I guess she didn't like her welcome," mumbled Rafel. He was sitting up again, despite the sickly tinge to his skin.

The captain glanced quickly at him, then, apparently satisfied that he wasn't seriously injured, turned back to Savina, examining her with a critical eye. "That's a nasty looking cut."

Savina nodded, her teeth clenched shut. She couldn't afford to think about it right now, not if she wanted to keep the contents of her stomach down.

"Best deal with it, then, before you lose too much blood. You too, Rafel, you're going to get fixed up before I trust you to pilot us anywhere. Come on, let's get both of you strapped down, and Beni and I will see what we can do."

"It's no worse than when those smugglers took after us in Belo," Rafel grumbled, but his wan, shell-shocked expression belied his words, and he did as Joska asked.

The captain was clearly accustomed to treating injuries—she worked quickly and efficiently, calling out orders to Beni, and soon both Savina and Rafel were bandaged and sitting up.

Joska wiped her hands on a towel, still frowning. "How did she manage to get close without the scanner picking up anything? And how did she get through the ship's airlock?"

"I have no idea," Savina muttered. "But—" Grimacing, she reached into a pocket and pulled out a small disc. Her hands shook, and it took more effort than it should have to switch it on. "This might help. It took a scan of everything on her—documents, weapons, tech."

The captain raised an eyebrow, watching as Savina flipped quickly through the glowing pages.

"She has delta-level cloaking," said Savina absently as she paged through. "That would explain how she got on here, at least, and why the *Dolphin's* sensors didn't pick anything up. But—"

She broke off suddenly, staring down at the glowing words floating in front of her.

The agent had a DNA scanner. And Savina's blood was scattered in tiny droplets across the cabin, and caught on the agent's blade.

And the warrant—there was a copy of that, too. The official that she'd send her report back to. Chief Justice Alba Espina.

The moment the agent's latest report came in, it would match, immediately, with the mission-ship's database.

And there was something horribly, stomach-clenchingly familiar about the name of the mission ship.

Nicolau's ship.

The moment the report went back to the judge, his secret, the secret even he didn't know, would be out.

And he would die.

"Beni—" she whispered.

"Vina?"

Savina turned to the captain, her voice distant, clinical and calm. "Do you know if the news packets mentioned the name of the diplomatic ship?"

The captain frowned. "Is it important?"

"Very." Her voice was still calm, somehow.

How long did they have? Minutes? Hours? Days? She had no idea how often the agent sent in her reports.

The woman who'd be reading the reports was the Judge of Heresies. The woman whose very existence threatened Savina's family and everyone she cared about. The woman who'd set a government agent after her.

The woman who would watch as Nicolau died.

For a brief, breathtaking moment, a memory flashed in her brain —her own mother bending, tears running down her cheeks, to lower a tiny squirming bundle into a hole in the ground. Her baby brother's thin wails as the shovelfuls of dirt landed on his tiny body, his flailing arms, his face.

The way the grass and pebbles cut into her hands as she and Beni scrabbled frantically in the dirt once the adults were gone, the sweet, sick relief that flooded her chest when he'd blinked his tiny eyes and drawn in a choking breath and whimpered, nuzzling his dirt-streaked face against her shirt.

It wouldn't happen again. No one else would stand by to watch Nicolau die, not if she could stop it.

The captain was still watching her, but finally she gave a faint shrug. "I can check, I suppose," she said, tapping her wrist to activate the wavelink.

She listened for a moment, eyes distant, then nodded. "Here," she said, bending over the screen and tracing a line with her finger. "The ship is called the Firedawn. This is their rout."

Savina glanced it over it quickly, the calm, icy cold still gripping her chest.

She'd guessed right. It was his ship. Of course they'd have

conscripted his ship.

The route wasn't far from where they were now, maybe twenty-four planetary hours distant.

"They shouldn't get in our way, if that's what you're worried about," said the captain. "And even with what happened, we can still make—"

Savina cut her off. "There's been a change of plans," she said curtly. "We're not going back to Colorida."

Now all the eyes in the cabin were on her, expressions ranging from curious to concerned.

"I thought—" Joska began, an odd tone in her voice.

"We're going to meet up with the diplomatic ship," said Savina, tone still pleasant and very distant. "We're going to get aboard it, somehow. And we're going to kill the Chief Justice."

20

Alba

They reconvened the next morning a grim, silent group. No one looked like they'd slept, with the possible exception of Yosip, and even his face showed sharp lines of worry. Istvay stood protectively close to Aran.

"I am no longer sure that we are intended to survive this mission," said Feliu at last, his normally dour face carved even more so by worry and exhaustion.

Alba almost snorted. Leave it to Feliu to come up with a way to make an already terrible situation sound even worse.

Still, he may not be wrong. The thought sent an unexpected thrill of fear through her, like a gulp of too cold water on a too hot day.

"Then I suppose we'll have to figure out how to survive it anyway," said Yosip. He smiled, but his smile looked more strained than usual.

Alba took a deep breath. "We don't have many options, it appears, but let's review the ones we do have. We could find a way to get ourselves off ship if and when we stop by a planet for supplies."

Yosip shook his head slowly. "I already talked to someone I know who works in the nav crew. There are no planned stops between here and the portal."

"I ... we could—" Ines stopped, looking down quickly as Alba turned her eyes on her.

"Ines, please," said Yosip, his voice gentle and encouraging. "We can use any ideas right now. Even if they don't work, maybe it'll help us think of something."

Ines glanced up at him gratefully, swallowed, and nodded. "I ... I only thought, if we could mess with the supplies, sabotage them, maybe—" her voice faltered.

"That's ... not a bad idea, actually," said Istvay thoughtfully, looking away from shooting irate glances in Alba's direction. "The moment the crew learns we're running short on supplies, I don't think they'll agree to keep going, captain's orders or no."

"It's not a bad idea, maybe," Feliu snapped. "Assuming the captain isn't willing to simply let us and the crew starve to death in deep space. And I'm not sure we can assume that's the case any longer." He turned to Alba. "Madam? What do you think?"

Alba sighed.

This was exactly the question that had kept her awake the previous night.

"I ... don't know," she said at last. "I suspect Cavaco intends for us to get to the planet, and then sabotage the mission. However—" she paused a moment, forcing her voice not to tremble, "We can't discount the possibility that, as Feliu suggested, he simply intends to have us killed on the trip over."

Alba had faced countless threats over the course of her career— threats to her reputation, to her career, threats to make a fool of her, to cost her an election or an appointment. But this—something about the crass physicality of this threat had awoken a primal, instinctual fear, something that made her muscles tremble and her voice shake unless she kept an iron hold on herself.

Yosip shook his head again. "I don't think they'll dare do that. According to people I know in the communications bay, there's enough contact back and forth for family and friends, news packets, so on, that it would be difficult for the captain to monitor all the feeds. There's no guarantee that word wouldn't slip out, no matter how careful they were. If you were killed—if any of us were killed— word would get back to the planet. Perhaps they felt safe attacking Aran because, brilliant as he is, he's not the only scientist on board. They could make an argument that the mission should continue without him. But the Chief Justice murdered—" He shook his head. "They couldn't risk it. If the General wants the mission to fail, and to turn the failure to his advantage, he'd have to make it appear that the trouble came from the aliens themselves, not from your own crew."

Alba gave a curt nod.

What he was saying made sense. But it wasn't a simple thing to convince her nerves of that.

"Even so," said Feliu, "if we sabotage the supplies, we're gambling the lives of everyone on the ship. Do we want to take that risk?"

For a few moments, no one spoke. At last, Aran stirred and glanced up. "Listen," he said. "What if, instead of sabotaging the supplies, we just tell the crew what we've found out? I mean, the results of our particulate research, and our hypotheses? I … there are people on the ship who'd probably listen to me." There was something slightly grim in his tone, as if this was an unpleasant fact, and one he didn't like to think about.

Alba stared at him.

As far as she had observed, not only were there people on the ship who'd probably listen to him, every single person on the ship would hang off every word he deigned to speak to them.

Clearly, he either didn't realize this himself, or he preferred to pretend he didn't.

He cleared his throat, obviously uncomfortable. "If the crew understands the potential danger of going in without further study, it might have more or less the same effect as Ines's suggestion."

Feliu nodded, looking faintly impressed. "They'd have a mutiny on their hands," he said. "If someone like Aran says something—from the rest of us, it could be construed as politics. But everyone knows Aran's commitment to science. There's no possibility the captain can spin it as some self-interested trick. He'll either turn around, or he'll go through the portal with no crew. I doubt even someone bought and paid for by Cavaco would be that heedless of their own mortality."

Istvay hadn't spoken for a while, but now they looked up. "That means we'd go back to Colorida, correct? End the mission. Not just pause to re-supply."

Alba looked over at them, frowning. She couldn't read the expression on their face, but she caught their quick, unconscious glance towards Aran, the mix of concern and worry and something desperate that she couldn't tell whether was relief or disappointment in that look.

Alba nodded. "Yes. I suspect that is exactly what it would mean."

She didn't have to say the rest—that if they went back, the chance that another diplomatic mission would be sent out was virtually nil.

It meant the loss of the culmination of her life's work. The failure of a final, definitive proof that diplomacy could triumph over aggression, that wars could be won by speaking, rather than with weapons. From now on, the argument that first contact with a new species could be dealt with without the military, and that the Military Committee could be disbanded, would be set back, possibly forever.

But that wasn't all. If this mission failed—if they went to war against these aliens, or even if the portal disappeared and both parties were left in peace—the chance to find the cure for the defect would be gone forever.

Aran was staring at the floor, clenching and unclenching his hands.

"Aran—" said Istvay in a low voice.

Aran closed his eyes. "I'll … do it, then," he said, raising his chin and conspicuously avoiding looking at Istvay.

"I'm sorry," Alba said without thinking, and then stopped, wondering where that had come from. Her, apologizing to some young biologist who wouldn't even look her in the eye.

"I suppose there's not much more to discuss, then, at least until we find out if this works," said Yosip at last. "But we'll need to be careful. I don't think they'll dare kill the Chief Justice, but we can't be sure. And that goes double for the rest of us." He turned, looking at each of them in turn. "Until we know who we can or can't trust, don't go anywhere alone. Don't let your guard down. Lock your door to your cabin when you sleep. And keep a weapon on you at all times."

Feliu nodded and reached under the desk, pulling out a large, bulky box. "I wasn't sure what we would be facing on this trip," he said stiffly, avoiding Alba's eyes. "I took the liberty of procuring some weapons. I hope they're acceptable."

Alba raised an eyebrow in surprise as he opened the box, revealing a disturbing number of what, at least to her inexperienced eye, looked like highly lethal objects.

Yosip crossed over to stand beside him, then glanced over at Ines. "Have you used a weapon before?" he asked, his voice low and reassuring.

Ines looked up at him and gave a quick little half-nod. "My—my father used to take me out shooting redbirds when they were eating the crop," she said, in her quiet voice.

Alba frowned. The girl, though rather a pathetic thing, was clearly educated. And Alba had simply assumed that meant she was from Vila Nova do Sol, or at least the Belt. She knew, intellectually, that people in the Rim Mountains were just as likely to be intelligent and educated, it was simply that—

She shook her head, pushing down the mildly disconcerting self-reflection.

Yosip nodded, still smiling that reassuring smile. "Good. Come pick something you're comfortable with, then."

Throwing a timid glance in Alba's direction, the girl did as Yosip asked, pulling out a serviceable-looking pulse pistol.

It took Alba a moment to realize that the glance had been one of something close to pleading. As if the girl didn't know what Alba's reaction would be, but cared desperately.

The thought sent an odd twinge through her.

She'd all but ignored the girl up until now, treating her as nothing more than a necessary tool. But Yosip hadn't. Yosip had seen her, spoken to her. He wasn't surprised by the revelation the girl was from the Rim Mountains—he'd likely already known.

"Only use it if you need to," Yosip said. "But if you do need to, don't hesitate to use it. If someone is trying to hurt you, it's no sin to defend yourself."

The others stepped over, choosing their own weapons. Feliu looked uncomfortable holding his, but Aran and Istvay took their own with a familiarity that showed their experience.

Of course, judging from the lives they'd led, Alba would have been surprised had they not been familiar with weapons.

She stood back, watching, until at last Yosip turned to her.

He held out a small, deadly looking pistol, offering it to her. "Madam Chief Justice. I expect you haven't had to use something like this previously, but I think this one should suit."

She had to force herself to take it from him, and she wasn't sure she concealed the way her fingers trembled. The small, unfamiliar shape sat cold and heavy in her palm, the weight of it somehow menacing.

Yosip smiled at her, his gaze surprisingly gentle, and said, "I don't imagine you use pistols that often in your line of work. Would you like me to walk you through it?"

She gave a short nod, absurdly grateful that he'd offered, rather than forcing her to admit that she had no idea what to do with the small, deadly thing in her hand.

"It's not overly complicated," he said, taking it back from her for a moment. "This, here, will charge it. This trigger will release the pulse. Point it where you want to shoot, and pull the trigger. You can discharge it a dozen or so times before it needs to be recharged—as long as the green light is blinking, it'll continue to fire when you pull the trigger. Once it's fully discharged and the light goes off, push the lever forward and pull it back again. It will take a few seconds, so try to do it at a time when you're not in the middle of being shot at." He was clearly trying to keep his tone light. But she could hear the worry in it, and she understood the import behind his words.

As a judge, she'd condemned people to sentences that would lead to their deaths—if not directly, certainly indirectly. It was a statistical inevitability that some percentage of convicted criminals would take their own lives if condemned to a lengthy prison sentence, or banished from the city or town where they'd been raised. But when she sentenced them, she'd managed not to feel guilt—she was only carrying out laws that had already been written. And even when she was the one writing the laws, she did so with the firm conviction that the law she was writing appropriately balanced the needs of the few and the needs of the many.

But bringing up a weapon, discharging at someone in front of you —the brutal, immediate violence of it made her feel queasy.

Yosip walked her through how to set and release the safety, then handed the pistol back to her. "And that's all you need to know. With luck, you won't have to use it."

She nodded, and, checking carefully that the weapon was charged and the safety on, tucked it into her reticule.

"That will be our plan, then," she said sharply. "As Yosip said, be careful, and watch out for yourselves and each other. We'll reconvene here when Aran has started the rumours spreading." She paused a moment. "Good luck, to all of you."

They murmured it back to her and shuffled out of the room.

When they'd all left, even Feliu, she locked the door behind them and sank down on the hard-backed chair at her desk.

The weight of the weapon in her reticule was heavy and uncomfortable, as hard and cold as the knot in her stomach.

21

Aran

The door to Aran's cabin slid shut behind him. He glanced quickly around the room, every muscle in his body tense, then pulled the weapon off his belt and laid it on the cot.

Ani squeezed out from the tiny space under his bed and made her way delicately over to him on the tips of her tentacles, her movements holding the furtive, diffident curiosity she exhibited when she could tell he was upset.

He smiled despite himself and gestured to her, and she swarmed up his leg, around his back, and pulled herself onto her customary place on his shoulder, pressing her bulbous body against the side of his face. He sighed and reached up, tickling her gently under the chin, and her tentacles went a deep, satisfied green.

"Here's the thing, Ani," he said, crossing over to the small drawers at the foot of his bed. "Maybe the Chief Justice is right, and this whole trip was set up to fail. But that blood sample was real. And—" he shook his head. "Ani, it's the best chance I've ever had. The only damn chance I've ever had. I'm not going to let Istvay die. I won't. I don't honestly care about the damn consequences."

Ani stroked his arm soothingly with her tentacles, and he managed a small chuckle.

She didn't have to understand what he was saying to know he was upset, and that was all that mattered to her.

Ani, he could understand. Hell, he'd take being poisoned by tentacle spikes on accident any day over dealing with people, with their bewildering lies and jostling and positioning, for reasons he frankly couldn't comprehend, no matter how much he tried. He knew, intellectually, that power and influence were considered objectively desirable. But he'd be damned if he understood why. Yes, he knew perfectly well what it felt to be so hungry you thought your stomach would eat itself from the inside out, and he knew what it felt like to be shivering, and cold, and have nowhere to go to get out of the rain and the wind, and no idea if you were going to stay warm enough overnight, or if at some point you'd shiver yourself to death, hypothermia slowly gripping your muscles and turning them sluggish, convincing your brain there was nothing to fear, that you were warm and comfortable, and you should sleep, a sleep you'd never wake from. He could understand trying to survive.

But this? This, he'd never understand.

"The Chief Justice wants to turn back," he said, as Ani peered over his shoulder with a decent approximation of someone hanging on his every word. "I can't blame her—there's some plot to kill her, or sabotage the mission, or something along those lines." He pulled open the drawers and glanced through them.

After years of field work, in conditions that tended to be too harsh even for drones, he'd learned how to pack light. Most of what he'd brought consisted of gear he'd scrounged, modified, or constructed over the years to suit his needs—ugly, probably, and a bit unconventional, but effective. He sighed, pulled open his battered rucksack, and began shoving items into it in the practised manner of long familiarity.

"It's my fault that they want to turn around. I was trying to find something that might help Istvay, and I ended up screwing things up," he said quietly. "But we're not going back, not the two of us. Not until we find whatever's behind that portal. Maybe whatever it is does shoot down ships. But something as small as an escape pod, I think we have at least an even chance of getting through unnoticed."

He couldn't think too hard about what he was planning to do, because terror would freeze his muscles and panic would turn his brain to mush. But he had experience planning expeditions that terrified the hell out of him—hell, that was basically the story of every expedition he'd ever planned.

Ani gave a sort of purr that he chose to take as agreement.

"We'll do what we promised, get the crew to refuse to go on, get everyone headed back safely. And then, just before the ship turns around, we'll slip into a pod and take off. I looked at the specs. It should work."

He had looked at the escape pod specs, compulsively and in depth, over the course of their journey, during far too many nights when the excitement of their daily research had faded and he was left with the lingering horror of the realization that they were hurtling through a vast, empty vacuum that would leave you a crystallized corpse, choking on your own bodily fluids as you died.

And right now, he was planning to voluntarily strap himself and Ani into something barely bigger than this cabin and take off into the centre of that void. The pod had an oxygen generator and enough fuel cells and ration packs to hypothetically keep a person alive for a month or more. But he had no idea what was on the other side of the portal, or how long it would take to reach it. For all he knew, the small, claustrophobic pod would become his coffin.

He closed his eyes for a moment, steadying himself against the sudden wave of terror-induced nausea.

"It should be fine," he said. "The pods are perfectly safe."

He couldn't help the way his voice shook at the last words. But then, there was no point in pretending to Ani that he wasn't abjectly terrified. It was his mood she picked up on, not his words, and she was attuned to the subtlest hints. There was nothing he could do to convince her he wasn't afraid.

And in the end, it didn't actually matter. There was one thing, and one thing only, that scared him more than getting into that pod. And that was watching Istvay die.

Ani tightened her tentacles a little firmer around him and made a protective sort of clicking with her razor-sharp beak. He sank down on the cot for a moment, pulling her off his shoulders and into his lap, and stroked delicately down her long tentacles. She purred in pleasure, flattening her body slightly, her skin going an even deeper green.

Aran chuckled. "I'm sorry, Ani. I haven't been paying enough attention to you lately, have I? Well, pretty soon it will be just you and me, and then you'll get all the attention you want."

She grumbled a little, but it was half-hearted, and he could see her eyes closing to slits of contentment.

There was a tap at the door, and Aran jerked his head up.

"Aran? Are you in there?"

He jumped to his feet, spilling Ani onto the floor. She growled in annoyance, grabbing at his leg to keep her balance.

"I'm—I'm here, I'm just—" he began frantically, bending to disentangle himself from Ani, and then the door slid open and Istvay stepped inside.

Aran straightened guiltily as Ani scrambled back to her perch on his shoulder and Istvay took in the disarray of the small cabin.

For a long moment, neither of them said anything.

Aran clenched his teeth, trying to think of some explanation, but when he saw Istvay's face he knew it was useless. They'd guessed what he was doing. They'd probably guessed before they'd come to tap on his door.

He closed his eyes for a moment, bracing himself for Istvay's furious lecture.

When Istvay spoke, though, their tone carried no anger at all, just a sort of sadness. "Aran?" they said quietly.

He looked up, meeting their gaze, and, like always, those brown eyes seemed to pull him in until he felt like he was drowning. "Istvay," he mumbled, "I—"

Istvay shook their head. "I can't talk you out of this, can I?" they said. "Even if I tell you it's probably going to kill you."

Aran gritted his teeth. "You're dying, Istvay," he said, his voice harsh. "We both know that. And if there's a chance—even the slightest, most ridiculous chance—I'm going to take it. You'd have to kill me to stop me."

Istvay managed a small smile, their expression one of mingled affection and misery. "I know," they said, even more quietly. "I know there's nothing I can do." They reached out, and when Aran nodded, they put their hand on his arm. "But you're not going alone. I'm coming with you. And before you say anything, I'm going to quote your own words back at you—you'd have to kill me to stop me."

Aran stared at them for a moment. He opened his mouth to protest, then closed it again.

Istvay was right—Aran knew better than anyone how damn stubborn they could be. He wouldn't be able to force Istvay to stay behind any more than he would Ani.

So at last he nodded, with a rueful smile that matched his best friend's.

Istvay squeezed his arm gently. "I checked the escape pods already," they said. "Since I was pretty sure you were going to come up with something ridiculous like this. We can take one of the four-person pods. It should give us a little extra life support, in case it takes longer to get where we're going than we think, and it'll give Ani some extra room. Although I don't know that she'll need it, since she usually refuses to get more than a few centimetres' distance from you, even if you're greeting a government minister in front of your hotel." They paused. "And. Um."

They rummaged in their pocket, and pulled out a small, wrapped package, holding it out. "Butter taffy. Your favourite. They had some in the kitchens, and I figured you'd be stressed, so …"

Aran stared at his friend for a moment, speechless. Istvay chuckled, and Aran was struck, suddenly, at how the sound made the cloying, nauseating, unassailable terror of what he was planning so much less debilitating.

He smiled reluctantly and took the candy, shoving it into his mouth. The buttery sweetness spread across his tongue, and he closed his eyes and breathed in through his nose, the familiar, homey taste grounding him.

It only took him a few minutes to finish his packing. Istvay waited for him, leaned back against the doorframe and reading through something on their palmscreen.

When Aran turned back to them, Istvay glanced up, studying him for a moment. Then they leaned forward, fixing the collar of Aran's jacket in a familiar gesture. The back of their hand brushed Aran's throat, and for half a second, he couldn't seem to pull in oxygen.

Istvay straightened, grinning. "You ready to start a mutiny?" they said.

Aran drew in a shaky breath, and smiled back despite himself.

Ani had obviously picked up on the fact he was getting ready for a journey, and didn't want to risk being left behind. And although he'd spent three years working with her, the fact of the matter was that if an inherently lethal killing machine like Ani—whose species had managed to keep an entire, otherwise perfectly habitable planet from human colonization, who ate radiation like candy, and who seemed completely insusceptible to most modern forms of weaponry— decided that she was going somewhere … well, she simply did. She spread across his back, tentacles gripping his shirt, blended herself in with the colour of his clothing, and stubbornly ignored his pleas for her to wait in the cabin.

He sighed.

At least with her ability to camouflage, she wasn't as noticeable as she could have been, although she did end up leaving him looking distinctly lumpy in ways that it would be difficult to mistake as natural.

Istvay tucked their pistol inconspicuously in the back of their belt as they stepped into the corridor, and Aran shoved his pistol into his waist holster as well. True, Ani was the best protection either of them had, but there was no point in taking chances.

The weight of it against his hip served as an ominous reminder that however dangerous this stupid mission had been before, it was a hell of a lot more dangerous now.

"Aran," said Gilda warmly as he stepped into the lab. She went to put a hand on his shoulder, and he stepped back quickly—he didn't want Ani startled in this mood.

She gave him a quick smile of apology. "I saw you'd been down lab last night. Did you find anything interesting?"

"I did, actually," he said.

There must have been something in the tone of his voice, or else everyone had been craning their ears to overhear the conversation, because the lab went suddenly silent, every face turned towards him.

He walked over to the table and powered up the screen. "This is probably something everyone should see," he said, pulling up the data from the night before.

By the time he finished his explanation, the expressions around him ranged from faint scepticism to outright horror.

"I can't dispute your findings," said one of the scientists, an older man, his gravelly voice slow and cautious. "But before we make any sweeping assumptions, we'd better be sure that the sample wasn't contaminated, and that the results are replicable."

Aran nodded. "And even if they are, this isn't the only possible hypothesis. But I think it at least calls for a more in-depth analysis before we plunge ahead."

"Have you mentioned this to the captain?" asked another of the scientists, a younger woman with thick black hair and a normally friendly smile, now turned into a frown of concern.

He gave a short nod. "He doesn't want to take the time to pursue this further. I think he's making a mistake."

There was a murmuring among the assembled group. "Maybe if he hears it from more than one of us, that will help," said the first man who'd spoken. "My husband's one of the diplomatic aides, so I'll see if I can't get some of the diplomatic corps to bring up the matter as well."

Aran shook his head in sudden panic. He'd seen the fear on Feliu's face when he talked about the corps having been infiltrated by the General's people, and he remembered all too well the tickle of spiny insect legs against the back of his neck. "No! No, I don't think that's a good idea. The diplomatic corps probably won't be pleased with the idea of delaying the mission, and they might try to convince the captain of entirely the wrong thing."

The man hesitated, then shrugged. "You're the famous one. You'd know better than any of us what the bigwigs are like. If you think it's best—"

"I do," said Aran fervently. There weren't many times that he was grateful for his unwanted notoriety, but if it kept this man's husband from winding up in a corridor with a slit throat, he'd take it.

"How many other people know?" asked an older woman.

He shook his head. "Not many. You know, the captain knows." He'd never been good at lying, but this wasn't exactly a lie, so it flowed a little more easily over his tongue.

She nodded, still watching him, and he turned away quickly, making a pretence of shutting down his screen. "Anyway," he said, his eyes fixed on the table. "It would be unbelievably helpful if you could convince the captain to turn around, or at least pause to give us time to look into this farther. I want to find a cure as much as anyone, but it won't do us much good if we're blown out of the sky the moment we pass through the portal."

He took his time shutting down his equipment, and he could hear the scientists talking quietly, heading back to their desks, or, more frequently, ducking out the door.

At last he and Istvay and Ani were alone in the lab.

"I think you convinced them," Istvay said quietly. "We'll have to hope it's enough." They paused, glancing around at the deserted lab. "I guess now we go talk to some of your friends in the crew."

Aran nodded grimly.

If he were being honest, the thought of walking out onto the crowded, noisy, bustling main deck set his teeth on edge and made his limbs heavy with dread. But Istvay was right—they had a duty, at least, to keep as many people as possible alive. If that meant marching out onto the main deck and letting the crew swarm around him to congratulate him on his latest and likely much embellished exploit—well, he may not like it, but he'd do it.

Istvay smiled. "It'll be fine," they said, a touch of affection in their tone. "Get this done, and then you won't have to be around anyone but me and Ani for the next—who knows how long?" They chuckled. "Although by the end of it you might get so tired of us that you wish you'd thrown us overboard in the first week."

Aran gave a half-hearted chuckle, shaking his head, but it was slightly easier to force his legs to move him towards the door.

They'd made it about halfway down the hallway when he caught, from the corner of his eye, the faintest movement—a shift in the pattern of light and shadow. Ani hissed, tightening her tentacles on his back, and he dropped to the ground on instinct as something hissed over his head.

From behind him, he heard Istvay's startled exclamation.

Then they grunted in pain, and Aran, terror catching in his throat, rolled to his feet in time to see them stumble, barely catching themself against the wall of the corridor.

"Istvay," he shouted, grabbing for his friend.

Istvay's face had gone grey, sweat forming on their forehead. They opened their mouth as if to speak, specks of foam at the corners of their lips, and then their eyes rolled back into their head and their body went limp.

Aran caught Istvay as they fell, and swore, his voice shaking. He lowered his friend gently to the deck, looking them over frantically for a sign of what had happened. It took him a moment to see it—a slender needle, like one you'd use to tranquillize an animal in the field, lodged in the fleshy part of Istvay's upper arm.

With another curse, Aran yanked off his jacket and tied a makeshift tourniquet at Istvay's shoulder, cranking it tight. Better for Istvay to lose an arm than lose their life to whatever the hell had been on the needle. The tourniquet done, he jerked the needle free, fingers fumbling for the kit at his belt.

"Ani, watch Istvay," he snapped, and for once she obeyed, slithering off his arm and dropping to Istvay's chest at the command. With her there, nothing would dare come close to Istvay while he was gone, and if anyone did, they'd be dead before they had time to go for a weapon—he knew how fast Ani could move when she wanted to.

He was already running back towards the lab as he plunged the needle into his test kit.

It spat out a result as he shoved through the lab door and sprinted for the first aid cupboard, and he glanced down at it and swore again.

Spiny-wasp venom. Fast acting, and it would stop Istvay's heart in less than a minute.

He fumbled through the antivenin vials, knocking them over in his haste. He snatched out the correct one, then grabbed a long, thick needle and sprinted back towards where Istvay lay.

They were mostly still by now, face slack, spittle foaming at the corners of their mouth, the only movement the slight jerking of their limbs. Aran was still swearing under his breath, every curse word he knew and some he had to invent. He bent over Istvay, feeling for a pulse.

Nothing.

He swallowed against the sick pit of dread welling in his stomach.

It wasn't too late. He'd been fast, and Istvay's heart couldn't have been stopped for more than a few seconds.

Hands shaking almost too hard to manage, he fixed the needle to the small vial and felt carefully down Istvay's rib cage. He closed his eyes, picturing where he'd have to place the needle to reach Istvay's heart. Then he positioned his fingers gently as a marker, took a deep breath, and shoved the needle in with a sharp jerk of his hand. When he was sure it had reached its target, he depressed the back of the vial, and watched it drain.

Istvay's chest gave a quick jerk under his hands, like a startled animal, then stilled.

Aran swore again, yanking a small vial of artificial adrenaline from his pouch. Without removing the needle, he slipped the vial of antidote carefully off the end of it and replaced it with the adrenaline, and depressed the back of the vial once more.

This time, he felt Istvay's heart jerk and stutter a couple more times, like a frightened bird.

He closed his eyes. "Please," he whispered, to whoever might be listening. "Please."

For a moment, Istvay's heart seemed to still. And then it jerked again, then again, and then settled into a weak but rhythmic motion, the needle in Aran's fingers twitching at each beat.

Aran let out a long breath, almost dizzy with relief, and with trembling fingers, yanked the needle from Istvay's chest.

Beneath the tourniquet, Istvay's fingers were turning a dark purplish. Aran untied his jacket, massaging the blood gently back into Istvay's hand. Their face was still slack, their eyes closed, their muscles limp under his fingers. He could feel the weak stutter of a pulse, and every beat he was terrified would be the last.

"I'm sorry, Pishti," he muttered, fighting back the sharp sting of tears. "I shouldn't have ducked, I should have been more careful, I should have damn well listened to you in the first place—" his voice choked. Without really thinking, he'd switched to the language he'd known as a child, the Mountain Dialect he'd only been able to speak when he was alone. "You can't die on me, Pishti," he whispered. "I —I don't know how to live without you. I don't know how to survive if you're not here. You always tease me about why I haven't found someone yet, but—but dammit, Istvay, it's because I love you. I've loved you since we were kids, and I've never been able to say it, because you don't want me to and I don't know why. But I've never loved anyone but you, and if you die, it will destroy me."

He felt a faint movement under his hand, and he looked up, wiping his sleeve quickly across his face. Istvay's eyes had blinked opened, and they were looking around in disoriented confusion.

"Aran?" they croaked, their voice hoarse.

The sudden rush of relief was almost enough to make Aran lightheaded. "Istvay? Istvay—" his voice choked again.

"What … what happened?" they asked, voice still rough.

"You were poisoned." Aran's voice came out sharper than he'd meant.

"I was—" They fell silent for a few moments. Then they frowned up at him. "Just now. You were saying something—"

Aran felt the blood rush to his face, and silently thanked any deity that might be listening that he'd been speaking Mountain Dialect. "I … was just saying I hoped you'd get better. Because I don't want to go talk to the crew by myself."

Istvay's eyes had fallen closed again, but at his last words, they opened them again, fighting to raise their head. "Aran," they muttered. "I … don't think we'd better talk to the crew." Their expression was grave. "If someone was willing to kill you over what we found—because I'm certain it was you that poison was aimed for —they won't hesitate to kill anyone in the crew who speaks up. If we could find a way to tell them all at once, maybe, but now—" They shook their head weakly. "We'd just be deciding who to fix the target on next."

Aran stared at them, his stomach knotting. "We'll have to come up with a new plan," he said at last. He held out his arm for Ani, and she swarmed up it, returning to her usual perch. The pouches under her eyes were puffed up, and she made no attempt to blend into his shoulder this time, instead hissing like an angry cat.

He helped Istvay to their feet, and the two of them walked slowly back towards their quarters, Istvay leaning heavily on Aran, steps stumbling. Aran helped them onto their cot, then locked the door and shoved something against it to hold it shut.

"You should … you should go back—" Istvay began in an exhausted voice. But before they finished the sentence, their eyes had drifted shut, and they were asleep.

Aran hesitated a moment, then pulled up the small chair from behind Istvay's desk and sat, his pistol in his lap—although Ani, perched on his shoulder and puffed up like a beach ball, still hissing angrily, would probably take care of any potential threat long before he had time to.

He watched the slight rise and fall of Istvay's chest as they lay on the bed, the exhausted droop of their eyelids, the unhealthy grey that lingered in the tips of their fingers and around their mouth and eyes.

There was something cold and hard and furious inside him, now that the panic had died away.

When it had been only him in danger, he could deal with that.

He'd dealt with threats his entire life, and he wasn't afraid—or rather, he was terrified, but it had become such a familiar state that he'd learned how to push it to the back of his head.

But this was different. Istvay had almost died.

Even the thought still closed up his throat with panic.

He clenched his fists until the fingernails bit into the soft flesh of his palms, the pain of it steadying.

They'd almost killed Istvay.

He couldn't let this happen.

But he wasn't sure, anymore, that anything he could do would stop it.

22

Savina

"Provide your shipping code, please," said a businesslike voice over the ship's communication system.

Savina raised her eyebrows at Joska, who sighed and leaned forward, tapping the line open. "57489. Ship's license, 87D. Registration, 55994872. We're running a short-term supplies and communications drop."

There was a pause, and Savina found her heart beating a little faster.

Beni had pushed through an information packet to the ship which should have showed the *Dolphin's* route, but it listed Joska as the captain—probably better for all concerned not to have Savina's name showing up in the database.

"Alright, you're clear to come aboard," said the voice, sounding slightly mollified.

Ahead of them the bay doors slid open, revealing the gaping entrance to a massive loading dock. Joska glanced at Savina, and Savina could read the tension in the woman's posture, the obvious reluctance with which she was carrying out the orders.

"Listen, Savina," she said quietly, her voice that wry, husky rasp that had become so familiar over the last few days. "There has to be another way to—"

Savina shook her head, pressing the muzzle of her gun a little harder into the back of Rafel's head.

He winced, and swore. "Giving me new bruises isn't going to make your gun work any better," he grumbled.

Savina was tempted to turn the pistol and hit him across the head with it, but she refrained herself. She still needed these two—no point in antagonizing them more than necessary.

She tried to ignore the small pang of guilt at the thought.

It wasn't like it would stop her from doing what needed doing. Still, guilt wasn't a feeling she was accustomed to, and it unnerved her.

Anyway, she couldn't afford to worry about it right now. Right now, the most important thing was keeping Nicolau alive. Which meant killing the judge. Everything else she could deal with later.

Joska brought the ship in and set it down gently on the bay floor, and they waited until the outer airlock doors had sealed shut behind them and the sensors on the inside of the ship flashed green.

Savina removed the pistol from the back of Rafel's head and holstered it. "Beni, make sure these two behave. I'm going to get us IDs and uniforms. I'll be back soon."

Beni nodded, coming to take Savina's place. "I've set the restraints and shut down the communications to outside the ship," they said, but there was a look on their face that said they were almost as unhappy about this as the captain was.

Savina sighed.

Beni was smart, and they were good at what they did, but they were far too trusting. They'd have been killed a hundred times over without Savina protecting them. And Savina planned to continue doing so, disapproval or no.

She gave Joska and Rafel a friendly grin, straightened her sundress, and raked her fingers through her hair. Then she sauntered down the loading ramp, looking around her with the wide-eyed wonder of a planet-side girl on her first trip to space.

"Identify the securities officers," she whispered into her wavelink. A moment later a catalogue of translucent pictures popped up in the corner of her retinal screen. With a flick of her eye, she scrolled through them until she found a woman slightly older than herself, but of similar height and build. The name 'Maria Cortez' flashed beneath the picture.

"Take me to her," Savina said, and waited a moment while the device scanned. It beeped softly, a red blinking light indicating the location of Savina's quarry, and she widened her smile and started off down the hallway.

When she reached the woman's office, she tapped politely at the door.

"Yes?" called someone from within.

"I'm here to drop off some discs," Savina called back. "Reports from the officers on night watch, I think."

The door hissed open and Savina stepped inside, peering around her with wide-eyed amazement.

The woman at the desk smiled at her. "First time on a ship like this?" she asked, a trace of kindness in her voice.

Savina nodded, still staring around her.

The woman stood. "You get used to it soon enough. Although I'm not sure you'll ever set foot on a ship with a mission like this one has again," she added, a touch of wryness in her tone.

"I heard," said Savina, turning the full effect of her smile on the woman. "I guess I'd better give you these, then."

The woman returned her smile and held out her hand. Savina rummaged in her pocket, frowning as she stepped around the desk to stand beside the woman. "They should be right—"

In a practiced movement, she pulled her other hand from under her sleeve, a long, needle-thin knife clasped between her fingers, and drove it through the woman's back, activating the electric shock at the moment she knew it touched the heart.

The woman's eyes widened for a moment. Then she toppled forward on her desk.

Savina counted to ten, then withdrew the weapon, the puncture wound so thin that only a few drops of blood welled and soaked into the woman's uniform.

Good. Not having to clean the uniform would be a definite plus.

Within a few minutes, she was dressed in the security officer's uniform. She checked her retinal screen, and when the hallway was empty, hoisted the limp body onto her shoulders with a grunt of effort and staggered down the hallway to the nearest airlock. With the woman's identification and passcode, it was easy enough to get the lock open, and she laid the body out on the floor. She stepped out of the airlock, closed the inner door, hit the outer door open, and counted to ten to give the body time to be sucked out. Then she closed it again, wiped her hands on her trousers, and, smiling cheerfully, stepped back into the deserted corridor.

One uniform and identification down. Three more to go.

By the time she got back to the ship with the stolen IDs and uniforms for Beni, Joska, and Rafel, she was whistling cheerfully, her good humour fully restored.

It was nice to be doing something she was good at again.

She walked briskly up the loading ramp and onto the *Dolphin's* flight deck. It felt a bit strange navigating the ship in full gravity, after their time in space.

When she entered, everyone was where she'd left them.

"I've got everything," she said cheerfully, zipping open her bag and dumping its contents onto the floor. "A uniform and ID for each of you."

Joska took the uniform reluctantly, her eyes hard. "There's blood on the jacket," she said quietly. Her eyes found Savina's, and there was an accusing look in them.

Savina found she couldn't quite meet the captain's gaze. She shrugged easily. "Nothing that won't come out with a bit of cold water. It shouldn't be noticeable anyway, but I do have some enzyme spray if you want to clean it up tonight."

Joska didn't say anything, but there was a dark look in her eyes as she shrugged the jacket on.

When they'd all dressed and Beni had set the IDs to their biometrics, Savina stood. She let her eyes linger for a moment on Joska, who was looking faintly mutinous, and Rafel, who was looking sullen.

"I'm here to kill the Chief Justice," she said, her voice hard. "The two of you may agree with me, or you may not—I don't care. But right now, you are wearing stolen uniforms, and you are carrying stolen IDs. If they find me, or Beni, or any single one of us, I can promise you that they won't listen to a word of your defences. You be locked in the brig, and I am very capable of making sure you die before you get home for them to hold trial." She gave a quick, mocking grin, glancing between Joska and Rafel. "And if you aren't concerned for your own safety, please remember, it's not just your own life at stake. If one of you speaks, both of you die."

Joska's eyes were hard with—not fear, but a sort of disgust. Savina wouldn't have thought that would matter, but for some reason, she found it hard to look the woman in the face. But the captain didn't say anything, just gave a curt nod.

Rafel grumbled his assent as well, and Savina nodded, smiling. "Excellent. The details of your roles should pull up on your wavelink screens as soon as you tap into your IDs. I tried to find people who were off duty tonight, since I figured we'd want some time to plan before we make our move. So. Shall we go?" She beamed at them with her most infectious, innocent smile, and gestured them out into the corridor ahead of her.

23

Alba

There was a grim silence in the small cabin as the door closed behind the young scientist.

Aran had given his report with a brusque efficiency Alba had never seen in him before, his expression flinty, and the moment he'd finished answering their questions he'd left to go back to where his friend was still sleeping. When Yosip had asked him, in some concern, if he was sure he'd be safe, he'd said, "If anyone wants to try to get past Ani, they're welcome to." And she'd had the sudden, uncomfortable recollection that this quiet young man was travelling with a creature that could probably wipe out a small city if sufficiently provoked.

He was on their side, nominally. But the idea was still not a comfortable one.

Almost a pity, really, that they couldn't use that destructive power against their unseen enemies. But the fact was, they still had very little idea who on the ship was a friend and who a foe, and an indiscriminate killing of the human population of the ship would hardly forward their goals. And she'd gathered enough to understand that releasing an irate Ani would be akin to releasing a wildfire in a dry forest—in both terms of the destruction it would cause, and their ability to control it.

"Istvay was right, though," said Yosip at last, his friendly face creased with concern. "Any attempt to subvert the crew will just lead to deaths. We can't risk it. Aran's already told the scientists, and there's not much we can do about that. But I doubt the General would risk killing all the scientific corps, and honestly, if he does intend for Aran to die, he'll need most of the remaining scientists together to make up for Aran's rather unique skillset. So I suspect—I hope, at least—the General's people will find another way to keep them quiet."

Alba nodded, trying to push back the cold that seemed to have settled permanently in the pit of her stomach. "Either way, it's out of our hands at the moment. More important to focus on next options."

She paused, chewing on her lip—a nervous gesture, and one she'd thought she'd left behind years ago. But something about being trapped on a ship with unknown enemies who clearly had no compunction about killing, was, she found, bringing back more than one nervous habit she'd thought she'd overcome.

She stopped herself with an effort and looked up. "The obvious solution is to send out a general broadcast to the ship. But if there are as many of the General's people on board as we suspect there are, there is a high chance that the moment the broadcast is begun, whoever is transmitting the broadcast will die. I do not believe we're quite that desperate yet." She paused. "I'm going to have to call Ander. We must work from the possibility that we will not be successful in getting the ship turned around before we reach the portal. I'm still hopeful that, since we have advance warning that

Cavaco's up to something, we may be able to somehow salvage the mission. It's possible, too, that our resident scientist is being overly paranoid—the fact that the aliens sent something through the portal with at least nominally peaceful intent leaves open the possibility that, in this case at least, they merely want to open a dialogue. But we can't rely on either of those possibilities.

"However, if the President is made aware of our situation, it may be that with this additional information he will be able to rally the public to our side. I imagine that no matter how popular Cavaco's made himself in my absence, with both myself and their folk-hero scientist on board, the citizenry will be outraged at any suggestion of sabotage, and doubly outraged at these murder attempts. If the ensuing furor doesn't force the General to rescind his orders to the captain and bring the ship back, at the very least it will mitigate the effectiveness of his overall strategy. I can't imagine he will realize any political benefit from his scheme once word gets out that he's intentionally sabotaged the diplomatic effort, as well as attempted to murder Aran Romeu."

Feliu nodded. "I don't suppose we have a better option at the moment," he said reluctantly. "It's not a solution. But perhaps it will buy us time to come up with one."

She gave a brusque nod, turning to Yosip. "When is your friend on duty in the communications bay?"

Yosip frowned, tapping his left temple to and muttering, "Time?" He nodded, a small smile tweaking the corners of his mouth despite the overall grimness of his expression. "She'll be coming on duty in half an hour or so. We'll give her half an hour to get settled, then I'll take you down."

In the end, all four of them went—Feliu refused to leave Alba alone with only Yosip for protection, and Yosip refused to leave Ines by herself. Ines's face had taken on a permanently stunned expression, but Alba could see her relief at not being left alone to be the next potential murder victim. So they made a larger group than Alba would have liked as they walked down the corridors towards the communications bay.

It was probably simply the time of day, but the corridors felt ominously quiet, the ship's normal bustle conspicuously absent.

She shook her head. She was seeing danger where there was none—at least, she was seeing signs of danger that were likely inaccurate, although the danger itself was certainly real enough. Still, the long walk had taken on a sinister air, every pair of eyes from a crew member or an officer brushing past them, every respectful nod to her, every quiet, friendly greeting to Yosip, a veiled threat.

When they reached the communications bay, Yosip gestured them to stay back. "I'll go talk to her, make sure that she can put me through. There are times they monitor the feed more closely, and don't want to risk her safety."

Alba nodded, and the three of them stood in a close huddle in the corner of the corridor as Yosip tapped on the door to the communications bay.

A moment later the door slid open, but the person standing there was not Adela. "What do you need?" the man asked in a bored tone.

Yosip gave him that easy smile. "Diogo," he said. "What are you doing on duty? I thought Adela was on duty today."

The man's face, which had relaxed at the friendly greeting, turned grim. "Didn't you hear?" He paused, his voice softening slightly. "I'm sorry, Yosip. She's dead."

Alba felt like a giant hand had taken hold of her chest, and was squeezing.

"Dead?" repeated Yosip softly. She couldn't see his face, but she could hear the strain and disbelief and genuine sorrow in his tone.

The man nodded. "I'm sorry to be the one to break the news. It happened three days ago. There must've been something in the rations she was allergic to—anaphylactic shock, she was gone before anyone could get to her." He shook his head. "We sent word back to her partner and their daughter. It's too bad. Her kid wasn't very old."

Even through her sudden panic, Alba could see the weary slump of Yosip's posture. "I'm … sorry to hear that," he said, his voice heavy. "My condolences, to you and to her family back on planet."

The man nodded. "Thank you." He paused. "And to you. She spoke about you frequently."

Yosip turned away as the doors slid shut behind him, and there was a weariness to his posture that hadn't been there before.

"Can you ask him to let us put a message through?" Feliu whispered urgently, but Yosip shook his head.

"No. He's not one who'd let protocol slide."

Alba could hear in his voice that even if the man would have agreed, Yosip wouldn't have been able to bring himself to ask.

"It … wasn't your fault," she found herself saying, as they walked silently back to her cabin. "You had no idea this would happen."

Even as she said the words, she could feel the discomfort in them —if it had been someone's fault, it was hers. She'd asked for the political message to be sent. She hadn't known at the time what the implications would be, but she'd certainly been best positioned to have guessed.

Yosip turned to her with a small smile, but there was a sadness in his eyes that was far deeper than she would have expected.

"She had a daughter," he said quietly. "Thirteen years old. The same age my grandson would have been, if he'd lived."

There was nothing to say to that.

Alba nodded, and they finished the short trip in silence.

Once the door had closed behind the four of them and Feliu had locked it tightly, he sank down into a chair at Alba's small table. "I don't know what else to do," he said, his voice hollow with despair. "We're just over twenty-four planetary hours away from the portal. Once we pass through it, who knows if we'll be able to send word back at all?"

"There … there might be one more thing we could try," said Ines, in her timid voice. "We could sabotage the ship. Not the supplies, I mean, but the ship itself."

They all turned to stare at her, and she shrunk under the weight of their combined gaze.

Then Yosip smiled that gentle, friendly smile, his eyes regaining a touch of their usual twinkle. "Ines," he said. "You're brilliant."

The girl looked up eagerly at his words, the hope in her face almost painful.

"I don't see how that—" Feliu began irritably, but Alba raised a hand.

"No," she said. "I think the girl might have a point. I'd like to hear what she has to say."

Ines froze, the look on her face one of blank astonishment, and Alba narrowed her eyes slightly in irritation. "I'm not doing you a favour, girl," she snapped. "But your idea is a good one."

Ines, who'd shrunk a bit at the sharpness in Alba's tone, nodded humbly.

"Go on," said Alba impatiently.

The girl swallowed hard, clearly bracing herself, then looked up. "They're going to need an extra push of propulsion to get through the portal I think, from the supplementary thrust system—at least, that's what they're saying. We can't just destroy fuel cells, because we need enough to get turned around and started back for home. But the supplementary thrust burners use a different fuel. We could destroy that. I don't think they'll dare try to get through the portal without them."

Alba raised her eyebrows in surprise, and gave the girl a brusque nod of approval. "Not bad," she said, and again, Ines froze. But the glance she turned on Alba a moment later contained a gratitude that was both unexpected, and, Alba was forced to concede, completely undeserved.

Alba narrowed her eyes at the small twinge of guilt that followed the thought, and snorted at her own foolishness. She turned to the others. "I think, as Ines said, this is our best option. I suspect having the scientist along as an extra pair of hands would be helpful, so Feliu, would you please call him on his wavelink? We'll have to do it tonight. As Feliu has reminded us, our time is quickly slipping away."

She didn't voice the rest of her thought—that perhaps, too much of it had slipped away already. Perhaps they were already too late to prevent what was coming.

24

Savina

No one stopped their small group as they walked, and Savina was glad—one look at the captain's mutinous expression told her that had she shot down an innocent crew member in front of the woman, Joska may well have crossed her arms stubbornly and refused to move a step farther, threats notwithstanding.

As it was, though, no one cast them a second glance in their crew uniforms, and she didn't even need to use the stolen IDs.

On a ship this big, they could simply blend in.

She herded her captives into a small, neat cabin which had apparently belonged to her victim, and closed and locked the door behind them. Then she leaned against it, crossing her arms and smiling.

Reluctantly, Joska and Rafel took their seats on the small cot and the chair in front of the desk, and Beni sat as well.

"I checked through the ship's log with my access from the new ID," Savina said once everyone was seated. "The ship will be through the portal in just over twelve planetary hours. I, for one, have no intention of being trapped in alien airspace. So." She turned to her sibling. "Beni? Have you looked at the security protocols surrounding the judge?"

Beni nodded. "Yes. Like we guessed, the entire diplomatic floor is covered by advanced security. It's nothing you and I haven't dealt with before, but it will take me some time to work through it—I'm usually more familiar with the systems before we go in." They paused a moment. "I checked the records on Nicolau as well. He's safe, at the moment."

Savina breathed a quick sigh of relief. At least word hadn't gotten back yet.

"I assume the Chief Justice follows the ship schedule?" she asked.

Beni nodded again. "Morning watch to evening watch, and she sleeps during night watch, it looks like."

"Midnight ship's time is in about ... six planetary hours," said Savina. "Can you do what you need to by then?"

Beni hesitated. "I'll do my best," they said at last. "But I can't make any promises. It would be easier if I had more time."

Savina bit her lip. "What if I were to sabotage the ship, give us some extra time?"

Beni gave her a small smile. "Like we did on Almeda?" they asked.

Savina grinned at the memory, the knot in her chest loosening just a little. "Just like on Almeda."

Beni nodded. "I'll go through the ship's databases and send you some specs. We just want to slow it down, right, no need to disable it entirely?"

"I wouldn't mind disabling it entirely, if that was the easiest option," Savina began, but Joska, who had been scowling silently at her through the course of the exchange, said quietly, "We're too far out in space for a rescue. You'd very likely be condemning this entire ship, and every person aboard it, to a slow, agonizing death. And I don't believe you'd do that, Savina. Because if you did, believe me that I would blow up my own ship rather than let you walk away from this."

Savina rolled her eyes heavenward. "Fine. Just to keep Joska from scolding us all day, try to find me something I can break that will be fixable."

Beni, who appeared to be fighting back a smile, nodded.

Savina turned her glare on Joska. "And you two are bloody well going to help Beni, like good little crew. And you're going to be very, very careful not to arouse any suspicion. Because right now the plan is that Beni and I will do our best to keep the ship functional. But if something were to happen, and someone got suspicious, I'd have no more incentive for people not to get hurt."

Joska returned her glare with interest, but nodded curtly.

Savina gave her a friendly smile. "Good. I knew I could count on you." She ignored Joska's dirty look and turned back to Beni. "The ID I got you should get you into whatever database you need. If you can't get into somewhere, I'm in security, so I can probably extend your access authorization." She gave the others her trademark friendly smile, then turned and slipped out the door.

She pulled up the crew list on her retinal screens as she strode down the corridor, flicking her eyes to scan through it until she saw a familiar name.

Nicolau Oller.

Her heart skipped a little in her chest, a rush of memories washing over her—her baby brother's tiny, chubby face looking up at her from a mess of dirty blankets. Beni's horrified expression as they ran their small hands over his face and shoulders and pudgy arms. The strange, empty ache in Savina's own arms when she lowered her bundle gently onto the doorstep of the bright, cheerful farm cottage, then tapped on the door, grabbed Beni's hand, and ran.

A half-caught view of a toddler laughing as the farmer spun him around in the farmyard, her eyes soft with affection, his bright with excitement. A cheerful, pudgy five-year-old tossing pebbles at a fencepost with a small dog following at his heels, the sight of him obscured through the branches of the tree Savina was hiding in.

The terror on the farmer's face at Savina's whispered warning from the roof of the cottage, the way the woman's eyes had gone wide in the moonlight. How she'd snatched up the sleepy, crying Nicolau and hushed him as her husband threw food and clothing into a bundle.

The woman's quiet tone as she's told Savina they'd take her with them if she wanted, despite the fear clear on her face.

The way Savina's chest had ached with the desire to say yes. How she'd forced herself to shake her head no. Because Nicolau wasn't safe, not yet.

A few hours later, standing in front of the now-abandoned cottage, looking up at the grim-faced men and women from the compound who'd been sent with her. Widening her eyes, telling them she was sure the farmer and her family were inside, hiding. She'd been a good liar, even at twelve.

And then, when they'd entered the empty house, bending quickly over the stacks of straw doused with lamp oil they'd set at the door, a lit incendiary in her hand.

The plex windows of the farmhouse twisted and melting, the door gaping open, flames shooting from the roof. The screams from inside of the adults who'd accompanied her, the sharp pain of her fingernails cutting through the skin of her palms.

It had been the first time she'd killed someone.

The expressions on the faces of the others in the compound when she'd returned alone, explained there had been an accident—the family with the kidnapped Old Believer child had been killed, of course, but the others who'd been sent with Savina had been caught in the blaze.

She'd always been skilled at looking innocent.

She'd kept track of Nicolau since then, of course, but she'd never tried to find him. The Head Order of the compound had been suspicious of her story, even after seeing the burned farmhouse, and she and Beni had thrown themselves into the business of the compound with all the fervour they could muster. Because not to do that might confirm the Head Order's suspicion, that Nicolau had survived.

Nicolau hadn't been important, not really—an infant meant to die. But the fact that he hadn't—the fact that he'd been raised by a family of Orthodox—was a stain on the compound that couldn't be washed away in anything but blood.

And so she and Beni had stayed. Their lives for his. And she'd never seen him since.

And now, here she was.

Her hands shook, just a little.

He was working the main deck, and she found her steps slowing slightly as she approached it. She closed her eyes for just a moment, took a deep breath, and stepped inside.

She hadn't seen him, not in person, for years. But she picked him out almost immediately—a tall, broad-shouldered young man with a friendly smile and light-brown skin, its tone a match to her own. But

—

She had to put a hand to her mouth to stifle a quick gasp.

His hair. It wasn't black, like it had been when he was a child.

It was a bright auburn.

Like hers.

Like Beni's.

And he probably didn't even realize the danger it put him in.

She clenched her teeth.

Thank goodness she'd come back—she and Beni would have to think of a way to deal with this. But only after. First thing was to keep him from getting killed.

He had a provisions sack slung over one shoulder, and was laughing, his face turned towards another crew member working alongside him.

Something caught in her chest as she watched him, a stinging ache growing behind her eyes.

She and Beni had saved him, but he'd never known them. He had his own life now, his friends, his world.

And she was going to blow it to pieces, because it was that, or let the judge kill him.

She watched until he had crossed the deck with his long, leisurely strides and disappeared behind one of the doors. Then at last, slowly, she turned.

"I found him," she whispered into her wavelink.

"You did? How is he?" Beni answered immediately.

"He's … fine. He looks happy." She cleared her throat. "Anyway, now that we know he's safe, I'm going to go through the security protocols."

She made her way back to the office where she'd found her uniform and ID. By the time she reached it, she'd regained most of her composure, and when no one was in the corridor to see, she slipped inside the office. She closed and locked the door, sat down in the comfortable seat behind the desk, and, bringing up the ship's system on the desk's holodisc, tapped into the system.

She smiled to herself as she paged through the information. The planning part of a job was familiar and soothing, a reminder that despite everything that had gone sideways in the last few days, she knew her work and was good at it.

At last the lights in the ship shifted, signalling the upcoming change to the night shift. Savina pushed back her chair, preparing to stand and stretch the kinks from her back, when a small, flashing communication on the screen caught her eye.

She frowned, pushing her chair back into the desk and tapping open the communication.

The timestamp read half a planetary hour ago.

Her frown deepened.

It was a request to come aboard.

She'd checked and double checked as they approached the ship. There was no legitimate reason for someone to request to board, let alone for the request to be accepted. That's why Beni had had to work so hard to forge their qualifications.

Cold grew in the pit of her stomach as she tapped the screen, examining the underlying file more closely.

The request had come in forty-five standard minutes ago. It had been granted half a standard hour ago. The ship had docked, the file had been closed.

And some part of her knew, even before she pulled up the specs on the unknown ship, who it would be.

A small, one-person ship, with a modern design and heavy weaponry. Registered to a Reka Soler, government agent.

She closed down the communication, and for a few moments she sat at the desk, staring at nothing.

At last she murmured, "Activate." When her wavelink came

online, she whispered, "Beni?"

"Savina? What's wrong?" Beni's voice radiated concern.

"We're going to have to speed this up," she said quietly. "I'll sabotage the ship as soon as I can get through. Once the ship's alarm goes off, it should be easier for me to slip past the judge's security. We have to kill her tonight, and get off the ship."

"What—" Beni began, then stopped suddenly. "It's her, isn't it?" they said at last in a small voice. "How did she follow us here?"

Savina shook her head grimly. "I don't know. But it doesn't really matter. We kill the judge and get out, or we all die. And Nicolau dies as well."

25

Aran

Aran surveyed the small company assembled in the corridor, his stomach churning uneasily.

They'd all simply assumed that he'd be the one leading them. Which was honestly absurd, considering he was pretty certain not a single one of them, not even the girl—Ines?—who looked like she'd startle if someone blinked at her, was as viscerally uncomfortable with human interaction as he was.

He let out a short, quick breath of combined nerves and frustration.

Not like anyone in the group had anything to recommend them, when it came down to it.

Their sabotage team consisted of himself, with whose flaws he was thoroughly and intimately acquainted; a timid, nervous Ines; Yosip, who had to be at least seventy years old, and who, although adept at leaning against the corridor wall and striking up a friendly conversation with anyone who had time to burn, did not look like someone who'd hold his own in a physical altercation; and Istvay, whose face was still drawn and pained, and who seemed to have trouble standing up without holding onto something. Aran had tried to insist they stay behind, but they'd got that stubborn look on their face, and he'd realized, with a sinking feeling, that it was useless—Istvay was coming, whether he liked it or not.

And Ani, of course. She was huddled on his shoulder, currently making herself as small as possible, having obviously picked up on the mood of the group.

"Well," he said, "I … guess we should get going."

He started down the hallway, the others following his lead. He'd put Istvay in the middle of the small group, where they were protected by him and Ani in front, and Ines and Yosip behind. It wasn't much, but it made Aran feel a little better, at least. The glare Istvay shot him told him they knew exactly what he was doing and were not impressed, but at this point Aran couldn't possibly have cared less.

Just let Istvay get out of this alive, and then they could be as angry about it as they wanted.

It was the hour of shift change onboard the ship, and the corridors were quiet. They picked their way carefully, Aran keeping an eye on Ani for any sign that she'd noticed a threat. But she stayed huddled into a ball on his shoulder, her tentacles gripping his shirt with the tightness of nerves, but not of alarm.

The engine room was five floors down, on its own separate deck. He hadn't been down there before, although Istvay probably had—they'd always been fascinated by how things ran.

The trip itself couldn't have taken more than half a standard hour, but it felt like forever. By the time he stepped off the lifts onto the first floor, Aran's nerves were wound so tightly that he could have sworn each footstep was loud enough to alert the guards.

"Everything on this floor is technically the engine room," Istvay whispered from behind him. "The fuel storage is about halfway down this corridor on the left-hand side. It'll be its own sealed room, near the centre of the ship."

Aran nodded, and they started forward again.

At the door Istvay indicated, Aran stepped back and Yosip took his place in the front.

Yosip pulled out a small electronic lock-pick kit and set about fastening it to the door lock, and Aran watched him, eyebrows raised. From the way Yosip used the lock pick, he obviously had some familiarity with it.

"Got it," Yosip said at last, satisfaction in his voice. He straightened, tapping the lock pad, and the door slid open quietly.

Aran glanced around again at their small group and sighed. "Ines," he said at last. "Can you stand watch? If there's trouble, just give us warning. Don't try to be a hero."

She gave a trembling nod, her fingers fidgeting unconsciously with the religious icon on the chain around her neck.

At least she could move quickly if someone or something appeared, which couldn't be said for anyone else in the group but him and Ani.

He contemplated, for half a moment, leaving Ani to stand guard with her, and then realized it probably wouldn't make the girl feel any better.

"We'll be as quick as we can," he whispered awkwardly.

She nodded again. Yosip laid an encouraging hand on her shoulder, and then he, Aran, and Istvay slipped inside the room.

"What are we looking for?" asked Aran once they were inside. Istvay squeezed their hand to activate their palm screen, frowning down at it. "The supplementary fuel cells look like this," they said, raising their palm so the others could see. Yosip and Aran peered over their shoulder.

"We'll split up, then," said Aran, and the three of them separated and began pulling down the bulky storage boxes to sift through them.

By the time an hour had gone by, Aran's back ached from bending over, and the three of them had hardly made a dent in the number of storage boxes—on a trip like this, there was no wasted room.

And then, from the other side of the room, Istvay called, "I found it!"

Aran and Yosip joined them as they pulled a long, smooth canister out of one of the jumble of cases on the floor and held it up triumphantly. Aran let out a quick breath of relief, then he and Yosip joined in with a will, pulling down the heavy boxes and wrenching off the lids.

"According to Ines, we'll need to destroy at least seventy-five percent of the canisters to be sure," said Yosip. "They'll have brought some extra, but even so, that should give us a safe window." He shook his head. "Destroying them all would be best, but we've spent too much time down here already. The sooner we get done and get out, the better."

"How many will they have brought, do you think?" Aran grunted, pulling one of the heavy containers from the top of a stack and lowering it to the ground with a *thump*.

Yosip shook his head as he pulled it open. "I was talking to one of the boys who works in the cargo and resupply, and he estimated there were at least a hundred and fifty cells. That should be about —" He paused, calculating. "Thirty cases, give or take."

Aran nodded grimly, then turned to snatch the edge of a crate that looked like it was about to fall from Istvay's wobbling hands.

"For heaven's sake, Istvay, let me get the boxes down," he snapped. "You can hardly stand up."

"How are we going to sabotage them?" Istvay grunted as they and Aran set the carton on the ground. They swayed a little as they straightened, and Aran grabbed for their arm.

"We're going to get Ani to spray them with her acid," he said through his teeth. "I checked through the chemical fingerprint of the supplementary fuel—her acid should ruin the cells without causing them to explode. Istvay, for the love of everything holy, go sit down."

Istvay shook their head stubbornly. "We don't have time."

Aran sucked in a short, exasperated breath, then glanced over to where Yosip was pulling down a carton that looked heavier than he was.

Aran swore through his teeth and strode over, helping the older man lower the crate.

He should have left one of those two out in the hallway, since apparently Ines was the only other able-bodied person on their damn sabotage crew.

They'd only gotten about ten cases opened when there was a sharp tap on the door.

Aran glanced up absently from where he was working. He'd finally managed to convince the others to let him take down the boxes, so Yosip and Istvay were unloading the cylinders, and at first he thought someone had dropped one.

And then he realized, and swore, tapping his palmscreen. "Ines? What is it?"

"There are people coming down the corridor," she whispered, her voice shaking. "They're not here yet, but my scanner's picking them up. There's at least a dozen of them, and it looks like they're armed. They'll be turning the corner any second."

Aran swore again. "Run! Just get away, we'll deal with what happens in here."

"There's … nowhere to run." Her voice was almost too quiet to make out. "There are more people coming from the other side."

"What is it?" asked Istvay, turning.

"Get in here, then," Aran whispered. "We'll lock the door from the inside. If it's a regular security detail, they should just pass by."

The door opened a crack and Ines slipped inside, her thin body shaking with nerves. She closed the door behind her and hit the lock, and the four of them stood, listening in frozen silence for the footsteps.

A moment later they came, the sharp click of heavy boots along the corridor. Even through the locked door, Aran could hear the muffled murmur of their conversation.

He took a deep breath, stroking one of Ani's tentacles to quiet her.

It was probably just the regular security detail. As long as there was no noise to alert them, there'd be no reason for them to—

The footsteps stopped directly outside the door.

Aran glanced around quickly, then shoved Ines towards Yosip, who was frantically beckoning them back into the maze of boxes.

No time now to try to hide what they'd been doing.

He grabbed Istvay by the shoulder, pushing them ahead of him, and sprinted after Yosip and Ines. Istvay pushed through the small gap where the other two had disappeared, and Aran followed as the door hissed open.

There were a few moments of silence as whoever had entered the room took in the scene.

"What the hell is going on in here?" a harsh female voice snapped.

The question was clearly rhetorical.

Yosip had found a narrow opening through boxes, and although it meant they'd all had to go down practically on hands and knees to get through, the four of them had managed to wedge themselves in close beside the rear wall of the fuel storage.

Aran turned, peering into the centre of the room through the cracks in the boxes.

Then he frowned, and beside him he felt Istvay stiffen as well.

"Those aren't ship security," Istvay mouthed. "They're soldiers."

Aran met his friend's eyes. Istvay looked as grim as Aran felt.

Whatever this was, it didn't bode well for either the sabotage attempt, or the diplomatic mission.

One of the soldiers was bending over the pile of cylinders Istvay had been laying out on the floor in preparation for Ani's acid to do its work. "It's the supplementary fuel cells," he said in a gruff voice, straightening. "I don't know what they were doing with them, but—" He broke off suddenly.

"If that damn scientist is behind it, or that bloody Chief Justice, it has to be sabotage," said the woman who must be the captain. Her voice was flat and deadly. "We obviously interrupted them—it looks like the seals aren't broken on all the cases yet."

She glanced over her shoulder at the other soldiers. "Spread out and find them. There's a good chance they're still in the room. But it's a damn good thing that government agent walked in and introduced herself, just in time for us to lock her up—even if we have to move sooner than we expected, at least we had a heads up that old cow of a judge was planning something."

Aran cursed under his breath.

The soldiers spread out and set to work, pulling down boxes methodically.

There were a dozen of them, and they were working much faster than he, Istvay, and Yosip had managed. It wouldn't take them more than thirty standard minutes to clear the room, and there was no way past them to the door. And watching them, Aran was suddenly very certain that, if the motley sabotage team was found, they wouldn't be taken to the brig and brought before a tribunal.

They wouldn't leave this room alive.

Something stirred on his shoulder, and he clamped his mouth shut on another curse. "Ani, no," he whispered, grabbing instinctively at Ani's tentacles, then loosening his grip before she could sting him.

Ani could kill the soldiers, certainly, every last one of them. But they had military-class uniforms with embedded sensors, and if even one of them was killed, an alert would go up across the entire ship. It wouldn't be long before the place was crawling with soldiers with guns. And yes, Ani would be happy to take on the entire ship if given the motivation, but she couldn't take all of them out at once. Even if she survived the resultant shootout, he and Istvay and the others almost certainly would not.

Besides which, he wasn't sure he was quite ready to turn the ship into a bloodbath. And if Ani went on the rampage, a bloodbath it would be.

Yosip, his face grim, had reached into his jacket, and was pulling out his pistol. "Aran," he whispered, "If you and I stay here and start shooting, we may be able to hold the soldiers' attention while the other two run for it."

Istvay's eyes narrowed. "Like hell I'm going to—" they began.

Ines interrupted them. "I've … I pulled the ship's schematics while we've been waiting," she said, her voice barely a whisper. "There's a cooling vent opening, not too far from where we are right now. It's wide enough we should be able to fit inside, and it'll bring us out somewhere near the lift. I—I know it's not perfect, but at least it's something."

They all turned to stare at her.

Aran cursed himself quietly. Why hadn't he thought to go through the ship's schematics, instead of sitting there watching the soldiers like a damn fool?

"Could you find the vent opening for us, do you think?" asked Yosip gently—the girl was squeezing her religious icon so tightly Aran was almost surprised it hadn't snapped.

She nodded and gestured for them to follow. The four of them crept along the walls, sucking in to squeeze through the narrow gap. At last Ines crouched in an area that had obviously been left to allow air to circulate. "Right here," she whispered.

Yosip crouched beside her, pulling out his lock pick, and Aran glanced worriedly at Istvay. His friend's face was drawn, their teeth clenched in grim determination, and they looked almost dead on their feet.

When he glanced down again, Ines and Yosip had removed the vent, and Yosip was placing it gently on the ground. "You go first," he whispered to Ines. "You know the way. The rest of us will follow."

Ines bobbed her head in a tiny nod and started off down the gaping tunnel on hands and knees.

Aran gestured Yosip forward. "Ani and I will go last."

Yosip nodded and started after Ines.

"You next," whispered Aran, turning to Istvay.

For a moment they looked like they were going to argue.

"You really think anything could hurt me with Ani on my shoulder?" Aran hissed in irritation.

Istvay let out a long-suffering sigh, but they dropped to their knees and followed Yosip.

Aran looked dubiously into the dark tunnel, and took a long, steadying breath.

Being killed by soldiers was objectively worse even than small, dark spaces, he reminded himself.

He dropped to his hands and knees and started after the others, pausing to reach awkwardly around behind him and set the grating loosely against the vent opening.

It wouldn't fool anyone for long, but it might give them a few additional seconds.

It was pitch black inside the ventilation tunnel, and the sounds were abnormally loud in the darkness—the scuff of knees and boots against the smooth surface of the tunnel, the way their breathing echoed. The smell of his own sweat and fear, a soft curse from ahead of him where Istvay must have bumped against something. The walls were narrow enough that Aran could feel the roof against his back, and his shoulders almost brushed the walls on each side. He closed his eyes, even though in the dark it made no difference whatsoever, and began counting backwards from one hundred.

Eighty-seven. Eighty-six. Eighty-five.

His fingers tapped a soft rhythm on the floor in time with his count.

He wasn't going to panic. They weren't going to be in here forever, they'd get to the end soon. His breath was coming faster, his throat tightening.

"Aran?" Istvay whispered over their shoulder, concern in their voice. "Are you alright?"

He couldn't answer—at least, not truthfully. He was so far from alright it was laughable.

And then, from ahead, Ines's timid voice. "I'm at the end."

Aran took a deep breath, refraining himself with an effort from shoving his way forward until he could push through into the open air.

He'd be out in a moment. It would be fine.

He could hear the shuffling as Ines and Yosip switched places, the soft, metallic ting of the lock pick. And then the striated shadows ahead were replaced with a solid square of light through which he could see the white of the hallways.

He sucked in a breath, only the residual dizziness making him realize how long he'd been holding it.

He waited until Istvay was out, then forced his shaking muscles to move at a deliberate pace, rather than a panicked rush, as he clambered out of the dark hole.

He straightened in the corridor, leaning up against the wall, and closed his eyes against the sickening dizziness. He felt Istvay's hand on his arm, and he clung to the sensation.

It was fine, they'd all be fine.

When he'd recovered sufficiently, he opened his eyes and turned to the others. They were watching him, and he tried to force a smile. "Let's get out of here while we still can," he whispered.

Yosip, who was crouched on the floor replacing the vent cover, stood, shaking his head grimly. "There's no way we get back down here again once we leave, not with the security they'll put in after this."

"We'll deal with it when we get out of this alive," said Istvay through their teeth. "Let's go."

Aran set a quick pace for the lifts, and the others followed. He could hear, faintly, the noise of a dozen soldiers from inside the fuel storage room, but apparently no one had noticed their escape yet.

When the lift let them out on the second floor, he could feel his muscles go weak with relief.

They'd made it out alive. Istvay was right, the rest they could deal with later.

Their small group started briskly down the almost empty corridor, Aran in the lead, to the lifts that led to the diplomatic section of the ship. Aran turned a corner, and almost ran into a young woman in the uniform of a crewmember. She had wide eyes, a broad, pleasant face, and an innocent smile, the picture of a country girl fresh from the mountains.

"Hello," she said in a friendly voice. She paused a moment. "I'm sorry to bother you, but I saw some soldiers heading in the direction you're coming from. Is anything wrong?"

Aran give a quick shake of his head. "No. I … think they were headed for the engine room."

She hesitated, then sighed. "Well, I don't want trouble with soldiers. I'll come back later." She paused a moment. "I didn't realize there were that many soldiers on board."

"Nor did I," said Aran grimly. "If you'll excuse me—"

She nodded and stepped to one side, and they made their way quickly past her.

They were almost at the main lift. Aran could feel the tension in his shoulders loosening, just a little.

And then, just as they reached the lift doors, a voice called out from behind him. It was so entirely unexpected, and so impossibly, horribly familiar, that he froze.

"Aran," said Emeric. "Where are you going in such a hurry? I think we should sit down and have a talk."

26

Savina

Savina stared after the ragged group stumbling towards the lift. Half of them looked terrified out of their minds, and the other half looked like they were about to keel over.

But their words had confirmed the sense of unease that had been tightening around her chest.

Something was wrong. Something was very, very wrong, and it appeared sabotage was suddenly off the table.

For a long moment, she hesitated.

In the end, it wasn't much of a choice—she didn't have time to spare. She had to kill the judge, tonight, and then she and Beni had to get off the ship.

"Beni," she whispered into her wavelink. "There's been a change of plans. I'll have to go straight to the Chief Justice."

There was a moment of silence from the other end of the line, then Beni's voice. "Alright," they said, worry thick in their tone. "I have all the specs, and I'll send them through to you. But without any distraction, the plan I came up with—"

"It's either I go in now, or we're all killed before we can leave this damn ship," Savina snapped. "I'd rather take my chances with the judge."

Beni didn't answer.

A moment later, the security details flashed across Savina's retinal screen. She scanned through them. "Thanks," she said shortly. "If you don't hear from me in three hours, something's gone wrong. Get Nicolau if you can, and get off the ship."

"Call me if you get into trouble, please," said Beni.

The familiar worry in their tone stiffened Savina's resolve.

This wasn't about revenge, although she had to admit that killing the woman who had haunted her nightmares since childhood would be immensely satisfying. It wasn't even about money.

This was about keeping Beni and her baby brother alive. This was about everything she'd worked for and suffered for her entire life.

This was a matter of survival.

She remembered the government agent's face, her cold smile and mocking eyes. The way she'd tried to slide her knife across Savina's throat, and how Savina had for a moment been unable to breathe, half because of the knife, and half because of the breathtaking antagonism in those cold eyes.

She shivered at the sudden, unsettling thrill of the memory.

A very immediate matter of survival, in her case.

Getting past the security between the second and third floor, and then into the diplomatic section of the ship, took longer than she'd expected. Still, it was only half an hour past midnight, ship's time, when she stepped at last into the corridor where the Chief Justice was housed. She wiped the blood fastidiously from her fingers onto her dark trousers—she liked dark trousers for the fact they didn't really show bloodstains—and then started at a nonchalant pace down the hallway.

Beni would have disabled the cameras, and the blood on her fingers bore testament to the fact there would be no guards coming down the hallway until the next shift.

She reached the judge's door and pulled out a lockpick, slipping it into the sensor and moving it deftly. A moment later the lock clicked, and she pushed the door open just enough to allow her to slip through.

Once inside, she blinked to activate the infrared on her retinal screen and scanned the room.

She frowned, scanning it again more slowly.

Then she swore.

Alba wasn't here.

"Savina? Did something happen?" Beni's voice was even more worried than usual.

Savina couldn't blame them—neither she nor Beni was used to a single job going as badly as every last damn thing had gone over the past few days.

"Where the hell would a seventy-something-year-old woman go at bloody midnight?" she whispered through her teeth.

"She's gone?" The worry in Beni's tone was sharpening.

"If that damned Joska warned her—" Savina began, murder in her voice.

"She couldn't have. I put a block on her wavelink. She couldn't have contacted anyone but me." Beni paused. "Maybe the judge moved to a different schedule, and it wasn't updated on the databases."

Savina gave a grunt of irritation and tapped the wavelink off.

Wherever she was, the woman couldn't possibly stay out all night. It didn't matter when she was killed, really, as long as it was quick.

She glanced around the small cabin.

The judge's desk, and in it, a locked drawer that looked around the right size to contain a holodisc safe.

In a few deft motions Savina had the lock on the drawer open, and then a few moments later, the safe itself. The judge had decent security, but Savina had broken into so many safes she could have done it in her sleep.

She found the mission discs relatively quickly, and pulled them out. They were encrypted, of course, but the codebreaker set into her wavelink was the most advanced on the market, and it made short work of even the government ciphers.

She pulled one open and tapped it to her wrist, and watched the transcribed words scroll slowly across her retinal screen.

"… diplomatic mission to the aliens, in order to bring back a cure for the defect."

"… confident that a peaceful solution is possible, and indeed vital, if we wish to advance our overall objective to remove the military's position as a branch of government."

"… wisest course of action, taking into account the fact that there have been no wars or major hostilities in the past several decades. The last major episode of inter-group hostilities was the Cleansing, the sectarian violence inflicted by the Orthodox Church against the so-called Old Believers, or Corpus Dei sect, at the turn of the last century."

"… can prove diplomacy's ability to solve problems without resorting to bloodshed, as long as …"

A cold unease spread through her as she scanned the briefings.

She'd known, from the moment she'd heard about this so-called diplomatic mission, that it was a front to finally wipe out the Old Believers. The Orthodox Church and its government supporters wouldn't admit it publicly and risk warning their victims, of course, but in the Judge of Heretics' private briefings, they'd have no such concerns.

But it wasn't there.

—no wars or major hostilities in the past several decades—the Cleansing, the sectarian violence inflicted by the Orthodox Church against the so-called Old Believers—the turn of the last century.

It was a lie, just like everything else. It had to be. Orthodox propaganda, something to make her and the rest of the Old Believers let down their guard. There was no way everything her mother had told her, everything she'd learned as a child, every terror-filled nightmare she'd woken from, sobbing, only to see the confirmation of her fears in her parents' faces—there was no way that could be false.

It was impossible.

The purpose of the mission was to kill the Old Believers. It must be.

But—

She found herself scrambling desperately now, pulling up the rest of the handfuls of discs.

More of the private files, private Council notes from the days and weeks leading up to the mission.

"… highest priority must be to maintain the ability of the government as an entity to preserve a peaceful and orderly society, which leads to the inescapable conclusion that General Cavaco and the military branch be disbanded …"

She read through the words again. She must have missed something. She had to have missed something, or misunderstood the words. Why would the Judge of Heretics want the Military Committee disbanded?

It made no sense. General Cavaco would be the one leading the armed forces to seize the Old Believers when Alba made her pronouncement, that's what they'd always told her in the compound.

Maybe the Chief Justice just wanted the military under her own control, that was all. Maybe she was worried that even General Cavaco would balk at the orders she was planning to give.

But even as Savina thought it, it felt uncomfortably false.

It was the Judge of Heretics and the head of the Military Committee, working hand in hand, who'd destroy the compound and everyone in it, torture the children to death in front of their families' eyes and then burn the adults alive. That was what the Head Order had preached Savina's whole life.

But … it had been the Head Order of her own compound who'd decided her baby brother should die. Her own mother who placed her crying infant, no more than a week old, into a hole in the ground, to be buried alive as he screamed in terror.

It had been Savina, twelve years old, who'd burned people alive for it.

"… work towards outreach and education for cult-members and fanatical groups of whatever religious or other persuasion, and, by reducing the influence of the military in decision making, avoid a repeat of the Swan River Massacre a decade ago. We are confident that with increased educational opportunities, as well as community outreach, we can …"

There was a picture further on in the briefing, President Ander Seguer. He was pale-skinned, with mousy-brown hair. And standing behind him in his circle of ministers was another man, clearly a councillor, brown skinned, but with hair of an incongruent bright auburn.

An Old Believer, then. Or at least someone from Old Believer stock.

She reached up unconsciously, touching her own hair.

How long had she kept its colour hidden? Her whole life? Because she'd known it would single her out. Make her a target, whenever Alba and Cavaco finally made their move. They always told her, in the compound, that anyone she saw outside with that distinctive auburn hair and brown skin was a dupe at best, a slave at worst.

But this was a member of the government. One of the President's own ministers.

A dupe, maybe. But a powerful one if so.

It was propaganda, lies, it must be. It had been planted here for her.

Except it hadn't. Because the judge had no idea she'd be coming. No one had known.

The warrant Reka had been carrying hadn't mentioned Savina's religion. Just her career, and the councillor she'd killed three months ago.

Savina hadn't lost sleep over that killing, any more than any other —the woman had been Orthodox, and Savina had known, deep in her bones, that the woman would have done the same to her if given the chance. She wouldn't have needed even the slight justification of a payment. She was Orthodox and a councillor, and therefore her whole life had been dedicated to the destruction of Savina and everyone like her.

Except—

Except surely Alba's private briefings would have mentioned … something. Surely if this had all been part of the plot to kill the Old Believers, it would have been mentioned, at least.

Scattered throughout the briefings and Council notes, there were some relevant articles from the recent news packets. She scanned through them, unable to make herself stop.

Celebration of religious freedom in the capital—parades move down the Vermelhas Boulevard.

Monument to those killed in the Cleansing raised in Floras de Memoira Square.

Under the headline, a picture of a glowing holostatue, where tired, noble-looking people—adults and children both—sank down to their knees, hands outstretched, faces resolute at the prospect of death. The plaque under it read, i*n memory of those who died for their convictions.*

Numbness was spreading through her, so she wasn't sure, really, if her body still belonged to her.

She'd known about these things. She'd read them in the news packets, seen the statue herself. She'd always assumed they were a ploy, a cynical manipulation on the part of the people in power to lure the remnants of the Old Believers into complacence.

But now—

No matter how far she read, no matter how deep into the briefings she searched, there was no mention of a plot against the Old Believers, except for what had happened a century past. No mention of religion at all, except as a side note—a news article about preparations for one of the customary religious holidays, where a holographic icon would be paraded through the streets to cheering crowds, perhaps, but clearly more an excuse to celebrate than a demonstration of religious fervour. A mention of a man attacking a youth, shouting slurs about their beliefs, and a note that the man had been taken into custody and charged.

When the scrolling stopped, Savina sank onto the cot, her legs suddenly unwilling to hold her up.

Her head was spinning, her stomach uneasy with nausea.

It couldn't have been a lie. It was her whole life. It was everything she'd known, everything she'd ever been told. Her whole life had been based on an existential struggle, her and her family and their small, remote compound against a system engaged in a holy war, dedicated to their destruction. It had been the only thing that had given meaning to her desperate fight for survival, the beatings she'd endured and the ones she'd watched Beni take. Perhaps it had been bad, but it had been better than the alternative, better than the horrific, corrupt system outside their compound. It gave her something to hold onto while she stifled her sobs and curled in on her bruises—when she was young and stupid, it had been for the Mystery's sake, the Mystery made flesh who'd smiled down on her benevolently and blessed her suffering. And then when she'd grown too old to believe that, it was because the rest of the world was a place that would kill her because of the beliefs of her parents. The world was evil, and what she'd suffered was acceptable, because it was better than what would have happened to her outside.

She felt like she was floating, her mind not quite attached to the rest of her.

"Savina!"

The voice through her wavelink jerked her out of her stupor, but it took a moment for her sluggish thoughts to recognize the voice as Beni's, and the note in it as panic.

"Savina, you have to get out of there! There are people—"

The communication broke off abruptly. Savina jerked to her feet. "Beni? What happened? Beni, are you—"

The door to the judge's cabin burst open, and a group of grim-faced soldiers stepped through.

"Who are you?" snapped the leader, turning to glare at Savina. "Why are you in Alba's cabin? Are you colluding with her? We caught that government agent she called in. Are you working with her?"

"This must be one of the crew she's subverted," said another of the soldiers. She turned over her shoulder. "Take her."

Soldiers grabbed for her. Savina slipped easily free of their grasping hands, the threat waking muscle memory, even if her brain was still sluggish and slow. She yanked out a short, deadly sharp knife, plunging it into the throat of the soldier who'd grabbed for her, and as the woman collapsed, choking in a spray of blood, Savina spun, jerking her pistol out of her boot. She got off three shots, and sent three soldiers down, before someone else sprang forward.

She turned with the knife, slashing at her attacker's arm, but their body armour turned the blade, leaving only a surface-deep cut. The soldier grabbed her, yanking her arm around behind her back, but she stamped her foot on the floor, a small blade in the toe of her boot clicking out, and kicked, aiming for soft tissue below her captor's knee. The man dropped, grunting in agony, and Savina yanked her arm free—and then something slammed into the back of her head, and she staggered, the world wavering in front of her eyes. There was the whistling hum of a bolas, and a thin cord caught around her ankles, the three hard balls slamming painfully against her calves. She stumbled, and another bolas struck her and wrapped around her torso, pinning one arm to her side.

She yanked a knife from the sheath behind her neck with her free hand and flung it, and had the satisfaction of watching a soldier stagger back, clutching at her face. And then someone had her by her other arm, and slapped an electric tranq onto her wrist.

The shock jolted through her, freezing her muscles. By the time it released, she was thoroughly bound.

The leader stepped forward, his eyes narrow, and slapped Savina hard across the face. Savina spat out a curse against the pain of the blow, but it was half-hearted.

Even the sight of the cabin, spattered now with blood, wasn't enough to rouse any emotion other than a faint, distant despair.

What did it matter, at this point?

She was dragged out of the cabin and down a corridor, then another. She couldn't force her numb mind to pay attention to the twists and turns.

It couldn't be a lie. Her entire life couldn't be a lie. The looks on her parents' faces, the fear, the sorrow—

The soldiers shoved her roughly into an empty cabin. She lost her footing and fell hard on her face, unable to catch herself with bound hands.

The man who'd shoved her laughed. "Don't worry," he crooned. "I'm sure we'll find a way to make your death painful. You like violence, you showed us that. We'll see how much you enjoy it when it's turned on you."

He stepped back, and the door slid shut. There was the click of a lock, then another click which must have been an exterior lock.

Even if she still had her lockpick somewhere on her, she wouldn't be able to get through that.

She rolled painfully over.

Now that the adrenalin of the fight was fading, she could feel the bruises rising across her face and along her body, the latest ones on her knees and elbows where she'd tried to catch herself as she fell, the throbbing ache in her shoulder from the pulse wound two days earlier.

She could guess, now, why Beni's communication had cut off so quickly.

It looked like the soldiers were going through all the crew who they hadn't predetermined were on the General's side. Which, thanks to her disguises, likely meant Beni, Rafel, Joska, as well as her.

They hadn't asked for any of this. Joska had been dragged into it, and, despite Savina's lingering irritation over the thruster repair and the payment of past fees—she'd saved Savina's life. She'd done it more than once.

And now she'd die for it.

Savina lay where she'd fallen, staring up at the blank, sterile white of the ceiling in the cramped ship's cabin that had become her prison.

This time when the tears burned at the corners of her eyes, no amount of blinking would push them back.

27

Alba

"Where the hell are they?" Alba snapped.

Feliu looked up, faintly shocked.

He shouldn't be. Just because she put on a refined face for the idiots on the Council didn't mean she couldn't swear when the occasion demanded.

But then, Feliu had seemed genuinely shocked earlier that day at being gestured by Yosip, who had clearly meant it as a friendliness, to sit in the chair. He'd stood stiffly at her back for a while, and finally, at her irritated insistence, taken a ginger seat on the edge of one of the smaller stools.

"I'm … not certain, Madam," he said at last, and she heard the concern in his tone.

"Time," she snapped, flicking her eyes to activate the wavelink, and glancing at the retinal display in the corner of her vision.

Well past 2300 hours, ship's time.

The others had been gone three full hours by now.

She shook her head and pushed herself from her chair. "Has

anyone contacted you?" she asked the clerk.

He shook his head. "No, Madam. I'm sorry."

She leaned against the desk with one hand, closing her eyes for just a moment.

There'd been four of them on the sabotage team. Aran, ridiculous as he was, was obviously skilled in matters of survival. His friend too, probably. And Yosip was friends with every person on the entire ship, apparently, and Ines, timid though she was, was smart.

But …

She'd seen them, gathered in the hallway—Istvay, their face drawn and unhealthy, looking barely able to stay on their feet; Yosip, smiling and kindly, but as old as Alba herself, and certainly not a fighter; Ines, practically shaking with nerves; and Aran, with soul-deep terror lurking behind his eyes.

"How long should this have taken them?" she asked.

It wasn't the first time she'd asked the question. But Feliu knew better than to remind her of that when she was in this mood, and merely sighed.

"I think we calculated that it could take them up to two hours by the time they got to the fuel storage room, found what they needed, destroyed it, and then got back up here."

And it had been almost three hours.

"Something's gone wrong," she said.

Feliu shifted uneasily. "Madam," he began, then paused.

He wanted to contradict her, she could hear it in his voice. But he couldn't.

Because the fact was, she was almost certainly right.

"Madam," he began again. "Be that as it may, I'm not sure what we can—"

She straightened, pushing back her shoulders like she had decades ago when, as the youngest member of the Judiciary Committee, she'd had to try to fool people into thinking she wasn't terrified every time she stepped into the Council Building.

She was terrified, honestly. But she'd been considering this possibility ever since the others had left. Ever since she'd seen them standing there in the corridor, and realized what a slim chance they had of making it out of this successfully.

Or even alive.

She ignored the thought, because somehow, she couldn't bring herself to imagine any one of those four lying still and cold on a sterile corridor floor. Aran, with his quiet, dreamy smile; Istvay, who watched Aran, when they knew he wasn't looking, as if he was the most important thing in their world; nervous, timid Ines, with her bright smile when praised, and her clever ideas spoken in a barely audible whisper; Yosip, the way his eyes twinkled, the way he had of making everyone around him feel at ease—even her, although she'd never admit it, even to herself.

The thought of any one of them dead, body stiffening, eyes blank and staring—

She shook her head resolutely.

No. She wouldn't think of it.

"Well," she said sharply, turning to Feliu, "thankfully, I have a secondary plan."

He stared at her blankly. "Madam?"

"If they're not back by now, and have not contacted us, the likelihood is that they've either been stopped somehow, or captured." She didn't speak the other possibility aloud, and was unreasonably grateful when Feliu refrained as well.

"Therefore, it appears our opponents are determined to do whatever it takes to advance their agenda, the rest of us be hanged.

We tried warning the crew piecemeal and learned quickly that was no solution at all. If they'll kill their lead scientist, certainly they won't hesitate to kill members of the crew. However—" she paused a moment, steeling herself. "If I am able to broadcast the information via the general communication lines, I believe that might do the trick. I understand my name still holds some sway, even on this ship on which I'm apparently not the final authority. I very much doubt that even our bloodthirsty friends will be able to kill the entire crew —logistics of the matter aside, they can't very well pilot the ship without assistance."

Feliu was staring at her. "But—" he began. "Madam, we talked about this. If you are broadcasting, they'll know—"

She glanced at him sharply. "Yes. They'll know who it came from, and where to find me. At the time we discussed the option, we were not out of alternatives. However—" she paused a moment, to be certain her voice wouldn't shake. "However, it appears the others have not succeeded at their mission. And if getting this ship turned around and the general population alerted to General Cavaco's perfidy requires me to be locked up or—or otherwise incapacitated, I hardly think I can countenance regret at such a sacrifice."

He was staring at her, his mouth half open, an expression of horror on his face.

Something twisted in her chest, but she couldn't decide if it was gratitude, or affection, or fear, or guilt. "Don't bother trying to talk me out of it," she said briskly. "I can tell you right now you'll be wasting your breath."

"I'll—I'll come with you, of course, Madam." His voice was uncharacteristically husky. "Besides, you'll need someone to set up the broadcast system."

She hesitated.

But he was right. She'd never needed to know how to set up communication equipment. And there was at least a solid chance that, as she'd be the only one broadcasting, she'd also be the only one whose death would be a necessity.

"If you choose to come, your assistance would be appreciated," she said at last. There seemed to be something caught in her throat, making speaking more difficult than usual.

The old clerk nodded and reached down to pick up the pistol on the table. But she caught the suspicious glint in his eyes, and found her own eyes watering unaccountably.

He brushed his sleeve quickly across his face, and after a moment, cleared his throat respectfully. "Madam," he said, his voice gruff. "I'm ready if you are."

"Very well. No use in waiting around, then." She stepped to the door, and it hissed open at her command.

She took a deep breath, touching the small, delicate pistol tucked into her coat pocket.

She wasn't certain, if it came to it, that she'd have the stomach to use it.

Best to hope, then, that she wouldn't have occasion to find out.

She stiffened her back and stepped forward in the hallway, Feliu following close behind.

The moment she stepped out of her cabin, she knew her suspicions were correct. Something was wrong. The ship was a flood of noise and confusion, shouts coming over the general ship lines and through the amplifiers, footsteps running heavily down adjoining corridors.

She forced herself to keep walking.

She was doing nothing wrong, she reminded herself. Only an evening stroll.

The distance to the broadcast dock was not far, according to the directions on her retinal screen. But the moment the lift doors opened, she almost stepped directly into the path of a company of grim-faced soldiers, escorting a small huddle of crew in restraints down the corridor. She stepped back quickly, but thankfully they didn't glance in her direction.

"Madam," Feliu whispered from behind her. "I'm not certain we'll be able to get through at all, let alone in time to make a difference. We're only a few hours away from the portal."

She fixed him with her coldest stare. "Do you intend to spend your time prophesying doom, or do you intend to help me?"

He straightened, shutting his mouth abruptly, and she turned to the corridor.

It was empty, at least for the moment, and she stepped forward, praying to any deity that might be listening.

Her legs were shaking, but she fought not to let it show.

Just before they reached the booth, a soldier rounded the corner at a run and almost plowed into them. Alba shot the woman such a look that the woman mumbled an apology and slunk back like a scolded schoolchild, apologizing shamefacedly before continuing down the corridor.

But it wouldn't last. No amount of bluffing could last forever, Alba's lifetime in politics had taught her that.

And then they were standing in front of the doorway to the broadcast booth. She braced herself, then placed a hand on the sensor and stepped through the door as it hissed open.

The three communications officers turned to stare at them, and Alba gave them a frosty glare. "Please conduct me to a booth, immediately," she demanded, praying that none of them were in the General's pay.

"Who—" one of the men began, but the woman next to him elbowed him, and Alba heard her name hissed in a sharp whisper. The man's face went suddenly slack with terror. "I'm—I'm sorry, Madam Chief Justice," he said hastily, straightening so quickly it was almost comical. "Right away, come with me …"

She and Feliu follow the man down to the booth. He opened the door and let her in. "Will you be needing anything else?" he asked nervously.

She glanced around. She had no idea how to work any of this equipment, but Feliu caught her eye and give a quick shake of his head.

"No," she said. "That will be all, thank you."

He nodded and left, sidling through the door as if she were a dangerous creature he didn't dare turn his back on.

When he was gone, Feliu locked the door, his shoulders sagging in relief. "I didn't think we'd make it this far," he muttered. "But let's not push our luck."

"I assume that you know how to set up this equipment?" she snapped, nerves making her voice sharper than she intended.

He nodded and set to work, placing his pistol on the table to free his hands. She dropped into the chair at the booth, closing her eyes and leaning her head back wearily. Her legs were so shaky she wasn't sure how long they would have held her up anyway.

Two weeks ago, the thought of sitting here in a communications booth on a ship that carried thousands of people towards an uncertain future, in full expectation of her death, would have been laughable. If someone had told her, she would have assumed they were drunk, or possibly mad.

But here she was.

This would be her legacy, then. Not the woman who'd dismantled the military branch of the government, but the woman who'd been murdered trying to prevent a coup. And whether she was vilified for it or lauded for it would depend entirely on whether or not she succeeded.

"Madam." The huskiness was back in Feliu's voice, and he was avoiding her eyes, as if that was enough to keep her from seeing the sheen of tears. He cleared his throat. "Madam, it's ready."

She closed her eyes for just a moment, and for just a moment, allowed herself to regret what had brought her here.

But she found, in the end, she couldn't. If she were given these decisions to make again, she would have made each of them in the same way she had.

In the end, perhaps that was a satisfying way to go to one's death after all.

Alba nodded, took a deep breath, and leaned forward as the light above the booth flickered green.

"Officers, diplomats, members of the crew," she began in the firm, ringing tones she used to address the Council. Her voice was old now, but still clear and resonant as it passed through the communication system, booming out across every amplifier on the main deck. "This is Chief Justice Alba Espina. I was appointed by the council to lead this diplomatic mission. However, I am afraid that both you and I have been sent here under false pretences.

"The captain of the ship, among others, is working under the employ of General Cavaco. And it appears the General has an interest in our failure, if not our deaths. During the course of our flight, our lead scientist, Aran Romeu, discovered fragments of crewed ships that were destroyed on the other side of the portal. We do not know yet what this indicates, but common sense dictates that it is not news to be brushed aside. The captain has refused to turn the ship around despite my clear orders, nor will he allow us to pause and reconsider our options in light of this new information."

She paused a moment. "I understand this is an irregular message. However, due to attempts on my life, this was the only option open to me. I would ask, therefore, that as you value your lives, you take matters into your own hands. The ship cannot run un-crewed. I ask —"

The green light blinked out abruptly, the equipment going suddenly dead.

Alba turned. "Feliu?" She was unable to hide the worry in her tone.

"Madam," he said. "I don't know—"

There was the *crash* of something slamming into the locked door.

"Madam," Feliu began, straightening quickly. "You must—"

There was another crash, and this time the door burst open, sagging in on its tracks, the lock shattered.

In the doorway stood at least a dozen soldiers. The three in front were carrying heavy shock-rams. Behind them the other soldiers held their pulse rifles, the small, deadly muzzles pointed directly at her.

Alba swallowed down her fear and forced herself to push back her chair. She stood, straightening to her full height, which was still barely at the level of Feliu's shoulder.

A strange peace had settled over her.

She was going to die. She'd never know now whether or not she'd succeeded.

Perhaps it was for the best.

"Alba Espina?" the lead soldier snapped. "Step away from the communications booth, now."

Alba raised her chin. "May I ask the meaning of this?" she said in her iciest tone.

For a moment, no one moved.

"Stop talking! Get away from the booth!" one of the soldiers shouted, his voice shaking with nerves. Before she could move to obey, she saw his finger tighten on the trigger, his muscles tense as he pulled the gun in tighter to his shoulder.

"Madam Chief Justice!" Feliu began, his eyes widening in horror. He threw himself across the room towards her even as she opened her mouth to shout at him to stay where he was.

The barrel of the gun twitched slightly with the kick, and, as if in slow motion, she saw Feliu stumble as he stepped in front of her, saw his body sag, saw the red blossom across the crisp white of the shirt he always wore. She saw him slump to the ground, and she heard shouting around her, and saw the soldiers moving forward, but for some reason, she couldn't seem to pay attention to any of it.

All she could see was her old clerk's body, limp on the floor.

It was all she could see even as they grabbed her roughly, pulling her arms painfully behind her back and fastening them with restraints, as the captain screamed at her subordinate, as someone hauled Feliu up like a cargo sack and shoved Alba ahead of them through the door.

"All right, Madam Chief Justice," said the squad captain, when Alba was pulled up in front of him. "You've caused enough trouble, I think. From now on, you'll stay in your cabin." He grinned. "Don't worry, we cleaned the blood off the walls just for you."

She was pushed down the corridors, soldiers in front of and behind her, muscles aching at the unaccustomed abuse.

But still, all she could see was Feliu's limp body, scarlet staining the pristine white of his shirt.

In the end, her pistol had done her no good at all.

28

Aran

Aran turned slowly, his heart pounding.

Yosip and Ines stood in front of him, frozen.

And behind him stood Istvay, one hand supporting themself against the wall, a gun shoved against the back of their head.

Emeric smiled at him from the centre of the corridor. "Aran," he said again. "Lovely to see you again. But I really think you should consider—"

Aran could barely hear him through the fury pounding in his brain.

"Don't damn well touch Istvay," he hissed.

Emeric just had time to look surprised before Aran launched himself forward, slamming into the man standing behind Istvay. The pistol went flying, and Aran and the man landed on the ground, grappling.

Distantly, he could hear shouts and the dull sound of blows, and he realized, dimly, that the entire corridor behind him had broken out into fighting.

He didn't care.

He drove his fist into his opponent's face, over and over. The man was spitting blood now, but didn't stop trying to push Aran away and grab for Istvay.

Something slammed into the back of Aran's head.

His grip loosened, his vision momentarily blurring as a woman leaned over him, a grim smile on her face, a metal baton in her hand.

There was a hissing sound, too, like a dozen teakettles steaming at once, and for a moment he thought the blow had affected his hearing—and then he blinked up in time to see Ani boiling across the floor, eye-pouches puffed out, whole body turned a furious orange and electric green.

She swarmed up the leg of the woman who'd hit him, barely slowing as she moved from the horizontal to the vertical, and then she was horizontal again as the woman went down, foaming from the mouth, her body stiff and welts like green warning signs flecked up her skin where Ani's tentacle spikes had made contact.

Ani launched herself from the woman's convulsing body as she fell, spreading her skin flaps to sail across the corridor and land on the face of a man who was in the process of bringing up a pistol to point at Aran. The man sputtered, gave a choked scream, and died, his muscles jerking even in death.

The man Aran had been fighting twisted to watch, his own fight forgotten, his face an almost comic picture of horror—or it would have been comic, if the situation hadn't been so thoroughly horrific —and then Ani had landed on his back, and his face tightened in a rictus grin, his hands loosening from Aran's throat as his body began to spasm.

"Ani, come here, Ani, it's—" Aran began frantically.

From the corner of his eye he saw a man yank out a pistol, levelling it at Ani and Aran as he backed down the corridor. Ani must have seen it too, because she ducked under Aran's outstretched hand and slithered towards the man, tentacles pulling her along in a snakelike motion that was deceptively quick.

"Ani!" shouted Aran, but it was no use. She wasn't going to listen to him when she was wound up like this.

Emeric stood halfway down the corridor, and there was calculation on his face, under the shock.

As Aran watched, he reached out, pressing the airlock control. The inner door hissed open, just in time for the man with the pistol to back into it, apparently hardly noticing where he was going, his full attention focused on the hissing Ani slithering towards him.

Aran realized what Emeric intended a split second later. He scrambled to his feet, heart stuttering with horror as Emeric hit the button again, sealing Ani and her victim inside.

He sprinted down the corridor. "No! Emeric, please, just—"

It was too late. Emeric hit the control, and Aran could hear the pressure in the airlock suck away as the outer door slid open.

He threw himself against the door desperately, just in time to see, through the plex porthole, the tip of a tentacle, orange with alarm, grasping at the edge of the door.

"Ani!" he screamed.

The tentacle tip slid free, and she was gone.

There was a *hiss* as the outer airlock door slid shut behind her.

Aran slumped against the inner door, his mind gone blank with despair.

Everything around him was strangely foggy.

Ani was gone.

He couldn't quite make himself believe it was real. Maybe this was a nightmare, and he'd wake up to her quiet, chirruping purr as she nudged his face, begging, in her unsubtle way, for food.

When he had the strength in his legs to straighten, he turned wearily.

The bodies of the people Ani had killed lay twisted on the ground, their skin a gruesome purplish-green where the poison had spread. Someone had grabbed Istvay, now that the danger was over, and again a pistol had been shoved up against the back of their head. Istvay's eyes were wide with shock and pain, and this time, Aran didn't try to fight.

It would have been useless, anyways.

Yosip and Ines were being held as well, arms pulled roughly behind their backs.

"Do you want to see someone else you care about die for you?" asked Emeric, his expression one of mocking sympathy. "Or are you ready to come nicely?"

Aran gave a dull nod. They approached him warily at first, but he didn't struggle, just let them grab his arms and fasten them behind his back with a restraining cord.

He didn't struggle as they were shoved along the corridors, and when the door to his cabin was pushed open and he and Istvay shoved inside, he didn't try to fight back. They'd pushed Ines and Yosip into the cabin next door, and he'd seen Ines's frantic gaze, pleading for him to do something—but he hadn't.

The door slid closed, and someone attached an external lock.

He glanced quickly over at Istvay. They were slumped on the cot, their face bloodless, their eyes closed, as if the effort of staying conscience was all they could muster.

They weren't bleeding, at least, and Aran couldn't really bear to look at them anyways.

He dropped wearily into his chair and stared at the wall.

Ani was gone. Ani was dead. She'd only been trying to save him. It wasn't her fight, she'd been trying to protect him. And when he should have saved her—he hadn't. He'd watched her die.

Just like he hadn't been able to save Istvay. Just like he hadn't been able to save anyone.

To think he'd imagined, once, that he could be the one to find the cure, save Istvay and everyone in the system with the defect.

He should have damn well known better. But it was too late now. Everything was ruined, and Ani was dead, and it was his own damn fault.

He wasn't sure how long he sat there, staring blankly at the wall. He wasn't sure he cared, honestly.

He thought he heard, for a moment, the distant sound of Alba's voice through the amplifiers outside, but before he could catch what she was saying, it cut off.

Whatever she'd tried to do, it hadn't made a difference. If he hadn't just imagined it in the first place.

At some point, the noise of the ship's engines shifted slightly, their whine taking on a deeper note, and the ship shook a little, like air turbulence in an in-atmospheric transport. Aran glanced up dully in time to see, through the plex of the small porthole window, a swirling wall of energy.

Istvay had glanced up as well, their face taking on an expression of slight interest.

And then the sky outside the porthole settled, looking once again like it always had, an endless expanse of nothing, with stars glowing and burning through it.

"We're through the portal," said Istvay, trying for a smile. "Farther than anyone in the system has ever gone."

Aran didn't have the heart to smile back, just turned and dropped his chin in his hands, staring at the blank wall in front of him.

"So," said Istvay at last, quietly. "What are we going to do now?"

For a moment, Aran sat in utter disbelief.

Then he turned abruptly to face them. "We're not going to do anything," he said harshly. "We're going to damn well sit here and not do a single thing, because every single damn time I try to make things better it makes it worse. I can't fix this Istvay. I can't fix anything."

Istvay stared at him. "Aran, what are you talking about? You're bloody brilliant! You're a damn legend. You've gotten both of us out of scrapes worse than this hundred times before."

Aran stood, knocking his chair backwards. "Don't be stupid," he snapped. His voice was shaking, a mixture of anger and self-loathing. "You're my friend, I know, I get it. And yes, I can do crap like pulling us out of a volcano, after I got us into trouble in the first place, but anything else? Anything real, any problem I didn't create myself? I can't solve those. I let you get poisoned, Istvay. I let Ani—" His voice choked for a moment, but he forced himself to keep going. "When I was a kid out on the streets, running scared from my foster parents, I couldn't stop them from hurting me. But you found me. And your mom helped. You never asked for a damn thing in return, neither of you, and when she got sick, I didn't even know until she was so far gone that—"

He swallowed hard, turning away for a moment. "If—if I'd been in time, maybe I could have thought of something, maybe I could have done … something. But I didn't. She died, and I couldn't do a damn thing. And you should've hated me, kicked me out and left me on my own, but you didn't. And now you're sick, and I can't bloody well save you either, just almost get you killed. Like … like I got Ani killed."

Istvay was staring at him, eyes wide with surprise, and Aran couldn't bear to meet their familiar gaze. He turned away in disgust, dropping back into his chair.

"Aran," said Istvay at last.

"Don't try to make me feel better, Pishti," he said dully, without turning. "Nothing you can say will change it."

There was another long pause. At last Istvay said, "Aran. I've known you since we were both about five. So I'm not going to bother telling you that the genetic defect isn't your fault—you already know that, you just don't care. And I'm not going to bother reminding you that you were ten when my mother died, and the entire system had been searching for a cure for the defect for five centuries. I'm not going to say anything about the fact that you couldn't possibly have stopped Ani from doing what she did just now, once she saw you were in danger. Hell, maybe you're right, maybe despite the fact that you've done things our classmates didn't even dare dream of, you're really a complete failure, deep down. Maybe everything is your fault, maybe you're not nearly as good as everyone thinks, maybe you've just been faking it this whole time." The cot creaked slightly as they stood.

"But dammit, Aran, there are people on this ship who are going to die. So for hell's sake, fake it a little longer. Because even if you won't believe me that you're the best person on this damn ship—they don't have any better options right now."

Aran turned, caught off guard.

Istvay was supporting themself on the desk with one hand, their face still drawn and bloodless, and Aran sat blinking at them for a few moments.

Istvay was wrong.

He couldn't do this.

After everything that had happened, everything he'd already failed at, after watching Ani die, he couldn't make himself stand up and start figuring a way out of the cabin, going to rescue Yosip and Ines and maybe even that Chief Justice who Istvay hated so much.

"I—" he began.

And then he noticed the way Istvay was looking at him, that stupid, blind faith. He remembered the pleading in Ines' last desperate glance.

And he couldn't bring himself to finish the sentence.

He couldn't let Istvay down, not again. Not without at least trying.

He took a deep breath and pushed himself to his feet. "Alright, Pishti," he said, trying to smile. "I guess we see if we can fix this. Even if—" he broke off.

Istvay was still watching him. "Aran," they said quietly. "I'm sorry about Ani. I can't tell you how sorry I am. I know how much she meant to you. But she died fighting to save people she cared about. And I know you. No matter what happens, you're not going to do anything less." Their voice choked a little. With an effort, they grinned. "Alright, then. Now that's settled, what are we going to do?"

And despite the drawn look on Istvay's face, and the desperateness of the situation, the sight of their grin was unaccountably reassuring.

Aran took a deep breath, pushing back the heavy knot of grief, and went through a quick mental inventory of the supplies in his belt pouch, which Emeric apparently hadn't thought to confiscate before he'd shoved them in here.

"Well," he began after a moment. "I suppose I could—"

The ship shook, hard enough to send both him and Istvay to the ground.

They stared at each other for a moment.

"What the hell—" Aran began.

The ship shuddered again, and in the distance, he could hear the sharp shrill of alarms.

He scrambled upright and crossed to the small porthole window, peering out at the blackness beyond.

Istvay joined him a moment later, still unsteady on their feet.

The two of them stared at the black of space beyond the plex window for a long moment without speaking. Something cold had wound itself around Aran's chest, and squeezed.

The gash in the fabric of space, the portal that had been their destination for this entire trip and that now marked their only chance of return to their old life, was sealing shut behind them. Energy sparked and crackled from it like it was alive, and as Aran watched, it let off another snap of whirling energy, and the ship rocked again.

"What—" he began again, panic almost choking the words in his throat.

And then there was a final burst of energy, so bright Aran staggered back, shielding his face with his arm. He blinked, momentarily blinded, and squinted through the white sunburst seared across his vision.

The portal was closed.

And then the burst of energy hit, and the ship rocked and bucked as if it were a desperate animal trying to throw off a predator with jaws latched around the back of its neck. Aran and Istvay went sprawling a second time as more alarms howled to life, joining the chorus.

Aran lay dazed for a moment, his head aching where it had hit the corner of the desk, then blinked and pushed himself into a sitting position.

Istvay had already picked themself up, and was scrolling desperately through pages of information on their palm screen.

They looked up at Aran, their face suddenly very, very grave.

"The ship's breaking up," they said quietly. "The life-support systems are on redline, and the hull is cracked in half a dozen places. The ship has a self-sealing system to isolate the breaches, but with this level of damage that will only prolong the inevitable. We have to get off, now, or we die."

The ship lurched again, and the cabin door swung free, sliding loosely on its hinges as the ship rocked. Aran caught a glimpse of the door's external lock, broken and useless after the power surge.

"Well," Istvay said at last, pulling themself to their feet. "I guess that solves the problem of the door."

Aran gave a grim nod. "Come on," he said. "Let's go."

29

Aran

The scene outside the cabin was pure chaos—people running and screaming, soldiers with guns shouting orders, some trying to regain control of the situation, others simply shoving past everyone else in a blind attempt to get to the escape shuttles first.

Aran and Istvay pushed their way through the mayhem to the cabin where Ines and Yosip had been locked up. Their lock, too, it seemed, had been fried by the power surge, and Istvay yanked the door open.

"Come on!" shouted Aran. "We're getting off the ship, now."

To their credit, Yosip and Ines didn't pause to ask questions, just jumped to their feet and followed Aran and Istvay out the door.

"What in the system—" began Yosip in tones of shock as he surveyed the chaos around them.

"The ship's breaking up. Let's talk about it when we're on an escape pod," snapped Istvay.

As the four of them approached the lifts, they slowed—the space around them was crammed with pushing, shouting people, the lifts themselves so full that the lift doors couldn't close, hanging uselessly open and unable to move.

Istvay swore. "What the hell are they doing?"

"The ship's officers were probably locked up too, at least the ones who weren't on Cavaco's payroll," said Aran grimly. "No one to keep things organized."

Istvay sighed, glancing around in indecision. "We can't just leave them like this."

Aran yanked a flare out of his pouch. "Look, take this, shoot it off. When you have their attention, get them moving down the stairs. You can mark the path like we do when we're trying to get ground-pigs out of their burrows. I have a set of the marker lights here …" He dug through his supplies pouch.

Istvay glared at him. "And what the hell will you be doing?"

Aran looked up, shoving a handful of marker lights into Istvay's hands. "Crank the setting up to the brightest they'll go. It should be enough to attract their attention. I'm going back for the judge and Feliu. I'll meet you at the pod we were originally going to take—it's on the deck above where the shuttles are, so it'll probably be less crowded there. I already loaded it with some of my supplies."

Istvay hesitated, and Aran could see they wanted to insist on coming with him. But the pallor of their face and the slight trembling in their hands made it clear that they weren't going to be all that much use, and they knew it as well as he did.

Instead they muttered, "You can't damn well go back there by yourself. You'll bloody get killed in this crowd."

Aran shook his head in exasperation. "I'm pretty sure I remember someone telling me, just a few minutes ago, that even though I might be a pretty crap option, I'm the only—"

"Yosip can help Istvay get people to the loading docks," said Ines in a small voice. "I'll go with Aran."

Both Aran and Istvay turned to glare at her reflexively, and she shrank under their combined gaze.

Aran sighed and forced the irritation from his expression. "Thank you, Ines. That's a good idea." He turned to Yosip. "Can you—"

Yosip was smiling that irrepressible smile, the wrinkles around the corners of his eyes deepening. "I'm not a famous explorer, but I think I can take instructions from one."

"Good," said Aran. "Istvay, once people are heading for the loading deck, get the hell out of here, okay?"

Istvay gave a brusque nod. Their lips were pinched tight, but they didn't argue.

Aran took a deep breath, then plunged back into the crowd, heading towards the Chief Justice's cabin.

He shouldered his way through the rushing torrent of people, Ines following in his eddy. It felt like pushing upstream through a neck-deep river, and more than once he thought he'd be bowled over. Once someone bumped into him so hard that he almost lost his balance, and only Ines catching him and shoving him back upright kept him from being pulled under and trampled.

At the very least, he thought grimly, Cavaco's soldiers, who he saw now and again through the crowd, seemed too worried about saving their own damn lives to try to kill anyone.

The crowd thinned as the two of them pushed through the general section of the ship towards the diplomatic quarters, and Aran frowned as he and Ines broke into a sprint.

There were hundreds of people on this floor. Surely they hadn't all—

And then he noticed the external locks on the doors, and swore. Ines turned to him in barely concealed panic, and he gestured with his head to the doors.

"It looks like the soldiers locked everyone up, and didn't bother to release the locks before they ran off. The power surge killed the locks in our sector. Looks like in this one, it locked down the emergency system instead."

Ines's eyes grew wide with horror as she realized what he'd said. "You mean they were just going to—"

Aran nodded. "They were going to leave them to die. Let's get to Alba first, and then we'll deal with this."

Ines gave him a quick, frightened nod, and they ran on.

The blaring of the alarms was like a physical force, pounding against his head, stopping him from thinking.

They skidded to a stop outside the judge's door.

"Stand back," said Aran over his shoulder. He ran a hand lightly over the exterior lock, feeling for the mechanism. When he found it, he grabbed a detonator from his pouch and fastened it to the surface, then tapped on the door. "Chief Justice," he shouted. "Can you hear me? This is Aran and Ines. If you can hear me, stand back. I'm going to blow the lock."

He stepped back sharply and hit the controller. There was the quiet *pop* of the detonator, and then the active light on the lock flickered and died.

He stepped forward, jerking the door open. "The ship's breaking up. We need to get out, now."

Alba stood at the door, looking older than he remembered, her face set and grim. "I'm afraid," she said quietly, her voice barely audible in the shriek of the alarms, "that it won't be quite as easy as that."

She gestured behind her, and Aran frowned.

The cabin was too dark to make out the interior properly—the lights must have gone out in the breakup—but there was blood on the floor.

"What—" he began, his eyes flicking to Alba to check for injuries.

"Madam. I may have been injured, but I'm not quite ready to die just yet," came Feliu's weak voice from within.

"Nonsense," snapped Alba over her shoulder. She turned back to Aran. "He decided to be a hero, and got shot. He's lost a lot of blood, I'm afraid. I don't know enough about first aid to know how bad the wound is."

Aran swore under his breath and pushed past her into the cabin, squeezing the light on his palmscreen to illuminate the small space.

Feliu was propped up against a wall, his face pale and blood staining his shirt. Aran crouched beside him, yanking out his mediscanner, and took a brief scan. He glanced at the readout just long enough to assure himself the wound wasn't immediately fatal, then turned back to Feliu. "I'm sorry," he said. "We have to go. I'll help you stand."

"Be careful," Alba snapped from the doorway.

"If we don't bloody get him out, he's going to die here anyways," said Aran through his teeth, as he hoisted Feliu to his feet. "We have an hour at most before this whole damn ship breaks apart."

Feliu grunted in pain, his face drawn, but with Aran's arm around his back, he managed to stagger out of the cabin.

When they were all gathered in the corridor, Aran looked up and down at the closed doors, teeth clenched.

"I'll take them. You get the doors," came a small voice by his elbow, and he jerked around, startled. Ines stood there, her face fixed and determined.

He hesitated half a second, then nodded, shifting Feliu's weight from his own shoulder to hers. The man moaned again, sweat standing out on his forehead, and Ines staggered a bit under his weight—she was a slight girl, and Feliu was no lightweight—but she caught her balance.

"You know how to get back?" asked Aran.

Ines nodded grimly, then gestured with her head. "Follow me," she said, and started forwards. Alba hesitated, then went after her.

"Tell Istvay I'll catch you up as soon as I can," he called after them, then he reached into his pouch, pulled out a handful of detonators, and started down the hallway.

He blew the lock on the next cabin down the hall, yanked the door open, and shouted, "Get down to the loading dock, quick as you can! Take the stairs, the lifts are no good. Go!"

The older man huddled inside didn't wait to be told twice, just jerked to his feet and started down the corridor.

By the time Aran reached the end of the long hallway, the unsteady movement of the ship under his feet told him better than words that their time was running out.

"Aran!" came Istvay's voice in his earpiece. "Where the hell are you!"

"I'm on my way," he said, squeezing his hand to activate his own wavelink. "Just getting people out."

"We don't have any more damn time," Istvay hissed. "Get the hell down here!"

Aran glanced around him uncertainly.

There were more corridors he hadn't checked, where the doors may or may not be unlocked …

"I swear to you, Aran, if you don't promise me right now that you're on your way, I'm damn well coming after you."

Aran let out a quick breath. "Fine. I'm on my way. Did the others make it?"

"Yes. We're heading to the pod. Meet us there."

Aran took one more quick glance around, but Istvay was right. There wasn't time to explore the ship and see which cabins were open.

He'd just have to hope that the other locks had broken, like they had in his and Istvay's sector, rather than sealed shut, like they had in the diplomatic quarters.

He turned and started back down the corridor at a run.

The passageway to the upper deck, where the smaller escape pods were stored, was much less busy than the clogged corridors leading to the stairs to the loading dock, and Aran only had to dodge around one or two people on his way to the stairwell. The deserted corridors were almost eerie, his footsteps echoing, no noise of shouting or talking to cut the high-pitched wail of alarms.

Just get to the stairs, meet up with Istvay. The two of them could figure things out from there.

He'd almost reached the stairwell when a voice stopped him.

"Aran!"

He whirled around, the knot in his stomach tightening.

He recognized that voice.

Emeric stood in the passageway, a wild look in his eyes. But the pistol in his hand was steady, and it was pointed directly at Aran.

30

Alba

Alba, Ines, and Feliu stumbled down the hallway in the direction Aran had indicated. It wasn't crowded at first, but it was only a few moments before other panicking people were running up from behind them, pushing past in a desperate effort to get to the stairs, and soon they were wading through a sea of absolute chaos.

Beside Alba, Ines stumbled as someone shoved past her, and more came in their wake. Feliu gave a gasp of pain as the girl almost lost her footing, and Alba reached out unconsciously to catch them both. The weight of them made her stagger, but she pushed herself upright.

"Ines, get behind me," she snapped.

"I—but you—"

"Do as you're told!"

This time, the girl did, pulling Feliu with her to stand behind Alba. Alba took a deep breath and stepped forward, pulling herself to her full height and planting herself in the middle of the tide of bodies.

"Step away from us this minute!" she shouted, with every ounce of authority she'd accumulated from her decades on the Council.

It almost wasn't enough. The people around her paused, taken aback, and then surged forwards again, panic stronger than any lingering capacity for intimidation.

But it gave the three of them enough space to push through to the corridor wall, where they were sheltered somewhat.

Feliu sagged against Ines, his eyes half closed, blood leaking through the front of his shirt. Ines's shirt, as well, was streaked with blood, and the girl's hands were wet with it.

Alba fought back the sharp sting of panic, forcing her mind calm. "Ines. Where are we going? I'll lead."

The girl nodded and whispered the coordinates, and Alba narrowed her eyes and started forwards.

"Activate," she snapped into her wavelink. "Yosip, where are you?"

"Madam?"

It was strange how the sound of that voice, with its friendly, cheerful overtone even through the grimness, sent a rush of visceral relief through her.

"We're on our way, but Feliu is injured, and we're struggling to get through to the stairs."

There was a moment's pause. "We'll meet you by the stairwell, then," said Yosip at last. "It's on our way."

Alba deactivate the wavelink and glanced behind her.

Feliu's face was completely bloodless now, his breaths ragged and gasping. He was leaning against Ines so heavily that Alba could see the girl's legs trembling under his weight.

"Let me help you," she said, stepping back beside Ines and draping Feliu's other arm over her own shoulder.

"Madam," he choked, but she gave a sharp shake of her head.

"You, Feliu, will be quiet, and you will do as you're told until we get you somewhere safe," she said grimly. "And right now, I am instructing you to lean on me so that we can get down this damned corridor and up to the shuttles."

He nodded weakly, and she could feel him trying, and failing, to straighten at the tone in her voice.

She could tell they were getting closer as the mass of people packed more heavily into the corridor, any semblance of order turning into frantic chaos. And then she heard Istvay's voice, weak, but still loud enough to ring out over the noise. "For hell's sake, down the damn stairs! Line up and stop damn well pushing, and you'll all have a chance to get off this bloody wreck!"

They were standing at the stairwell, a point of stillness in the rushing, eddying chaos, and beside them she could make out the bristly grey of Yosip's head.

Alba raised her voice desperately. "Yosip!" she shouted. "Istvay!"

She saw both their heads turning, searching for her, but neither could see her through the press.

"Yosip!" she shouted again, louder this time. Bodies were pushing up against her, dragging the three of them forward against their will. Ines was gasping with effort, and Alba could feel herself being pulled away from the girl and Feliu, despite her desperate efforts.

And then the two at the stairwell must have seen her, and Istvay was pushing their way through the crowd towards her.

"Where's Aran?" they snapped as they reached her, looking around quickly as if expecting Aran to be bringing up the rear.

"The doors in the diplomatic section were sealed closed. He said he was going to try to get people out," said Ines in a low voice.

Istvay swore. "I'm going after him," they began, but Yosip shook his head, placing a hand on their arm.

"You can't. You won't do any good, and by the time you reach there, if he hasn't started back, neither of you will stand a chance. Let's get to the escape pod and hold a place for him. That's the best we can do."

Istvay's face was cut with indecision. At last, though, they nodded, squeezing their palm screen to activate the wavelink. "Aran, where the hell are you?" they said through gritted teeth, leaning over to take Feliu's weight off Alba's shoulders. They staggered a little as they took the weight, and Alba was reminded that they'd been poisoned scant days before. They managed to straighten, though, jerking their head forward, and Alba and the others fell in behind them as they shoved through the crowd.

"We want to get to the upper deck," Istvay shouted over their shoulder. "The escape pod Aran and I were preparing is up there."

Alba frowned. "The—"

Istvay scowled. "Not important right now. Let's go."

She bristled at the tone in their voice, but they were right. She swallowed her retort and nodded.

The General's soldiers were mingled in with the crowd, and fistfights had broken out here and there. She turned at a sudden, gasping scream, just in time to watch a soldier yank out his pistol and fire directly into the face of the woman beside him, a woman Alba recognized vaguely as one of the diplomatic aides.

She turned quickly away, feeling sick.

"Are you alright?" asked Yosip, turning to her with concern, but she pressed her lips shut and nodded.

There would be time to think about all this later. In the meantime, the important thing was to keep moving.

Pushing up the stairwell, past the steady flood of people stumbling in the opposite direction, was a terrifying, breathtaking endeavour, but between Istvay's bull-headed shoving, Ines's terrified stubbornness, and Yosip's sturdy frame, they managed it, and finally pushed out into another corridor.

Istvay came to a sudden halt. "We can't go this way," they said, tension bleeding through their tone.

Peering past them, Alba could see why—the corridor was completely packed, a mass of frantic, pushing, struggling people.

"We'll have to go all the way around," said Istvay grimly. They hesitated, clearly reluctant. "If we go up one floor, maybe two if we need to, we may be able to get across the ship and come down on the other side. But it'll take a lot longer, and I don't know how much time we have."

"I—I think I know another way, that might be a little faster," whispered Ines, her voice trembling.

Alba turned to her. "Yes, girl? Tell us."

Ines's face was stricken, and Alba, sighing internally, added, "Your ideas so far have been good, and I have no doubt this one is as well."

Alba wasn't sure if that actually lessened the stunned look on the girl's face, but Yosip shot Alba a quick, approving smile, and she was surprised at the warmth in it.

"If—if we go down that corridor back there, it'll take us through to the main deck. I know it will be crazy there, but it's a lot of open space, so if we stick to the edges we should be able to get through. There are crew ladders there that lead up to the emergency docks."

Istvay nodded brusquely and turned, only staggering a little as they pushed back towards the corridor Ines had indicated.

Alba and the others followed in their wake.

Ines's intuition had been correct—once the group of them were able to break through to the relatively clear passageway, they went at a stumbling half-run. Alba's breath caught painfully in her chest, her heart pounding at the unaccustomed exertion. And then they were there, and Istvay shoved back the door onto the main deck.

As Ines had predicted, the main deck, though crowded, was large enough that they could weave their way across the floor, even with Istvay half-carrying Feliu and staggering with the effort. The muscles stood out in their arms and shoulders as they supported his weight, and despite everything, Alba smiled faintly to herself. She might be seventy-three, but she still had eyes. She could guess at least one reason Aran was so obviously smitten by this one.

When they reached the ladder, Istvay stumbled to a halt, panting.

"Feliu isn't going to be able to—" Yosip began.

Istvay nodded, their face grim, and without a word, bent and hoisted Feliu bodily up onto their shoulders. Feliu gasped in pain. Istvay grunted at the effort, but straightened unsteadily, grabbing onto the ladder for support. "I'll go up, then I'll help the rest of you," they said, voice strained.

Despite the fact they'd been poisoned mere days ago, they were still the most physically capable of the group.

It was a depressing thought.

Alba watched with trepidation as Istvay scaled the ladder, their pace agonizingly slow, and then lowered Feliu to the ground, where he lay gasping, his face almost grey.

"Madam Chief Justice?" said Yosip, gesturing her forward.

Alba stepped up to the ladder and took a deep breath, steeling herself.

Her legs were shaking so hard by now with a combination of nerves and exhaustion she wasn't sure her knees wouldn't simply give out on her, but she grasped the rungs of the ladder in both hands, and, sending up a quick prayer to the Great Mystery, started up.

Halfway up, her hand slipped, but Istvay, down on their belly and leaning over the edge, caught her wrist before she could fall. They half-helped, half-pulled her up the rest of the way, their face pale with the strain.

Ines scrambled up next, followed by Yosip, and then Istvay had hauled Feliu back to his feet and the group of them set off again at a stumbling run.

As they rounded the corner to the pod station, Alba could feel the tight knot of tension that was choking off her breath begin to loosen. Most of the people on the ship must have scrambled for the emergency shuttles, which were both larger and more capable of surviving for an extended period of time in space. There were surprisingly few people gathered around the smaller individual pods.

And then she slowed, a sudden weight forming in her stomach.

In front of her, Istvay staggered to a halt, Feliu groaning faintly against their shoulder.

Half a dozen soldiers stood in front of the airlock door. Their guns were trained on the five of them, and there was a look on their faces that told Alba they wouldn't hesitate to use them.

31

Aran glanced around, then yanked open a door to one of the supply cupboards, placing it between himself and Emeric. It was thick enough, probably, that Emeric's shot wouldn't get through it.

"Emeric. Get out of the way," he said. His teeth were gritted, his heart pounding.

Emeric had killed Ani.

But there was no time to think of that now.

Emeric still hadn't moved, his pistol held steady.

"The ship is breaking up, Emeric." Aran tried to keep his voice calm, like he was soothing a frightened animal. "Whatever it is you want, you can't get it if we're both dead. Just get out of the way, and we can deal with this later."

From somewhere below him, he could hear the hiss of loading doors opening, releasing the first of the emergency shuttles.

Emeric's face was drawn with terror, but there was a fixed determination under the fear on his face. "I'm sorry, Aran," he said. "I wish I didn't have to do this. I've never wanted to kill you, I just wanted you to stay out of the way. But you wouldn't. You don't understand the stakes. You have to die."

Aran stared at him. "The portal has closed. We're all stranded here, and the ship is breaking up. Every last damn one of us is going to die if we don't get off. This isn't the time or place to worry about whose damn side anyone's on. Just move over and let me past. We can both get to an escape pod, there's still time."

He moved as if to start forward, but Emeric stepped in his way again, pistol held steady.

"I'm sorry. I have to kill you. I don't have a choice. But I don't have to kill anyone else, not even Istvay. I won't do anything to stop them, I promise, I won't even try to stop the Chief Justice. If you don't try to fight, everyone else can walk away from this."

The ship shuddered as if to punctuate his words, and both of them staggered.

Aran's breath was coming too quickly.

Damn it to hell, he didn't have time for this, neither of them did. Maybe it had all been too much for Emeric. Maybe watching Ani kill his companions had been too much and Emeric's mind had broken from the strain.

Gently, Aran eased his own pistol from the holster on his belt.

"Don't," Emeric snapped. "I know where Istvay and the judge are. I have my people stationed in front of your escape pod, and they've been instructed not to let your friends pass until I give the word. Step out where I can see you, show me you're not going to fight, and I'll give the word, I swear it. I don't mean them any harm. But I need you dead."

For a long moment, they stared at each other.

There was a cold knot in Aran's stomach, and he found his hands shaking.

Emeric wasn't crazy after all. And he wasn't bluffing. Aran had seen this expression on him before, when they were classmates. There was something he wanted, something he thought he deserved, and he'd step over the body of anyone who got in his way without so much as a twinge of conscience.

Istvay was down there, and Ines, and Yosip. They were headed for the pods, and they had no idea there were soldiers waiting for them.

"If you say so much as a word through your wavelink, I'll tell my soldiers to shoot them down," said Emeric, as if reading his mind. "I told you, I don't need them dead. But by the Mystery itself, I wouldn't shed a single tear for them either." He took a step closer. "You can save them, though. It'll be easy, you won't feel a thing. I don't hate you, despite what Istvay thinks. This is only business. Don't let someone else die for you."

And just for a moment, Aran almost did it. For a moment, he pictured Ani, that glimpse of her tentacle slipping from the airlock door. The look on Istvay's face when they woke that morning, years ago, and their mother didn't, the drawn, skeletal outline of her body that still woke Aran from nightmares. The way Istvay's face was slowly gathering the ghost of that same look, day by inexorable day.

Istvay would get off the ship, and they'd take Ines and Yosip and the others with them. Istvay would be safe.

Except—except they wouldn't, not really. Whatever General Cavaco had decided to do, it was obvious that Emeric, at least, believed it wasn't over. And who knew what awaited the others, if the rest of them did find a planet to land their pod? Istvay was smart, but Istvay was still recovering from being poisoned. And none of the others had any damn idea how to keep themselves alive in the field, he'd be willing to bet on that.

He gritted his teeth and swore quietly.

Damn Istvay to hell. If they hadn't harassed him half to death in the cabin, maybe he could have just stepped out into the corridor with a clear conscience.

But he couldn't.

He'd failed Ani. He'd failed Istvay's mother. Maybe Emeric was right, and he was nothing but a useless failure after all.

But he was all Istvay and the others damn well had. And he couldn't bloody leave them.

He took a deep breath. Then he threw himself forward, yanking his pistol out as he went.

Emeric stepped back in surprise, and Aran slammed into him.

"Activate—" Emeric began in a choked voice, then Aran hit him in the mouth with the butt of his pistol. He winced as blood spurted from Emeric's nose, but he couldn't let him get through to the soldiers.

Emeric's hand grabbed for Aran's neck, his grip surprisingly strong, and Aran barely managed to shove him aside. Emeric lunged upwards, shoving Aran off him, then turned, dropping his knee into Aran's stomach. Aran grunted in pain, the breath knocked out of him.

"Activate," Emeric mumbled again. "Captain Da Costa, you need to—"

Aran grabbed Emeric by the shoulders and shoved, using his momentum to roll them over until he was on top again. He grabbed Emeric's hair and slammed his head into the deck, and his words choked off.

"Sorry, Emeric," he gasped. "I told Istvay I was going to meet them. I'm not going to let you make me a liar. So you're going to have to get out of the way, or we're both going to die here."

Emeric struggled, trying to break free, and managed to yank a hand out of Aran's grip. He grabbed for something, then slapped his open palm against Aran's shoulder.

Something sharp and painful jolted through Aran's entire body. For a split second, he wondered if Emeric had been holding a knife, or maybe a needle with a nerve-poison—

He tried to move, only to find his muscles frozen.

An electric tranq. He'd used them before on animals, if it was that or let them be killed, but he hated it—despite the professional reassurances, he hadn't been able to imagine an electric current running through your muscles, even one routed specifically to avoid cardiac damage, wouldn't be painful.

Apparently, he'd been correct.

Emeric rolled out from under him, shoving him off to one side. Aran couldn't move, couldn't speak, his jaw clenched so tightly that his teeth ached from the pressure, couldn't even turn his head to see what Emeric was going to do next.

Still, that probably wasn't necessary. Emeric had made his intentions abundantly clear.

From the corner of his eye he saw Emeric stagger to his feet. He was bleeding from the mouth and nose, bruises already rising on his face, but even through the blood and mess, the cold hatred in his eyes shone out like a flare.

He'd said this wasn't personal. But, Aran realized suddenly, he'd been lying.

Istvay had been right all along. Emeric hated him, and from the look of it, that hatred had taken on the sheen of religious fervour.

Emeric steadied himself against the corridor wall for a moment, wiping the blood from his face with his sleeve, then reached into a holster at his belt and pulled out another pistol.

Aran's heart pounded, his stomach a cold, sick knot.

He didn't want to die. He hadn't realized, until just now, how much he didn't want to die.

But then, that wasn't really up for discussion anymore. He'd done what he could, and it hadn't been enough.

From behind Emeric, in the direction of the loading docks, came a strange hissing sound, hardly loud enough to be audible over the alarms.

Aran tried to frown, but the muscles in his face were too frozen to allow for it.

Maybe he was imagining things.

The hissing grew louder.

He strained to move his head, even a couple centimetres, but he couldn't.

He wasn't imagining things, though—Emeric had half-turned, glancing in the direction of the noise.

And then Emeric's face went completely bloodless. He shoved the pistol back into his belt, and Aran heard his panicked footsteps pounding away down the corridor.

Aran's heart was pounding fast and uneven, his pulse loud in his ears.

Whatever the hell it was, he wasn't going to get away from it. Or maybe it wasn't something coming at all, just the sound of the pressure breaking somewhere ahead of him, and he'd be sucked out into deep space, another frozen testament to the brutality of whatever the hell lurked behind the portal ...

Something touched his arm, and he would have flinched if his muscles weren't held solid by the current.

It touched him again, and he thought maybe he'd actually pass out in terror.

And then whatever it was gave a soft chirruping purr, and for a moment he wondered if maybe he'd died after all, and this was some sort of post-death hallucination.

The gentle, probing tentacles—he recognized the touch now, even though it was completely impossible—moved down his arm until they reached the device Emeric had slapped onto his arm.

"No, Ani, that'll hurt you—" he tried to say through gritted teeth, but of course, no sound came out.

There was a small jolt from the device, and Ani's tentacle jerked back, then touched the thing again.

And then she growled happily, her tentacle suckers closing down on it, and suddenly Aran was free.

He jerked upright, staring around wildly.

Ani was sitting on the floor beside him, patterns of bright, electric colours rippling through her body in soft undulations as she purred in contentment.

For a few moments, he just stared at her, too flabbergasted to form a thought.

"Ani?" he said at last.

She turned to him, and there was the quick, electric jolt through his body as she let go her hold on the tranq device for just a moment. The shock of it brought Aran back to himself, and he reached over and broke the thing free of his skin.

Ani grumbled, the electric patterns wavering out through her tentacles and dying.

"Ani!" His voice was choked in a mixture of disbelief and happiness. "Ani, how the hell—I saw you die!" He picked her up as he spoke, turning her over gently to inspect her for injuries.

She was battered, and he could see half a dozen small cuts on her body. There was an odd glint under one of her tentacles, and he turned the tentacle over and examined the suction cups more closely.

There were bits of metal caught in them, a smooth, shiny silver colour.

"Ani?" he said again, frowning. "Is this from the ship's hull? Did you—" He broke off, staring at her. "Ani. How did you survive that? It's impossible for a life form to survive in space without a suit, at least that's what we've always assumed." He pulled one of the metallic slivers gently free and turned it over in his fingers, a sudden excitement welling in his chest.

He'd have to test it to be sure, of course, but on a cursory examination it looked like the same material as the hull of the ship.

"Were you out there this whole time?" he asked, turning back to Ani. She'd settled herself in his lap, and was pushing her bulbous head under his hand, begging for pets. "How the hell—"

Of course, the airlock doors had been opening and closing almost non stop for the last half-hour, ever since people started getting off the ship. Hypothetically, if she'd managed to attach herself to the hull, she could have crawled inside when one of the external doors opened, then come through to the ship's interior after the external door closed and the internal one re-opened …

What this would mean to science—what they could learn from a creature who could survive in deep space …

The ship shuddered again, and he started, glancing around.

Ani might be able to survive in deep space, but he damn well couldn't.

"Come on, Ani, we'd better go. We'll talk more about this later," he said. He held out his arm, and as she pulled herself to his shoulder, he scrambled to his feet. Then, with one last glance around, he sprinted down the corridor towards where Istvay and the others would be waiting.

32

Alba

"What is this?" Istvay asked the soldiers, in a voice that was trying to be calm. But something about their tone told Alba that Istvay had guessed exactly what this was.

So had she.

Despite the cold in her stomach, spreading slowly down her limbs and through her body, she stepped forward and touched Istvay on the shoulder. They turned, frowning at her, and she gave them her most imperious glance, even though she was still gasping for breath.

"Let me, if you'd be so kind."

Istvay hesitated a moment, then, apparently reading the look in her face, stepped back so she was standing at the front of the tiny, ragged group, facing the soldiers.

Her legs were still trembling badly, adrenaline pulsing sick and heavy through her body, but she refused to put out a hand to support herself against the wall.

"Soldiers," she demanded. "Please explain the meaning of this at once."

The soldiers didn't answer, just shifted their grips on their weapons, their postures ready, faces grim.

"You aren't to come any closer," said the captain, her voice cold and businesslike.

"Alba. It's fine," said Istvay, their tone strained. "We'll find another pod, and I'll come back here to tell Aran where we—"

The captain jerked her head at her subordinates, and they spread out, blocking off the exits. "I'm sorry," the woman said. "We've been ordered to hold you here. You're not to get onto an escape pod until I'm given the word."

"Come now, none of us want to die on this ship, us or your soldiers," said Yosip, stepping up beside Alba. "If there's a problem, I'm certain we can work it out once we've solved the immediate issue." His smile was as friendly as always, but the calm in his expression was belied by the worry under his tone. "You need to get your soldiers out of this alive, and I'm sure you as their captain wouldn't willingly bring them to harm. You're welcome to this pod. Just let us go and we'll find another. No one needs to know we were here, and whoever is giving you orders can't possibly argue that you didn't do your duty by keeping yourself and your soldiers safe—"

"Shut up," the woman snapped. "Or you'll be the first one I shoot."

Alba glared at the woman, surprised by her own unexpected surge of anger.

From the corner of her eye she saw a hint of motion, Istvay's hand reaching slowly for their pistol.

But it wouldn't matter—it wouldn't be enough. There were six soldiers. No matter how good Istvay was, it would turn into a massacre.

She straightened her shoulders and fixed the captain with her iciest stare. "You," she began, her tone crackling with a mix of icy formality and haughty indignation, "will address me as Madam Chief Justice, if you please. I happen to be one of the joint heads of your government. And while you may answer to the General, his authority ultimately passes through the Council, and therefore, through me. I am not accustomed to being disobeyed."

The woman stared at her.

"I am not accustomed to being spoken to in this manner. And I am not accustomed to being treated like this," Alba snapped, her temper rising with her words. "I am embarrassed by you, and I am embarrassed by every soldier on this ship. I had expected better of any person who claimed to act in the name of our government. I have, and always have had, nothing but respect for the efforts of our soldiers to keep peace throughout the system. But I had been led to believe that legitimate soldiers followed the proper chain of command. You, young woman, are a disgrace. A disgrace to your company, and a disgrace to our system. Following orders that you know are seditious, in order to gain standing with someone in the process of committing treason. You can't tell me this is what you are taught in our military academies. Your instructors would be ashamed of you. I am ashamed of you."

The woman was still staring.

Alba took a step forward, drawing herself up to her full, if not particularly impressive, height. "As your head of government," she said, enunciating each word, "I demand that you get out of my way." She turned to the other soldiers. "And you. Stop embarrassing yourselves. Put down your weapons this instant."

There was a moment of silence.

The soldiers' faces were slack with shock.

Alba turned back to the captain, and had to hold herself back from starting in surprise.

Behind the captain, her face screwed into an expression of miserable determination, Ines was raising a piece of broken metal tubing, gripping it tightly enough that the tendons in her hands stood out against her skin.

Alba grasped her composure with an iron grip and resolutely avoided looking at the girl. "Furthermore," she began, but she was flustered, and her voice had lost its tone of command.

"What do you think—" the captain began, rallying.

Ines swung the metal tubing like a bat, slamming it into the side of the captain's head with enough force to knock the woman sideways and send Ines staggering backwards.

The captain landed hard on the corridor floor, and Yosip stepped neatly past Alba and plucked the rifle from her nerveless fingers. From the corner of her eye, Alba saw Istvay snatching the guns from the hands of stunned soldiers, their own pistol held steady at the soldiers' faces.

It was over in moments. Yosip had turned the captain's gun on the disarmed soldiers, and Ines had grabbed a gun from Istvay and was pointing it at the fallen captain with a shaky determination.

Istvay's breath was still coming quickly, their eyes narrowed, violence in their expression and a gun in their hand. Yosip stepped up beside them, shaking his head gently. "Let these people go. They're not worth our lives."

Istvay hesitated for a moment longer, then nodded.

Yosip turned to the captain. She was lying where she'd fallen, blinking blood from her eyes, her expression dazed.

"I'm sure you're a good woman," he said quietly. "You were doing what you thought was your duty. But you've lost. Now, get your soldiers out of here before anyone gets killed. None of us have time to waste fighting."

As if to punctuate his words, the ship shook violently, and through the plex in the interior airlock door Alba saw a huge mass against the black of space. For a moment she stared at it, confused, before she realized what it was—the entire port section of the ship, swinging ponderously to one side as it broke partially free.

The captain staggered to her feet, hand pressed to the bloody wound on her head, and gestured curtly to her soldiers. They jumped forward to support her, and the whole half-dozen of them disappeared down the corridor.

"Come on, get in," snapped Istvay, hitting the control. The airlock's interior door slid open, and Alba and the others stumbled inside, Istvay and Ines half-dragging the unconscious Feliu between them.

Istvay's hands were full, between Feliu and the pistol they were still holding, but they harangued the others ahead of them into one of the tiny four-person pods, coming in last with Feliu and Ines.

Alba looked around at the cramped space.

Meant for four, and already they were five and waiting for a sixth.

Still, it couldn't possibly be worse than the alternative.

She dropped wearily onto a bench. Ines and Istvay laid Feliu out on one of the open sleeping pods, and Yosip dropped into the pilot's seat. A few moments later, the small pod hummed to life.

Istvay glanced up quickly at the sound, their face set. "I'm going out to wait for Aran," they said shortly. "He's not answering his wavelink. He should have been here by now."

Alba and Yosip exchanged glances, but neither of them spoke.

Alba could already tell it wouldn't do any good. They'd have to drag Istvay away kicking and fighting, and she, at least, wasn't physically capable of it.

"From what I'm seeing on the readouts, we have maybe three minutes to get off before it's too late," said Yosip quietly.

"Then if I'm not back in three minutes, leave without me," said Istvay through their teeth, and disappeared out the door.

Again, Alba and Yosip exchanged glances.

The seconds dragged by.

One minute.

Two.

Yosip was glancing back at the loading ramp where Istvay had disappeared, and she could see the strain and indecision on his usually cheerful face.

Would he be able to bring himself to leave Istvay, if it came to it?

Alba was suddenly, sickeningly grateful that she wasn't the one who had to make that decision.

Two and half minutes.

Yosip pushed himself up out of the pilot's seat. "I'm going to—" he began.

And then Aran stumbled up the loading ramp and through the hatch, Istvay at his heels and that awful tentacled murder-beast clinging to his shoulders. Istvay hit the control as they staggered in, and the hatch slammed shut, sealing with a hiss of pressure.

"Go!" Istvay shouted, and Yosip, who'd already slid back into the pilot's seat, hit the controls.

The outer airlock doors slid open, and the escape pod launched itself free of the massive ship's death spasms, and out into a cold, pitiless black expanse that was entirely and utterly unfamiliar.

Alba kept her eyes fixed forward, and refused to consider, just for now, the incalculable mass of humanity that was dying along with the ship.

33

Savina

At the first shock, Savina had rolled to her feet, trying instinctively to see if the door latch had been disabled. But it appeared to have sealed shut, stronger than even the lock her captors had set.

She hadn't been able to try it more than half-heartedly anyways with her hands bound, and the restraints on her wrist had been set to block off her wavelink.

But they'd gone through the portal, she'd felt that. And whatever they'd found on the other side—something had happened to the ship.

She could hear the shriek of alarms through the door, the panicked shouts, the orders to evacuate. And she knew, instinctively, that if something had happened, the soldiers wouldn't risk their own lives setting their prisoners free.

So she sat in the corner of her small prison and waited to die.

Being captured had been bad enough. Being captured had meant a trial, prison—possibly death, if the ship's captain or the judge decided bringing her back was more trouble than it was worth, and made it clear they'd turn a blind eye towards an 'accident' in her cell.

The thought made her mildly ill—she'd seen the hatred in that soldier's eyes. It wouldn't have been a quick death.

But the others, at least, likely would have gone free, eventually. There was nothing connecting Beni to Savina's crimes—Savina had made very, very sure of that. And Joska and Rafel—well, all they had to do was tell the truth. There was plenty of evidence of the veracity of their claims, and no one would disbelieve them, knowing Savina's history.

But locked in the cabin on a ship that was being evacuated—there was nothing she could do to salvage this situation.

She'd never realized, until just that moment, how afraid she was to die. She'd teased death her whole life, dancing along the edge of it like a rope dancer, revelling in the danger. But now that it had arrived—now that she'd lost her balance and was tumbling over the edge—she realized that the thing that fed the thrill, that brought the pleasant racing of her heart at a dangerous prospect, was terror. And she was plunging into it, over her head. Drowning.

Since she was a child—since she was seven years old, holding a tiny, dirty, bundled baby in her arms—she'd never felt this cold fear, the kind that overtook her and curled itself around her until she was smothered in it.

"I'm sorry," she whispered. And she wasn't sure if she was talking, in her head, to Beni, or to Nicolau, or to Rafel, or to Joska—a woman who'd shown herself to be a truly good person, the kind of person Savina had never even aspired to be.

There was a pounding on the cabin door, and Savina jerked her head up in shock.

"Savina? Savina, are you in there?"

For a moment, she just stared. Then she shouted, her voice

cracking with desperate hope, "I'm here! Help me, please."

"I'm trying. Give me a moment."

Savina recognized the rough voice, with its dry humour.

There was a small *pop* from outside, then the door was yanked open and Joska stood silhouetted in the opening. Blood ran down her face and into her eyes from a shallow cut on her forehead, and she was bleeding from a long gash down one arm, but her grim face was somehow the most wonderful thing Savina had ever seen.

Behind her stood Beni.

Savina blinked at them for a moment, and for just a moment she thought she might start crying.

"Come on," Joska snapped. "The ship's breaking up. We have to get off. The portal closed, and the energy wave hit us hard. You and Beni head back to the ship, I'll meet you there."

Savina jumped to her feet at the urgent tone in the woman's voice. "Beni," she said. "Can you get the restraints off me?"

Beni nodded and stepped forward, finding her unerringly. Their hand ran down Savina's arm until they located the restraint, then they yanked a sparker from their pocket and clipped it on. A moment later, the restraint popped free.

Savina rubbed her wrists, glancing up at Joska. "Where are you going?"

Joska shook her head grimly. "I'm going back for Rafel. Beni found where he's being held, but I can't get through to him on the wavelink, so I have to assume he's locked up." She glanced at Savina. "If he and I aren't back and the ship looks like it's going, you two get out. Don't wait for us." She paused, a rueful smile pulling at her lips. "Although I suppose I don't have to tell the two of you that. You seem quite adept at saving your own skins."

What she'd said was only the truth, and a week ago, Savina would have accepted the offer without hesitation.

But she found herself shaking her head.

"No," she said. "I'm going with you to find Rafel."

Joska stared at her.

She rolled her eyes. "We have to find Nicolau anyways, and besides, I don't know how to pilot the damn ship."

Joska's eyebrows, already raised, practically disappeared into her hairline. But she nodded gravely, a small smile twitching at the corners of her mouth. "As you say."

"If Savina's going, so am I," said Beni, the softness of their voice betraying their own terror.

Savina glanced at them reflexively, but one look at her sibling's face told her she wouldn't be able to talk Beni into staying behind, and there wasn't time to try.

Joska glanced between the two of them, then gave a curt nod. "I won't lie and say I wouldn't be grateful for your help." She jerked her head towards the long corridor. "Let's go."

They sprinted down the corridors, dodging around panicked clusters of people, crew and passengers and soldiers mixed. The soldiers were screaming and shouting in a desperate, futile attempt to keep order, weapons out, some of them firing indiscriminately into the crowd in their panic. Joska slowed a moment, indecisive, then shook her head grimly and kept running.

"Rafel's being held in the port stern deck, floor three," she said over her shoulder to Savina. "Where's this Nicolau, or whoever he is?"

"Beni?" gasped Savina.

Beni nodded grimly. "I'm already scanning for him," they said. "Should only be a minute or two more, I think—there are a lot of records to go through."

Savina nodded, and activated her own wavelink with a flick of her eyes. "Directions to port stern deck, floor three," she snapped, and a moment later a pulsing red dot blinked on her retinal screen over the transparent overlay of the ship's schematics. The translucent arrow in her field of vision pointed her down a side corridor. She followed it, and the others followed her.

Shoving through the chaos got more difficult as they approached the centre of the ship, near the exits to the emergency bays. But when Savina pulled out her longest knife and her widest smile, the crowds parted for them with surprising rapidity—the three of them weren't here for the escape shuttles anyway, so it wasn't as if they were trying to take a place in the corridors that anyone else was competing for.

Joska glanced at Savina, eyebrows raised and a wry expression on her face, but didn't say anything.

The crowds lessened as they neared the stern of the ship. Savina led them to a crew ladder and slid down, not taking the time to wait for the lift, then started down another empty corridor, the others' footsteps echoing behind her.

"Nicolau is on the main deck," Beni gasped out behind her. "We'll have to get through there to get back to the *Dolphin*."

Savina nodded. "We'll grab him on our way out, if he hasn't already evacuated." The ship was shaking and groaning, the wail of alarms a wall of sound that pummelled her eardrums. "Give me the coordinates to where Rafel's being held."

A moment later, they popped up on her retinal screen.

She turned down a corridor and pulled to a stop in front of a door the translucent marker on her screen had overlaid with a bright red.

"This one," she panted.

Joska stepped past her and banged on the door. "Rafel!"

"Captain?" There was disbelief in the familiar gruff tone.

"Stand back, I'm going to blow the lock," Joska said tersely. She clipped a small detonator to the door fastener. "You two, stand back as well," she said over her shoulder. She stepped back herself as she hit the controller, and there was a puff of smoke and a small *pop*.

When the smoke cleared, the door was swinging loose. Joska yanked it open, and Rafel stumbled out.

He looked worse for the wear, one eye swollen all the way shut, a bruise spreading across the side of his face. He cradled one arm as if it pained him, and his breaths came shallow and rough—probably a broken rib, or a dozen.

"Come on," said Joska again, her voice tight, and he nodded and followed her out. Savina was certain she caught, just for a moment, the shine of tears in his eyes.

The ship shook violently, and Savina was thrown against the corridor wall and Joska and Rafel thrown to the ground.

"What—" the captain began, pulling herself painfully to her feet.

The ship shuddered again, and they all grabbed instinctively for the walls.

The hallway lights flickered and died, plunging them into complete darkness.

Savina felt her feet leave the floor, that dizzying, disorienting sensation of zero gravity.

"They've lost emergency power," said Joska grimly from the darkness. "All the emergency systems will be going soon." She paused a moment. "There are handholds on the ceiling and walls, for when the gravity system gives out. We'll have to use them. We don't have much time."

Emergency lights flickered on, running along the sides of the corridors, and in the dim yellowish light, Savina could make out

Beni, who'd already grasped the handholds.

Of course—the echolocator in her sibling's wavelink wouldn't work any differently with or without light.

The ship shuddered again, and Savina was jostled into Joska and Rafel. Beni reached out and grabbed Savina's arm, dragging her up to the handholds, and Savina grabbed on with both hands.

Someone screamed from one of the cabins at the far end of the corridor. Joska turned back, but Savina grabbed the woman's arm and shoved her forwards. "There's no time, you said so yourself. We get out now, or we die with them."

"We can't just—" Joska began, but Rafel shot Savina grateful look and snapped, "Captain, she's right. You can't save whoever that is— by the time you got down there and set the detonator, you'd both have lost your chance to get out. And so would I, because I'm not damn well going without you. Come on!"

Joska's face was tight with indecision, but Savina didn't give her time to think about it, pushing herself forward along the handholds and dragging the captain behind her.

By the time they got to the end of the corridor, Joska must have realized it was hopeless. She shook herself free of Savina's grip and grabbed the handles as well. She was better at it than Savina and Beni, and Savina tried to imitate her smooth motions—pull, glide, grab, pull, glide, grab—a little like the monkey-bars she'd played on as a child in the worn-out playground in the compound.

The ship was shaking, each jolt threatening to pull them free from the handholds. Savina clung on grimly, keeping an eye over her shoulder for Beni as she went, ready to grab her sibling if necessary.

And then there was another jolt, even larger than the last two, and Joska's face went bloodless.

"It's broken up," she choked. "We're too late."

Savina glanced past her, and saw, with a sick horror, what the captain meant—the entire port section of the ship had broken off, held to the main ship only by the slightly flexible interior lining. The lining itself was strained to its limits, the material groaning like a living thing in pain. It would be mere moments before it broke open, sucking them and everyone else on the port deck into deep space.

And there was no way across the stretched broken section—no handholds, nothing.

"I'll push Rafel across first," said Joska grimly. "If he makes it, I'll try with the rest of you."

Savina gave a snort of exasperation and shoved past the woman, reaching into her belt. She pulled out a small cable gun and squinted, judging the distance.

It should be long enough, barely.

She depressed the trigger, and the compressed coils shot out, the magnetic tip catching the wall on the far side. Savina glanced around, then shoved the pistol through the largest of the handholds and twisted it around the cable, tying it as firmly as she was able.

"Go!" she snapped, and the others didn't wait to ask questions, pulling themselves hands over hand along the cable.

The groans from the strained interior lining grew to a sound akin to a shriek of pain. Savina pulled herself along faster, gritting her teeth against the enveloping terror that threatened to overwhelm her.

And then they were at the other side, and she was pulling Beni and Rafel through and onto the handholds that led to the closed-off blast door. Joska swore, and Beni pushed past her, tapping something into their wavelink and then running their fingers down the door until they touched the lock. It spun, and the doors hissed open, and the four of them fell through, gravity once again in effect. Beni rolled to their feet, and Savina grabbed their hand, guiding it to the controls. Beni hit them frantically, and the noise of the door slamming shut was overshadowed by a grinding, tearing sound, the scream of tortured metal, as the entire port section of the ship broke free.

Joska pulled Rafel to his feet, and the four of them took off at a dead run down the now almost-deserted corridors.

"Is that man you want to save still aboard?" the captain panted from ahead of her.

"Beni?" Savina gasped.

"He's still on board. Still on the main deck," Beni called.

Joska nodded and turned down a corridor. "It won't take any more time to get back to the *Dolphin* going through the main deck than around it, I don't think. But you'd damn well better find him quickly."

From the screaming and shouting below them as they approached the deck, it was obvious that more people were trapped on board still than had gotten off.

They broke through onto the main deck, and Savina muttered something into her wavelink. A moment later, a shining translucent halo of red appeared on her retinal screen over the head of someone near the back of the crowd. Savina pulled out her knife and shoved her way through towards it. "Joska, take Beni and Rafel around the edge and meet me on the other side of the deck," she called over her shoulder.

She pushed her way through the panicking crowd until she reached the tall, auburn-haired young man, his face drawn with shock and horror, and grabbed him by the arm.

"What—" he began.

She didn't give him time to finish, simply slapped a restraint on his wrist and jerked him along. "I'm trying to save your life," she hissed as she shoved him ahead of her. "Don't try to fight or I'll damn well paralyze you."

"But the others—" he began.

She sent a small warning shock through the restraint, and at last, his shoulders tight with strain, he let her push him forward.

Joska and the others waited at the mouth of the corridor that led towards the hangar bay. When Savina reached them, they set off along it at a run, none of them bothering to speak.

By the time they reached the hangar bay entrance Savina's breath was sobbing in her throat, a sharp cramp like a knife between her ribs. Beni hit the control, and the doors slid open. A few dozen crew members who must have been trapped inside rushed for the opening, but Joska, too breathless to speak, held up a hand, gesturing to the ship.

"Get on if you want to come with us," Rafel growled, pain making his gruff voice even harsher than usual. The hapless crew members glanced around in panic, then seemed to decide that any vessel that would get them off the dying behemoth was safety enough. Before the loading ramp was even finished lowering they were scrambling on board, packing into the cramped space that had been built to house five, maybe six people.

Once everyone was inside, Savina hit the controls, sealing them in. Joska had pushed past Savina and was already on her way to the flight deck, Rafel close behind her. Savina snapped at the panicked crew members to sit still and shut up, then glowered at Nicolau. "You can damn well make them behave," she said, then she and Beni followed the captain.

"Strap in, if you can," Joska said briskly over the amplifiers, her hands dancing across the controls. "Beni, if you would get the outer airlock door—"

Beni nodded, dropping into a seat and muttering something into their wavelink. The ship hummed to life, and a moment later, the outer doors hissed open.

"And I guess this is where we find out if they bothered to lock down our ship when they locked us up," said Joska. "Savina—your ship. Give me control if you want me to get us off."

Savina tapped her wavelink through to the ship's controls. "Authorize Joska to pilot," she snapped. Joska hit the controls, and the ship lurched up and forward.

Savina barely had time to notice, with a hint of relief, the government agent's ship still parked in the hangar bay, and then they were out, the airlock doors sliding closed behind them.

She watched the ship's screen as they shot out into the darkness.

The dying ship behind them glowed like a beacon on the screen. The small flickers of escape pods flared brightly for the briefest moment as they left the airlocks, tiny dots against the main ship's massive hull, which itself was a tiny dot in comparison to the expanse of space surrounding them. They flickered out like fireflies as the *Dolphin* shot forward, Joska bent grimly over the controls.

And then there was a burst of blinding light, swallowed up almost as quickly by the vacuum as the brief flashes from the fleeing escape pods.

Then there was nothing at all, except a halo of dust and debris, expanding slowly outward.

Savina stood stunned for a long moment. At last, she glanced around the cabin at the others.

"Savina?" asked Beni in a small voice. "What happened?"

"The ship's fuel storage must have lost pressure," said Savina. Her own voice sounded hollow in her ears. "They're gone. The ship. All of them."

Beni's face was cut with shock, and looking at them, Savina felt a quick pang of worry.

Rafel sat stoically, staring straight ahead, but she could once again see the hint of tears in his eyes. And Joska—even without gravity, her posture was slumped, the expression on her face raw, sick horror.

34

Alba

Alba stared out the plex window of the pod into the blackness of space surrounding them.

The remnants of the ship expanded outward in a sparkling arc, like the drift of tiny seedlings from an angel-hair flower plucked by a child and puffed free from its stem for a wish.

It was hard to comprehend the violence and death that accompanied that gently expanding halo.

"More space dust to float through the next portal that opens," murmured Aran, a note of bitterness in his voice. He was stroking the hideous, venomous creature that was currently cuddled in his lap, its tentacles wrapped protectively around him.

"Maybe that's all it was, after all that," said Istvay quietly. "Just ships broken up by the portal itself."

Aran glanced up at them with a quick, brief smile. "Maybe."

Alba could hear in his voice that he didn't believe it. To be honest, neither did she. But she found she was grateful to Istvay for making the comment regardless. It was something, at least, to hold on to.

And the Great Mystery itself knew how badly they needed that right now.

She glanced around the tiny, cramped pod.

It had been built to fit four, and had been designed for utility rather than comfort. Aside from the pilot's seat, the only places to sit were on the small sleeping pods, which were stacked almost atop each other, or on the narrow strip of bench between them. With Feliu laid carefully in one of the sleeping pods and Yosip in the pilot's seat, the other four passengers, plus the tentacled death-beast, were packed in shoulder to shoulder.

Alba turned back to stare out the window, a strange hollow emptiness sitting in her chest.

She'd traveled off-planet before, of course, in the execution of her duties. But this—cast adrift in an overcrowded escape pod, in a place so remote that without the portal none of them would have reached it in their lifetimes or their grandchildren's lifetimes even on a generation ship; so distant, in fact, that with the portal closed, their chances of getting back were virtually nil, and even if they found a planet, with no idea whether its inhabitants would help them or murder them—if someone had told her that she'd find herself in this position, she would have laughed in their faces.

And yet, here she was.

She'd lived through plenty of hopeless events in the course of her life. And each time, through a combination of iron determination and sharp intelligence, she'd been able to force things to work out in her favour—or at the least, had survived them. And she'd come to conclude that nothing was really as hopeless as it seemed, once the dust settled.

She glanced over at the unconscious Feliu, with a slightly bitter smile.

He'd been right. She'd come to believe in her own invincibility.

She sighed, and leaned wearily back against the uncomfortable side of the pod.

One look at Feliu reminded her of how very false her own vision of her abilities had rung, when it came down to it.

There was a sharp, insistent beep from the pod's control panel, and Alba's mind jerked back to the present.

Yosip turned quickly to the control panel, and she could see the tension in his shoulders as he bent over it.

She could feel the tension in her own shoulders.

What else could possibly go wrong? Or more to the point, how much more of things going wrong would any of them survive?

And then his tense form relaxed, and he laughed softly, turning back to them. "We just might have had a stroke of luck. We just might have had been unbelievably, incredibly lucky."

"What is it?" Aran asked, standing quickly.

"There's a planet ahead. It was hidden behind the ship, but it looks like it's within easy range of the pod's capabilities. Maybe thirty, forty planetary hours away—well within the capacity of our supplies and oxygen."

Aran had come to crouch beside Yosip, and she could see the blossoming interest on his face, rapidly drowning out both the terror and the despair.

"I have some equipment we can hook into the pod's sensors." Aran's voice was brightening with excitement. "It doesn't have a long range on its own, but added to the pod's capabilities, we may be able to pick up whether or not there are lifeforms as we get closer. Granted, the presence of lifeforms doesn't mean the planet's habitable for humans," he added, glancing reflexively at the oddly shaped lump on his shoulder, its tentacles dangling down his back.

"But at least it raises the chances."

Yosip nodded, and Aran bent over the controls beside him, pulling what looked like a sort of scanner from a pouch around his waist.

Alba glanced around the cabin again.

Istvay was leaned back against the pod's side, eyes closed, body slack with exhaustion, mouth hanging slightly open. Ines hunched in her seat, a disc opened in front of her with a thick spread of documents displayed on it, some of which Alba recognized as the strange scratchings that might have been a language that they'd found on the box that had passed through the portal. She looked just as young and timid as ever, but Alba had spent enough time around her to know that neither youth nor timidity would affect the keenness of her mind.

Alba smiled to herself softly.

It took its own type of courage, really—to keep going even when you felt so far out of your depth it could take your breath away.

Feliu was still resting where they'd laid him. His eyes were closed, but his chest rose and fell more evenly since Istvay and Aran had treated the wound. Aran had assured her the wound was a clean one, and it should heal quickly. Perhaps he wasn't a doctor, but he was clearly very familiar with biological processes, and besides that— well, she found she trusted his judgement.

She turned back to the window, staring out at the place where the portal had been. It was now gone so thoroughly that she could only identify it by marking the place of the spreading cloud of debris that had once been their ship.

There was something cold inside her, a chunk of ice in her chest that wouldn't melt.

Just as well. If it did—if for one moment she allowed herself to contemplate the enormity of what had happened—her heart might simply stop beating with the horror of it. The sheer number of people killed, their bodies scattered through space, no remains to bring home to loved ones who might spend their entire lives never knowing what had happened.

And she'd been the one to propose this mission.

It had been Cavaco who'd forced them to go forward when she would have turned back. But she couldn't escape the cold, hard fact that if it hadn't been for her, those frozen, lifeless bodies might still be warm and alive.

"You should get some sleep, Madam."

She started, and glanced up to see Yosip, crouched in the narrow confines of the pod. He was smiling at her, lines of good humour creasing around his eyes.

And she found herself smiling back, despite everything.

"So should you," she said.

His smile broadened. "I intend to. I've set in a course, and the pod should do very well on autopilot until we get closer."

Alba glanced around the cabin once more.

Ines was still huddled over her translation documents, but Aran seemed to have taken Yosip's advice. The sleeping Istvay had been transferred to one of the pods, and Aran stretched out on the floor beneath them, the murder-beast splayed out on his chest and eyeing the rest of them suspiciously.

That still left them short one pod. Alba hesitated, but Ines looked up from her work and managed a small smile.

"It's fine, Madam Chief Justice," she said. "I won't be able to get to sleep until I've gone over these documents a couple more times, and that'll take me a few planetary hours."

Alba raised an eyebrow, but the girl looked so pitifully hopeful, like a puppy waiting for a bone, that Alba gave a curt nod. "Thank you,

Ines."

She climbed into one of the remaining sleeping pods, pulled it shut, and drifted into an exhausted slumber.

She woke to Aran's excited exclamation, and rolled over stiffly, hitting the button to unseal the sleeping pod. It sprang open, and she blinked at the disorienting flood of light in her face.

"Look!"

She could make out Aran's words now, instead of just the tone.

"Look at the concentration right there—that's got to be a settlement of some sort. And that's only the side of the planet that we can see from our position." The young scientist sounded utterly delighted, as if the prospect of running into an entire settlement of alien lifeforms with questionable motives was the most wonderful thing he could imagine.

Alba sat up, blinking the sleep from her eyes, to see Yosip and Aran huddled together over the control panel.

"I suggest putting us down around here," said Aran, leaning over to touch something on the screen. "It's within a day or so's walk of the settlement, and it looks like there'll be shelter. We can set up the protection screen and gather all the survivors together, and then see if we can make contact with the life forms and determine whether or not they're sapient."

Yosip nodded. "I'll put out a beacon for the other pods and shuttles."

"You want to give the soldiers who were bloody shooting at you another chance?" Istvay's voice was groggy with sleep, but still managed to sound grumpy.

Alba turned to see them sitting up in their pod, looking pale and weak and thoroughly irritated at the world in general.

"Istvay. We can't just leave people to die," said Aran. "Anyways, you saw what happened last time Ani got angry. I don't think they'll bother us too much."

Alba shot the scientist a quick look.

She was somehow quite certain that this was a story she did not wish to hear.

Istvay snorted, but Aran had already turned his attention back to the scanner, his eyes lit with interest.

Alba found she was smiling, despite herself.

"Madam?"

She turned to see Feliu, sitting up rather stiffly. His voice was hoarse and cracked, and she could hear the pain in it. But, as Aran had predicted, he seemed to be recovering—at least, his face had regained some of its natural colour.

"What are your plans now?" he asked softly.

She wanted to sag back into the sleeping pod, close her eyes, and just for a moment pretend the weight of this entire mission didn't rest on her.

But she couldn't. In the end, she was responsible this: for everything that had happened up to this point, and everything would happen after. And perhaps that weight—the weight of the lives lost, and the lives still to save—was too great for one person to bear. But bear it she must.

She took a deep breath. "As far as I'm concerned, nothing substantial has changed. I am still the leader of a diplomatic mission. We still have a strong chance of making contact with the beings who, presumably, sent us the items through the portal in first place. I intend, therefore, to attempt to regroup as much of the diplomatic party as possible once we arrive on the planet, and then initiate contact with any sapient life forms we may encounter."

"The—the portal is closed, Madam," said Feliu.

"Well, if the life forms behind the portal are responsible for its closure, perhaps they can be induced to reopen it. And if it is purely a natural phenomenon, perhaps they will at the least be able to give us an idea of when it might reopen on its own. I refuse to give our situation up as hopeless until I have a much stronger cause to do so," she said briskly.

She could feel all their eyes on her now, and she hoped, vaguely, that she sounded more certain than she felt.

"Yes, Madam," said Feliu at last. "I suppose you're right."

Alba sighed and leaned back against the wall of the pod.

Despite her brave words, she was at heart a realist. She knew very well that, in the end, the final objective of her grand efforts may shift to simply a desperate bid to save the lives of the five other passengers sharing the escape pod with her.

But as she looked around at their weary, exhausted faces, she realized with abrupt clarity that if saving these people was the only thing she accomplished—in the end, she would not feel the loss of her hoped-for grand legacy nearly as sharply as she would have imagined.

When at last the escape pod burned through the atmosphere and set down gently in a clearing amid the dense greenery of the planet, everyone in the pod had their faces glued to the plex windows. Aran, in particular, looked almost ready to faint for joy at the prospect of likely losing his life to some vicious alien life form.

"It looks like the atmosphere is oxygen-based, if we couldn't already tell from the plant life," he murmured, studying a sensor in his hand. "And I don't see traces of any dangerous gasses. We should be able to breathe without assistance."

Istvay had already gotten to their feet and was pulling down the emergency kits. "First item of business is to get to a shelter. Something stronger than this pod, if possible—maybe a cave? Yosip, put out the scanners and see what you can find."

Yosip nodded and turned back to the control panel.

"Aran," said Alba quietly.

He turned to her, eyes still lit up with repressed excitement, and she sighed.

"Aran. What are your intentions going forward? May I—may I count you as a member of our diplomatic party?"

For a moment, he hesitated, and she saw the way his eyes flicked to Istvay.

She followed his gaze. Even her untrained eye could see the unhealthy hollows under their cheekbones, the deepening circles under their eyes that were far too prominent to have come simply from the strain and exhaustion of the last few days.

"My intention is to find the cure," said Aran in a low voice, turning back to her. "That's why I came on this mission in the first place. I'll get the rest of you somewhere safe first. And as long as it looks like diplomacy is our best option for finding the cure, I'll be whatever part of your diplomatic party you want me to be. But I am damn well finding that cure, if I have to die to do it."

There was a fierceness to his expression that left her in no doubt of his sincerity.

She studied him for a moment, then nodded. "I suppose that's acceptable," she said quietly. And for the first time since she'd known him, he flashed her a quick, genuine smile that changed the entire look of his face.

Istvay turned back, holding out a loosely filled knapsack. Aran took it and slung it over his shoulders, the murder-beast shifting out of the way for it then resettling herself in what was clearly a practiced dance.

"I found something, not too far distant," said Yosip, looking up from the scanner. "I think it might serve. I'll send the coordinates through to you."

A moment later, Alba's retinal screen blinked with the alert for an incoming transmission.

Istvay gave a deep sigh, shouldering their own pack, and glanced at the door with clear reluctance. "Well, I suppose we'd better," they said.

Aran nodded, clearly giddy at the prospect of stepping out into the jungle hellscape waiting for them. He tightened his grip on a stun pistol, and the murder-beast gave a small hiss, pulling herself more tightly down on his shoulders.

"Aran—" Istvay began.

Aran turned to them, rolling his eyes. "I know, be careful. I get it. But Pishti, there's probably things out there no one has seen before —"

"You're not making me feel any better about this," Istvay grumbled. With obvious hesitance, they hit the controls for the hatch, and it hissed and sprang open.

The wet heat of the jungle, rolling up the short loading ramp, hit them like an oncoming transport, and Alba almost staggered under it. Aran hardly seemed to notice, though, his gaze fixed on the scenery outside, his grin almost wider than his face. The moment the ramp descended, he stepped outside cautiously.

They all watched him as he reached the end of the ramp and took a few steps into the jungle. He pulled out a sensor and turned in a slow circle, holding it out, then turned back to the ship.

"There are life forms everywhere, but I haven't calibrated this thing to the new environment, so it'll be picking up everything— insects, worms, what have you. You may as well come on out, since —"

His words cut off abruptly, and he spun around as something burst through the trees behind him. Alba caught a confused impression of a mass of muscles, claws, and fangs, and Istvay shouted in alarm, starting down the ramp. And then something launched itself from Aran's shoulder.

The massive, cat-like beast howled as whatever it was landed on its back, and it twisted to tear at its tormenter. Then its body went rigid, and it dropped to the ground, twitching.

Aran looked horrified.

"Ani!" he scolded. "We've talked about this! There were a hundred other ways we could've dealt with the problem. Now look, it's dead, and I didn't even get a chance to—" He yelped, jumping forward, and pulled Ani, now turned a deep green, off the monster with some effort, as she clung on with her tentacles. "Don't eat that! You don't know what it is, it might make you sick!"

It took Alba a moment to realized, with some bemusement, that the scientist wasn't horrified by the fact he'd almost been taken apart by something longer than the entire escape pod, with fangs the length of his hand, but for the fact that his tentacle-beast might get a stomach-ache.

Grudgingly, Ani allowed herself to be pulled away, and Aran gathered her gently in his arms, stroking her.

"Like I said, you can come out," he said over his shoulder.

In front of him, the monster's form was slowly flattening, presumably as its insides were liquefied by whatever Ani had injected into it.

Istvay sighed, shaking their head. "He means well," they said wryly. "I suppose he's right, we may as well go out. He and I both have stun guns, and the rest of you can take the rifles from the soldiers. And there's always Ani, if things get bad."

Alba glanced around at the terrified faces of the others.

If she were being honest with herself, her own legs were feeling distinctly shaky after the last five minutes. But she straightened, taking one of the rifles from where Istvay had laid them on the seat —although what good it would do her, she had no idea, considering it would take her probably five minutes to figure how to work the damn thing—and forced her feet to move her towards the exit.

Aran held out a hand to help her down, and she took it graciously, steadfastly avoiding looking at Ani, who was snuggled in the crook of his other arm.

When they'd all disembarked, they had to wait another few minutes as Aran studied, with every semblance of complete fascination, the dead creature lying before them, and then launched into a technical discussion with Istvay which Alba couldn't follow, and didn't care to.

At last, though, she cleared her throat loudly. "It appears the sun is sinking below its zenith. If we wish to find shelter before dark, I suggest we start immediately."

Aran looked up, clear reluctance on his features, but he nodded. "You're right. Yosip, the other pods and shuttles should be coming down close to where we are, correct?"

Yosip nodded. "I set the beacon, at any rate. If they're looking for a safe place to land, they'll probably try to set down near it, seeing as we made it down in one piece."

Aran nodded, glancing around at the thick vegetation surrounding them. "Alright. I'll go with you to the shelter and help get things set up. Once we've done that, I'll come back to look for survivors.

Tomorrow we can start towards the settlement, see what we can find."

Alba closed her eyes for a moment.

For some reason, huddling in a shelter as the sky darkened overhead, without the exuberant presence of the young scientist and his frazzled best friend, was a more daunting prospect than she liked to admit. But he was right—any other survivors would likely need their help.

She looked up and nodded. "Thank you, Aran. That is acceptable." She took a deep breath. "Now, if you would be so good as to lead the way …"

35

Savina stared straight ahead out the window as the *Dolphin* made its slow way towards the gentle curve of the strange planet ahead.

Now that they were safe—or at least, as safe as they could be, considering they were in an uncharted universe—her adrenaline was giving way to that strange, dull numbness.

They were alive, yes, by some frankly unfathomable stroke of luck. But they were trapped, so far beyond anything she knew that there was no way her brain could even comprehend it.

Joska sighed, looking up from the control panel. "Well, at least we resupplied when we got the thrusters repaired. But this ship wasn't meant to hold more than six people. We have limited fuel, and no idea how long the supplies will have to last us."

"The ship's in bad shape herself," Rafel muttered. "We when we got caught in that aftershock, it blew some of the systems. Nothing major, but we'll be limping along at about half our normal speed until we find a place to put down and fix her."

Joska tipped her head back against the seat wearily. "Well, this may be the worst mess we've been in for a while. But considering our run of luck lately, I can't say it's entirely unexpected."

There was a dry humour to her tone that almost made Savina stare.

This woman had been ripped away from everything she knew, and shoved into a nightmare. In her place, Savina would have been furious, vowing vengeance on whoever had brought her there.

Which meant in this case, of course, herself and Beni.

But the captain didn't seem particularly angry, just resigned. And once again, Savina wondered what this woman's life had been like that this was her reaction to a disaster of this magnitude.

"Joska," she said at last.

The woman glanced up at her.

Savina took a deep breath. "Why?" she asked at last, bluntly. "Why did you come back to save Beni and me?"

The captain studied her for a moment. At last she shook her head and gave a soft, rueful chuckle. "I suppose I'm a glutton for punishment," she said. "Seeing as you hijacked my ship, threatened to kill me more times than I can quite frankly count, and got all of us into this mess in the first place."

Savina narrowed her eyes, and the captain's chuckle turned into a genuine laugh.

She turned back to her controls, punching in a couple more coordinates, then leaned back. "I guess I couldn't bear to see two kids blown up in an explosion like that, not even terrors like the two of you," she said at last, not looking at Savina. "You're a bad one, through and through, and you've proved it to me. But I have a niece who'd be around your age. And—" she shrugged. "I guess maybe I know what it's like to be young and scared. And so maybe I can't blame you as much as I should. Probably be the death of me one of these days."

Savina stared at the back of the woman's head, the grey streaked through her thick black hair, pulled back into its no-nonsense ponytail.

A week ago, she would have brushed the woman's words off as nothing but a cynical ploy to get Savina to let down her guard. She'd known you couldn't trust someone who was Orthodox. You couldn't trust anyone. If you didn't hit first, and hard, you'd be killed, that was how the system worked.

And then this damn woman, who she'd kidnapped and threatened, had saved her life. Beni's life, too, when Savina wouldn't have been able to herself.

Rafel stiffened suddenly, glancing over at Joska. "Captain," he said, a twinge of excitement in his voice. "Now the debris is cleared and our sensors are working, I'm picking up a beacon. It's saying there's a safe place to land, and survivors." He reached forward, his thick finger marking a pulsing dot on the outline of the planet's surface on the screen.

A slow smile spread across Joska's face. "Well, that's the best damn news I've heard all day." She paused. "Not that there's been a lot of competition for the title." She glanced around the cabin. "I'll set a course for the emergency beacon, unless I hear any objections."

Savina wasn't inclined to disagree, and Beni didn't speak, just faced out the window, their expression still glassy with shock.

"It'll still take us a while to get down there," said Rafel in his gruff voice. "No need to stay on the flight deck the whole time."

The dismissal was rude, perhaps, but Savina didn't really care. Her brain was too full, too many thoughts swirling insistently through her head for her to be able to make sense of them around anyone else. So she just nodded, and made her slow way back to her cabin.

Nicolau, under Joska's orders, was organizing the survivors, directing them into anywhere on the ship with room. Savina paused a moment, watching him, and something tightened in her chest.

Her baby brother.

She could still see in his face traces of the five-year-old who'd played in the yard of the farmhouse near the compound.

But he wasn't a baby any longer.

He straightened and glanced over, catching her eye. She dropped her gaze quickly and went to brush past him, but he grabbed her arm.

"Wait. Please. I … I need to talk to you." Nicolau's voice was rough, and she glanced up despite herself. His face was set and pale, and there were tear streaks down his cheeks. Again, her chest tightened painfully.

He'd been happy before she arrived. She'd never meant for this to happen. She'd never meant for him to have a reason to know who she was.

"Look," he continued. "I don't know you. But you saved me. Only me. My … my friends were back there, and now they're dead. Why?"

She studied him for a long moment. "Are—are your parents safe?" she asked at last.

She wasn't sure why she'd asked the question. Only that he'd looked so happy with them, the last time she'd seen him.

He nodded. "Yes. They're back on Colorida." He paused. "Do … you know them?"

She gave a quick, brusque jerk of her head. "Yes."

He nodded slowly, releasing her arm as if he took that as her answer.

It wasn't really a lie. And he didn't need to know the rest, not right now.

Maybe not ever.

The tiny cabin that Beni and Savina shared had been left empty, and she pulled herself down the corridor and slipped inside.

She was alive, and Beni was alive, and they'd saved Nicolau. She should be desperately grateful. But she found it difficult to feel anything at all.

She wasn't sure how long she'd been sitting there when there was a soft tap on the door.

"Yes?" she called listlessly.

The door opened, and Joska poked her head in. "Mind if I come in?" she asked, and Savina didn't have the energy to tell her no.

The captain pushed herself into the room, glancing around, then, with a shrug, pulled herself down onto Beni's cot, anchoring herself with the straps.

For a few moments, neither of them spoke.

Finally, Joska said, "So. Who's Nicolau? A lover?"

Savina almost laughed. "Brother."

"And he doesn't know you?"

She nodded, and didn't offer an explanation.

Joska didn't ask for one, just gave her a wry smile. "Well, he seems like a nice enough boy. Goes to show it's not all about genetics."

Savina turned to glower at the woman, and she chuckled, then sobered again, still watching Savina.

Savina turned away, not willing to let the captain see her discomfort.

For a few moments more they sat in silence. At last Joska said, "You alright?"

Savina looked up in surprise at the sympathy in her tone.

Joska's gaze was sharp, but kind. And for just a moment, Savina was tempted, for the first time in her life, to open her mouth and tell this strange, quiet woman everything—about her family back home, about the compound, about the dull, routine terror of growing up in a place where everything was a threat and everyone a danger. About trying to keep Beni safe.

About what she'd done to keep Nicolau safe.

How she'd always been certain there'd been meaning behind what she'd gone through, but that now, suddenly, she didn't know anymore. How she didn't know, anymore, what was true, and what was a lie.

How lost she was. How afraid. How alone.

Joska didn't speak, her eyes thoughtful, her gaze penetrating.

Savina managed a quick smile. "Nothing's wrong," she said. "Just a bit of a shock, is all."

The captain was still watching her, and it was obvious she didn't believe Savina's reassurances. But she only nodded noncommittally. "Nothing wrong except for the obvious, you mean," she said with a small grin.

Savina's smile grew genuine for just a moment, then she looked away.

Joska shifted on the bunk. "So," she said quietly. "What do you suggest we do next? Since this is your ship."

Savina turned to stare at her, and Joska chuckled again. "No need to look at me like that. We're together now, at least until we can figure out a way to get out of this alive. I'm assuming you won't stab Rafel and me in the back until you know you won't need us any longer."

There was a hint of amusement in her voice, though, that told Savina she wasn't really serious.

"Rafel's been taking scans of the communications," Joska continued. "The diplomatic party survived, it appears—or most of them, anyway. From what I know of Alba, she's bullheaded enough to try to start negotiations, portal or no. Joining up with them might be our best hope. At the very least, if we're in a group big enough, the aliens might not be able to kill us all at once."

Savina sucked in a breath at the mention of Alba's name, and she wasn't prepared for the quick, hot surge of rage that flashed through her.

Damn that woman to hell.

Everything had been fine before Alba had sent an agent after Savina, cobbled together a mission through the portal that had dragged Nicolau along. And since then, Savina's entire life had gone up in smoke—everything she'd known, everything she'd believed, everything she'd been sure of, gone in the course of a few relentless days.

Even if everything had been a lie, even if Savina was only collateral damage and the warrant for her issued as payback for a murdered councillor, with the thoughtless confidence of a bureaucrat trying to solve a political dilemma, it didn't honestly matter. Alba knew Savina's past. Alba was a judge with a reputation for harsh justice. Alba would kill her, and Beni and Nicolau would be caught up in the aftermath, if they weren't simply killed as well.

Whatever had happened, whatever the reason for it—Alba had to die.

The captain was still watching her.

Savina nodded absently. "You're right. That's probably our best option—get around as many people as we can, and hope there's safety in numbers."

"And I doubt anyone will recognize us, unless that government agent of yours managed to get on her ship and off that place in the few seconds before it blew up."

Savina nodded again, and felt a small smile growing in the corner of her mouth.

Joska had been right—they were in this together, at least until they found a way back. But that might come sooner than the woman imagined. And even if it didn't—well, they'd all be mixed in with the rest of the survivors soon enough. She'd no longer be Savina's responsibility, certainly.

And out here, far away from everything they knew, everyone guarding the judge would be watching for aggression from alien life forms. Which would make things much, much easier.

"You're looking happy," said Joska, a note of question in her voice.

Savina turned to her, letting her dimples show. "I've been thinking about what you said. You're right. You never know, we may survive this after all."

Joska nodded warily, unstrapping herself from the seat. "Well, if you're in agreement, I'll head back to the controls. We'll reach the planet in fifteen or so planetary hours, give or take."

Savina nodded, still smiling, as Joska left, closing the door behind her.

A few more hours.

Then Alba would be dead, and Savina would be free. And everything else she could work out from there.

She hummed to herself quietly as she gathered her things in preparation for their landing.

36

Aran

Aran sighed, and leaned wearily against one of the strange, rough-barked trees. He'd learned from experience that the trees with smooth bark were less "trees" than they were "carnivorous predatory botanical hunters lying in wait for unsuspecting prey," but honestly, he'd take the long cut down his arm in a heartbeat in exchange for the absolutely fascinating look at the inside of the thing's mouth.

Ani had tried to eat it in return, and he'd barely managed to pull her off.

Ani, perched on his shoulder, made an inquisitive sound.

He shook his head. "It's nothing, sweetheart," he murmured. "Just tired."

Tired was an understatement.

He'd left the others at the edge of a large overhang of rock at the base of a cliff that rose twenty metres out of the jungle. He and Istvay had examined it for danger, and then set up the protective force-field. With the rock at their back, it should hold off even whatever it was that Ani had killed when they'd first arrived. The two of them had helped the others set camp inside the safety of the force-field, then Aran had left the rest of the party with Istvay and headed back into the jungle to search for survivors, much to Istvay's vocal dissatisfaction.

In the end, though, Istvay's poison-induced weakness aside, it had been painfully clear that the tiny, helpless group of survivors wouldn't last long alone. None of the others, with the possible exception of Ines, knew anything at all about surviving in the wild. And nor could Aran and Istvay abandon the other potential survivors in the jungle, especially not with night coming on.

Besides, Aran had pointed out reasonably, he had Ani. Only something very stupid would make the mistake of attacking him while he had Ani with, and it would only make that mistake once.

Istvay had at last, reluctantly, agreed, because they hadn't really had any choice.

Since then, Aran had shuttled three groups of survivors back to the shelter through a jungle thick enough that each step was an effort. And now, as dark was falling, he was coming back for one last sweep before true nightfall.

He didn't mind being alone with Ani, though. He needed the time to think.

Alba was right—trying diplomacy was probably the first step, at least until he could understand the language and knew the lay of the land. But as he'd trekked back and forth through the jungle, Istvay's words had rung over and over in his ears.

"Even if you won't believe me that you're the best person on this damn ship— they don't have any better options right now."

And that was exactly it. He was the only one Istvay had. If they wouldn't take this seriously—if they insisted on being more concerned about Alba's diplomatic mission than finding a cure—it didn't matter. Because Aran might be all they had, but they did have Aran.

He would find the cure, or he'd die trying. And if it meant slipping off into the jungle on his own, the moment it became clear that Alba's solution wouldn't work, so be it.

The thought should terrify him, probably. Honestly, when he had time to think about it, it probably would. But right now all he could feel was a weary sort of resolve, that had hardened into something steely and unbendable.

He would save Istvay, no matter what that took.

He flipped on his sensor again. He'd calibrated it to scan for humans, and while that meant it wouldn't show him any potentially hostile animals approaching, he wasn't overly concerned—he had Ani, and he had a stun gun, and he'd managed pretty well so far.

The sensor beeped, and he sighed and straightened. "Looks like we found someone, Ani."

The sensor led him past where most of the other pods had come down, and into a small clearing. And in the clearing—

He frowned.

It wasn't a pod at all, but some sort of a ship.

But it was definitely occupied, and the occupants were definitely human—a young woman stood on the loading ramp, waving at him frantically.

She stopped when he turned her way, and shot him a brilliant smile. "We heard chatter over the wavelinks that someone was bringing survivors in." There was no mistaking the raw, exhausted edge to her voice. "I was hoping you'd come through one more time. I—don't particularly like the look of this jungle."

Aran smiled back. "It's not as bad as all that. But you're right, you can get yourself in trouble if you're not careful."

"You can come out, someone came for us," she called back into the ship, and one by one, other figures emerged—first, a tall individual who looked a little younger than the girl who'd hailed him, with an androgynous appearance, dark hair, and enough rings and spikes in their lips and ears and eyebrows that they looked a little like they were growing their own defensive armour; then an older man with light skin, a limp, and a scowl; and then a middle-aged woman with a frank, matter-of-fact expression that Aran found himself liking even before she'd said a word.

The woman looked him up and down without any trace of awkwardness, then nodded and stepped forward. "I'm Joska. This is Savina and Beni, and this," she gestured to the older man, "is Rafel. The others I don't know—we picked them up from the ship on our way out."

Aran shot an inquisitive glance at the ship, and the young woman who'd first hailed him caught the look. "We were on a supply run when everything went sideways," she said with a small shudder. "I never dreamed they wouldn't let us off before they went through the portal, but I guess we got caught in the middle of something. Some soldiers locked us up, and I wasn't sure we'd get out alive at all."

Her face was friendly and open, her smile pleasant, her attitude one of guileless cheerfulness.

But there hadn't been any supply ships scheduled. Aran knew that from the records Istvay had pulled up.

"I'm sorry you got caught up in it," he said at last, watching them surreptitiously.

Still—he couldn't exactly leave them to die in the jungle, whatever their reason for lying.

"I'm going to make a final sweep, and then I'm heading back to the shelter for the last time," he said. "Would you prefer to wait for me here, or would you prefer to come with?"

"Come with, please," said the young woman, and something about her tone told him that this, at least, was no ploy. Whatever else she was, she was legitimately terrified of the jungle.

He couldn't blame her. If it hadn't been so damn interesting, he probably would have been paralyzed with terror himself.

"Alright, bring what you need. But only what you need," he cautioned. "Walking is hard, and you'll have to carry everything yourselves. I'm going to need both my hands free if I want to keep us alive."

Two return trips through the jungle had showed him this was no exaggeration.

When everyone had gathered what pitiful belongings they had, Aran gestured with his head. "Let's go," he said, and they started off into the jungle.

"Aran, isn't it?"

He looked over, startled, to see that the friendly young woman— Savina?—had come up beside him.

He frowned. He wasn't accustomed to anyone being able to walk quietly enough to startle him. But then, he was tired, and probably hadn't been paying all that much attention.

"Yes," he said warily.

She smiled, pleasant dimples appearing on her face. "I've heard so much about you. It's so nice to actually meet you, although I have to be honest, I'd have preferred other circumstances."

Aran smiled ruefully. "As would I," he murmured.

They walked in silence for a few moments. He hoped against hope that she wouldn't start asking about his exploits, or flirting with him —always awkward, since he never seemed to be able to figure out when it was happening, which meant it usually ended badly for all involved. But she didn't appear to be contemplating any of those things—instead, she looked as if she was deep in thought.

At last she looked up again, the dimples on her cheeks reappearing. "You—haven't seen the Chief Justice, have you?"

The way she asked the question, the delicate hesitation in front of it, made him frown. But—it wasn't a secret. And even if it had been, it would have gotten out as soon as they reached the shelter.

"Yes," he said. "She's with the others."

The girl's smile widened, a happy, infectious grin, and he almost found himself smiling as well, despite everything.

"Oh, that's excellent!" she said exuberantly. "I've been wanting to meet her ever since I heard she was on the ship."

He glanced at her curiously, but he couldn't read anything from her face.

He shrugged, and turned his attention back to the scanner.

He'd bring these people to the shelter, and tomorrow they'd start out for whatever settlement the ship's scanner had picked up. And then, somehow, he would find Istvay a cure.

The scanner beeped, indicating another group of survivors, and he turned towards the sound, the ragged group of travellers following close behind.

37

Epilogue

The beast crouched in the jungle, watching the black smoke that curled from the wreck of the tiny craft. The thing had landed ungracefully on the jungle floor, nose first, and tumbled over and over itself before finally coming to rest against a stand of carnivorous trees.

The beast had never seen anything like it. But it couldn't be much of a threat—the entire craft was barely longer than the creature's own body.

It crouched, its only movement the flicking of its long tail. The smell of burning made it cautious, but it wasn't long before it determined that the thing, whatever it was, wasn't going to move.

It padded across the jungle floor in the moonlight, twenty-centimetre-long claws retracting delicately. When it was close enough, it reached out and swatted at the mangled metal, then drew quickly back.

Still the thing didn't move, and the beast padded closer, curious. It nudged the craft again, then reached down and nipped at it, making a disgusted face at the taste of burnt metal.

And then the craft rocked, and the beast crouched, tail lashing in alarm.

From the side opposite, a hatch hissed open. The beast watched warily, and just as it had made up its mind to investigate, a figure emerged from the hatch.

It was a woman, with black hair and a tailored grey suit that the creature's eyes skipped over strangely. There was blood smeared across the woman's face and clothing, but she didn't move as if she was badly injured. She stepped out onto the jungle floor, glancing around her languidly and brushing ash off her clothing, and the beast crouched down, sniffing the new scent on the air.

The woman glanced at the small sensor strapped to her wrist, and her lips curled up into a smile. She turned towards the darkest part of the jungle, stepping around the carnivorous trees with hardly a glance in their direction, and started into the thick undergrowth.

The beast crouched lower, its powerful front quarters bunching.

This was something new, certainly, but it smelled eminently eatable. And certainly nothing to pose a challenge to the creature's own supremacy in the jungle.

Letting loose a triumphant roar, it leapt.

The woman turned casually over her shoulder, pulling a small gun from a holster in her sleeve, and fired.

Reka hardly glanced back at the twitching body scant metres away, just slipped the gun back into her sleeve and continued forward, following the small beep of her sensor.

By the time half an hour had passed, it had led her to an open clearing some half a kilometre distant, where the vegetation had been burned away. What had caused the damage became apparent a few steps further on—an old, battered spacecraft, gleaming dully in the bright light of the planet's three moons.

She smiled grimly.

Cavaco had pinned all the blame for the job gone wrong on her, and one day, when that Chief Justice fulfilled her promise and gave Reka her life back, she'd pay him for it.

But Savina had been the one who caused the job to go wrong in the first place. And she'd always have to be the first one to pay.

Reka paused at the edge of the clearing, tapping the scanner on her wrist to check for life forms.

Nothing. But then, she hadn't expected there to be, not now.

She stepped warily into the clearing, and paused at the ship's loading ramp, which gaped open, abandoned. Then she climbed inside.

The corridors of the ship were deserted, and dirty, as if they'd been trampled over by several pairs of feet.

Reka frowned.

She'd looked up the information on the woman who'd shot her, the captain Joska. She couldn't blame the woman for getting dragged into Savina's schemes, and when she shot, the woman had clearly not been aiming to kill. She wasn't the type to kill. And everything Reka had read on her told her that Joska was the type to try to save survivors.

But the fact that Savina hadn't stopped her was … curious.

She paused a moment, then crouched and did a quick DNA scan of the walls.

Enough people had touched it that the DNA signatures were a muddled mess. But after a moment, she was able to pick out a familiar signature.

She glanced down at the screen, then raised her eyebrows.

There was the signature she was looking for. But there were two others as well, too similar for it to be a coincidence.

Slowly, she smiled. "Savina," she said. "Traveling with family, I see."

That was a piece of information she hadn't been given. How interesting. If she'd had time to run her DNA scans after the failed attack, how differently would this job have gone?

Interesting to contemplate. But it was a consideration for the past, and there was no point worrying about it now.

She made her way back outside and knelt, running her fingers along the broken grass that marked the travellers' footprints.

Maybe five, six hours since they'd left here.

She was late. Still, considering the damage her small craft had taken, she was lucky to have made it at all. And she wasn't one who generally counted on luck to carry through with her plans.

The portal through which they'd come had disappeared, but she was practical enough to realize that a portal that could be opened once could be opened again. And when it did, she fully intended to have cleared her name, and Savina's debt.

The warrant had been flexible on whether Savina needed to come back alive.

She hesitated a moment, then slipped a small holodisc out of her slim jacket pocket and tapped it open.

The warrant blinked and glowed to life, bright against the dark of the night, and she studied it.

A frank, innocent-looking girl with plump, comfortable curves and a dimpled smile rotated gently. Lifelike, yes, but the holoimage couldn't convey the wickedness in those wide, innocent eyes, the satisfaction in that dimpled smile as Savina plunged her knife into flesh.

Reka expanded the screen with her fingers, studying the woman more closely.

Savina had proved herself to be more intelligent, and more dangerous, than Reka had expected. Still, Reka hadn't earned the reputation she had by being afraid of a challenge.

"I'm looking forward to our next meeting, Savina," she whispered.

She tapped the disc, and the holograph disappeared. She slipped it back into her jacket pocket, and glanced around the small clearing one last time.

Her lips curved in a slow, dangerous smile, and she stepped out into the jungle, following the bent trail of footsteps.

Book two, The Observer Effect, coming soon!
Preorder available on Amazon

You might also enjoy The Ungovernable series, also by R.M. Olson.

A mouthy ex-smuggler pilot, a grumpy demolitions expert, a tech genius and a hacker. They're pulling a job on the most dangerous weapons dealer in the System. They're stealing tech that could change the course of history. And every one of them has something to hide.
What could possibly go wrong?
"Spectacular and thrilling! Olson's debut novel is filled with compelling characters and endless excitement." -SD Simper, author of the Fallen Gods series

You can order book one, Zero Day Threat, on Amazon.

I also have a Patreon, where I post character art, short stories, sneak peaks, and other fun stuff. You can get in on it for only $3/month, so if you're interested, check it out here!
https://www.patreon.com/rmolson

9 781990 142116